BEACHY KEEN

ALSO BY KASEY STOCKTON

Contemporary Romance

Cotswolds Holiday

I'm Not Charlotte Lucas

I'm Not His Style

Love on Deck

Falling in Line

Cabin Crush

His Stand-in Holiday Girlfriend

Snowed In on Main Street

Melodies and Mistletoe

Snowflake Wishes

Regency Romance

A Noble Inheritance

A Forgiving Heart

All is Mary and Bright

Bradwell Brothers Series

Hearts of Harewood Series

The Women of Worth Series

The Ladies of Devon Series

Myths of Moraigh Series

BEACHY KEEN

FALLING FOR SUMMER

KASEY STOCKTON

This is a work of fiction. Names, characters, places, and incidents either are the product of the author's imagination or are used fictitiously. Any resemblance to actual persons, living or dead, events, or locales is entirely coincidental.

Copyright © 2024 by Kasey Stockton
Cover design by Melody Jeffries Design
First print edition: June 2024

Library of Congress Control Number: 2024911675
ISBN 978-1-952429-52-1
Golden Owl Press
Boise, ID

All rights reserved. No part of this book may be reproduced or used in any manner without written permission of the copyright owner except for the use of quotations for the purpose of a book review.

This one goes out to melty popsicles, hot sand on the beach, and salt in your hair

WELCOME TO SUNSET HARBOR

Sunset Harbor is a fictional island set off the west coast of Florida. Each book in the Falling for Summer series is set in this dreamy town and uses crossover characters and events, creating fun connections throughout the series. Be sure to read all seven books so you can fully experience the magic of Sunset Harbor.

CHAPTER 1

Cat

RUNNING IS FOR RICH PEOPLE. It's a pastime used by office bros and yoga moms to bring purpose to their mornings, since the rest of their day is taken up with meetings and lunches and sitting in comfortable swivel chairs.

I haven't sat in a swivel chair in my entire life—never had the opportunity or the need.

I also don't need to run *intentionally* to keep up my cardiovascular health, because I spend my days in continuous motion like an Energizer bunny with a to-do list five feet long. My job consists of legitimate manual labor at our B&B—from cleaning rooms to washing up after guests are done eating and Uncle Otto is finished blowing through the kitchen like a leathery tan tornado who makes breakfast.

The man is in his fifties. He's been cooking at Keene Bed & Breakfast for thirty years and still hasn't mastered the concept of rinsing dishes *as you go*. The amount of dried batter I've had to scrape off mixing bowls could make enough pancakes to build a castle.

My batter-scraping muscles have been honed through cleaning three other houses on the island, too—one of which is almost always empty and pays better than the other two houses combined, thanks to the prestigious owners being Sunset

Harbor's most famous family, the bougie Belacourts. Their money is older than the island. It's grown with the help of a massive real estate portfolio and a chain of elite resorts, vainly named The Belacourt Resort, they started a few generations back. We have one—the original, I think—in Sunset Harbor. It's small and posh, but aside from the odd wedding or event I've attended there, I avoid all things Belacourt. Their reality TV show, hotels, social media, ads...

It's not easy, but I do my best.

Sometimes Belacourt news is so prevalent in the island gossip it's impossible to ignore, like last year when the only Belacourt son officially made billionaire status in his own right. Noah Belacourt, billionaire bonehead. He's a year older and a thousand million dollars richer than me.

So, obviously, I hate him.

No, that's not fair. I hate *his sister*. He gets second-hand dislike for being related to her. Thankfully, the Belacourts my age never stay in the family house. When they're around, they stick to the resort.

I stick to my family B&B. Cleaning, cooking, and on the side, I manage Otto's calendar and errands, which isn't strenuous. He doesn't have too much of a life here on our little Floridian island of Sunset Harbor.

Everything Otto needs—mostly grocery shopping or moving guest bookings from our website to the ancient reservations book he insists on using—can be achieved at home or on a bike. A necessity when the small island where I was born and raised doesn't allow cars.

Yeah, you heard that right. No cars. We have golf carts at the B&B for guest use, so I take one of those when they're available. Most of the time, my trusty yellow bicycle and white basket serves me well. Hear that? Even more cardio.

Which is why, *right now*, it makes zero sense why running on the beach has absolutely winded me. I am dead. Gasping for air, legs on fire, lungs screaming to get back on my bike and out of this foot-grasping sand.

But I can't yet, because I'm the idiot who wore my mom's red scarf today, rolled up and tied around my blonde ponytail. The wind stole it right from my hair and is threatening to dump it in the ocean.

The actual ocean. If I don't reach my scarf in time, it will be lost forever. Since my parents both died more than ten years ago and didn't leave much behind, it's fair to say losing the scarf is not an option.

I pump my legs harder, watching the thin, silky red material land on the wet sand in front of the receding surf. Twenty feet away. Fifteen. Twelve.

So close. If I'm fast enough, I can reach it before it's taken by the wa—

Nope, the wind picks it up again. It dances through the air, over the clear blue water like someone is out there with a mega vacuum and sucking it out to sea.

No.

Panic edges into my body. My legs go shaky. I don't have time to kick off my shoes, so I run into the water with them on, following the dash of red in the wide blue expanse.

The mid-morning sunlight glares into my eyes. A wave crashes over my knees, slowing me, but I keep my gaze glued to the red scarf while it floats on the top of the water.

Until it starts to sink.

I scream, jumping into the next wave and swimming hard against the wall of tepid water. I never was a super strong swimmer—the ocean and I have a love-hate relationship since it killed my parents—but I can hold my own under normal, calm circumstances. Like swimming pools. In this moment, though, something possesses my body, propelling me forward at a speed

I didn't realize I was capable of. Maybe this is one of those high energy moments you see in a TikTok but don't know whether to believe, like a mom lifting a car to save her baby.

Adrenaline can do crazy things in moments of need.

Like how it makes me swim into the deeper blue where my scarf is slowly sinking. I swipe through the water, screaming with victory when my hand connects with silk.

Another wave crashes, filling my mouth with the bitter, salty sea and drowning out my triumph. But I don't care because I have the scarf! Coughing, I kick to stay above water and lift the scarf, just to make sure I'm not celebrating a silky strand of seaweed. My body relaxes in relief.

Until a hand comes out of nowhere and grabs my arm. "I've got you!" a man yells.

Another wave crashes over my head, pushing water up my nose and making me cough again.

The man pulls me against his chest—his very naked, very firm chest. I can feel his skin pressing into my bare shoulder.

I shake off the water and glare into the sunlight, but it's impossible to see. My eyes sting, and I don't know if it's from the saltwater or my non-waterproof mascara. "I'm *fine!*"

His grip slackens, but he doesn't release me. His strong arm is slung across my chest, holding me steady. "You screamed."

That's true. I kick harder, trying to get away from him, but he holds fast. "It was ...uh ...for something else. You can let go!"

He releases me, swimming backward. I think the waves dislodged one of my contacts. I can't see through my stinging eyes anyway, so I start swimming away.

"Are you trying to go ashore?" he calls. If I'm not mistaken, I detect a hint of amusement in his voice.

Freak, my eyes burn. Am I going the wrong way? I wipe at my eyes, but that doesn't help. They sting *so badly*. "Yes."

"This way." He gestures, but he's blurry. "Do you need help?"

Not from him. I don't recognize him through the blur of missing contacts and saltwater. I know *everyone* who lives on this island, and I can't place him, which means he's probably a guest at the ritzy Belacourt Resort just down the road.

If there is one thing I don't do, it's bother the rich kids.

Or rich *men*, based on his hard, well-defined chest.

Ugh. I wipe my eyes and squint until I find the tan blob that resembles the beach. Yep, both contacts are definitely gone now. I swim in what is probably the right direction, lifting my hand every rotation to check I still have the scarf. The sand shifts like sludge beneath my sneakers when I make it to shore. I wish I didn't have an audience, but Richie Rich's attention is keeping me from collapsing into a puddle right there in the surf.

I swam *in the ocean*. That'll need to be unpacked when I'm alone later.

"Ma'am," the guy calls behind me, much closer than I realized. "Are you okay?"

Great. He probably just noticed my shoes and the jean shorts that definitely aren't meant for swimming. The do-gooder probably wants to make sure the crazy lady screaming in the ocean isn't an escapee from the nearest mainland mental health facility and in need of an escort home.

"I'm fine, thanks." I tug down my blue tank and keep walking. I'm not fine, but I can't afford to think about the fact that I was just swimming in the *ocean*.

If this guy knew the whole scarf story, he wouldn't think I'm crazy. Not that I care. I consider myself mostly stable.

"That didn't seem fine." His voice is still way too close.

He's *following* me?

I whirl on him and immediately regret it. He's not expecting my swift change in direction and can't stop before colliding with me. He puts his arms around me mid-air as we fling to the ground, shifting us into a roll and taking the brunt of the fall.

We roll to a stop on the white sugar sand with me laying on top of him.

On *top* of Richie Rich.

His chest is firm underneath me. His lungs are having a party, moving in and out so quickly it's like I'm on a tiny trampoline. But his heart, man. It's beating wildly beneath my ear, and if he wasn't a posh snob, I would probably enjoy it.

Then, because this day can't possibly get any worse, I lift my head, dazed and dizzy. With him *this* close, I don't need my contacts to see. Two inches from his face, I can tell exactly who I practically mauled, and it's worse than Richie Rich. It's worse than a Belacourt Resort patron or president of the yacht club or my third-grade teacher who smelled like Greek yogurt and frowned all the time.

It's Noah Buttmunch Belacourt.

Yes, immature name calling on my part. I know. I coined Buttmunch Belacourt at least twelve years ago and the karmic rhythm of it stuck in my head.

He's one of the heirs to the Belacourt fortune, son of the hotel chain moguls, and older brother to the girl who made eighth grade my own special level of torture.

Remember? He's the guy who just made billionaire status thanks to his software company—among other things—according to *Forbes*.

But it gets worse.

He's the man whose parents' house I have to go clean *right now*.

My expression must display the feelings coursing through me because Noah frowns. His deep brown eyes bore into me, and his hair looks dark, messier than usual, dripping with seawater. Recognition flashes over his face, and his hands tighten on my back. Probably some caveman impulse.

"Sorry," I say, unsure of what else to do. I can't let myself think about how it feels with my legs all tangled in his. He is the enemy. His legs do *not* feel great.

Fine, I'm lying. He feels fantastic. I'm getting all sorts of tingles I haven't felt since Dax Miller winked at me last year.

I try to push up, but we're at an awkward angle, and he's not letting go of me.

"A little help?" I ask.

Noah seems to shake off his stupor and releases me. I push against his damp chest, untangling our legs and pulling my knees forward until I'm sitting up. As soon as I realize I'm straddling him, I scramble to my feet.

He jumps right up like he's an action star or a CrossFitter. Water drips from his dark hair onto his bare chest. I would assume he'd already been swimming when I got here, but he's in running shorts and socks. He must have kicked off his shoes at some point before diving in to save my life.

If he had known it was me out there screaming, would he have just kept running by? His sister would have, for sure. Thank the stars she isn't here.

"So, that was weird," I say, taking a few steps back. The farther away I move, the blurrier he gets, which is helpful. "But I'm really late for work now, and I have to go change."

"Can I help you?" he asks, his voice deep. "Give you a lift?"

Oh, nice. So his voice has only gotten hotter in the last few years, too. That's cool and irrelevant.

"In what?" I ask. If he has some special pass to drive a real car on the island, I'm going to call my friend Jane in the mayor's office and revolt. No one deserves special privileges just because they have a fat bank account.

He hitches a thumb behind him. "I have a golf cart up at—"

"I'm good." I keep backing away. I have to get out of these sodden jean shorts anyway. Like I could *ever* show up at home in a cart with Belacourt Resort emblazoned on the side. Otto would flip.

Noah just stands there, watching me back away like a nervous child. I give an awkward wave and climb up the sandy slope to where I dropped my bike when my scarf decided to take a cruise. I'm late to cleaning my client's house—Noah's *parents'* house—but since they aren't scheduled to be in residence right now, it probably doesn't matter. I really just keep the dust from settling too long between their visits, anyway.

Work was a good excuse to get me the heck off the beach, though.

I pick up my bike and put Mom's scarf in the basket, shifting my water bottle to sit on top of it so it doesn't fly away again. Swinging my leg over the bike seat, I position myself and glance back at the beach.

Noah still stands there, watching me.

Weird.

I kick off, riding down the slope toward Keene Bed & Breakfast. My shorts stick to my legs, wet and uncomfortable. That's got nothing on the tingling still sweeping through my body.

A few minutes ago, I was lying on Noah Belacourt. Actually lying on the guy.

And his reaction was to stare at me like I was crazy.

After the months of insults I endured from his sister's judgmental sharp tongue in middle school, I can only imagine the laughs this little episode is going to supply the Belacourt siblings. My face burns. I pedal harder, like I can ride away from the embarrassment.

Yet I can't get the image of a blurry Noah on the beach out of my head. He's probably standing there now, texting all the details of our run-in to all three of his sisters. I knew them before they all went off to their fancy boarding school and, fool that I was, I thought they were cool to begin with. I spent exactly six weeks being best friends with the middle sister, Olive, at the start of eighth grade until she showed up on the ferry one day on the way to school and wouldn't sit by me anymore. She wasn't just done being my friend—she wanted to be Enemy Numero Uno. It hardly mattered that the day before we'd walked through the town square eating ice cream cones and talking about boys. From that moment on, her only goal was to make me feel like a snail on the bottom of her yacht.

That's in the past. Most of the Belacourt family live in New York now and aren't seen around the island much anymore. I only know this because their stupid ads for the upcoming reality show *Bela-babes Take Manhattan* are everywhere. TikTok. Instagram. In between *The Office Superfan* episodes. Just everywhere.

I ride to the front steps of my pale yellow house and lean my bike against the stilts. The white porch wraps all the way around the front and side, and the white shutters make our B&B look like a dreamy beach house. I was born in this house. We lived here with Uncle Otto since he ran the B&B with my mom and dad. After my parents died, nothing changed, except that Uncle Otto became my guardian and couldn't take off for surfing trips whenever he wanted to anymore.

My sneakers squelch with each step as I dart inside and up to my room, my stomach starting to churn. Now that I'm away from the beach, safe in my room, anxiety is taking over my body. I swam *in the ocean*. I don't do that. I *can't* do that. But something about the idea of losing Mom's scarf had me jumping in the water before I could think twice about it, and now that I'm safe at home, fresh realization washes over me like a tidal wave.

I don't have time to sit in these feelings, because I need to get to work. I hang Mom's scarf over the end of my bed—I'll have to figure out the best way to clean it later—and shut the bathroom door. I wheel around to turn on the shower and freeze when I catch my reflection in the mirror. I lean close to the sink to see better.

Oh. My. Gosh.

I'm not just wet and droopy; I'm a drowned rat. My hair is

plastered to my head and my face is streaked with black mascara. It's smudged around my eyes and lining my cheeks.

Noah stared at me because I looked like a terrified raccoon. And not the cute kind.

Great. Absolutely fantastic.

Well, I learned two things today. First: Noah Belacourt is here, hanging out in places besides his private beach. It's a handy bit of info that will help me avoid him, because second: I can never face him again.

CHAPTER 2

Noah

WHEN I JUMPED in the water to help the swimmer in distress, I hadn't expected to end up entwined on the beach with Cat Keene, the *one* girl I wouldn't mind wrapping my arms around on this tiny island. She'd felt way out of my league in high school, and that definitely hasn't changed. Our tumble in the sand had my blood pumping way harder than my workout allotted for, and it took a good deal of time standing on the beach and waiting for my heart to slow before I could search for my shoes.

I still don't know why she was flailing around in the ocean, screaming and coughing like she was drowning, but she was pretty annoyed when I dropped everything and ran to help her.

Well, I didn't drop *everything*. My pockets weren't empty, so my phone is now at the bottom of Sunset Harbor's beach line, buried in the sand. Maybe a crab has taken it. Or an octopus. Do we have those here?

I have no idea. I didn't pay much attention in marine biology.

It doesn't take book smarts to discern that Cat was hiding something when she ran away, her face all streaked with black like she had forgotten she'd put makeup on and rubbed her eyes repeatedly. We're talking zombie eyes. I had no idea if it was better to warn her or not before she fled. I have sisters. I've seen plenty of mascara mishaps.

Yeah, I should have warned her.

Cat can say she's fine all she wants, but what I saw was definitely some level of distress. Even-keeled people don't scream in the ocean or swim in their sneakers. Besides, I know the woman can swim. She dated my next-door neighbor Jake for a few years when we were teens. I spent half of my high school years at boarding school in Massachusetts, but when I was home for holidays or long weekends, I saw Cat. A lot of Cat.

I doubt she ever saw me, though.

She basically took up residence at Jake's pool back then, and I have a good view of his backyard from my bedroom terrace. I'm not a stalker. I just like the view up there. Since we aren't on the Florida-facing side of the island, it's pretty much just turquoise blue ocean as far as the eye can see. It makes for some great sunsets and snooping on your neighbor's high school parties, if you're a creep.

I'm not a creep, either. I just love sunsets. And you can't help but look when your neighbors are shouting the lyrics to "Baby Got Back" or playing shriek-infested games of Marco Polo.

It was a good day for me when Jake went off to Yale.

The parties stopped. I had peace in my room again. No more distractions while I hung out with my boarding school friends over *Halo* or got lost in World of Warcraft.

Holding my running shoes by the laces, I inhale a deep breath of sea air and jog back to my family's private beach. It's mostly used by the resort patrons, but there's a little cove they don't know about. I spend most of my time there when I'm visiting Sunset Harbor.

Now that I'm here for the entire summer, I'm going to have to find other ways to blow off steam. Not too much steam or my therapist won't be thrilled, since I'm supposed to be taking a break, but enough to keep me from going stir-crazy. I need Dr. Stein to be happy so she writes me a favorable report at the end of the summer.

I climb the wooden steps up to the resort, then pass the infinity pool, sunshade cabanas, and wall of windows looking into the restaurant. The walkway turns toward the resort, but I keep straight and unlock the gate to the seaside path toward the house I grew up in. I wasn't planning to stay in the house all summer, but a friend needed my suite at the resort while she hides from paparazzi, and the house is empty anyway.

The big, giant, echoey beach house has too many rooms and too much space for one guy. I hate being here alone, but not as much as I hate being here with my entire family. Generally, I don't mind being by myself—I'm pretty used to it. But *this* house? It's a glaring symbol of everything that's gone wrong in my life.

Currently, it's the center of my parents' divorce arguments, which makes climbing the back porch steps from the path to the house unpleasant. I saw more texts come through our family thread this morning, but I stopped reading them about a month ago. *Now* I really can't read them, since my phone is chilling in the ocean somewhere. My older sister has an Android, so that group chat won't come to my iPad. For all I know, Mom has claimed the property already and is en route with her squad of wealthy wives to trash the place in Dad's honor.

I can't think about it anymore. The irritation is raising my heart rate again, and I can't have that.

Just trying to keep my anxiety from mounting is anxiety-inducing all on its own. If I want to keep my position as a well-respected CEO of my tech company, Scout, I need to get a handle on it in the next three months.

Board of directors' orders.

I stop in the kitchen to make a protein smoothie, then carry it upstairs. A long, hot shower will chill me out and remove the sound of Cat's panicked screams from my head. Maybe it will get my mind off Mom and Dad's divorce negotiations and my impending job loss, too.

Wow, I'm a real catch. No wonder Cat ran from me like I carried a bucket full of camel spiders.

Not that she'd be interested if I carried a bucket of baby goats or something else women universally seem to adore, though. Apparently, she hates me. The disdain in her eyes on the beach earlier spoke volumes to how she feels about my particular brand of human. I have no idea what I've done to earn that scowl, but there's no mistaking her intent, since it didn't show up until she seemed to recognize me.

I toss my running clothes on the floor and turn on the shower. Ten minutes in, the steam isn't doing anything to push Cat out of my head. When was the last time I saw her before today? A few years ago, at least. We were at the public beach on the south side of the island. She'd been there with friends playing volleyball, and I was pretending to learn how to surf from my sister's boyfriend. He clearly didn't know what he was doing, but I let him think he was teaching me so I didn't seem like a jerk. Our family's reality show had been filming us at the time, which meant best behavior all around.

Most of my life has carried that theme. People are watching: chin up, shoulders back, monitor what you say, and keep your face neutral. Dad's two most repeated phrases are *don't do anything to give the family bad press* and *keep an eye out for gold diggers*.

Ironic, given who he's dating right now.

Cat's life has always seemed the opposite of mine. She's carefree, cheerful, and nice because she wants to be and not because her dad stood behind her with a stick, prodding her into good behavior. I used to be envious of her sheer freedom to be whoever she wanted to be and how much her uncle supported her. That envy transferred straight to Jake when they started dating, and I realized I didn't just want Cat's life. I'd wanted *her*.

Teenage me had a fat crush on this girl. Can you blame me? She wasn't just sweet and outgoing and fun; she was just as beautiful then as she is now. It had to have been two years ago when I last saw her on the beach, but I distinctly remember watching her jump into the arms of a tall blond guy and kiss him after her team won the volleyball game. She's probably married to the guy now. Someone called Bradley who makes kombucha and plays the piano and recycles his *Wall Street Journal*. You know, perfectly well-rounded.

Why is this guy living in my head? I don't even know him. The day I saw them on the beach, we hadn't even talked. I remember chatting with my good friend Tristan and a few other island friends on the opposite team, but Cat hadn't even acknowledged me. The guy didn't either, but he clearly hadn't grown up here or I'd know him. He'd worn board shorts and no shirt and acted like Cat was his property. Apparently, that's all my brain needs to spin a stupid backstory for him.

Go home, anxiety. That's enough for today please.

I give myself another ten minutes in the shower, closing my eyes and dropping my head back under the water to soothe away my stress.

Did I have a crush on Cat back in the day? Yes.

Did she notice I existed? Nope.

Does that even matter now? Not at all.

Except for the fact that my stupid heart went buck wild when we went down on the sand. Hello, tangled legs. I can't push that image out of my mind no matter how hard I try. It's much better than reliving her gargled screams.

When the shower has been on longer than I care to admit, I shut it off and towel dry. My iPad rings from my dresser, so I wrap the towel around my waist and move to answer it.

Mom is calling. Her name and face flash across the screen. It's a photo from her 60th birthday party a few years ago, blonde hair pulled back into an elegant style and pearls encircling her throat. I reach for the iPad, but my hand hovers before making contact. I can't talk to her now. I *just* chilled out, and the last thing I need is a forty-five minute diatribe on Dad's latest trip to Cancun with his newest model "friend."

Guilt slithers in, though, and I reach for the iPad again just as it stops ringing. Well, I tried.

I'll call her back when I'm dressed. Or when I have a phone again. My second-in-command, Gina, wants to go over the latest updates on our new dating app, and I told her I'd make time for her this afternoon.

I pull on pants that are appropriate for the office, then search the closet for a good tie to go with my blue shirt. I probably brought too many clothes to Sunset Harbor for a summer-long move, but I like to be prepared for anything. This also means needing to worry about laundry less often. Since I'm not good at laundry, that's important.

Mateo usually handles those things for me, but he can't be out here all the time while we're trying to launch the app. He might be my personal assistant, but I'm happier when his focus is on the office.

I reach for a tie and pause when a thud draws my attention. It sounds like it came from downstairs, so I lean toward the closet door and listen.

The front door snaps shut.

Think of the devil. Mateo must be early. Or... is he? I think I told him to meet me at the office for the meeting with Gina. But he tends to know what I need before I do half the time, so he's probably here with a paper that needs an ink signature or important dry cleaning or a sandwich.

Man, I hope he's here with a sandwich. I didn't realize how hungry I am until now.

Footsteps tap up the exposed wood staircase.

Tossing the tie around my neck, I slip my arms into my shirt and start toward the hallway. "I hope you brought me something to eat."

Stepping into the shaft of sunlight from the long window in the hallway, I'm aware of three things in rapid succession:

First, it's not Mateo. It's a woman.

Second, her shriek tears through the house, shrilly reverberating through my bones.

Third, she has a bucket in her arms, and she throws its contents at me, drenching me in warm, soapy water.

I hope it's soap, at least, and not poison. It does *smell* like Dawn.

"You?" she squeals. I don't know why, because my eyes are stinging from the soap, and I can't open them. "Noah Butt—" She clears her throat. "Why are you here?" she asks, her tone sounding more whiny than scared.

Her voice sounds familiar. I scrub my hand over my face and squint.

I make out a woman, average height, slender, with a frowning, scowling forehead, blonde hair thrown up in a ponytail, and —if I'm not mistaken—bright red cheeks.

Catalina Keene. Inside my house. Holding a now-empty bucket.

Weird. "Did you follow me here?" I ask, clearing the water from my eyes.

She straightens, leaning back slightly. She's changed her clothes since jumping in the ocean. Now she wears a baggy Princess Peach T-shirt and shorts. It was obviously a stupid question.

"I'm here to clean." She says this like it's obvious. She has a pair of yellow rubber gloves in one hand, so maybe it is.

At least that explains how she has the code to my parents' house. I wipe a hand over my face to get rid of more water. "You're the cleaning lady?"

She crosses her arms over her chest, and the sassy pose proves she still doesn't like me. What did I *do*? "I've been cleaning your parents' house for the last few years," she says.

Every new word that comes out of my mouth is digging my hole deeper and deeper. I check out her hand and don't find a ring. Guess she didn't marry Beach Blondie.

Does this mean she's single? Would it matter if she was? She's still staring at me, so I better say something. "They didn't tell me."

"Why would they?" Her eyebrows pull gently together in genuine confusion.

My ears warm. Idiot. Why *would* my parents think to tell me that some random island girl was hired to clean the house? They don't know we knew each other—kind of—in school. That my sister Olive used to be her friend until I slipped and mentioned I thought Cat was cute. The next day they weren't friends anymore.

My parents never kept tabs on my sisters' friends, and they certainly didn't keep any on mine either. Not to mention no one comes here much anymore, so I doubt Cat's in regular communication with them.

But still, they should have given me the schedule. What if she'd walked in on me in the shower? Or getting dressed?

"I'll be here for the summer," I say. "They didn't tell me when you'd be cleaning or I would have made sure to stay out of your way."

Her eyebrows hitch up. "The summer? All of it?"

I'm still dripping on the floor, but she doesn't seem to notice, so I don't mention it. "Yeah. Until the end of August."

Cat puffs out her cheeks and blows a long breath. "Okay. Good to know." She does a sweep of my clothes, her eyes widening as if *just* noticing she threw a bucket of water on me. Her eyes linger on my chest, and I have to actively avoid flexing. "Oh my gosh. I'm so sorry about the water. You startled me, and—"

"Don't worry about it."

She pulls her bottom lip between her teeth. "Let me help you clean that up."

I raise an eyebrow and glance down. "You want to help me with my wet shirt? Or did you mean you want to dry my chest?"

Her cheeks go pink. "No. I mean, yeah... that's not what I meant."

She's cute when she's flustered.

"I need to get back to it," Cat says.

"Cleaning? Or ogling me?" For the first time probably ever, I feel like I have the advantage over her.

Her cheeks are really red now and I love it. "I wasn't *ogling*. I was looking to see how much damage I did."

"None, as you can see." I put my arms out to the sides to showcase that I'm perfectly undamaged. Physically. It pulls my shirt open further.

Cat checks me out again before her eyes snap to mine. "We use a Google calendar to keep the schedule, Mr. Belacourt. If your parents need to add cleaning days or anything, they do it there, and I move them if I need to. Maybe if you request access to that, you can let me know what days I shouldn't come while you're here."

Mr. Belacourt? What the actual heck? If that's her attempt to keep things professional, it's a little too late for us. But she's clearly uncomfortable. Maybe if I get her info, I'll have a way in. A form of communication. I can text her. "Can you send it to me?"

She pulls out her phone and taps a few times before glancing up. "Email address?"

Well, that ruined that plan. I was hoping she'd have to text me the calendar. I rattle off my email address, and she finishes typing it into her phone.

"If this is a bad time, I can come back another day."

"I'm just heading out," I tell her. "You're welcome to stay."

"Just leave your wet clothes in the bathroom, and I'll take

care of them," she says, turning back down the stairs. Probably to refill her bucket and not at all because she needs to get away from me as fast as humanly possible.

I watch her walk down the stairs, her hair bouncing with each step. My instinct is to follow her, but my brain knows better.

It's not smart to mess with island girls, no matter how cute they are or how pretty their smile is or how much I want to make them laugh. Island girls like Cat want to stay here forever, and I definitely don't.

I do what any smart guy would do in my shoes. I turn and walk away from her, and I try really, *really* hard to push her out of my head.

CHAPTER 3

Cat

BAD THINGS usually come in threes.

One, the scarf-ocean debacle.

Two, Noah startling me into sloshing water all over him.

Three is coming. Something *will* happen. It's a law of nature and karma. Until it does, I'm going to assume the next time I see Noah, I'll have poppyseeds in my teeth or I'll run into his mailbox with my bike or I'll accidentally turn all his white shirts pink in the laundry.

I don't know why I'm doing his laundry in this situation, because that's not my job, but karma has made worse things happen, so it's best to be prepared. I haven't seen Noah since a few days ago, and thanks to the calendar we use for scheduling cleanings, I can probably avoid seeing him for the rest of the summer. If I'm crafty.

I'm nothing if not crafty. They don't call me Clever Cat for nothing.

Okay, no one calls me that. But they should.

"You busy?" Otto calls from the kitchen.

I'm sitting on a wicker porch chair, the waves crashing on the beach in the distance and sea air ruffling my hair while I peel peaches. "Just making jam."

"You almost done, Cattywampus? I need to talk to you."

Okay, that *is* one of my nicknames, and it's far more apt.

I glance down at the three full buckets sitting at my feet waiting to be peeled. "Not even close. How about you grab a peeler and come help me? We can chat in the sun."

Otto steps outside, letting the back door swing shut behind him. His hands are up like he can push away the manual labor. "These old hands? I'll mess something up."

I lower the peeler. "You're literally a chef."

He squints, tilting his head to the side so his overgrown white hair flops over his shoulder. He's always been suited to island life, with his leathery skin and shoulder-length blond hair. He's a Beach Boys surfer bro to the bones. It's unclear if his hair has gone white from age or was bleached by the sun. "Am I, though?"

"Yes. You're a chef. It's your job." His *only* job, but I don't add that part. Over the last few years, he's been sloughing more and more responsibility from the B&B onto my shoulders. I don't complain. It means I get paid more than what I made as a teen, when the only thing I'd do was clean the guest rooms after school. When Otto had cancer a few years back, I took on more responsibility so he could meet with doctors and focus on chemo. He was diagnosed with skin cancer, but it moved to his lymph nodes. It was a scary time for both of us and I stepped up a lot. Some of those job assignments sort of stuck after he got the all-clear.

So, I'm not complaining. But let's call an orange an orange here. The man can peel peaches.

"Why didn't you blanche them first?" he asks, watching my peeler. "Much easier to get the skin off that way."

"I'm following Mom's recipe to a T."

Otto nods. "I need to head out."

"I thought you wanted to talk."

Otto sits on the other wicker porch chair. He's in orange board shorts and a green Hawaiian shirt he hasn't bothered to button. And people say *my* style is eclectic. "After we talk, I want to head out."

"Surfing?" I ask, but not because of his attire. This is daily wear for Uncle Otto.

"No."

"Skating?"

"No," he says, defensively.

"Then where?" It's not Saturday, so there's no farmer's market, and his fishing buddy just had a hip replacement, so they're on a small break.

"Golfing," he says quietly, like he's been caught singing to Taylor Swift while making scrambled eggs.

That happened last week.

But *golfing*? That's not embarrassing. The man is in his fifties and spends more time outside than in. He can golf in the middle of the day if he wants to—even if it means stepping on Belacourt land. We only have one family checked in to the B&B currently. They've been spending their days at the beach, so Otto isn't really needed here. Besides, we keep our phone numbers in each of the rooms in case we aren't home when a guest has a question.

"I'll be around for a while. This jam takes forever. If the Carmichaels return and need dinner recs or whatever, I'll cover."

"Okay." He leans back, letting out a weary sigh. It stands the hair on the back of my neck to attention. I have a feeling the golf wasn't why he came to talk to me. Unless he's ashamed? Mom was forever harping on the Belacourt greed, and Otto never was a fan of them either... but it's just golfing.

I take a sip from my cold LaCroix, then pull out another peach and start peeling so I'm not staring at him. "What did you want to talk about?"

Otto stretches his legs out and crosses them at the ankles.

When I look up from the peach, he's staring at me. "What's wrong?" I ask.

"Nothing," he says, a little too quickly. "Just wanted to check in with you. See how things are going."

"At the B&B? I feel like it's pretty much the same as usual. We're slow, but that's to be expected right now."

"And the cleaning business?"

"I don't know if I'd call it a business, but—"

"You would." Otto gives a decisive nod. "It's a company your mother would be proud of, even if she hated who you clean for."

My cheeks warm and I focus on the peach again. I only clean one of the rich houses on the island, and that gig only came about by chance. Mom was opposed to families like the Belacourts, people with so much wealth they couldn't spend it all if they tried. She thought they didn't do enough to help others.

She was right, of course, but I don't plan on quitting for that reason. I'll gladly take their money.

The other two ladies I clean for adored Mom, and she loved them.

"Stella would have gotten a kick out of how much you charge them, though," Otto says, clearly still thinking of the Belacourts.

I swallow, afraid I'll blush. It's a curse of my fair skin that I turn red so easily. I shouldn't charge the Belacourts as much as I do, but they didn't balk when I quoted my price, so here we are.

"You're happy, then?" Otto asks, his blue eyes raking over my face.

My pulse spikes. If his cancer is back, I'm going to throw up. I lower the peeler. "Who's dying?"

He sits up. "No one. Well, everyone is to some degree, but no one we know is close to the grave."

No cancer, then. "Why are you being weird?"

Otto frowns. "I just wanted to make sure you're happy, Cat."

"I'm happy." My smile strains, stretching over my face. "How could I not be? I get to live here with you, doing the things I love most."

He cringes but covers it quickly. "Making peach jam?"

"Yes. Jam is the thing I love most."

He looks at me suspiciously. "Any boyfriends?"

"You'd know," I say, focusing on the peach again. I'm not in the mood to deep dive into my single life.

"So, no?" he says.

"No one right now." I was hoping Dax Miller would ask me out, but so far it's been crickets from him. I go out of my way to ride my bike past him on the way to work—the man fixes boats shirtless, ladies—but the most I've ever gotten was a wink once when I waved. To be honest, I'm not entirely sure he wasn't just squinting into the sun. I guess me on a bike isn't all that enticing.

Shocker.

When you live on an island like this, there aren't a whole lot of dating options. It's retired men or guys like Beau and Tristan, whom I've known since I was in diapers. I've tried apps before and spread my radius to include the mainland guys, but none of those dates ever developed into anything real. I'm not past my prime. I don't need to worry about a lonely existence yet. I'm only twenty-seven, for heaven's sake.

My parents were married and had had me by the time they were twenty-one, but they were high school sweethearts. Totally different situation.

Did I once see myself following in their footsteps and being married with five kids and a happy beachy life by now? Maybe I did, but some dreams have to pivot when the high school boyfriend turns out to be a tool and you're well past twenty-one without any romantic prospects.

Besides, guys these days are just not the same. Give me James Dean leaning against a car any day.

In my dreams, obviously. That's probably why I've had a thing for Dax. He totally has that bad boy vibe going, with his hot smolder and his shoulder tats. I pull out my phone and text my friend Holland.

> CAT
> Wanna watch Rebel Without a Cause tonight? I've got a hankering.

"If you ever need a night out, Cat, take it," Otto says, getting to his feet with a few creaks and a long groan. "There are plenty of cool, hip places to hang out on the mainland. You don't need to stick around for me."

I lower my phone and look up at my uncle. Cool, hip places? Like... clubs?

Oh. My. Gosh. He's trying to get me to go out. Is he *worried* I won't find anyone and I'll be stuck living with him forever? Okay, maybe it's been a few years since I've had a boyfriend, but I like our situation here. We're happy. It's been me and Otto against the world for so long, we're a real team.

But apparently, both of us don't share that opinion, and one of us thinks I'm a spinster.

Are my feelings hurt that my fifty-four-year-old uncle thinks I need to get out more? Maybe. Or maybe he's onto something and I don't want to admit it.

Remember that dream about the husband and five kids? I won't ever admit it out loud, but it's still what I want more than anything. Which is a struggle when *there are no men to date*.

"I'll date," I say. "When I find the right guy."

"How will you find the right guy? What's your plan?"

I toss my finished peach into the bucket and pluck out another one. "I was hoping he'd show up at the house one day and I'd just know."

Otto narrows his eyes, clearly unsure whether to take me seriously or not.

I mean, it's a solid plan, right? We have a fairly steady stream of customers staying here. They're usually married or vacationing with significant others, but you never know when a hot, single, eligible guy might drop in on you.

It happened to me *literally* just the other day.

Well, I don't know if Noah is single, and I certainly won't call him eligible.

Why am I even thinking about him?

"I'll go on a date," I say quickly, mostly to end this conversation. At book club last week, Jane tried to convince me to give island guys another shot. Maybe she was onto something then. "I won't give up and go buy six cats."

Otto makes a repulsed face. "One Cat is enough for me."

"I know." I roll my eyes. He's said that so many times over the course of my life. "What about one Cat and one kitty?"

He shudders in revulsion. I don't know why he's always hated cats, but he has. I wanted one *so* badly in fifth grade, and it's one of the only things he put his foot down on—which is saying a lot, because that's when I was still reeling from my parents' deaths and Otto would have done nearly anything for me. He claims to be allergic, but I'm ninety percent sure that's a lie.

"I'm leaving," he says, going for the door to let himself back into the house.

"Good luck with your golf swing. That's a thing people say, right?"

"Not sure," Otto says. "I'll let you know."

The door swings shut behind him just as my phone chimes to indicate an incoming text. I pull it out and swipe it open.

> HOLLAND
>
> Or we can go out so you can meet a real man. Jane might not have been entirely wrong at book club, you know.

I totally expected Holland to want a night in, which is part of why I texted her instead of Ivy, who's been one of my best friends most of my life. But Ivy just returned to the island and probably needs time to settle in anyway.

> **CAT**
> Fictional men will do fine for me right now
>
> Hot ones in black and white, preferably

HOLLAND
> I'll bring the popcorn

> **CAT**
> I need to fill you in on Noah Belacourt, btw

HOLLAND
> DID YOU SEE HIM?

> **CAT**
> Yes. Worst day ever

HOLLAND
> Were his sisters there? I kind of want to see if they look as plastic in real life as they do on screen

> **CAT**
> You're not missing anything there, Holls.

HOLLAND
> Wait. So are the Belacourt sisters here or not?

> **CAT**
> It's just Noah so far. But he's back FOR THE ENTIRE SUMMER and I've already embarrassed myself in front of him twice. So I need popcorn and you and James Dean

HOLLAND
> I'll be there at 8

FOUR HOURS and eighteen sealed jars of jam later, I'm tossing used dishes into the giant stock pot in the sink so they can soak. I love me some peach jam, but the amount of effort that goes into one little jar is unreal. This is a favorite among our guests, though, so I won't stop making it. The process is soothing, anyway. I like doing it.

I'm a regular Betty Crocker. Minus the husband, the two perfect children, and the apron.

I wash sticky sugar from my palms before going to the front door and picking up the pile of mail that has been pushed through the slot. Most of the letters are junk, but two have come for Otto, so I take them into our small office. After my feet cross the threshold into the room, I freeze, my eyes skimming over the return address.

Killigan Hammer Cancer Institute.

Those four words make my stomach turn over. It's been three years since Otto came home clean and free of all cancer, thanks to chemo, radiation, and surgery to remove some of his lymph nodes. Why are they sending him letters now, and *why* is there a red-stamped "final notice" on the front of the envelope?

Silence echoes in the empty house as I cross to the desk pushed up against the wall, reaching behind the pot for the key to Otto's top drawer. He probably doesn't know I'm aware of this key, but I've seen him put it away so many times that he's either in denial or trusts me.

I glance down at the bill from Killigan Hammer and frown. Evidently, he doesn't trust me *enough*.

It doesn't take very long to rifle through the drawer and find previous bills from the same place. I lay them across the desk, picking my jaw up off the floor. Each of the bills are the same, with varying levels of unpaid notices stamped across them. The number grows with each late fee, but it's so big to begin with it doesn't change a whole lot. There are way too many zeroes involved, and according to the statements, Otto hasn't been making his monthly payments for a while.

Ninety-two thousand dollars. The price for saving his life.

I open my banking app and check out my finances, but they look the same as they did yesterday. I'd been so proud of the little nest egg I'd slowly been building, but up against these outstanding bills, my six thousand is a drop in the bucket.

I close my eyes and lean back in the stiff leather chair.

Why didn't he tell me? Why doesn't he trust me with this?

Voices outside indicate that the Carmichael family has returned. I sit up quickly and shove the bills back into the drawer, locking it and putting the key away. Sliding Otto's latest bill between two pieces of junk mail, I leave the stack on his desk.

He'll come home, find it, and pull me in to talk again. Maybe that's why he came out on the porch before he left. If I give him time, he'll confront me on his own, then we can sit down and make a plan. Together. Team Keene.

I turn just in time to put a large smile on my face and welcome the Carmichaels home from the beach.

But they aren't alone.

They have a billionaire with them.

CHAPTER 4

Cat

THE LAST THING I want to see while I'm stressing about money is a man who has so much of it he could pay Otto's bill ten times over and not even feel a dent in his finances.

Stupid buttmunch billionaire.

I mean, what's the point of amassing that much money? So he can buy more designer suits like the ridiculously well-fitted one he's wearing right now? Good freaking grief, the man is on an *island*. Why is he walking around like he just stepped off an episode of *Suits*?

Why is he walking around my house at all?

I'm in cut-off shorts and Birkenstocks, so next to him I look like little orphan Annie. I could use a Daddy Warbucks right now though. So I'll take it. Maybe the outfit will bring me some good karma.

"Kylie *loved* the ferry," Meg Carmichael says, carrying the baby on her hip while her husband leads the toddler through the door. They aren't much older than me, but they clearly have their life together. I recommended they ride the ferry to the mainland for the three-year-old and the dolphins.

Connor Carmichael grins. "You'll never guess who we found on our way back to Sunset Harbor. My old college buddy."

Noah. He went to school with *Noah Belacourt*. That's fun.

"Oh, how nice," I say, my smile straining as I force it wider. I shut my lips, thinking of the bad luck poppyseeds. It's time for bad thing number three and I'm not prepared.

Or maybe I'm off the hook. Noah Belacourt standing in my house on the tail of me finding out that my life might be imploding is pretty awful. Connor's "old college buddy" is famous, irritatingly handsome, and uber rich. And he's judging me from the foyer of my quaint, creaky, hundred-year-old island house that I might lose if Otto can't find ninety-two thousand dollars. That's what happens when things say final notice, right? The bank takes your house to pay off the cancer-curing treatments.

Hey, sorry you're homeless, but at least you're alive.

"Yeah, he's the reason we're here," Connor continues, unaware of the turmoil in my head. He flicks his head toward Noah since his arms are full of bags and a little girl. "He recommended your place."

My gaze shoots to Noah. "You recommended my B&B instead of your own resort?"

He clears his throat, looking uncomfortable. He slides a hand effortlessly into his pocket, his dark hair impeccable, his brown eyes shifting to his friend, then back to me. "It was a while ago."

A while ago, as in long before I mauled him on the beach, then threw a bucket of sudsy water over his face? Noah's family wasn't a fan of me already, but I'm guessing his dislike has only grown in the last seventy-two hours.

"Don't be modest," Meg says. "You told Connor we'd love it here, and you were right."

Noah clears his throat and moves his weight to the other leg. He's uncomfortable, and something about that makes me ease into my skin a little better.

Where's flirty Noah now? He's no longer accusing me of admiring his pecs—and I, for the record, am actively ignoring the way his Oxford shirt fits like a glove or remembering how his back forms a V. Definitely not thinking about shirtless Noah right now.

"We didn't expect to see him though," Connor grins, slapping Noah on the arm and bringing me back to Earth.

"I didn't think I'd be around." Noah catches my eye for a second before looking at his friend again. "It's pure luck I bumped into you on the ferry."

The ferry? Noah doesn't take a private boat when he wants to hop over to the mainland? For some reason, that surprises me enough to make me pause.

"Our luck." Connor grins. "I wish I brought something better to wear to dinner though."

"Don't worry about it," Noah says.

Meg starts for the staircase that leads up to their room, then pauses, moving the baby to her other hip. "Hey, Ms. Keene?"

"You can call me Cat."

"Cat." She smiles. "You don't offer babysitting services here, do you? Or know of someone who might? Noah invited us to dinner at his resort. He says it's fine if we bring the kids—"

"It *is* fine," Noah interrupts.

Meg goes on as if he hasn't talked. "But I know he's just being polite. If we could find someone to watch them, that would be easier."

Babysit? I haven't babysat since the Nelsons lived next door... probably five years ago. Meg mentioned that their baby Willow recently hit the six-month mark, which meant nothing to me, because I had no idea what a six-month-old baby was capable of. But, apparently, we need the money. How hard can it be? The Carmichael girls are cute—and the Carmichaels are clearly wealthy. "I can do it," I say, trying for a confident tone. Holland won't care if I reschedule our movie, especially after I tell her why I need the money.

"You can?" Meg grins, her shoulders sagging in relief. She looks at her phone, then up at the ceiling like she's calculating.

"If I feed her now, we have until eight before she'll want to eat again." She gives me an apologetic nose-scrunch. "She's nursing."

"Not a problem," I say, because I'm not sure why it would be. She knows her kid's schedule. She just has to tell me what to do, and I can handle it.

Connor doesn't look as confident. "You sure, Meg?"

"Yeah. If Willow gets hungry, we can come home early."

"Or—" Noah starts, then looks at me uncertainly. I guess he chooses to power forward. "If Cat watches the girls at my house, they'll be close to the restaurant."

"Oh, would you?" Meg asks hopefully, her wide eyes rounding. "We haven't left Willow yet, and I'm still a little anxious about how she'll react."

Should I tell her yes, but only if she pays double? The idea of spending my evening in Noah's family mansion gives me the ick.

"Unless being in a stranger's home makes you uncomfortable," Meg says, not reading my hesitation accurately.

The problem isn't Noah; it's that he's a Belacourt.

Okay, so the problem is that he's Noah *a little*.

He must feel the shift in my energy, because he takes a small step closer to me. "Cat's familiar with my house. She's been there a few times."

He forgot to add the part about me cleaning it because I'm the help.

"You two are friends?" Connor asks, looking at me appraisingly.

"We know each other," Noah says.

"Everyone who grew up on the island knows each other." I give him a look I'm hoping he'll accurately translate. I'm trying to say, *Let's not make this sound like something more than it is.*

He picks up what I'm laying down because he drops the subject. "What do you say, Cat?"

Money. I need money to the tune of ninety-two thousand dollars to save my uncle and my home. Anything helps. "Sure."

Meg crosses the entryway and pulls me in for a quick hug. The baby grabs a fistful of my hair and yanks. I suck in a breath while pain reverberates from my scalp.

"Willow!" Meg says, taking her pudgy fist and unfurling her fingers. "Sorry, Cat."

"No problem," I say through my teeth.

So apparently six-month-old babies are capable of *that*. I'll have to put my hair up before we head over.

Noah watches the whole interaction with a guarded expression. I hold my breath while his friends take their girls upstairs to change for dinner and re-pack their diaper bag. It might be the opposite of how I really want to spend my evening, but the Carmichaels have money, so I'm hoping they'll pay well.

Noah looks around the house, his eyes trailing from the wooden floorboards and floral runner to the quirky wall decor and seafoam green wallpaper. Trying to look at my house from his perspective, I can see why our B&B gets so many reviews commenting on the quaint, beachy, hip-grandmother vibe we have going here, and I'm proud of it. We might not be worth a billion dollars, but our house vibes and people love being here.

That's a lot more than I can say for his cold, sterile, modern resort.

In his eyes, this place is probably heavy on the grandmother and light on the trendiness. The smell of boiled peaches isn't helping, either. His eyes are sweeping over everything, but his face is a wall of impenetrable blankness. Judgy McJudgerson, just like the rest of his family.

Noah's eyes flick to the floor, then meet my gaze. He takes a tentative step toward me, bringing attention to all six-something feet of him in his sleek suit. "Listen, Cat—"

Willow wails upstairs, her cries piercing the house and

making us startle. I look up and wonder what I got myself into here.

"She has some lungs on her," I mutter, a little disappointed that the baby cut him off from whatever he was going to say.

Noah catches my eye and smiles. "So, you babysit, too? What *can't* you do, Catalina Keene?"

His use of my full name sends a zing of awareness through me. How does he even know it? We might have known each other for a long time, but we were never friends. The way he's looking at me now, his brown eyes deep and piercing, makes my skin itch.

Instead of answering him—I'm not sure if it's weird teasing or an attempt at conversation—I brush past his shoulder to lock the back door and fetch my phone.

I might need the money, but I *don't* need to sit here and let him judge me and my house. I've dealt with that from his family enough for a lifetime.

Noah

THE RESTAURANT at the Belacourt Resort has been fine-tuned to create a soothing atmosphere and delicious, Michelin-star quality food. Chef Gotier would have that star if she worked in a big city instead of our little island, for sure.

Seated next to the open windows with the sunset on the horizon and the breeze coming in off the water, we're listening to waves crash on the beach in between the tinkling of silverware and soft din of conversations. My family's resort is small, but it's high-quality, and even in the island's off-season, we're never empty.

A blessing and a curse.

It's been great catching up with Connor and his wife over dinner, but I haven't missed the way Meg has checked her phone every ten minutes or looks outside like she's eager to return to her kids. It's sweet that she loves them so much. Someday I want a wife who enjoys being with her kids, too.

Connor has kept the conversation running on a steady stream of college memories and gossip about some of the friends we shared when we went to school. He cuts a bite of his prime rib and chews, giving me a once-over. "So, you and our B&B host?"

"Her name is Cat," Meg supplies.

"You and Cat," Connor says, chewing his steak. He leans back a little in the seat and smiles. "Do we have a leg up on Page Six?"

My stomach roils at the thought of any magazine linking me with Cat, mostly because of how much she'd hate it. I haven't had many relationships over the last decade. I learned quickly that not all women are into me as much as they like my no-limit black card and easy entrance to New York clubs. It's cliché, I know, but when you find out your girlfriend cheated on you, then hear she misses your apartment more than you, you get a little wary of women and their motivations.

Not to say I don't date. I do. Somewhere out there is a woman who will enjoy my leather sofa and my laugh and not make fun of me when I get sucked into World of Warcraft until three in the morning. I'll date until I find her. But girlfriends? Linking my name to one woman so the people of Instagram can scrutinize our facial expressions every time we step out together? No thanks.

"I think your silence is answer enough," Connor says, grinning.

Being with Cat Keene is an old fantasy, not something I can afford to spend too much energy on imagining in my current life. It's almost laughable that Connor's mind would go there.

Did he not see Cat's reaction when I stepped into her house? I wouldn't have gone inside at all, except the Carmichaels were my ride home. My boat broke down on the mainland, and I had to hitch a ride back on the ferry to Sunset Harbor after work, where I conveniently ran into them. But since I had driven myself over to the mainland in my boat, there was no golf cart waiting at the ferry to drive home.

Connor offered me a ride. It would have been weird not to accept, and even weirder to hang out on Keene B&B's golf cart while the Carmichaels went inside to change out of their swimwear for dinner.

Cat didn't hide her feelings well when she saw me. I could tell the moment I stepped into her home that I'd made a mistake in going there.

"She's not into me," I finally say. "Even if she was, I'm not sticking around, so it doesn't make sense to start something with an island girl."

"Come on, Noah," Meg says, leaning forward on her elbows. "Have you ever had a summer fling?"

Had I? There were a few times I wanted to, but the girl was taken, and she was all over my next-door neighbor and his pool. I shake the mental image of teenage Cat in Jake's arms and paste on a smile, reaching for my drink. "Sounds like a recipe for disaster."

"Summer romances," Meg says with a sigh. "I miss those."

Connor raises his eyebrows. "What do you call this?"

"Family vacation."

"You want a summer romance? I'll give you one." He leans over, kissing her long enough that I have to look away. It's cute that you love your wife, but get your own table, man.

Meg pushes him away and leans close, but her cheeks are flushed. "Can we get the check? I know I'm being crazy, but Willow has never been away from me this long. I'm kind of eager to get back to the girls."

"I've got dinner." I lift my hand to Kendall, our waitress, and look out over the darkening sky while the sun slips to the other side of the earth. I'm eager to get back to the girls as well, despite how much Cat isn't feeling it.

Maybe there won't be a summer fling between us, but I can get to the bottom of her plain dislike while I'm here.

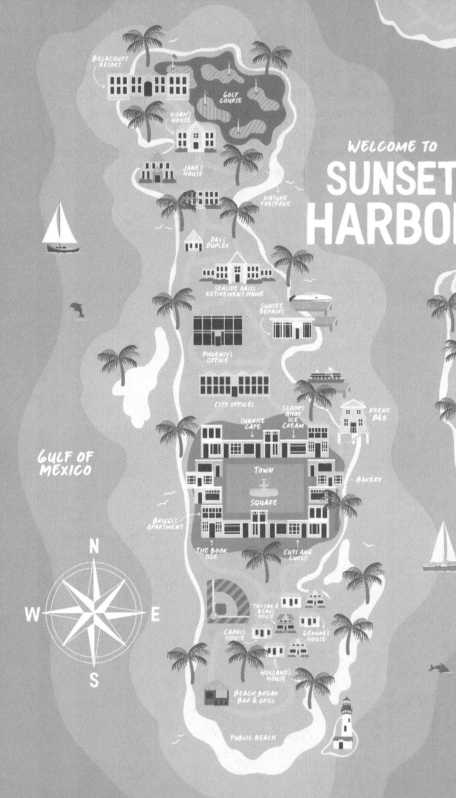

CHAPTER 5

Noah

THE IDEA of a summer fling with Cat is equally enticing and utterly laughable. Actually, legitimately laughable. The woman doesn't just casually dislike me—there's fiery hot loathing there. We get home from the restaurant to find her sitting on the living room floor with Willow spread out on a blanket in front of her. The baby is flailing her arms and giggling while Cat keeps bending down to blow raspberries on her tummy. It's just about the most adorable thing I've ever seen, second to Willow's thrilled laughter. But when Cat lifts her head to see us walk in, the light shining in her gorgeous, round blue eyes dims as they land on me, and her smile falls flat.

Just the *sight* of me ruins her mood, for some inexplicable reason. Does she hate my commercials? My company? My family's resort? *Me?* Why does her prejudice give me the sudden, pulsing desire to make her want me? I spend too much time working out and toning my abs not to get some use out of them. Given her reaction a few days ago, that just might be the only thing about me she likes.

The moment the thought enters my mind, it leaves again. I'm not ripping off my shirt just to get Cat's approval. *Get it together, man.*

"How were they?" Meg asks, dropping her purse on the counter and walking into the living room to scoop up her baby.

"Absolute angels," Cat says, sitting up to gather the Carmichaels' belongings. She glances around the kitchen and smiles bashfully. "Well, messy angels. But most of that is on me."

Willow starts crying, and Meg bounces to soothe her. "They're tired," she says, "but we'll stay and clean up first."

"Don't worry about it," I tell her. "You can get your kids home. I'll clean up."

"*You* will?" Cat asks, standing and resting one hand on her hip. "Or you'll get your cleaning lady to do it?"

That sends an irk up my spine. "I will."

"Thanks, man," Connor says, picking up the diaper bag and tossing their things inside. Kylie is glued to the television with one eye drooping as he scoops her up, leaving *Moana* on in the background.

I walk them to the door, trying to listen to what's passing between Cat and Meg, but I don't hear anything.

"Thanks for dinner," Connor says, shifting his toddler in his arms as she starts to doze. "It was great catching up. Maybe we'll see you around."

"How long are you here for?" I ask.

"Another few days."

"I'm sure I'll see you again before you head back to Boston."

Connor smiles before walking down the path toward the Keene B&B golf cart waiting in front of the house.

Meg follows him shortly, reaching up to kiss my cheek in farewell before taking her crying baby outside. "Thanks for dinner," she calls. "It was lovely. Good night!"

I hover at the door, but when Cat doesn't follow them, I close it and go in search of her. The TV is off. She's not in the living room or the kitchen, which looks and smells like someone made cookies for an army and left the mess behind. There's an empty bag of powdered sugar next to a can of LaCroix, which I don't keep in the house, so Cat must have brought it with her.

Dirty dishes are piled in and near the sink, with globs of dough on the counter and a trail of flour from the counter to the floor. What does a person even use to clean all this up?

The thought has hardly formed when Cat comes around the corner with a bucket of cleaning products and a broom. She doesn't pay me more than a passing glance while she sets it down and starts clearing up the kitchen.

"I meant what I said. I'll handle this," I tell her.

Cat hardly looks up from where she's pushing dishes into the sink. "So I can show up next week and have to do it all over again after the dirt has had time to set? No thanks."

"I'm not incompetent."

She pauses, glancing up. Surprise flashes in her eyes. "I didn't mean that."

Give me a break. My eyebrow goes up on its own.

Cat rolls her eyes, then she looks at me. *Really* looks at me, as though she's clearly seeing me for the first time instead of trying to peer through a foggy window. Her shoulders sag a little, and she shakes her head. "I made the mess, Belacourt. I'll clean it up."

"You're the one who threw flour all over my kitchen?"

"I was trying to make cookies. Kylie got a little flour happy. There was talk of flour-angels at one point, but I convinced her to save it for the sand."

I fight a little smile, imagining Cat negotiating with the three-year-old. "Her parents will love you for that one."

"I love me for that one," she counters, wetting a rag and dragging it over the counter. "Way less mess to clean up."

Cat's eyes are big and blue and making me freeze in place every time they wash over me. We're in my dim kitchen, but I feel like I'm sixteen and running into her at Sunrise Cafe, hoping she'll talk to me. Or fifteen and seeing her give her last Sour Punch Straw to her friend's little brother instead of enjoying it herself. Or seventeen and hosing off my back patio, overhearing her telling her boyfriend to invite a new kid in their class to swim with them so he can start making friends.

This girl is something else. I still can't seem to break the spell she has over me. Her attention is like a gift from above, and I need to savor it. I don't think I've ever met anyone with Cat's self-possession. She knows herself, she's confident, and from a guy who spends every free second stressing or being told to fix his posture and watch his tongue, I'm envious of that.

These abs only exist because my dad thought it would be a good idea if I toned up a little for our reality show. I might keep it up now for random photoshoots or the odd commercial here or there, but they're proof that my family has put a major emphasis on appearing perfect. I doubt Cat's ever done a sit-up in her life unless she wanted to.

I need to walk away before I get drunk on Cat's attention and do something I will undoubtedly later regret.

I move to the living room and start straightening it, putting pillows back on the sofa and folding my mom's leopard-print throw blanket.

Cat keeps cleaning the kitchen. She wipes the counters, puts away the ingredients, and fills the sink with water and a liberal dash of soap to soak the pans. I can't find anything else to clean, so I head to the sink to scrub the dishes while she's sweeping.

She pauses, leaning on the broom handle. "You don't have to do that."

"I know."

There's silence for a beat while she tucks a loose blonde lock of hair behind her ear. "I'm still planning to charge you for this."

My hand stills, the sponge resting against the metal mixing bowl. "Charge me to clean a mess you made in my kitchen?"

"Just doing my job."

"Which part?"

"Both."

Is she ridiculous or teasing? I can't tell. "The mess was your job?"

She shrugs. "Yeah. It falls under babysitting."

"The cleaning, too?"

"Yep. I'd file that away with my cleaning lady responsibilities."

Okay, so she's teasing. I can't help but chuckle as I reach down into the foamy water to scrub the mixing bowl. "What kind of discount am I looking at since I'm doing the dishes?"

"Discount?" She shakes her head. "No, you can pay me for that, too."

I stop fighting the smile. She's being ridiculous, but the edge of teasing in her voice while she's talking to me might be a once in a lifetime thing here, so I'm enjoying it while I have it. "Oh, can I?"

"We'll call it distracting the cleaner."

"If I'm going to be charged for distracting you, there are much more interesting ways I'd go about it."

Cat drops the broom.

I plunge my hand back into the water so I can look down and hide my smile a little better.

She clears her throat. "Fine. Ten percent off."

"You drive a hard bargain. I could use your negotiation skills at work."

"Done."

I flick a look at her. "Or maybe not, since it didn't seem too hard to convince you."

Cat picks up the broom and sweeps the flour mess off the floor around me. I can feel her brush past me and have to tell my heart to chill the heck out.

"Why'd you arrive so long before your family?" she asks. "I don't have them returning on my schedule until next month."

My pulse starts thrumming like it wants to keep time with her quick sweeping motions. The idea of telling anyone about my anxiety outside of the small group that watched me botch the meeting and lose our partnership with Genesis Investment Firm makes my stomach sick. I don't need Cat knowing what a failure I am. It's not a good look. "I just needed to get away."

"Here for some summer surfing?" she asks, not at all aware of the turmoil under my skin.

I swallow, my throat dry. I try to will my breathing back to normal, but it's out of my control. Once the anxiety train leaves the station, it's difficult to slow down.

I need a diversion. She'd make a good one if she didn't hate me. "Maybe."

Cat bends down to sweep the flour and probably a good amount of sand—we do live on the beach, after all—into the dustpan. "Are your sisters coming out too?"

I'm pretty sure I can detect hesitancy in her question, but I can't place why she'd feel that way. Does she *want* them to come out, or the opposite? "They aren't planning on it, as far as I know."

Her straight nose bunches up. "You guys don't talk much?"

"Keeping up with our family group chat would be a full-time job. I quit a while ago."

Cat laughs, the sound melodic to my ears. It chases away my suddenly rising pulse, putting me at ease. I want to bottle up that sound and play it when I feel low or nervous. There are probably healing powers interwoven there.

She gathers up the cleaning supplies and leaves to put them away while I finish rinsing the last bowl and place it face-down on a dish towel to dry.

I'm well aware that our conversation has been surface level, fishing for information—how long and which of my family members she'll be forced to endure this summer, mostly—but that doesn't mean I'm ready for the night to end.

Cat pulls her belt bag over her shoulder and starts toward the front door. "Good night, Belacourt."

"Hold up, Keene." Two can play the last names game. I follow her, drying my hands and tossing the towel onto the counter as I go. "I need to pay you."

She tosses a shrewd look over her shoulder. "I was joking. I'm not taking your money."

"But you stayed to clean up."

"That's part of babysitting," she says.

I reach for my wallet.

"Seriously," she says. "The Carmichaels paid me well. I was just finishing the job."

My fingers pinch a hundred dollar bill, but don't pull it out.

She shoots me a disingenuous smile and moves to leave. "Have a good ni—"

"How are you getting home?"

Cat stills, her elbow locking into place where it holds the door open. The dark sky behind her is filled with stars. There isn't much crime or traffic on our island, but Cat rode over here on the back of the Keene golf cart Connor was driving, and that golf cart is now back at Keene B&B.

"It's a nice night," she says.

"You can take one of my—"

"No, thanks."

How do I argue that? "Cat, really. Just take a cart. I'm not using all of them."

"It's not that." She runs her hand through her blonde hair, pushing it away from her face. "My uncle isn't really... I just don't want to have your golf cart sitting at my house."

Ah. So there *is* prejudice involved. "Then give me a second and I'll drive you home."

"That's okay, but thanks. See you around, Belacourt." She closes the door behind her, and she's gone.

I open the door but don't see her. Man, she's fast. I just need to be faster. I jog for the keys to one of the golf carts and hurry into the garage, sliding into the seat while the door opens behind me. It takes way too long to back out and race down the driveway, and by the time my lights shine on Cat's shorts, she's reached the lane.

I pull up right beside her.

Her eyes flick to me and away, but she doesn't slow down. "Nice wheels, Bezos."

"Bezos?"

"He's the first rich guy I could think of."

I fall in beside her, keeping my chuckle in.

"I don't need a ride," she says.

"I'm not giving you one," I say, keeping pace.

Cat keeps walking. "You're just out for a drive?"

"No, I'm following to make sure you get home alright."

She glances at me over her shoulder, her face glowing in the golf cart's headlights. "How do you know I'm going home?"

My stomach constricts. Does she have a boyfriend? It wouldn't surprise me, but I wasn't expecting the blow. "Are you?"

"Yeah, I'm going home." She stops in the lane.

I take my foot off the gas.

Cat faces me. "You're really going to follow me all the way home *just* to make sure I get there safely?"

"It's not that crazy." I start to feel defensive. Is it crazy? Lately I've been unsure where to draw the line and when my mind is crossing it. I have a feeling where Cat's concerned, that line is murkier than most.

"No." She shifts to her other foot. "It's sweet."

A slow grin spreads over my face. "Sweet? Catalina Keene thinks I'm *sweet*?"

She shakes her head and walks around the golf cart to slide onto the seat beside me. Her shoulder presses against mine on the narrow bench. "Just drive so this can be over faster. I'm charging by the minute."

A laugh bursts from my chest. "Since you wouldn't accept any cash for cleaning, I'm not too worried."

"If I had less pride, I would have," she mutters.

Something about the way she says it leaks into my chest and makes me let off the gas a little. Not just to prolong this ride, but because something feels off. I'm silent, trying to give her room to talk if she needs to.

Apparently, she doesn't feel the need to confide in me, because she stays silent.

"How's your uncle?" I ask, so I can fill the silence with her voice. "I heard about his cancer a few years ago."

She turns to look at me, clutching the front bar. "He's good now. I mean... yeah, no, he's good."

She was going to say something. What was she going to say? "He's in remission?"

"Yep, totally in remission. Totally alive. We had to pay a lot for him to be alive—*still* have to pay a lot. But at least he's alive, you know?"

I try to think of something to say, but it doesn't matter because she keeps talking.

"It's ridiculous, isn't it? People are *dying* and what do we do as a country? We charge them *thousands and thousands* of dollars to save their lives. Don't have the money? Don't worry about it! You can pay it off over the next thirty years."

Wait... what? I stop the golf cart and turn to face her. "What happened?"

Cat leans forward, resting her face in her hands.

I grip the steering wheel and watch the back of her head, searching for something to say. She hasn't yelled at me to finish driving her home, and she hasn't jumped out of the car, so I opt to sit in the silence and let her feel whatever she's feeling.

I kind of can't believe I'm sitting in a golf cart with Cat Keene, and I don't want it to end.

I guess my crush is alive and kicking after all.

CHAPTER 6

Cat

MY HEAD FEELS like it's going to explode. I don't know when the headache came on. One minute I was helping little Kylie Carmichael scoop cookie dough balls onto a cookie sheet, and the next thing I know my head is throbbing and the Carmichaels have taken their babies away, leaving me with Noah and a mess.

How did we get from there to sitting in the golf cart? Why didn't I just take his money when he offered after I cleaned up? Stupid conscience.

"You okay, Cat?" Noah asks, his low voice climbing over my skin.

I want to let it wrap around me like a blanket. Maybe if I make him fall in love with me, he'll give me access to the Belacourt vault in the basement of Disney World. That's where all the best things are kept, right? The thought leaves as quickly as it arrives because it's *awful* and I'm not that type of person. I have too much pride to be a gold digger, unfortunately. Maybe a little integrity, too.

Concern pulsates from Noah in waves. I just want a hug, and it's so tempting to weasel one out of him. I'll lean into his confidence instead. The more I've thought about it tonight, the more I feel like I can't share this with anyone. Not Holland or Ivy or any of my friends. Otto deserves more privacy and respect than that, and I've already broken it by sorting through his mail. It would be disrespectful to spread this around, especially without confronting Otto first.

But Noah? He doesn't run in my circles. He doesn't really know Otto, even if he knows *of* him. He's a safe sounding board for the overwhelming things I'm feeling right now. Plus, he's only here for the summer and then he'll be gone again.

Or maybe I'm drunk on the darkness and the waves crashing in the distance and the gentle, humid warmth of a June evening.

Yeah, probably that.

I rub my temples. Here goes nothing. "I found a medical bill today that Otto never told me about for a ridiculous amount of money I could never dream of paying back in this lifetime."

It slips out like a melted popsicle at the beach. Why did I just confide in him? *Him* of all people?

But he doesn't know my friends. He doesn't know Otto. He's quiet and he's listening and now that I've started, I can't seem to stop.

"I don't get it. Otto had no choice. He would have died without chemo. We found him a good team of doctors, they save his life, and now he's stuck with bills he can't afford. And the worst part?" I sit up, turning to face Noah. "He didn't tell me." I scoff, lifting my hands in the air like a crazed lunatic and hitting the top of the golf cart. My hand throbs, but I power through. "Why? I'm trustworthy. I'm *family*. Not even just family, but his only family. He has no one left here but me, and he's facing this huge thing, but he won't even tell me? Seriously? I have a right to know if he has a debt so big we could lose our house."

I'm seeing stars. The words are all out and there's no taking them back. I'm not even sure a man who allowed his life into five seasons of a reality TV show is the type of person you should spill huge secrets to, but it's too late now. Silence wraps around my admission, cloaking us in an awkward heavy cocoon.

"How's your hand?" Noah asks.

"It *hurts*." I shake it out, but I can feel the bruise already forming.

Noah pivots to face me better. I can't help but be grateful that the first words out of his mouth weren't *I'm sorry*. "Do you need ice?" he asks.

"No." Something about him letting me sit in the pain makes me want to talk more, and I can't seem to stop myself anyway. I can feel my ire dying and the relief from unburdening changing that awkward cocoon into a comfortable one.

Deceptively comfortable?

Probably. I don't care right now.

"It all hurts, Belacourt. The stupid part is I can't do anything about it." I laugh, the sharp sound cutting through the dark. "I took that babysitting job tonight for the money. Well, good thing I did. I'm fifty bucks closer to reaching my goal. Fifty bucks," I repeat, because it's pennies compared to what we need to come up with. *Pennies*.

"I'm sorry you're going through this," Noah says. His voice is soft but firm, and I suddenly feel ridiculous for complaining about money to a billionaire.

A billionaire.

He probably wipes his nose with fifty-dollar bills.

"Cat?" he whispers, his deep voice climbing over my skin.

"Sorry. Just have a headache."

"I have ibuprofen back at the house."

Why does he keep offering things? Paying me for cleaning, a ride, ice, meds. We aren't friends. It gives me flashbacks to eighth grade and Olive asking if I wanted a piece of gum, then putting it in her own mouth after I said yes.

That was the moment I knew things had changed.

I face forward. "Can you just take me home?"

Noah starts driving immediately. We proceed in silence, and the shame that follows confessions like this washes over my skin.

"You know," he says, pulling onto my road. "If you need a job—"

"I have a job. Actually, I have two jobs. Three? I don't know if you can count being a personal assistant to my uncle, but I do that too."

"You're his personal assistant?"

"Not in an official capacity, but yeah. I've been doing it since he was first diagnosed."

Noah's quiet for a minute, the golf cart slowing a block before we reach my house, a gorgeous two-story bed and breakfast close to the center of town.

Has he forgotten where I live? He was literally there hours ago. Maybe he's as awkward as I am and wants to end our conversation now. I start to climb out when his hand on my arm stops me, the warmth taking me by surprise. "I need an island PA."

Huh?

"I have an assistant already," he continues. "Mateo. He's amazing. But he's on the mainland, and he can't make it over here often and it's been... I need help locally. Don't answer me now."

My head is still pounding. I'm trying to make sense of his erratic speech.

"Take time to think about it," Noah presses. "But it will pay better than babysitting."

Think about *what*? Running all over the island managing his dry cleaning and doing his grocery shopping and being his yes girl? Disturbing. Mom is probably standing over my shoulder now, shaking her head. And Dad is probably trying to drag her away and reminding her not to meddle.

I was only nine when they were pulled into the ocean by a rip current and didn't make it back out alive, but I remember them clearly. Mom with her ideals and Dad with his calming, leveling presence. They were a good balance. My heart reaches out for them, and I hope they're nearby, even if I'm making a mess of myself in front of a Belacourt. I like to think I walk the world with two guardian angels and one earthly one. Otto still counts, even if I'm bugged with him right now.

Noah's hand is still on my arm, keeping me frozen in the cushioned seat, one leg out of the cart with my foot dangling above the blacktop.

"That seems... weird."

Noah's fingers tighten. "Just promise you'll consider it." He releases me to pull a phone from his pocket and unlocks it. After fiddling for a second, he hands me the phone open to a new contact form. "You can text me when you've thought it over."

Don't look, Mom. I type my number in and write *Catalina* under the name. I don't know why I do that, except that I like hearing him say it. No one calls me that. *No one.* Except for nurses, dental assistants, or substitute teachers reading rolls, the only person who consistently used my full given name was my dad.

He met my mom on Catalina Island, so it's kind of special to him.

I complete the entry and notice I'm one of three phone numbers in his contacts. "A little sparse," I say, before I can tell my mouth to shut it.

Noah takes his phone back. "It's a new phone."

Of course it is. Because people like Noah need to have the latest technology. I bet his old phone is sitting in a drawer somewhere, barely a year old. I could sell it and be one step closer to saving my uncle and my home.

Or I could run him coffee and fold his laundry.

Ack, Cat. *No.*

There's no way I could work for this guy. Even if he offers me ninety-two thousand dollars.

Well, maybe I would then, but that would also make him certifiable.

Noah drives me to the front of my house and pulls the cart to a stop. I hop out. "Thanks for the ride."

"I'll text you so you have my number," he says.

This is weird. I feel buzzy and uncertain. What I really need, more than anything, is for Otto to come clean. Maybe it's all a misunderstanding anyway and the medical bills are wrong or Otto *has* been paying them but the payments haven't gone through yet.

But he wanted to talk today.

Either way, there are other ways of coming up with the money. I just made a ton of jam. If I stick labels on the jars, I bet I could hike up the price and sell them at the farmer's market. After I take some out for the B&B and deliver jars to my favorite islanders, obviously.

I'd only need to sell roughly... ten thousand jars of jam. No biggie.

Noah watches me, waiting quietly for a response, and I can't decide how to feel about the way he doesn't rush me. I would have thought a guy like him would be all business, impatient to get to the point, but he lets me think before he requires responses. It's refreshing.

I start toward my house. "Thanks for the lift."

"Anytime," he says quietly. He waits until I'm up the steps and inside before he pulls away.

That was oddly chivalrous.

The first thing I do when I walk inside is check out the study. The pile of mail is gone, so Otto must have found it. Good. Maybe now he'll talk.

I find him in the unattached garage on the side of the house, his surfboard upside down on a padded sawhorse while he rubs wax along the bottom.

When he lifts his gaze, his face lights up. "Cattywampus! You're home. Did you hit up any cool hip places?"

I can tell he's making fun of himself. I love him for being such a goofball.

"Meet any guys?" he continues, waggling his white brows.

"My dates were tiny, cried a bit, and at one point I had to change a diaper."

Otto's mouth hangs open.

"I was babysitting."

"Who?" he asks.

"The Carmichael girls. I guess Connor knows Noah Belacourt from college, so they all went out to eat at his restaurant."

Otto pulls a face. "A little too highbrow for me."

Says the man who spent the day golfing.

"Did they enjoy it?" he asks.

"Probably." I open the stepladder and sit on the top with my feet up on a rung, resting my chin on my palms. My phone buzzes in my pocket, but I ignore it.

Otto keeps waxing his board.

"I feel like a Victorian spinster and you're the matron pushing me toward eligible men."

Otto looks up. "I can't be the handsome, studious guardian?" His shirt is off a button and his stringy hair falls over his face.

"Sure. Wanna explain why you feel a sudden desire to marry me off? This house isn't big enough for both of us or something? This isn't *Bridgerton*."

"What's *Bridgerton*?"

"Otto."

He puts his hands up. "Okay, yeah, maybe I was thinking it might be nice if you fell madly in love and brought home a nice guy one of these days. It's not because I want you out of the house. The guy can live here with us if you want."

I take a page from Noah's playbook and sit in the silence, giving Otto a chance to come clean.

"I just want you to be happy, Cat. I'm not going to be here forever."

"Do you have something to tell me?" I ask, doing some mad sea fishing for information right now. "Is the cancer back?"

He shakes his head, scoffing. "No, of course not. I wouldn't keep that from you."

Currently, that's not an easy thing to swallow. It rocks me because I've trusted Otto implicitly for my entire life. Yeah, he's not my father, but he raised me. He got to be both my mom and my dad. He brought me flowers at high school graduation, took me to the shop for pads when I started my period, let me cry on his shoulder in college when Jake ghosted me for Yale sorority girls. I have other aunts and uncles and even a set of grandparents in Georgia and a grandma out in San Diego, but I don't see any of them often. Otto is my family.

And, as far as I know, he's never lied to me before. He's never kept anything from me.

"You would tell me, right?" I press. "If you were in trouble, would you tell me?"

"Come on, Kit Kat. You know I would."

Okay. So. Either he's lying to my face, or he's not really in trouble.

Otto returns his attention to the surfboard. "Hey, I've been thinking of selling the old Beetle. What do you think? I don't really use it, and I can get a good amount from someone who might want to restore it or something."

My heart stops. "You want to sell your car."

"We have the golf carts, and I don't really leave the island, Cat. Why do I need to keep it? It just sits at the ferry lot, rusting away."

He does leave the island, though. He uses it to meet up with buddies and surf along the Florida coast. He used it a few months ago for a road trip out to a music festival in North

Carolina. I used it a few months ago with a day pass at Costco to see if a membership was worth it.

It wasn't. Not unless we got a different vehicle. The Beetle doesn't hold enough, and I drove home with toilet paper getting in the way of the gear shift.

No, he shouldn't sell his car. But telling me he wants to? That gives him away. Otto *loves* his yellow Beetle. He adores it almost as much as he adores me. Which means he owes a lot of money, and he's in trouble.

He's been lying.

"It's your car, your choice," I say lightly. I need to buy some time. "I'd wait until the summer is over at least. Aren't you meeting up with Phil and Hank next month down south?"

His face screws up. "You're right. I'll sell it after that." He gives me a broad smile. "What would I do without you, Cat?"

Lose your house, I think. But he won't, because I won't let him. He's not going to lose his car either.

I might not make ninety-two thousand dollars selling jam, but I'm smart, and I will find a way to get that money.

I hop off the stepladder and head for the house. "Good night, Otto."

"Night, Cattywampus. Love you, kiddo."

"Love you too."

My phone buzzes again, so I slip it from my pocket while I cross the dark yard toward the house. Willow is crying from the Carmichael room upstairs, so I climb the porch steps and sit on the wicker chair in the dark, pulling out my phone.

> UNKNOWN NUMBER
> This is Noah Belacourt
>
> I'm not offering you charity, Cat. I really do need an island PA. If you don't want the job, I'll look elsewhere.

> That was not intended to rush you into a decision. Take your time.
>
> And now I've texted you too many times.
>
> Chronic overthinker.
>
> Please don't feel like you need to respond to me tonight. But letting me know I have the right number and I'm not overtexting a random would be nice.

I consider letting him stew all night, but he said he's a chronic overthinker, and I should put him out of his misery.

CAT

> You have the right number. I'll call you tomorrow.

Noah gives my text a thumbs up, and I put my phone away.

CHAPTER 7

Noah

THE MAINLAND MECHANIC prescribed a new motor for my broken boat, but it's only a year old, so that didn't sit right with me. I had it towed to Dax Miller's shop in Sunset Harbor, because he can fix anything. It's not about the outlandish price the mainlander quoted me, it's the waste of it all. I'm not buying a new motor unless the boat needs it.

I'm standing on the dock outside of Dax's shop, waiting for him to finish looking at it. The sun beats down on the sparkling water, and despite my linen shirt and chino shorts, sweat rolls down my back. The water looks good, so I'm thinking it might be better to swim than kayak today. Or I could do both.

Both is good.

Dax fidgets with something in the motor, then straightens. "Give me a few days. I should have it running by Friday, depending on the availability of the parts."

"No new motor?"

He steps onto the dock, wiping his hands on a grease towel. "Nah. I don't know why you were quoted that. The issue is in the carburetor. Might need a new jet, but I'll know when I get inside."

"You're speaking another language, man."

Dax's mouth flicks into a half-smile. "I'll call you when it's ready to go or if I find any other issues. It shouldn't set you back too much."

We walk to the front of his shop, right in the center of town.

"I saw your commercial," Dax says.

The four words that make me want to jump in the ocean and swim far away. My face goes warm, and I hope it's not obvious that I'm blushing. I didn't realize the stupid commercial had started airing already. "My sister set it up for me," I mutter. "I didn't have the heart to say no."

"Sure, but is it really the *only* food your dog likes?"

"Dude, shut up," I say, laughing.

Dax seems to find this funny. "If you could just give me the line again, maybe mime throwing the frisbee—"

"I don't even have a dog. They brought the golden retriever in for filming, and he's very well trained."

The hum of an oncoming golf cart passes us before it slows, the big letters on the side singling it out as the one police golf cart on the island. Beau Palmer leans forward, grinning, one tan arm resting on the wheel. "When did you get a dog, man?" he says.

For real? "Has *everyone* seen it?"

Dax rubs the back of his neck. "Tristan sent us the clip last night."

"Of course he did." I shake my head, smiling.

I'm surprised Tristan hasn't given me crap for it already. The commercial is for Bone Appetit's new premier kibble, and I'm throwing a frisbee around with a dog, sans shirt, then I say my line. It's a short ad and it's corny. There was a woman on set whose job was to make sure my abs glistened *just* enough—they were selling more than dog food. But my sister Zoey is dating the grandson of the Bone Appetit owner, and I felt like I owed her after walking away from our family's reality show.

At least it's just the guys who saw me trying to look like a thirst trap and not—

Cat. She's walking this way. And she looks *good*.

"So when I take Xena to the park, I'm supposed to leave my shirt at home?" Beau asks. "I've been doing it all wrong."

I look at Dax, who is still wiping the grease off his hands. He's shirtless *now*, so I don't get why the jokes are on me. "Ask him. He has more experience."

Dax shakes his head, chuckling as he heads back to his garage.

I kind of wish I was shirtless. It's hot and the clear turquoise water looks good. My gaze flicks to Cat again. She's still walking this way. I haven't heard from her since she texted me last night. After her last message came through, I spent another hour going over everything I had said to her. I'm pretty sure I've scared her away. In trying to be chill, I seriously had no chill.

Cat's wearing a jean skirt and a yellow tank. Her hair is thrown up with a white scarf tied around it. She's wearing big, round sunglasses, so I can't tell if she notices me or not.

Probably not, because she's turning into the retirement center next door. My feet are already moving in her direction.

"Just messing around," Beau calls.

I lift my arm in the air, pointing out. "I'm laughing all the way to the bank."

Which isn't that funny, because I didn't get paid much for the stupid commercial.

"Touché," Beau calls. I can hear him laughing while I walk into the retirement center.

It smells like antiseptic and floral perfume. Cat is leaning on the welcome desk, her sunglasses pushed up on her head. She slides a jar of something amber forward. "It's good on ice cream, too," she says.

The receptionist grins. "I might not be taking this to the break room."

Cat rummages in her bag and pulls out a second jar. "Don't

tell anyone." She winks and turns down the hall. Fluorescent lights make her blonde hair glow.

My feet are following her before I can overthink it. That's new. "Cat."

She glances at me over her shoulder. "You."

"Me." I'm not deterred. I should be, but I follow her anyway. "Can we talk?"

"I'm in the middle of something."

"I can wait."

She looks at me over her shoulder, continuing down the hall. "Hang on."

I wait in the hall while she knocks on a resident's door and pushes it open. "Hey, Virginia. Brought you and Deedee some peach jam."

"Oh, yummy," an older voice says. "Don't tell Gemma."

"Your granddaughter? Why would I tell her?" she asks, her head falling to the side a bit. "Does she not want you to have jam?"

There's a shuffling sound and a drawer snaps shut.

"Why are you hiding it?" Cat asks suspiciously.

"You didn't see that," Virginia says.

"Is this a health thing?" Cat starts to sound worried.

Virginia ignores her. "Deedee's bringing over a new book. Sit down for a minute and she'll read us the best bits."

"Oh, look at the clock. Can't stay." Cat's voice rises as she backs from the room. "Get that other jar to Deedee for me?"

"Sure thing, honey. But you're missing out! This one has a *pirate*."

Cat slips into the hall and curls her fingers around my wrist, pulling me away from the room. "Quick, before she sees you."

"Why?" I can't get over the feeling of her hand gripping my skin, but I try to play it cool.

"Deedee's on her way. I'm still disturbed by her reading of *The Haunted Cowboy and Me* last week at book club. If she sees you, she'll make us read parts, and Jane won't be there to stop her when it gets spicy."

Not sure what that book is, but I have a feeling I wouldn't mind reading parts with Cat. "Jane Hayes?" I ask, remembering the girl from school.

"Yeah. She saved us all last time."

My smile grows. "This has happened to you before?"

"Not while I was alone, but I wouldn't put it past her." She looks at me, then drops my arm. "We're in book club together."

"Got it."

"Here, at the retirement home."

"Cool."

Cat's waiting for me to say something else, but I'm not sure what.

She blinks at me. "You aren't going to laugh at me for spending my free time hanging out in a retirement home?"

"I think it's sweet."

"It's not charity," she mumbles, waving to the receptionist. "See you later, Sandra!"

"Y'all have a good day," the lady calls.

We step into the sun, and Cat is already walking down the sidewalk. We wade through thick, warm air toward the town square. My golf cart is parked in the opposite direction, by the mechanic shop, but I'll worry about it later.

I want to ask if she's thought over my offer, but I don't want to rush her. It's unclear why this is important to me, but I've known Cat a long time and I want to help. She's too prideful to accept a blank check to cover Otto's treatments, and Scout's board of directors doesn't need another reason to label me incompetent and nutty. I'm on thin ice as it is.

We walk through the town square, the fountain in the center trickling with sea water that's been routed from the ocean. "You read a lot of cowboy books with the retirement ladies?"

Cat looks at me. "You wanted to talk?"

No more chitchat then. "Yeah, about my offer."

"I'm listening."

It's suddenly become so much warmer outside. I'm a man who can run a board meeting, has built a multi-million dollar company from the ground up, spent last Easter in Greece with my middle sister and her boyfriend, who is the biggest superhero movie star in the last five years—but facing *this* girl? I'm a goner.

Olive's boyfriend might be Superman, but I still have kryptonite, and her name is Cat Keene.

"Are you okay?" she asks, squinting into the sun.

I reach for her sunglasses and gently push them down from her head until the bridge is resting on her nose. She's gone silent.

Did I just cross personal boundaries? *Pull it together, man.* "I need help."

She stands there in front of the post office in our town square, one hand on her hip, the other holding her canvas bag of jam. "Let's talk responsibilities. What did you have in mind?"

My heart rate picks up. She's not saying no, and that's something. "Dry cleaning. Morning coffee. Small errands."

"I have responsibilities at the B&B, and I clean three houses during the week."

"I'm flexible, Cat," I say softly.

The bell jingles as someone steps out of the post office, so I tug her to the side, around the pastel clapboard building. We don't need an audience for this conversation.

"What about scheduling?" she asks. "Will calls come to me and I'll have to field them for you?"

"Not really. For the island job, I really just need small things. Someone to be able to get to the house if I have deliveries while I'm at the office. Sometimes things will come up, maybe, but Mateo is on the mainland and he'll still manage my calendar."

"So I'm really just an errand girl."

I hold her gaze—what I can see of it through the black tint of her round white sunglasses. Something about her defensive stance, the way her arms are crossed over her chest, tells me how much she needs for this to not be charity. Fine, Cat. She wants a boss? I'll be a boss. I'm pretty good at that.

"I'm hiring a PA," I tell her. "Which is more involved than an errand girl. I'm happy to be flexible regarding your other jobs, but you won't be getting paid for doing nothing. I'm willing to provide a list for you each night so you can schedule your day ahead of time, and you can let me know if I'm giving you too much. Communicate with me and we'll adjust."

Something about her posture relaxes. "This sounds like a lot. I expect you'll pay accordingly."

"I'm a busy man with a lot to do, and I'm hiring you to help me. You in or not?" Yikes, my voice was too crisp. Was that too much? That was probably too much. I got into Office Noah mode and powered through a little too strong.

Where was Office Noah during the Genesis Investment Firm meeting? On a mental cruise to Jamaica, pretending his life wasn't falling apart, that's where. But he's back for a minute now because Cat needs him.

"How much will you pay?"

I've thought this part through. She needs a lot of money, but I don't know how much. For cancer treatment, possibly surgery, I'm guessing it's somewhere in the hundreds of thousands. If I jump ahead with something like fifteen thousand a day, she'll run for the beach.

I play it cool. "Same thing I pay Mateo. Four thousand dollars a day."

Cat is frozen. Or time is frozen. Her lips are parted slightly, and they've captured my attention like clickbait. I can't look away.

"You pay Mateo that much?"

"He works hard," is all I can say. I pay him well, but not *that* well. Besides, this isn't forever. It's a summer job. I just want to help Cat and Otto so they don't lose their house. I can be a little frivolous for once.

Her stare is worrying me now. Did I go too far? Offer too much right out of the gate?

As long as Scout doesn't find out and add it to the list of reasons I'm unfit to run a company. But they won't. How could they? She's not tacky enough to walk around telling everyone how much money she makes.

"Is that not enough?" I can't help but say, trying to reiterate the idea that this isn't a ludicrous amount of money for running errands. I might be wealthy, but I'm not stupid.

"It's too much, Belacourt."

"I plan to get my money's worth." My voice comes out low and husky.

Her eyebrows rise above the white rims of her glasses.

"In an appropriate work-related way." I grin because her cheeks are starting to pink. "Not in the mood to be sued for coming on to my employee."

She shakes her head. "How long are you planning to stay in Sunset Harbor? Two months? Three?"

"Probably two." The new dating app we created at Scout launches near the end of July. If I can get through the launch and the big party without having a meltdown, Dr. Stein will write a great letter of approval, the board will be off my back, and I can return to life as normal.

I'll still spend a fair amount of time on the island, but my apartment is just over the bay on Florida's mainland.

"And the job ends when you leave?" she verifies.

"Yes."

Cat pulls her bottom lip between her teeth, chewing at it. She's totally captured me again. She's not just clickbait. Hook, line, and sinker, I've clicked the bait. I'm *all in*, scouring the article to find out *what* new routine the Rock is doing to build up his lats.

Only this is so much better.

"Two thousand," she says, her voice so quiet I don't know if I heard her. "Four is..." She shakes her head. "Crazy. Way too much."

"What?"

Cat straightens her shoulders and pushes her glasses up on her head to look me in the eyes. "Two thousand each day, and I'll do whatever you want. I'll run your errands, do your grocery shopping, wash your clothes, clean your house—we can include that in this fee—walk your dog..."

"I don't have a dog."

"I'll get you a dog, train it, and then walk it every day. I'll make your bedtime snack and tuck you in, Belacourt. You make me a list every night and I'll be your fairy godmother, making it come true the next day."

"Two thousand dollars each day?" I verify, making sure she knows this isn't a paid-by-the-week gig. I'd pay her ten grand if she asked. I don't care.

Cat swallows. "Yes."

Her voice is so firm, it's adorable. I'm distracted by the freckles dusting her nose and trailing under each eye, and I have the overwhelming urge to lean forward and kiss each one. But then I'd definitely be sued. She needs this to stay professional, and I can give her that. I reach for her, hand out, and wait for her to take it. "You have a deal."

Her shoulders sag in relief and she takes my hand, shaking it firmly.

I can't help but smile. She thinks I'm doing her the favor, paying her a ridiculous amount for handling my dry cleaning and coordinating the lawn guy's appointments. She doesn't realize I'm the one who wins here.

I get to hang out with Cat Keene all summer long.

CHAPTER 8

Cat

WHEN NOAH'S text comes in late at night with a list of job responsibilities, I'm lying in bed and feeling my first wave of panic. Why did I think I could do this? My plate is already too full. There's no room to add another job. How am I supposed to clean the B&B, tidy up after Otto destroys the kitchen making breakfast for the Carmichaels, be at Mrs. Finnigan's house for her weekly cleaning, and bring Noah a coffee from Sunrise Café all in one morning?

A little finagling, I guess. What choice do I have if I want to keep my house? I lay in bed and text Mrs. Finnigan.

> **CAT**
> Can we push your cleaning back to noon tomorrow?

> **MRS. FINNIGAN**
> I have water aerobics at noon, but you can let yourself in. Don't forget to feed the birds.

> **CAT**
> That's my favorite part! Thank you, Mrs. Finnigan. Enjoy that booty-shaking

> **MRS. FINNIGAN**
> I haven't shaken my booty in a long time, young lady. But I will try tomorrow, just for you.

I send her a kissy face emoji and a dancing lady, then go over the rest of Noah's list. Which, to be honest, is longer than I expected for the first day. I guess, for two grand, I should be doing things like spit-polishing his shoes and arranging his M&Ms by color.

I'll take things like grocery shopping and folding his jeans instead.

Does Noah wear jeans?

Maybe I'll just be folding his socks. Running shorts. Other things.

> **NOAH**
>
> Times are flexible, Cat. I'm usually back from my run by 7am, but if you beat me to the house, let yourself in. You know the code.
>
> Coffee with cream, no sugar.
>
> Laundry—baskets located in my closet. Dry cleaning in white, everything else in gray.
>
> I need flowers sent to my sister. I'll leave instructions on the counter.
>
> Dinner meeting. Can you find something at the market that I can heat and put on a plate for three people? No dairy or melon.
>
> Don't buy me a puppy

If I show up with a mini goldendoodle tomorrow, Noah only has himself to blame.

I text him back with a saluting emoji.

> **CAT**
>
> You got it, Zuckerburg.

Also, *beat him to the house?* What time does he expect his coffee? The man is a lunatic. If I'm alert before seven, I've been abducted by aliens and replaced with a more responsible life source.

I guess I'm becoming more responsible now. Noah has agreed to such a crazy amount of money, I have no choice but to be an early riser.

Maybe I'll get a sunrise out of it.

NOAH
Zuckerburg?

CAT
Creator of social media. Rich. Computer genius. Also, did I mention he's rich?

NOAH
I'll take computer genius. Have you been spying on me?

CAT
The ads for Scout are everywhere, Zuckerburg. Everywhere.

NOAH
That doesn't explain how I'm a computer genius.

CAT
Don't you have to be one in order to develop software like that? Don't try to say you hired someone to develop it for you. I read a BuzzFeed article.

NOAH
Ahh right. BuzzFeed never lies.

CAT
Everything on the internet is true.

NOAH

Good to know. I guess that means my sister really is pregnant with Travis Kelce's baby and the first ultrasound showed that the baby has an extra heart. I hope her boyfriend doesn't find out.

CAT

I knew that one was fake!

NOAH

Not possible. It was on the internet, Cat.

I chuckle, reading back over his message. I don't mention that the article I read about Scout was a few years ago and off the *New York Times*, of course, because I don't want him to know I'm a snoop. But come on. The guy isn't even thirty and he's developed software to fact-check anything you find on the internet. Scout gives sources too, and I have definitely used it a handful of times. His new dating app coming out—Scoutr—uses the fact-checking software to ensure all dating profiles are legit. There will be no catfishing or exaggerating on there because Scout makes it impossible.

It's brilliant. It's necessary. It's going to cut down on so many inappropriate messages and booty call wannabes.

Besides, I've seen Noah mentioned in multiple *BuzzFeed* articles. It's not a total lie.

CAT

I'll see you in the morning, Zuckerburg.

NOAH

That's already gotten old.

CAT

Noted. Good night, Trump.

NOAH
Good night, Cat.

I put my phone down and roll over. Noah is supposed to be a representative of corporate America, all the things that are wrong with the wealth and greed in this country. But, so far, he has been helpful—sometimes to a distressing degree; hello ocean when I *wasn't* drowning—and kind. He's still a billionaire with more money than sense. And he has a lot of sense.

So I kick the weird, bubbly feeling aside and go to sleep.

WHERE DO rich people get their coffee? From their fancy kitchen countertop machines if they live in Sunset Harbor, probably. Our coffee at the B&B is good, but it's just coffee, so I hop on my bike and head to Sunrise Café. Otto was in the middle of making breakfast for the guests when I left, so I told him to leave the dishes in the sink. I'll take care of it later.

Also, it's only ten minutes after seven, so I think I'm doing pretty good so far for the personal assistant of a guy who is *finishing* his run before seven.

Once the coffee is in hand, I pop a splash stick into the drinking hole and hop back on my bike. I like the Carmichaels, but once they head home we won't have a guest for a few days and I'll be able to use one of the golf carts again, which is always nice. Otto would probably let me take one even with them here, but we have a guests-first policy, so I usually leave the extra one for him. He's active, yeah, but he's not young. If one of us has to ride a bike, it might as well be me.

We live close to the center of the island. The ride through the town square and up Main Street toward the ritzy side of Sunset Harbor doesn't take too long, but it's already warm. By the time I reach the Belacourt mansion, the sun is out in full force, blazing down on me. Perspiration lines my forehead and rolls down my spine, gathering on the small of my back.

I really wish I had just taken the golf cart.

Using the edge of my T-shirt sleeve, I wipe at my forehead and slide my phone into my pocket. I'm in pink running shorts and a white shirt, my Birkenstocks keeping the look extra casual. Oh, no. Am I *too* casual? A personal assistant usually wears professional clothing, don't they? But I can't sport a pencil skirt while I mop Mrs. Finnigan's original wood floors, so this will have to do.

I knock on the door, hot coffee warming my already warm hand.

Should I have gotten it iced? It's too hot for hot coffee, right?

Get a grip, Cat. I've never over-thought anything in my life, but now I can't seem to stop. Can overthinking be contagious? Because Noah must be rubbing off on me.

The door swings open, and it is a glorious sight to behold. Noah's chest is heaving like he just sprinted inside from his run. He's holding the bottom of his shirt up to mop his sweaty face, not unlike I did a moment ago, except in so doing, he has revealed a full triangle of glistening abs.

The man exercises regularly, clearly. He must have an entire regimen dedicated to those beauties alone. If he'd been running on the beach alongside me when I'd lost my mom's scarf last week, he definitely would have caught it before it hit the ocean. Maybe there's something to this working out thing after all.

I mean, I can't look away.

I've seen his abs a lot, okay? We live on a long, narrow strip of land surrounded by turquoise ocean and white sand, so there are always the boating, surfing, and beach occasions for shirtlessness. Then there's the time Noah did a cologne ad when we were all in college that I might have found on YouTube and watched on repeat after a particularly bad breakup. I wasn't a *fan* of Noah, obviously. His sister ruined my life in eighth grade, and his whole family is wild and entitled.

But he's nice to look at.

Yet none of those previous occasions compare to the specimen that is before me today. I make a point of not objectifying people, just in general, since our worth shouldn't be tied to how we look or what shoes we're wearing or how many yachts we own, but for a long moment I allow myself this one small treat.

He drops the shirt. "Good morning."

And treat over. Time for professionalism. My arm juts out with the coffee. "It's still hot," I say. "Want me to pour it over ice?"

Noah's gaze runs over my face like he's frosting a cake. Did he catch me staring? By the small smile playing over his lips, he totally caught me staring.

"Ice sounds good," he says. "There's a pebble ice maker in the kitchen."

I nod once, trying to channel Anne Hathaway in *The Devil Wears Prada* when she's good at her job, and step past him into the house. If I hold my head high enough, he won't notice my running shorts—I don't run, they're just easy to clean in—and dingy old shirt with a dirty sweat-wiped sleeve.

"I just need a quick shower," he says, passing the kitchen and heading for the stairs.

I go in search of a tumbler and fill it with ice, then take the lid off the coffee to let it cool off. It takes me ten minutes to follow the instructions he left for Bree's flowers and order some online to be delivered later today with a note.

Good luck, Bree. You've got this.
—Noah

First off, I try not to find the encouragement adorable. I know Bree is Noah's youngest sister and she's in the middle of filming for *Bela-babes Take Manhattan*, but I can't help being curious about why he's sending her good luck flowers in *Nashville*. The girl isn't even in New York City. Maybe they're doing a travel episode.

By the time the flowers are finalized and paid for—with the card Noah left on the counter beside his note—the coffee is poured over ice and I've checked out what he has in his fridge so I can plan something for his working dinner tonight. He comes downstairs, bringing both laundry baskets with him. He's wearing slacks and a button-down shirt, ready for the office. Does he ferry into work every day? Does he work from home at a level of adulthood that means he wears the whole work outfit, even when Zoom meetings will only show him from the chest up?

I refuse to consider the thoughtfulness of his gesture in carrying down the laundry. He probably just wants his clothes washed so his workout shorts don't make his bathroom smell.

"Thanks." I take the clothes into the laundry room and get to work.

There isn't much, so it only takes a minute to sort and start the first load. When I turn around, Noah is leaning in the doorway.

His arms are crossed loosely over his chest, his shoulder leaning against the door jamb. "I'm getting you a card for expenses. It should be here by the end of the day. I have Mateo working on it."

I pop a hand on my hip. "Your other assistant?"

"Yeah, he handles those things most of the time. Also, can you make that dinner for four instead of three? Mateo will join us tonight."

"Sure thing."

His gaze sweeps over my clothes in a way that makes me second, no... fourth guess what I'm wearing, but there is zero judgment on his face. I want to say it's appreciation lurking in those dark brown eyes, but that's ridiculous. Obviously, the uphill bike ride in the heat has messed with my head. "Anything else?"

"I'll put keys to one of the golf carts on the counter."

Oh my gosh. He saw my bike, or my sweat, or something. He must be trying to save us both the embarrassment of me showing up sweaty with his dinner later tonight in front of his colleagues and the assistant who actually knows what he's doing.

But I don't need charity.

"My bike is perfectly—"

"It has nothing to do with your bike," he says, straightening. "Though you're welcome to leave it in the garage. The cart feels necessary since you'll be running all over the island for me. I don't expect you to bike around with my dry cleaning or my groceries, Cat."

He makes a fair point.

"You can use the one that doesn't have any Belacourt Resort labels, so Otto won't have to put up with my logos in front of his B&B."

My lips curl into a smile and my hand drops, my ire gone. Trying to balance his clothes on a bike would have been a hassle. Same with trying to bike up his dinner tonight once I figure out what it's going to be. I could totally do it, but a golf cart would make things easier.

It would also help me get around faster.

And be generally less sweaty, which is a good enough reason on its own.

"Think of it as your company vehicle if you need to."

I was sold five minutes ago, but I nod at this. "Okay. Thanks."

Noah looks away, shoving a hand into the pocket of his slacks. He seems uncomfortable with the gratitude, which makes me want to be more effusive all of a sudden. He clears his throat and looks away. "I need to get to work, but I'll see you tonight."

"What time is dinner?"

"Seven. I'll take the dry cleaning to the mainland, so don't worry about that anymore."

A whiff of something delicious floats my way, rich and deep and swathing us in hues of black and white. Did we just step into a men's fragrance ad? It smells like it.

Quick, Cat. Time to mentally get back on track. "Do your lists often change?"

Noah smiles guiltily. "Mateo and I have a fluid communication thing going, but if it doesn't work for you, I will try to be more consistent."

"It's great," I say, quickly backpedaling. I can tell right away that a flexible schedule is going to make it easier to juggle all the balls in my life, so I support Noah and I having a fluid thing, too. I put both thumbs up like The Fonz and make a weird throat noise. Have I mentioned how much I enjoy old shows and movies? Right now, I wish I hadn't watched *Happy Days* reruns last week and instead watched something that would make me seem smart and sophisticated, like Audrey Hepburn. Audrey wouldn't point two thumbs at herself like a fifties greaser.

Be more like Audrey.

But then Noah smiles, his eyes lighting up, and I feel like *maybe* he's not just laughing at me this time.

"Have a good day at work," I say, hoping it pushes him out the door. A little space and the chance to step out of this noir moment would be beneficial to my mental health.

Noah nods once, stepping back, his hand sliding into his pocket again. He has so much suave. He just *oozes* handsome charismatic business owner vibes. If he could bottle *that* and sell it as a cologne, he wouldn't need to work another day in his life.

Okay, so he already doesn't need to work another day in his life, but my point stands.

I smile broadly in what I hope is an *I'm definitely not affected by you or your smell or your thoughtful gestures or your gorgeous ocean view, Mr. Darcy of Pemberley.* Time to get my head back on straight. Otto's dishes and Mrs. Finnigan's birds are counting on me.

"Have a good day, Cat," he says, walking away.

"You, too, Scrooge McDuck."

He turns a furrowed brow back on me. It has the effect of looking half-smolder and fully attractive. "The uncle, right? The duck triplets' uncle?"

I swallow. "Yeah, the one who swims in a pool of money."

"Oh, so you've been to my basement?"

I let out a snort. Now I'm glad I didn't call him Christian Grey.

He smiles softly like he can read my mind. "Bye, Cat."

I'm just a little bit disappointed when I hear the door shut behind him.

CHAPTER 9

Noah

I'M DISTRACTED. I have Cat on the brain, and it's getting in the way of work. I literally drew a cat on my napkin at the beginning of this meeting, which is the opposite of what the board wanted when they gave me some forced R & R time.

I'm not even supposed to be in the office today. I'm only supposed to come in for twenty hours each week, max, and I'm using up too many of those hours today because I had to get off the island. I couldn't stay in the house with Cat there another minute, because being around her makes me want to say or do things I shouldn't. *Especially* now that she's my employee. I need to keep a strong, solid professional barrier between us.

Besides, this whole rest and relaxation stuff is not my thing. I'm supposed to be kayaking or meditating on the beach or something else emotionally productive, but it feels like a waste of time when we're about to launch the app that could skyrocket our brand and open the doors to more helpful apps in the future.

But since I came into the office today and moved the dinner meeting to now, Gina won't have to come out to Casa Belacourt tonight. The meal I asked Cat to get is unnecessary.

I want her to feel like she's earned her income, though, and I'd planned on asking her to stay for the meeting anyway. Maybe

I'll still have Mateo come out to the island. We can go over some things, and I can introduce him to Cat. They might need to work together at some point this summer, anyway.

"The meeting with Jensen Advertising has been moved up to tomorrow," Gina says, tapping her heel on the vinyl office floor. "But I have it under control."

I should be running point on that meeting, but Gina's taken over that responsibility until I've proven I'm not going to bomb another one. "The projections are set. Don't let them lowball us."

Gina tilts her head, her short dark bob swinging with the motion. Her feline smile is telling me I should know better than to say anything like that, because negotiating is her middle name. She's a shark, and I'm glad she's on my side here.

My phone rings, and I lift it when I see Bree's name flash across the screen. "We done here?" I ask, already rising.

Gina closes her computer. "I'll compile the ad budget for approval."

Nodding, I answer the phone and put it to my ear. "How'd it go?"

Bree lets out a nervous, tinny laugh.

"*Has* it gone?" I ask, gathering my computer from the conference room table and carrying it toward my office. The workday is almost over, so I assume she's already done trying out for a slot in America's next big country music duo. "Are you finished with the audition?"

"Yeah."

It's silent while I walk into my office and put my computer down. I don't have a good feeling about this. "What is it, Bree?"

"I bombed it," she whispers. "Totally screwed the whole thing up. I'll be lucky if I get a callback from *anyone* in the business after this. You know how people talk."

I sit in my chair and swivel to face the window. "It can't be that bad. I've heard you sing."

"It was bad, Noah." She makes a frustrated groan. "I've never been so nervous in my life. I think it messed with my vocals."

That's possible. Sometimes my anxiety gets so bad I can hear my heart beating in my ears, which can't be normal. If that was happening while I tried to sing, it would mess with my voice for sure. But I don't tell her this.

I haven't told anyone in my family about my issues lately. They wouldn't know what to do with the information. Besides, everyone is so busy with their own problems and companies and filming and divorces, I don't want to add to their plates.

After I botched the investor meeting by panicking and walking out in the middle of the pitch, I agreed to slow down at work and take time off in Sunset Harbor, per my board of directors' decision. I made them agree to keep it quiet, that my episode wouldn't leave Scout offices. Which means my family still doesn't know about my weird situational anxiety.

That's what the therapist called it, at least. She told me it was likely due to my circumstances and could possibly be eliminated if I re-evaluate and reorganize my life. Like an anxiety amputation. I can cut it off and be all better.

I'm still trying to figure out how to do that. The time out in Sunset Harbor is supposed to reset my brain and help me get there faster. But, right now, Bree doesn't need me moaning about my mental health issues. She just needs to complain, and I'm pretty sure she hasn't told either of our other sisters about her Nashville opportunity. They've got a weird besties-but-also-enemies thing going. I don't understand it, so I stay out of it.

Bree moans again, and I can picture her flinging herself onto her hotel bed with an arm over her face.

"I'm guessing it wasn't as bad as you imagine it was."

"You weren't there," she says, whining. "I feel like an idiot, Noah. An *idiot*. I wore cowgirl boots so I'd look more the part, but I think it just made me look like a try-hard. The producer's assistant gushed before the audition. I guess she's a fan of the show. That's the moment I should have known they wouldn't take me seriously as a country singer."

"They want money and talent. If you have talent—which I know you do—they won't see your drama on *The Belacourts* when they look at you. They'll see dollar signs instead."

"Unless I bombed it and didn't sound like I have any talent. Spoiler alert: that's what happened."

For the sake of her dreams, I hope that's not the case. "When will you hear back?"

"No idea. That assistant who gushed over our show? She told me they'll be in touch." There's a sniffing sound, and I'm pretty sure Bree's crying now. "I don't want to go back to New York. Zoey and her boyfriend are so annoyingly in love it's nauseating, and Olive is off on location with Dash while he shoots that weird dinosaur movie she was telling us about, and Mom and Dad are just—ick."

Ick? That makes my chest sore. "Have you seen much of them lately?"

"Gosh, no. Dad's been difficult the last few years, you know, but now he's straight up incorrigible. His latest girlfriend is the same age as me."

"Gross."

"Don't quote me on that. It might be plastic surgery. But she *looks* my age."

My parents have been quietly separated for a few years, so you'd think the divorce wouldn't be that violent. But something about officially announcing the end of their marriage made both of them take the gloves off in the sparring ring, and now everything they do feels like a direct hit intended for the other. My sisters and I are just caught in the crosshairs.

My sisters more than me, since I've silenced the family group chat and don't live in Manhattan most of the time. Hardly ever anymore, really. I should probably lease my apartment out or something.

I think of the advice Dr. Stein gave about my situational depression. *Go somewhere. Get out of your office and your head. Commune with nature and re-introduce yourself to things you used to love to do. Time and space and healthy breathing will heal this.*

That was the official advice she provided my board of directors too, and they used it to give me a few work-related boundaries.

Maybe it could work for Bree, too.

"Have you thought of taking a trip? Get out of town for a while and distract yourself. Find your inner peace. Maui is nice this time of year."

"Like I could relax on the beach right now. I'm a high-strung *mess*. I need to work. To do something."

"Write a book?" I suggest.

She laughs. "Like it's so easy."

"*Read* a book."

"I wouldn't be able to concentrate. Hey! I just had a thought. You're launching your app soon, right? Do you need ads? I can do them for you."

"We're meeting with Jensen tomorrow to go over that, but most of the campaigns are all planned out."

"I'm not picky," she says. I can hear her getting up and going through a drawer or something. Is she packing? "Where are you shooting? The Florida office?"

Is she serious? I love Bree, but I'm not sure having her headline my campaign is the best move. She gets a little flighty sometimes. "Don't know yet. I was thinking Sunset Harbor, actually."

I don't know where that thought comes from, except shooting the ads on our private beach would cut down on costs, which is always a bonus, and it means I can be at the shoot without using up any of my allotted in-the-office work hours. Also, if it's on the beach, Cat can help. I've had the feeling from some of our interactions that she doesn't take me seriously, and part of me wants her to see me working. Like maybe she'll respect me more if she can see how capable I am. That I don't sit on my golden throne and let all my minions do everything for me.

It sounds ridiculous, but it's how I feel.

"I haven't been home in years," she says thoughtfully. "Are you there now?"

I swallow. If I tell Bree about my mental health retreat, the whole family will know by dinner time. So I play it chill. "Just for the summer."

She sighs quietly.

I hold my breath. I don't want my sister to come here. She'll figure out that I don't have my crap together. But her sigh sits between us, and I have to say something. "If you want to help with the ads, I can let you know the dates once they're finalized. I'd love to hang out for a weekend."

There, that wasn't too obvious. It gives her a reason to come home for a few days without crashing my entire summer.

"Thanks, Noah! I was hoping you'd say that. You staying at the resort?"

I can't tell her I've lent my suite to a friend or she'll want to know who, and then the entire country will know where Presley James is hiding. "No, just the house." *Think, Noah.* "I wanted to stay in my old room."

Old room? Why did I say that? But she must buy it because she sucks in a quick breath. "That kind of sounds fun. Like we're kids again. I'll get a flight out as soon as I can. But you have to promise not to play your weird games too long and take me out kayaking, okay?"

I haven't had many opportunities to play my weird games at all this summer, so she doesn't have much to worry about.

It looks like I'm stuck with her now. "I have a perfect kayak for you."

"Yay!" Bree squeals. "This is just what I need. A distraction. See you soon!"

"Bye, Bree."

We both hang up. I slump back in my chair, looking out over the water in the wharf and the lighthouse in the distance that marks the southern tip of the island. I might have chosen a location off the island for my company, Scout, but we can still see Sunset Harbor in the distance, a long, thin strip of land floating in the glittering ocean. The sun glares against my window, making me squint. For the first time in a long time, I want to be there instead of here in my office.

I'm guessing the beach isn't the reason for that.

A knock sounds on my door, so I swivel away from the window. "Come in."

Mateo pushes it open. "I have the ad budget Gina mentioned. She sent a hard copy to the printer." He puts it on my desk, and I motion for him to be seated while I take a look at it.

"My sister offered to help shoot the ads. I'm sure she'll give us a reduced rate if we want to consider that." I speak absently, going over the numbers. So far, everything looks good. "If we shoot on the resort's private beach, we won't have location fees."

"I'll make a note of it," Mateo says, typing into his phone while I talk. "Which sister?"

"Bree."

"Got it," he says, still typing away.

"Gina won't be coming to the house tonight, but I think we could still meet." I try to make my voice sound normal. "I hired an island girl to help a little around the house—calling her a PA, but it's just a summer job while I'm staying out there. I thought if you met her, she could help you with some things."

Mateo looks up, his hazel eyes widening. The kid is fresh out of college and everything I could dream of in a personal assistant. I want to tell him his job is safe and I'm only trying to help this girl out, but something stops me. I don't really want anyone to know that Cat needs the money, and I think I'll sound unhinged if it gets back to the board that I hired someone to do small chores just so I could pay her uncle's cancer bills.

"Your job is safe," I say, looking back at Gina's ad development cost projections. "I just need someone to get me coffee in the morning and handle my dry cleaning on the island."

"So this is who the extra credit card is for? Catalina Keene?"

"Yeah."

Mateo looks to where the bank card is sitting on my desk. He got it for me this morning, because, as I said, he is good at his job.

"Great." He shoots me an overly wide smile. "Can't wait to meet her."

"You'll love her," I say, because it's true. Everyone does. She is sunshine personified. "Stop freaking out. She's not taking your job."

"You could tell?" he asks, cringing.

"You don't hide your expressions very well. Don't worry, man. This really is just a summer gig. She's helping out a bit around the island and nothing more."

Mateo nods, and I can tell he's more on board with the concept now.

"She'll probably need your help, so I want you to come meet her. I want her to be able to reach out to you with questions, since you'll be able to answer them better than I can half the time."

Feeding his ego is working, and I can see I've shifted the situation in his mind so he now looks at Cat like a young Padawan and no longer like a Jedi threat.

"Seven?" he asks.

"Yes." I stack the papers that now have my notations on

them and hand them back. "Bring the updated cost projections and we can go over them tonight."

"Will do. Should I pick up dinner?"

"Cat's taking care of that."

Mateo nods and slips out of the office. I shut down my computer and pack up, eager to return home.

To return to her.

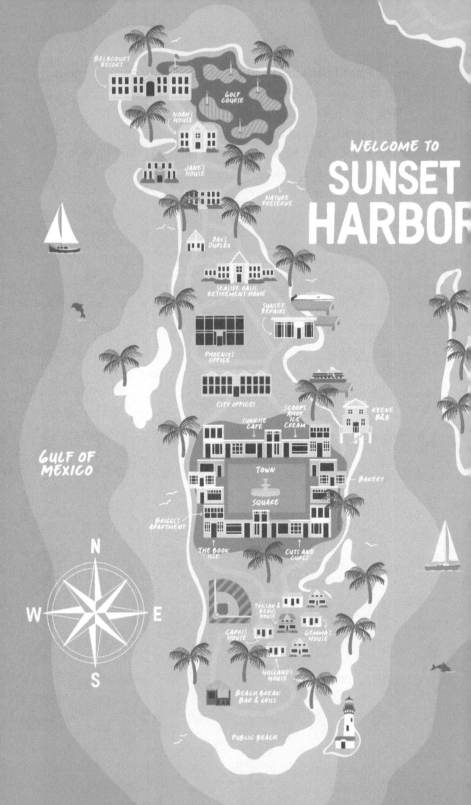

CHAPTER 10

Cat

HAVING Noah's house to myself while I'm puttering around being all domestic has done *weird* things to my brain. It's not like I have some fantasy of being the fifties housewife to Noah's working man, but I want to be a wife and a mom, okay? I refuse to be ashamed of that. It doesn't hurt anyone if I turn kabobs and mix a salad while imagining that the baby is taking a nap and the kids are riding their bikes out front and the husband—whoever he is—hasn't gotten home yet.

In this fantasy I'm also about three inches taller, have enough money to pay for Otto's cancer treatments out of pocket, and I'm not wearing a denim apron I found in the back of a kitchen drawer that says GRILL KING in bold red letters and still has the tag on it.

I guess Mr. Belacourt doesn't see himself as a grill king, since he's clearly never used this apron. Not surprising. I can't imagine Noah's dad making his own food.

I'm out on the back patio, grilling steak and pineapple kabobs and enjoying the sea breeze against my neck. I told the Amazon device in the kitchen to play 90s hits and have been jamming out to Whitney Houston and Nirvana while assembling dinner. The Backstreet Boys just came on to sing about being lonely, and I'm humming along while I shut the grill and return to the kitchen to cut the grilled corn from the cobs for a corn salsa.

The front door closes, and I glance at the time on the microwave. I have ten minutes before seven. Everything will be finished right on time.

I command Alexa to stop playing music.

"Something smells amazing," Noah says, coming around the corner with a briefcase in one hand and his jacket slung over his arm. Why does he even take it to work? It's like two hundred degrees outside.

I tried to dress more professionally after I finished cleaning Mrs. Finnigan's house and feeding her birds, but I'm still in shorts and a tank. Just a *nicer* tank over *nicer* shorts. It's still summertime in Florida, so let's be reasonable.

I suddenly see myself through Noah's eyes and cringe. This isn't professional. An anklet and Birkenstocks have never screamed professional, and mine are standing out like Whitney Houston in the middle of a 90s rock ballad. I tuck my anklet-clad foot behind my other leg and lean on the counter. "Steak kabobs and salad with chips and salsa. Is that too casual?"

He looks at me for a second, his brown eyes raking over my face. "Did you *make* dinner?"

Oh, no. I've crossed a boundary somewhere I didn't know about. Confidence is the best way to handle this, right? "Yes," I say. "I thought it would be better than a reheated chicken or something."

Noah sets the briefcase on a kitchen stool, looking at me. No, not just looking. Observing. Examining. I feel his gaze reach my bones. "It smells better than a reheated chicken," he says.

I step around the side of the kitchen island to pick up an onion and bring it to the cutting board. "I can't tell if you're mocking me or not."

"Definitely not," he says quietly, picking up his briefcase again. "I'm going to change. I'll be down shortly."

"Dinner will be ready in ten."

This isn't helping with my fantasies. He is *not* my husband. This is not my house. This is definitely not my apron.

The onion stings my eyes, but I don't wipe them. I don't need to lose my contacts or transform into a racoon again. I chop quickly and move onto the avocado and tomatoes. Mrs. Finnigan started putting on the Food Network while I cleaned a few years ago, and I got in the habit of sitting down with her when my job was finished and watching it for a while. The habit grew until I was putting it on at the Rojas and Belacourt houses while I was cleaning, if no one was home, and I picked up a few things. Yes, Otto is the chef in our family, but it's a fun pastime, and I like cooking for other people.

Noah returns downstairs in chino shorts and a plain navy shirt that hugs his chest and drapes down like the thing was custom made for him. I swivel away, retrieving the dressing I had made earlier from the fridge and drizzling it over the corn salsa. Stirring corn has never been so riveting.

Also, these bits of avocado. So green. So appetizing. If I focus on them, I won't ogle Noah. When did he get so handsome? I remember him in high school. He was hot then, yeah, but easy to ignore since his family was so full of themselves. They were bursting with pride and money and conceit. But *this* Noah? If he's an arrogant rich kid somewhere deep inside, he doesn't act like it.

"That salad looks great."

"It's salsa," I say, giving it another good stir before I carry it to the table. I've set one end of the long table for four, using wicker placemats and dishes I found in the cupboards. After the salsa is on the table, I pour a bag of chips into a wooden bowl.

"Can I help?"

I look up. Is he serious? "You're paying me to do this," I remind him. "I don't offer discounts."

He shrugs one careless shoulder. "I can still help. I fully

anticipated having to heat up and plate whatever you picked up from the store."

"Now you don't have to."

"That's a good thing for both of us. I can only really make one thing, and it's not the best summer meal."

I put the chips on the table and move to the patio door to fetch the kabobs. "What is it?"

Noah follows me to the back patio. "Fettuccine alfredo."

"I was expecting you to say scrambled eggs or toast."

"Okay, I can make three things."

"Then you're cooking next time."

"Deal."

I lift the grill and pull the kabobs off with the tongs. Once they're plated, I glance at Noah. "What did you mean by that?"

"Which part?"

"It's a good thing for both of us that I cooked. Why both of us?"

Noah rubs the back of his neck, his eyebrows rising. "Well, that's the thing. I was going to invite you to join in the meeting so you could meet Gina and Mateo and familiarize yourself with them since it's likely you'll work together sometime this summer. Gina isn't coming anymore, and Mateo won't be here for another half-hour. Which means it's just us for dinner." He hurries to add, "Unless you have somewhere to be, of course. We can do this another time."

I stare at him. This meal was supposed to be for Noah and his colleagues. Now it's like Noah saw my fantasy and decided to play along for a hot minute. Walking out the door and going home to have dinner with Otto isn't an option now, because Noah's my boss. He's paying me two thousand dollars today to do some basic chores and make him dinner. I realize I don't have to stay and eat. But imagining Noah seated alone at the table in this monstrous house eating a dinner I made for four people tugs at my heartstrings. I won't ditch him.

"Mateo's coming?" I ask, brushing past him to take the food inside.

He clears his throat and follows me. "He had to take care of something, but he should be here soon. Ish. He told me to start without him."

"Okay." I smile broadly and take the broccoli salad from the fridge. "Food's ready."

Noah pulls out a chair and stands behind it, looking meaningfully at me.

I stare at him. He's not sitting.

"Is there something else you need?" I ask, searching my brain for what the table might be missing besides the broccoli salad in my hands.

"This is for you," he says, dipping his chin.

"For me?"

His head tilts to the side like a golden retriever. "Has no one pulled a chair out for you before?"

"We don't do that at the grand Keene Bed and Breakfast, no."

"Well, we do it at Casa Belacourt."

He isn't moving, and it's just getting awkward, so I put the salad on the table and take the seat, letting him push my chair in. He's so smooth; he's clearly had practice. All those etiquette lessons at his fancy boarding school, no doubt.

He sits kitty-corner at the head of the table, and our meal starts off rocky. We pass around the dishes in near silence, making small comments about the food in an overly polite way. It feels like I'm fifteen and sitting down to dinner with my school principal. I would never choose to eat with Noah in a million years, so I don't want to be here. Yet, as my boss, he's someone I need to impress, so I crave a sign that he's enjoying the food I made.

If one of us doesn't start a conversation soon, this will go down as the worst dinner I've ever had, which is a shame because my kabobs are delicious.

What can I even talk to Noah about?

I'm clueless about yachts. I haven't ever driven a car that doesn't have rust on the rims or skied the Alps or hung out with famous movie stars. I don't know anything about tech, so Scout is off the table.

Noah's athletic, so maybe that's a safe space? "You run on the beach," I say. "That must be... hard, right?"

He chews his bite of steak, looking at me longer than necessary. Why is he always so *observant*? His deep brown eyes are mini X-ray machines, boring into me, making me wonder if I put my clothes on inside out. I want to text Ivy so she can psychoanalyze this situation with me. She knew Noah back in the day, and she would totally find this just as weird as I do. Maybe she'd have some conversation suggestions for the next time I'm stuck with him like this.

"I've been doing it for years, so it's not too bad," he finally says. "Used to be much harder."

Oh my gosh. This is more painful than eating dinner with a principal. It's cringey, like watching your friend get chatted up at a bar by a guy who laughs too loud and smells like wet dog.

Except Noah's chuckle is the right kind of manly and he smells like a dream.

We fall back into silence. Part of me is tempted to ask how his sisters are doing, but I also don't want to hear about their perfect lives.

"And you?" he asks. "Do you often swim in the ocean in your shoes?"

I can't be mad that this is the direction our conversation has turned when I'm the one who brought up that day on the beach. All I can think about is how scary it was to almost lose my mom's scarf, and how it made me jump in the ocean without thinking, which I haven't done in years. Fifteen years? Maybe longer.

It's just not something I do.

"I don't really swim," I say lightly. "So that was a weird situation."

Noah pulls a chunk of pineapple from his skewer and pops it into his mouth, chewing slowly. "You don't really swim," he repeats.

"Nope."

"That's funny. I remember you swimming at Jake's house *a lot* back in high school."

My body freezes. How can he remember anything like that? He wasn't there. Were he and Jake friends and Jake never told me? Just another thing that makes me feel like I never really knew my boyfriend. "That was a pool. I avoid the ocean."

"Oh." He looks at me like my words are hitting him belatedly, his eyes widening just so slightly. "*Oh.* Because of your parents?"

I guess we're just airing all my history right now. It's not a surprise he knows the story of how my parents died—everyone does. My mom was heading into the surf and a rip current pulled her out to sea. My dad tried to save her, but he was dragged away as well. They were close to the beach. I would have been with them if I wasn't at home with a sore throat that day. They had left me with Otto while they went for a picnic because it was their anniversary.

It was tragic. Two healthy adults. Two strong swimmers. So near the safety of the beach. But the ocean takes no prisoners. They must have fought the current too hard, forgot in the heat of the moment what they were supposed to do to free themselves. I've long since come to terms with the trauma of their deaths, thanks to therapy and Otto, but I stay away from the shore.

Noah being aware isn't weird, but I'm surprised he remembers it. "Yeah, I guess so. I've never... I just avoid it if I can."

"Do you still go out to the water, but you just don't swim? Or is the whole ocean off limits?" he asks, watching me so closely I can't slip away. "What about boats? Kayaks? That sort of thing."

I frown. I'm not sure I've thought about this before. "I don't know. I mean, I take the ferry, but that doesn't feel very dangerous. I've been out on boats plenty—I just don't get in the water."

"I'm sorry, Cat. I wouldn't have mentioned it if I realized—"

"Don't worry about it. We live on an island. Not being comfortable in the ocean isn't really typical around here, is it?"

"I've never cared much for what's typical," he says.

Why would he? When you have that much money, you get to be comfortable in your own skin. You get to do and say what you want and don't have to try to fit in with everyone else. People with money don't have to stress out on the first day of school when they're still wearing last year's sneakers or don't have the glitter gel pens that are in everyone else's backpacks.

Which is why Olive's friendship had been so exciting in the beginning. She'd shared her gel pens and complimented my bright yellow Converse—even though they weren't new—and we'd clicked. Until one day when we didn't, and she went from telling me my hair was cute to loudly asking on the ferry to school if I cut it myself because it looks like someone had taken a weed whacker to the back.

My uncle had trimmed my hair. It stung.

I still had Ivy, so I wasn't friendless, and Ivy never cared what my hair looked like or what shoes I was wearing. She was a real friend. But Olive Belacourt? She made eighth grade miserable for me, and I was never so happy as the day, a few years later, when I learned her parents decided to ship her off to boarding school.

"I like volleyball," I say brightly. "And I'm not too bad at it. There are other ways of enjoying the beach."

Noah looks at me over the rim of his glass, his dark brown eyes brooding. For a second I catch my breath, wondering what it is he's considering saying to me. He seems to shake himself. "You'll have to show me sometime."

My gut reaction is to refuse him, but now he's my boss. Yes, I know I'm not getting paid to hang out with the guy, but since he's my employer, I do need to be polite. Besides, these small sacrifices are worth getting Otto out from under the mountain of debt that is threatening my home.

"I'd be happy to."

CHAPTER 11

Noah

DINNER HAS GONE from awkward to worse. I never should have brought up the ocean or that day I tried to save her life—unnecessarily—or her parents' deaths. What was I thinking? I wasn't, obviously. The problem with this meal is proximity. Cat, right next to me, sliding steak from a skewer and snacking on her corn salsa like she hasn't spent the last hour or so cooking dinner for me.

I pay her. She's just doing her job. But seeing her pull the skewers off the grill and take them to a nicely set table got my blood fired up. You don't have to be a good cook to be a good wife or mother. That goes without saying. But something about Cat being a good cook and a great hostess has me wanting to imagine that it's just a typical day and I'm just coming home to dinner, which is archaic and probably breaking some sort of feminism code or something.

I still like it. Honestly, I like her.

That crush that developed when we were teens and lay dormant for the last few years had been fed some sort of rejuvenation serum when I saw Cat on the beach. It is now thriving, alive and well. I feel like I'm sixteen and trying to gain the courage to say hi to her in the market, except she's at my kitchen table eating a meal she cooked for me.

I can't act on my crush anyway, because she works for me

now and that's all sorts of wrong. She didn't cook dinner for me because she likes me. She cooked because I paid her to. I need to remember that. It's an important distinction.

Thank heavens Mateo is arriving. The house alarm chimes, letting us know someone is walking up to the front door, and I relax. We aren't alone anymore in our weird simulation of a date. Mateo opens the door and comes into the kitchen, looking frazzled.

"Please tell me you haven't eaten all the food. Gina worked me late, and I didn't have time to grab anything." He stops at the table and puts his things down, then reaches a hand across the table to Cat. "You must be Catalina. I'm Mateo."

"You can just call me Cat."

"Cat," Mateo repeats, shaking her hand, then pulling out his chair. "This looks divine."

"Let me heat the steak for you." Cat is on her feet before he can argue, taking the plate of skewers to the grill outside.

"Did you bring the updated projections?" I ask, needing a distraction so I don't keep watching her.

Cat returns to the kitchen and pours more ice water in our glasses.

"Yes." Mateo stops spooning the grilled corn salsa onto his plate and opens his bag, pulling out papers for me.

I flip through them, trying to note any financial differences, but really I'm just super aware of Cat leaning past me to take my plate and silverware. She's clearing the table now, and I want to help. I get up, taking her plate and carrying it to the sink.

She looks startled to find me beside her. "I'll take care of that. You finish your meeting."

"The meeting is for all three of us." Besides, there is something about her working that makes me want to jump in and help.

Cat looks up. "I'll do this later, then."

It's a compromise, at least.

She goes outside to retrieve the skewers, and I take my seat at the table again, trying to read Gina's updated numbers.

"When can Bree get out here?" Mateo asks. "Should I arrange her travel?"

"She has it taken care of." I slug the water, needing something to level me out. "I'm not sure when she'll come, but it should be soon."

Cat hovers with the plate of skewers behind her chair. "Your sister is coming?"

"Yeah. Do you know her?"

"Not really." She sets down the plate and pushes it toward Mateo. "Only Bree? No one else?"

Cat is still standing next to her chair. Is she in fight or flight mode? This is new. I can tell whatever I'm about to say matters. "Just her, as far as I know."

I'm desperate for her to sit down.

"We'll need to bring in some men and a few more women for variety," I say, pretending Cat's hovering isn't driving me crazy. What is bothering her?

"What is this for?" she asks, finally sitting down.

"The ad campaign for the new app."

"You haven't done it yet?" Her blonde eyebrows rise. "Doesn't the app release soon?"

"Middle of July. We had ads running—we have for a while—but this is a fresh campaign that will launch with the app all over the states." I lean back in my seat so I can see her better. "Yeah, we're cutting it close. We were supposed to iron this out and have it finished last month, but... things... got in the way."

That's a delicate way to say I had a breakdown and everything at work was put on hold.

Mateo pulls out his iPad and fiddles on it before turning it around to face both of us. "Should we choose the models now?"

Cat leans forward. "This is something I can help with."

"Filming will be on the beach, so we want relaxed and down

to earth," Mateo says, arranging the iPad case so it stands on the table. He flips to the first woman, a redhead with long frizzy hair and loads of freckles.

"Yes," Cat says. "She's gorgeous."

"They're all gorgeous," I remind her. "We need to choose people who fit the vibe."

"What's more vibe than frizzy hair on the beach?"

True. "Next?"

Mateo flips to a woman with long, sleek brown hair and a perfect smile.

"Next?" Cat asks.

Mateo flips again. And again, and again. After the first woman, Cat doesn't approve anyone else, but Mateo likes half of them.

We reach the men, and I put a hand up to stop him from going any further. "What's wrong with the models?"

Cat leans back in her chair, shrugging. Her mouth is closed tightly.

I look at Mateo, who doesn't seem to see the problem either.

"This is a safe space to share ideas and opinions, Cat."

She still doesn't speak.

Mateo looks at me, confused. Whatever Cat is thinking, she's alone in her opinion, but I want her to tell us. She's a regular consumer and that's valuable.

I lean back, watching her for a response. "From what I could tell, each of the models presented were standard, so I'm not sure I'm seeing what you are."

Cat scoffs. "Exactly."

I exchange a look with Mateo, but he's still just as lost as I am.

"They're all standard," Cat says, like this will make her point. When it doesn't, she makes a sweeping gesture with her hand. "Go back to the beginning and look at them again. Yes, they're beautiful. They're models. Is that who you're marketing to—people who look like this or want to date women who look like this? Because that last group will be disappointed when they're matched with someone on *your* app who doesn't look like a model. What about the regular women, Belacourt?" *Women like me,* she seems to say. "We aren't all tall, slender goddesses."

She's the most beautiful woman I've seen today, models included. "The redhead is still a model," I remind her. She approved that one.

"Yeah, but she's relatable. She has freckles and frizzy hair. If I was marketing a dating app, I would search for models with relatable traits. That's all I'm saying."

She makes a valid point. I want people to be enticed and intrigued enough to try my app, but I also want the follow-through to be satisfactory so they continue to use it and tell all their friends. Getting them to the app is only one step in the process. An important one, yeah, but it's not the whole story.

Why didn't I think about that when I was planning the campaign?

"We need to start over," I say.

Mateo balks, his skewer suspended midair. "Excuse me?"

"I get what Cat's saying. Our whole concept isn't going to give us the longevity and follow-through we want. It's just enticing."

"We don't want to entice people?" Mateo speaks slowly, like I've gone crazy and he's trying to subtly show me that.

I chuckle and lean back in my seat. "Of course we do. But we also want them to stick around long enough to use the app—repeatedly, if they need to."

"Expectations are part of that," Cat explains.

"So instead of couples looking *Vogue*, we can—"

"We like *Vogue*," Mateo argues, welding his skewer. "It goes with our brand."

"We get to decide what our brand is. If we were trying to sell our app to Manhattan, then yeah, the models fit our vibe. But we want everyone using the app. Our whole schtick with the fact-checking is to keep it real." As I explain, the idea settles more firmly. Why didn't I think of this myself? It embodies the foundation for my software at its core. "We should be keeping it real."

Mateo looks between me and Cat. "So you don't want models?"

"We want models," I say. "They're trained. It'll make the shoot go smoothly if they know what they're doing. But we need different models."

"A variety of people," Cat says.

"Doing what real people do on the beach. Picnics and surfing."

"A bonfire with someone playing the guitar."

I catch her eye. "A group playing volleyball."

"A couple kissing in the surf," she says, looking away.

Mateo sits back in his seat and looks between us. "Okay, I get it now. I can visualize this. We're making a montage."

"A summery, beachy, romantic montage," I say.

"This will take more than one day of filming, I think," Mateo mutters, pulling his iPad back toward him so he can type up notes on everything we've gone over. He and his notes are incredible.

"Good thing Bree is helping us out. She won't cost more for the extra work." I take a drink of my water and glance at Cat, who is picking at the wicker placemat in front of her. "Mateo, if you'll nail down the photographer and everything, I'll work with Cat on finding the right models."

"You will?" she asks, sitting up. "We will?"

"If that's something you're amenable to."

She only hesitates a moment, but it's long enough to give me a smidgen of doubt. Am I treating her too much like an employee? She is one, obviously, but she has a say here. She needs to have a voice or our relationship will be strained for the rest of our lives. At some point, Cat won't be my PA anymore, and I don't want things to be weird then.

Cat pushes her blonde hair behind her shoulders, looking between me and Mateo. "I'm happy to help. I just don't have any marketing experience."

"I wouldn't call Keene B&B's Instagram *nothing*."

Her face goes beet red, her cheeks mottling with a blush. "You've seen that?"

Mateo is already opening his phone, probably to check it out.

"Your followers aren't anything to scoff at," I say.

"Is Keene spelled—"

"With an E," I tell him.

He nods, typing into his phone.

Cat's blue eyes go round. "My account is small beans compared to something like this. It's not a national ad campaign. We just keep it up for the regulars. They like to feel like they're part of a community here on the island."

"We want people to feel that way about *Scoutr*," Mateo says, scrolling through her Instagram profile. "I agree, Noah." He looks up, resigned. "I think this is the right direction for the campaign."

"But...?" I can sense it. I know it's coming.

"Gina," he says. He's right. She can be difficult, and right now she's stepped in as unofficial interim CEO while I get my head back on straight. But I'm still in charge, and it's still my company.

"I'll handle her. Just get everything confirmed so we have a campaign."

"It's mostly scheduled, but I'll nail down a second day of shooting. I think we're going to need it. Where should we put everyone?"

"The resort, if there are enough rooms." I don't look at Cat when I continue. "Keene B&B is another local option."

She startles.

I shift my gaze to her. "Do you have space next week?"

"We're totally open," she says. "A family comes in on the 24th, but before that, we're free."

"Good. If we need more space, you can put people in our pool house."

"Gina?" Mateo asks.

"She'll want room service. You take the pool house, and we can order in if we need to."

"Done," Mateo says, typing again.

Cat gets up to clear the table, and I let her.

Mateo pushes his plate away and goes back to typing. "I'll have more model options to you by tomorrow."

"Great." I watch Cat stack dishes in the sink and open the dishwasher. "Will tomorrow work to go over models, Cat?"

She looks up, her blue eyes widening. "At the office?"

"Here," I say. "Anytime before noon, preferably."

She holds my eyes for a second and I find myself wondering which idiot rich guy she's going to use as my nickname today. It hasn't been lost on me that she's probably never used my first name. Is it a barrier she's putting between us? A wall to keep things professional?

No. I'm the one who has the crush and needs the constant reminders to keep things professional. Not her. She's just trying to save her house.

I bet it's proof there will always be a wall between us. I plan to enjoy this summer and any time I have to hang out with her, not worrying about it being anything more than it needs to be.

"That works for me," she says.

Inside, I soar. I get to hang out with Cat again tomorrow.

CHAPTER 12

Cat

THIS ENTIRE WEEK has included far more Noah time than I had expected when I signed on to be his PA for the summer. Running his errands and being around him occasionally was part of the deal. What I didn't count on was sitting at his kitchen table every day, choosing models and scene concepts and going over scripts and color schemes and wardrobes. There are so many components to putting together an ad campaign, and while Noah's team at the office is handling the details, he still has to sign off on them. Or, in some cases, provide notes and wait for an updated file to approve.

I'm only here to provide the notes. He likes my feedback—heaven knows why.

To be honest, the more time I spend in his company, the more comfortable we're getting. Like earlier this morning, when I made him a smoothie for his post-run snack while we debated the merits of eye-catching neon clothes, he let me have a sip of his when my glass ran out. It felt natural, which freaked me out.

I'm kneeling on Mrs. Rojas's bathroom floor, scrubbing the bathtub and thinking about that smoothie. No, the meeting. The ad campaign. Work-related things only.

Everything's coming together for the shoot. We settled on an array of models that look like a real group of friends but still seem like they'd vibe with Bree. Not that I know Bree personally, but I've seen a few episodes of *The Belacourts* over the years. She's the sister who acts like a hippie, with her cardboard water bottles and bamboo toothbrushes, but really just wants to pet sea turtles in her Gucci slides.

That was a few years ago, but I highly doubt she's changed much. Either way, Bree's way more palatable than Olive, the middle sister who's always dramatically proclaiming how much she *hates* drama while in the middle of gossiping about a guy or a friend or a sister.

I turn on the water to rinse out the suds and keep scrubbing. Cleaning is therapeutic for me. When I was ten, a few months after my parents died, I spiraled into a deep hurricane of depression. Otto took me to a counselor, who hooked us up with a psychiatrist specializing in childhood trauma. Together they got me sorted out and found the right medication to manage my depression. Over the years, I've had to shift medications occasionally to keep up with my life changes, but overall the thing I've found to consistently give me a sense of control is cleaning. I love it. It's cathartic to take something dirty and grimy and make it sparkle. There's probably something about the control it gives me, but it works. I don't mind cleaning at the B&B, but what I *really* love is being able to assist two women who can't get down on their knees easily to scrub tubs or clean toilets or wipe the dust from their baseboards.

The Belacourt job came my way because Mrs. Rojas is a friend of Noah's mom, and I really just wanted the money. But Mrs. Finnigan and Mrs. Rojas? These two old ladies make my days brighter and keep my natural serotonin levels up.

I moved on to the bathroom sink, scrubbing away the grime, when my phone rings. It's my friend Ivy, so I command Siri to answer it in my headphones. She's been back on the island for over a week now. We've talked a few times, but I haven't seen her since her cousin's wedding last week, where we chatted on the beach for a while.

"I'm elbow-deep in Mrs. Rojas's bathroom," I tell her.

"Please tell me she's not the type to leave eyebrow hairs all over the counter. I want to believe better from her."

"She's way too classy for that." I look back at the floor, where more fingernail clippings made it onto the tile than into the trash can. I'll chalk that up to poor vision and not incompetence, though.

"True."

I lean over the counter to spread cleaner along the second sink. "What's up?"

"Are we going to the beach soon?"

"I want to, but probably not this week. I'm swamped. Noah has me helping with an ad campaign for his new app and his sister is flying in for shooting. It's a lot."

"Olive?" she asks, her voice growing serious. She lived through eighth grade with me, when Olive was bent on making me feel less than human every day.

"No, just Bree. Do you know her very well?"

"Not really. She's super young, right?"

"A few grades under us, I think. I don't know exactly. I'm not looking forward to working with her, but the rest hasn't been that bad."

It's silent on the other end of the line.

I stop scrubbing the sink. "What?"

"The *rest*? Like working with Noah Belacourt? I thought he was a snob."

Should I tell her about how nice he's been? Offering me rides and ibuprofen and feeding me every time we have a meeting? He had muffins waiting for us yesterday. Tacos the day before that. But... *no*. I don't want Ivy reading into it. "He's turning out to be a nice employer, but I'm pretty sure he doesn't wear underwear."

Ivy laughs. "Do I want to know why you think that?" Her

voice grows serious. "He's not taking advantage of your position, right?"

"No. If anything, he's ultra careful. I'm doing the man's laundry. If he wears underwear, it's not coming through his washer."

"Maybe he dry cleans them."

I wipe the cleaner from the sink and straighten, looking in the mirror at my frizzy, platinum messy bun and zero makeup. The idea of Noah coming onto me is laughable. Him dry cleaning his boxer-briefs? "That's possible."

"I just reached the cafe, so I have to go. Call me when you're ready for the beach!"

"Volleyball?" I ask, hearing the hope rise in my tone. Maybe Noah can come. I promised to teach him, didn't I?

"Yeah. Too bad you aren't still dating whatshisname—that blond jock. He had such a great serve."

Maybe I won't bring newbie Noah. "I'll try to find a boyfriend in the next few weeks with an even better serve."

"That's my girl." Ivy laughs and we both hang up.

I haven't told her or Holland about Otto's medical bills or how much Noah is paying me, and it feels a little weird keeping those things to myself. At the same time, I don't want to talk about Otto behind his back. I only admitted these things to Noah in a fit of madness. I didn't think I'd see him again after that golf cart ride.

I was so wrong.

It takes another hour to finish cleaning the rest of the Rojas' house. I load all my cleaning supplies into the crates and slide them into their utility closet, then find the notepad near the fridge with Mrs. Rojas's shopping list and add Windex and dusting pads so she can replenish them before I come next week.

Noah's golf cart is sitting where I left it in front of the house.

My phone buzzes as I slide into the driver's seat and toss my belt bag on the bench.

Think of the devil, and he'll text.

> **NOAH**
> You busy tonight?

> **CAT**
> Depends on whether or not this job involves ice cream

> **NOAH**
> I'm open to negotiation

He made that too easy. I stare at his text, wondering when we went from business casual to banter. After a week of working together every day, things are easy between us. Too easy? My body stiffens, overthinking this. Also, who dry cleans their underwear? It's just weird.

It also makes me think about his underwear *way* too much.

That's so unprofessional. We've bypassed business casual-level conversation and have gone straight to flip flops and T-shirts.

> **NOAH**
> I want to scout a location for the shoot before the sun goes down. If you're free, I'd appreciate your input

> **CAT**
> I thought we planned to do it on your family's private beach?

> **NOAH**
> We will, but there are a few spots that could work. We need to nail them down ahead of time so the crew knows where to go

The photoshoot begins in two days. Every time I think we've got things done and dusted, he pulls another task out of the blue. His work never ceases, and there is no such thing as *business hours* for Scout, Inc. It's more like around-the-clock hours with some down time in between meetings when the rest of the country is sleeping. We don't work constantly, but very consistently.

I'm starting to see his need for high-salary employees. Noah can get away with this ultra flexible working schedule when he's paying twelve grand a week. Yeah, twelve. So far, Saturdays are working days. But each day chips away at the iceberg that is Otto's medical bills and gets us farther away from foreclosing on our house, so I'm not complaining.

At least I know he didn't hire me out of charity. He's working me too much for that. I'm grateful—I like feeling like I'm earning the paycheck.

CAT
Kind of last minute, Bruce

NOAH
Willis? Springsteen? Wayne? At least you've moved on to the heroes

CAT
Sure, all of the above

NOAH
Who were you thinking originally?

I'm not going to tell him it was Batman.

CAT
What time should I be there?

NOAH
Meet at my house in thirty minutes?

Yikes. Do I have time to shower? No. I can't shower. He'll

know I showered because he saw me in this exact outfit with this gnarly hair while I scrubbed *his* bathroom this morning and then sat at his kitchen island to look at models' wardrobe options while sipping a grapefruit LaCroix.

Like I said, this whole ad campaign thing is *involved*.

NOAH
Or whenever you can get here is fine.

CAT
I'll be there in thirty

After I shower, because I cleaned two houses and Otto's kitchen today, so I'm a mess. Not because I want to impress Noah. Just because I don't want to stink.

MY HAIR IS huge and frizzy by the time I reach Noah's house, because it's still damp and we're in Florida. I knock three times and walk inside without waiting for him to come to the door.

"I'm here," I call out, making my way to the kitchen.

There's no answer.

I put my bag on the counter and pull a glass from the cabinet, then fill it in the sink. I lean against the counter, sipping the cold water. The golf cart is handy—not that I'll admit it to Noah. I arrived today in minutes and not even a little sweaty.

Okay, maybe a *little* sweaty. Again, Florida.

When ten minutes pass and Noah still hasn't shown up, it starts to get weird. I text him but get no answer. I check all the downstairs rooms, the back patio, the garage, the pool house, the walk-in pantry, the theater room. He's not here.

Well, he's not downstairs.

"Noah?" I call from the foot of the stairs.

Nothing.

I should go up and make sure he's all right. I've been upstairs many times before, so it's not weird. I was supposed to meet Noah fifteen minutes ago, and in the week since we started working together, he's never been late.

My phone shows no response, so I start upstairs.

"Noah?" I call, mounting the stairs.

There's no response. There's no noise at all. The bathroom is open and empty, but Noah's door is closed, so I knock.

"Hello?" His voice comes from inside but sounds weird. "Oh my—hang on. Cat?"

He sounds so frazzled I can't help but smile. "Yeah, it's me."

"Time got away from me," he calls through the door. There's some noise inside, like he's rustling with something.

Should I go downstairs to wait?

"Coming," he says, and a second later the door opens.

I've seen Noah's room many times—like this morning when I vacuumed it—so this isn't weird, but what's different this time is the computer on a desk against the wall. It's big... no, it's *multiplied*.

"What did you do?" I ask, stepping past him into the room.

"Oh, that's not—" Noah steps around me and yanks a cord that makes everything go black.

But I saw things on the screens before that happened. Things with wings, a man in armor—not medieval, but some weird leather and brass armor—old scrolly letters, a screen entirely in code. It looked like *The Lord of the Rings* mixed with Vikings.

My gaze swings to Noah. "What was that?"

He looks at me, the power cord dangling from his hand. Well, that's incriminating. His brown eyes are wide and hold mine with a fierceness that takes me by surprise. His usually immaculate hair is mussed, and I'm guessing he was wearing the headset that is sitting on the desk.

He's hiding something. He's *definitely* hiding something.

I really want to tease him for it, but he's my boss.

Freaking work relationships. When is teasing crossing the line? When someone pays your salary, are you allowed to call them a nerd? I fold my arms over my chest, biting down a quip. Two thousand dollars. That's how much I'm getting to keep my mouth shut.

"Should we head to the beach?" I ask, hooking a thumb over my shoulder.

Noah drops the power cord and a sigh slips from his mouth. "Yeah, let's go."

He waits for me to leave the room before following me to the hallway and shutting the door behind us. I can sense the discomfort coming off him in waves.

My curiosity is rising. I walk down the stairs, biting my tongue between my teeth to keep the questions from spilling out of my mouth. When I reach the bottom, I give up and turn to face him.

Noah stops abruptly, and I didn't leave him very much room, so he's pretty close. Mmmm, he smells good.

Focus, Cat.

"What was that?" I ask.

"Just a computer."

"Like five computers."

"Five? Try three."

"Okay, Belacourt," I say patiently. "Why do you have three new computers?" My first assumption would be a home office, but I happen to know Scout doesn't have any tech involving Viking wizards.

"Well, three and a half. Kind of. If you count the laptop."

"I'll rephrase." I bend my neck to see his eyes better. They're so brown and deep and nervous. "What are you doing with so much technology and a ton of code?"

He swallows, pulling my attention to his throat. I've never actually been attracted to a guy's neck before, but Noah has a really nice one. Objectively speaking, he has a really nice everything, which has been easy to ignore until now because I can't stand his family or ideals or business practices or gobs of money.

Noah is starting to prove some of those things false—at least where he's concerned. Jury's still out on all three of his sisters.

His throat bobs again like he's nervous. It's right in my line of sight. What would it feel like to kiss him? Would he be as generous and thoughtful in that regard as he is an employer?

Okay, Cat. Pull back. This is getting into dangerous territory.

Noah's staring isn't helping either. Is he thinking *Move, chick. Get out the way?* Or is he thinking about how kissable I look, too?

NOT THAT IT MATTERS. Employer, employee.

Like magic, the door opens with the exact reminder I need to keep a steady distance between myself and Noah.

Bree Belacourt walks in on five-inch heels with a tiny dog yapping from her purse. She pushes enormous sunglasses onto her head and beams at us. "Honey, I'm home!"

CHAPTER 13

Noah

TRUST my sister to arrive at the worst possible time. She's had over a week to get here and *this* is the moment she chooses? Whatever was going on between me and Cat at the bottom of the stairs was heavy and thick with buzzing energy. I couldn't tell if she was staring at my lips or my neck, but either way, I was here for it.

If that connection and chemistry meant anything, she was here for it too.

Not that anything can happen between us while I'm paying her an exorbitant salary, but I was basking in the moment.

I'm playing the long game here.

Cat takes a hurried step back from me and goes into the kitchen to fill a glass with water and gulp it down. She's changed since this morning, and I like the relaxed collared shirt she has tied at the waist. It's coral and bright and so *her*.

I shouldn't stare. Bree's waiting by the door for her assistant Alonzo to bring in her bags, so I give her a hug. "I expected you like a week ago. This is what you meant by getting here right away?"

Bree flips her long dark hair over her shoulder. "I took a detour to Boston for a minute."

Cat looks up at this. She must know Bree was in Nashville since she sent the flowers for me.

"To see Mitzy?" I ask.

"Yeah. She's single right now, if you're interested." Bree waggles her sculpted eyebrows.

"Still no." I lean in to kiss her cheek. Her dog snaps at me, so I step back.

Bree seems to notice Cat for the first time—she never was very observant—and brushes past me, pushing her purse into my chest. The dog barks again, so I promptly set it down.

"Hi, I'm Bree." She puts out a hand to shake Cat's. "I guess Mitzy's really off the table."

Cat looks unruffled. "Mitzy?"

"My friend. She's been pining after my brother for ages. You are?"

"Cat Keene."

"That sounds familiar." Bree scrunches her eyebrows together.

I step in. "Her family runs the B&B downtown."

"Slumming with the competition?" Bree cackles. "I love it."

"We aren't competition," Cat says. "Our guest demographics are worlds apart."

"Cat's my PA for the summer. It's not—that is, *we* are not—" I clear my throat. "It isn't like that."

Bree looks me over, reading into my stammering. I might as well wear a sign that says how into Cat I am.

"You're *so* familiar." Bree's nodding, looking between us. "Were you friends with my sisters back in school?"

"Gotta go," I all but yell over her words. If Bree mentions Olive's failed friendship with Cat and ruins the progress I've made so far, she will be sleeping in the pool house. I don't know why they stopped being friends, but I do know that I mentioned Cat being cute and the next thing I knew Olive wasn't hanging out with her anymore. We really don't need to dredge up the past right now. "We're checking out locations for the photoshoot."

Bree lights up at this. "I haven't been to the beach in so long."

"Weren't you in Cabo last month?"

Alonzo lets himself in with two enormous rolling suitcases and sets them down. He gives me a nod and goes back outside, probably for more bags.

She rolls her eyes. "I meant *our* beach."

"Well, if you want to come," I say tightly, letting my words trail off.

"No, I need a shower. Airplanes make me feel grimy."

She probably had most of the plane to herself and her assistant, but that's irrelevant. I'm relieved I don't have to balance her and Cat at the beach. I look over Bree's head to where Cat is standing in the kitchen, gripping her empty water glass.

"Ready?" I ask.

She nods, then turns a wide fake smile on Bree. "Nice to meet you."

"Noah never stops working," Bree says. "If you're working with him, I'm sure I'll see you around."

"Probably," Cat agrees, her smile growing more strained.

Time to get her out of here.

Bree looks absently toward the door. "I should introduce you to Alonzo. He's with me all the time, so you'll need to—"

"We can do that later. He's busy." I'm walking toward the back door, and I hold it open for Cat. "Enjoy your nap."

Bree grins. "I said shower. I'll probably jump on the bike later, too."

"We both know what that means. A nap and a movie."

She spins away, heading for the stairs and leaving her dog behind.

"What about the puppy?"

"She likes Alonzo more than me," Bree says without turning around. "Joint custody."

When we step outside, a warm breeze brushes over my skin. I close the door and lead Cat to the gate that takes us to the beachside path.

"Are they dating?" she asks.

It takes me a second to realize she's referring to Bree and Alonzo. I'll admit the joint custody bit made it sound that way.

"Who knows." I unlock the gate and let her through before locking it again with the code. "He's been her assistant for a few years, and she's had boyfriends, but there's something weird between them for sure."

Cat doesn't say anything.

We walk the path to the resort, then pass through another gate and take the stairs down. We aren't here as early as I'd hoped, so the sun is starting to leave for the day. Sand coats the steps down to the beach and whips the salt through the air. Waves crash along the shore, bringing the white noise I love about this part of the world. There are a few couples in beach cabanas on the sand, so we walk behind them and keep going toward the cove.

I want to show it to Cat, but I don't really want to use it for the ads. It's not very big and it means a lot to me. It's the one place on the island that truly felt like it belonged to my family. Not in a possessive way, but because of the memories it holds. We spent most of our time there as kids, and even when we were teens, it wasn't a place we brought friends or hookups to. It was special to us, and bringing the photography crew there would taint it.

My family might be imploding, but that makes me want to protect the cove even more.

"Where did you have in mind?" she asks, sweeping her eyes over the beach. "We could use some of the chairs near the water. Have a few people make a sandcastle and then a wave comes through and drowns it."

Better save the cove for later. Cat's down here for work, so we should work. "That could be good if we can find someone to make a castle."

"I'll do it. We just have to build it early, then it'll be ready when the tide rolls back in to do the filming."

We walk side by side, moving closer to the water. I look at her while she analyzes the area. The sun is low and warm, making her skin glow. She looks up at me and my breath catches. This is not safe territory. I need to break the connection.

Clearing my throat, I stop walking and face the other direction. "Maybe we can quarter the beach so each shot has a different background. The teams can work to set up one section while the other is being shot. The castle, the bonfire, the volleyball."

"And kissing in the surf?" she says. "Or were you planning the picnic thing instead?"

"We can roll the sandcastle into the picnic." I can't think about kissing in the surf right now because that's all I want to do with her. My mind keeps flashing back to our tumble on the beach and how tangled we were. I need to get my brain onto something else, quickly.

"Great. Then the couple can stand in the water, kissing and looking happy. It'll show people the end goal for the app."

Right. The app. Because we're here for *work* and not because Cat has any feelings for me.

"Are you going to come clean about the computers, Millburn, or do I need to beg?"

I look at her sharply. "I don't know that one."

A slow grin spreads over her face, so mischievous I want to kiss it off.

Yes, I *know* I have a problem. This crush has been brewing for *years*. Cat shows up again in my life with her spunky smile and contagious energy and every bit as unaware of me as she was in high school, and I feel sixteen again. The years away from her were like sticking my crush on a back burner set to simmer.

Maybe I can cook four things. I make a *mean* taco soup.

"You're avoiding the question now."

"What question?" I ask, turning to face her again.

"What's with the computers?"

A laugh bubbles from my chest as I start toward the ocean. "Aren't you curious."

To my relief, Cat follows me. "You don't have to tell me. Even though I'm dying of curiosity."

I don't want to. Whatever impression she has of me being a Scout CEO businessman will crash and burn once I open the door to my most ridiculous pastimes. I'm not ashamed of my particular brand of nerd. I have enjoyed many games of Dungeons and Dragons, World of Warcraft, *Halo*, even *Warhammer 40k*. But *this*? It takes my nerdy to another level.

Most people don't develop their own games just for fun.

Or pay three of their employees to do it for them.

"You really don't want to know."

She bumps her shoulder into mine. "I do. But I'll respect that you don't want to share with me." She stops walking, looking out over the water. "We could do a boat scene too, if you wanted."

"On my yacht?"

Cat chokes. "You have a yacht?"

Okay, quick. Change course. "Or were you thinking a speedboat? Mine's been in the shop, but I'll pick it up in the morning."

"If we're going for down-to-earth, a speedboat might be a better choice. If that's another scene you want to film."

"I'll mention it to Christine."

"The photographer?"

"She'll know best if it's something we can pull off last minute."

Cat inhales a deep breath, her gaze out over the water.

My phone buzzes, so I pull it out, see my mom's name, and immediately put it back in my pocket.

"I haven't watched the sun set in so long." She glances at me. "I've seen sunsets, like daily, but it's been forever since I've sat and actually watched the sun go down."

This feels like a lead. I'm not about to miss an opportunity. "Do you have time now?"

"I'm supposed to meet up with my friend at the diner..." She checks her phone. "Yeah, I have thirty minutes."

We're far enough away from the incoming waves to make this stretch safe, so I sit down on the sand and Cat joins me. Pink and orange streak across the sky, blending down into the warm sunlight and reflecting off the water on the horizon. The sun slowly dips down toward the sea, growing smaller and deeper orange as it moves.

My phone buzzes again, so I take it from my pocket, see my mom's name, and silence it again.

"Do you need to get that?"

"Not unless I have two hours and a comfortable chair."

Cat brings her knees up to her chest and folds her arms over them. Leaning forward, she rests her chin on her arms. "Girlfriend?"

I laugh. "My mom."

"Oh."

"She and my dad are getting a divorce. I don't know if you've heard."

"I saw something about it." Cat tilts her head so she's looking at me and cringes. "Sorry. That was probably insensitive."

"We're the family who televised our lives for five years. It's not your fault you saw a commercial somewhere."

Cat watches me, her face not revealing anything about how she's feeling. I lean back on my hands and stretch out my legs, crossing my ankles.

"Still, this must be really hard."

At least I still have parents almost rolls off my tongue, but it's apples and oranges. Comparing our situations wouldn't be in any way helpful, and it's irrelevant. Our struggles are independent of each other, and contrasting the two wouldn't add anything to our conversation.

I decide to be honest. "It's been more irritating than anything else."

"Because of your mom's long calls?"

"Because of all the bickering and fighting and her wanting us to take sides even though she constantly says we shouldn't take sides. I know she really means that if we don't ditch my dad, it's a personal affront to her, but she won't admit it. I'm not sure she even realizes she might feel that way." I scrub a hand over my face, feeling the tension in my forehead. "Then there's the show. If she's not crying about the divorce, she's in a manic mood, bragging about her great single life and begging me to return to *The Belacourts* because they don't have a show with just a divorcée and three high-drama girls."

Cat's silent for a second. "You'd think that's all they need for a reality show. Do you feel like you balance them out?"

Well, I guess she never watched the show. It's not surprising, and I shouldn't be disappointed, but part of me is. I don't want her knowing the details of my dysfunctional family, but I wouldn't have minded her showing an interest.

"That's what my mom says."

"I can see it." Cat looks out over the ocean again. "Your sisters carry the gossip and drama, your parents carry the high-end class, and you carry the smoldering masculine charm."

Someone hold my drink. Smoldering? Masculine? *Charm?*

Her brow furrows slightly. "Not that I think your only value is your looks, because obviously people love all the Scout content on the show. You have both the brains and the beauty."

People love the Scout content? I grow very still. Maybe she had more interest in the show than I thought. Instead of asking about that, my mind snags on her compliment. "Beauty?" I ask, looking at her. I can't look away.

Her skin glows warm and rich with the sunset, her eyes sparkling and her smile relaxed. "Handsomeness doesn't have the same ring to it."

All I can hear is the fact that Cat thinks I'm attractive. Probably objectively speaking with no feelings involved, but I'll take it.

My phone rings again. I don't even take it from my pocket this time, I just reach in and slide the lever to put it on silent. The sun is so close to the horizon now, it'll only be a few more minutes. "Stupid ringtone. It's a relatively new phone, so I need to adjust the settings."

"You must be used to that, though," she says.

"Adjusting settings?"

"Getting new phones. Don't you techy guys always need the latest version of everything?"

For my gaming computers, yeah, but I'm not going to voice that one. "I've never really cared much about phones. I only got this one because—" My words die, shriveling awkwardly on my tongue. I don't want her knowing what happened to my last phone. She doesn't need to add anything to her responsibility list.

Cat shifts, facing me. "Why?"

"Just needed one."

I must not be good at evasion, because she can see through me. Her eyes narrow. "Why?"

"My last phone, uh, fell into the ocean."

"Fell into the—" She gasps, her pink lips forming an O. "It dropped when you thought you were saving my life?"

"Maybe."

"*Belacourt.*"

"Yes, okay. It fell in while I was swimming. It's not a big deal." I pat my pocket. "Just have to fix the settings on this one."

She shakes her head, scoffing quietly. "If you've had your new phone that long and still haven't personalized it, then yeah, I can believe you aren't the techy type who's constantly upgrading." Cat glances at me, tilting her head a little. "I'm sorry."

From her tone, it feels like she's apologizing for more than just the way I lost my phone. Maybe for misjudging me, too.

I need to change the subject before my muscles can tense any more. "How's Otto?"

She lets out a sigh. "Fine. Oblivious. He doesn't love that I took on another job, but he supports me doing what I want to do. He's just making his breakfasts and hitting the waves and living his life." She sounds tired. Am I working her too hard? "He golfs now, which is new."

"If you need to pull back at all, Cat, just say the word."

She looks at me quickly. "Are you kidding? You're an actual literal angel. I'm *dying* for the moment I get to tell Otto we have the money to pay off his bills, and this job is making that possible. Thanks for hiring me. I know you could have had someone more qualified."

Is now a good time to tell her that even someone more qualified wouldn't charge half as much as she is? No. That'll go with me to my grave. Besides, she thinks she's making significantly less than Mateo.

My phone buzzes again, and I'm tempted to chuck it into the ocean so it can hang out with my phone from last week. My stomach churns, wondering at all the reasons Mom is calling now. Did Dad text her again about the house in Park City? She doesn't even like skiing. I don't know why she's trying to hold on to it.

Either way, my blood is pumping and I just don't want to deal with it. I know I probably should, or Mom's frantic calling will only get worse.

"You should probably answer it."

"And ruin the sunset?" I pull my phone out, though, because she's right. There's a string of texts from my mom.

> **MOM**
>
> I need your confirmation for Tootsie's party ASAP
>
> It'll be at the Apollo Lounge
>
> Your father just RSVP'd. He's coming and he's bringing the model
>
> I will not survive the night without support by my side, Noah. Please come.
>
> Answer your phone!
>
> Shall I put you down for a plus one? Bree mentioned Mitzy?
>
> Mitzy might be messy. Should you come alone? That might be better.
>
> Celine hasn't RSVP'd yet.
>
> *a string of crying emojis*
>
> CALL ME
>
> Barbara needs an answer now so we can work on your suit!!!!!!

The last time I let her stylist dress me I ended up on a red carpet in an electric blue tux. We are not playing that game again.

> **NOAH**
>
> I'll wear my own suit, Mom. Count me in.

I groan, sliding my phone back into my pocket to the tune of more text vibrations. Or a phone call. When Mom texts like this, it's hard to differentiate between the two.

"Guess I'm heading out of town."

Cat looks startled. "Now? But the campaign—"

"Not for a few weeks. It's my aunt's birthday, and she likes to throw these lavish parties."

"That'll be fun?" she asks, like it's a question.

I watch the sun. "It's almost time."

Cat faces the ocean. Her arm brushes mine, and she leaves it there. I want to reach over and hold her hand and ask her to tell me about life in her beach house with Otto. It sounds cozy and idyllic compared to my stainless, sterile house.

It feels like such a shame that both of our hands are empty for the duration of the sunset.

While Cat watches the sun fall over the curve of the earth, I watch it through the reflection in her eyes. She's breathtaking, her skin glowing with an orange hue from the sunset and her hand trailing through the warm sand, heedless of the mess. She's so relaxed in her own skin. I would die to know how that feels.

I can't even get through one half of a texting conversation with my mom without feeling like I'm going to hurl.

My phone keeps buzzing, and I can't deal with it. Besides, Cat mentioned needing to meet a friend. A date? The sudden thought hits me like steel. I tear my gaze away from her and push myself up. "So you have a date tonight?" That was casual, right?

"Date? Ha. That's funny. No, just meeting a friend." She falls in beside me while we make our way past the beach cabanas toward the stairs. "Holland. Do you know her? She moved here a few years ago."

"I don't think we've met."

She nods like this makes sense.

I don't even have time to stress about the implications of that, because all I heard was the fact that Cat brushed off dating like it wasn't even on her radar. That meant she was single. Totally available.

Now I need to find a way to put myself on her radar.

CHAPTER 14

Cat

HOLLAND IS ALREADY SITTING in our regular booth when I arrive, digging into the same pancakes she always orders. I'm late, and I'm glad she didn't wait to order. Her blonde hair is falling over her shoulders, narrowly missing the strawberry syrup pooling on her plate. I search the cafe for Ivy, finding her at another table, setting glasses of soda in front of the people sitting there. She's wearing cutoff shorts and a white tee under her red and white pinstriped apron. Her messy, curly hair is tied up off her neck, and her cheeks are flushed. She's only been back and working in the diner for a few days, but it's like she never left.

"Cheeseburger?" she calls when she sees me.

"Extra fries."

I slide into the booth opposite Holland and melt into the seat.

She glances up, her brown eyes tracking the emotions running over my face. "Trouble in paradise?"

"Noah's house is literally paradise, Holls. A mansion on the hills that leads down to a private beach? His own yacht? The ability to buy a cargo ship full of Peloton bikes and not even feel the financial hit if it sunk to the ocean floor?"

"A ship full of bikes," she says, lowering her bite of pancakes and looking at me with concern. "You jumped to stationary bikes?"

"I've been thinking I need to work out more."

"More would imply you worked out before."

"I used to think cleaning houses counted as cardio."

"But then?"

"Then Muscles McGee constantly walks around shirtless, and it's clear I have some mass improving to do."

Holland lowers her fork entirely. "Do I need to be concerned?"

"What? No."

"You want to work out because your billionaire boss is cut." She reaches across the table to feel my forehead. "No fever."

"I'm not sick. He just makes me feel lazy," I say sheepishly, running my finger over a chip in the edge of the orange table. The amount of stuff that guy gets done in a given day puts even me to shame. And I *never* stop moving.

His workout regimen alone is layered. Running, lifting, the pushups and things he does on the back deck before he comes back inside after his runs. I'd imagine he was just putting on a show for me while I make power shakes and pretend to clean his spotless kitchen counter, but you have to work for abs like that, so clearly this is an old routine.

Ivy slides a hot cheeseburger in front of me and suddenly abs matter just a little less. Her dark eyebrows pull together. "Who makes you feel lazy?"

"Noah," Holland says around her bite of pancakes.

"You're like the Energizer bunny." Ivy crosses her arms.

This has gotten out of control. How do I describe the feeling of watching Noah walk in from his morning workout, his chest shimmering with sweat, his breathing rapid. It's like... not just attractive. I want to feel whatever he's feeling. Maybe my sudden desire to work out has less to do with wanting my own abs and something to do with wanting Noah's. Yeah, we need a convo change stat.

"Bree showed up tonight, and she brought an assistant and a tiny dog with her."

"Like a brunette Paris Hilton," Holland says.

"Excuse me, ma'am?" someone calls from another booth. Ivy leaves to help the other customers.

I take a bite of my burger. My teeth sink into it and I moan. "Delicious."

"Do I need to be worried?" Holland asks again, her blonde eyebrows arching high on her forehead. "For real."

"No." I drag a fry through mustard.

"Noah is..."

"A good employer, actually," I tell her. "I've misjudged him. He's so much nicer than I expected."

"He has to be, for you to take this job. I still don't get why you've done it."

To save my house. Because my uncle needs the money. How do I tell Holland without betraying Otto's trust? He hasn't even told me himself.

She peers at me, narrowing her eyes. "Why *did* you take the job? I thought after his sister bullied you in middle school you wouldn't want anything to do with that family again."

"I didn't. I still don't. But I need the money, and he's paying me crazy well." I shrug. "It's just for the summer."

That was the wrong thing to say. Holland looks worried. "Is the B&B okay?"

"It will be." I lean closer because I can tell this is something she won't drop.

Ivy returns and slides into the booth beside me. "Some people are crazy. That guy forced me to fill his Coke three times because he's convinced it's mostly soda water. Such a waste." She looks between us. "What's going on?"

Now or never, right? If I can't trust Holland and Ivy, then I have no one. I'm starting to think that telling them about the massive debt hanging over my head might take some of the pressure away. Or maybe I just need them to make me feel like I'm not taking crazy advantage of Noah and his generosity. He did offer to pay me much more than we agreed to, but it still feels like a lot.

I look from Holland to Ivy. "Otto still has cancer bills that are crazy high. I found them when I brought in the mail a few weeks ago. I don't know if he's ashamed or what, but he's keeping it from me. I kind of mentioned it to Noah, and now he's paying me enough to cover the bills by the end of the summer."

Holland just blinks. "So he's way nicer than we all thought."

"It's not just that, Holls. It feels *wrong* to take so much money. I'm not sure I'd ever feel like I'm doing enough to earn it."

"But he agreed to it, right?" Ivy asks, pushing a rogue curly dark lock off her forehead. "You told him everything. It's not taking advantage of him when it's consensual, Cat. It's a business transaction."

They are both oddly okay with this, and what they're saying makes sense. It helps ease the slimy feeling that I'd forced chivalry out of Noah, at least. I definitely didn't force him into anything. It was his idea.

"You know I'm not one to talk," Holland mutters before taking another bite of her pancakes. True. She has a lot going on in her life, but that's her story to tell.

The bell above the door chimes, and Ivy scoots out of the bench. "I have to get back to it, but don't stress so much, Cat. Let the guy help you out. He obviously wants to."

Let him help me. I was, wasn't I? I'd already been his personal assistant for over a week, and I was doing my best to earn my keep. He didn't hesitate to call on me at all hours to chat about various components of the ad campaign. I'd cooked him dinner twice, done all his laundry, fed him, sent out birthday flowers, and shopped online for a new rug since his bedroom one got a giant coffee stain on it that I couldn't get out.

I pull out my phone and set a reminder to be at the house in a few days to set up the rug after it gets delivered.

Holland reaches across the table and pilfers a fry. "You aren't backing out, right?"

"No, I won't back out. Are you?" She has an arrangement of her own to manage.

"I can't," she says. "I need the money."

We each take a fry and tap them across the table, a salty, carby cheers. "To us," I say, "and our sugar daddies."

"Just don't give him any sugar," she warns, chewing on her fry.

"I won't," I promise, but the idea of kissing Noah doesn't repulse me. It's not nearly as distasteful as it felt a few weeks ago. Good thing we have the ad shoot coming up and some solid time with Bree. If anything is going to remind me how much I can't stand that family, it'll be spending time with his sister.

I give Holland a hug and wave to Ivy across the room before making my way outside. We live close to the center of town, so I start walking home. The night is balmy. My skin is warm. My phone vibrates, and I pull it out to find a text from Noah.

NOAH
So that puppy training you mentioned…

CAT
…does not extend to your sister's dog

I hit send and hope I'm reading him correctly.

NOAH
I'll pay extra

I breathe a sigh of relief for accurately reading the situation.

Despite my promises to him when we made our employment agreement, I know next to nothing about dogs.

> **CAT**
> Did she soil the carpet? I can put in another order
>
> Also, your rug shipped. It should be here in a few days

NOAH
> She won't stop barking. She's clearly unhappy here
>
> Thanks for the rug. I can't wait

> **CAT**
> What about Alonzo? I thought he loved the dog.

NOAH
> He has a funny way of showing it. They're gone, Cat. They left right after you did, and this dog has been barking at the door ever since. Do dogs get separation anxiety?

I stop on the sidewalk in front of my house and pull up Google, because I don't know the answer to that offhand, and find a plethora of articles about pet separation anxiety. I copy and paste a few links and send them to Noah while I climb the stairs to our front porch and lower myself in the swinging hammock.

> **CAT**
> Have you tried comforting her?

NOAH
> How?

I laugh. Then, because of the dog and for no other reason, I hit the FaceTime button.

It only rings for a bit before Noah answers it. He's laying back on the couch, his head resting on his hand, so his bicep pops. Is that intentional? No, it can't be.

"Hey," he says softly.

"Hey."

The dog barks in the background, a high yippy sound. It jars me.

Noah cringes. "Yeah, that's been going on for an hour now."

"So that comforting thing I mentioned. Want to try it?"

"She'll bite me."

"Have you tried?"

Noah's arm drops, and he gives the dog a sidelong glance. The barking continues. I've only been on the phone with him for about a minute and I'm already over it. "Kind of."

"Think about the distress she's in. Her mom and dad left her in a giant echoey house with a stranger who clearly doesn't want her there."

Noah's face softens. "You think she knows that?"

"I think animals are intuitive." Got that from Google, too. And also the many, many animal-oriented TikToks that fill my feed.

He looks from the dog back to the phone. "Why is it so dark? Are you outside?"

"I just got home from dinner."

"I shouldn't be bothering you with this. You can go."

"For the sake of the dog, I feel like we need to resolve this."

"Okay." He stretches before getting up and padding toward the front door where the little Pomeranian is yapping.

"What's her name?" I ask.

"Peanut."

"You should get down and speak to her in a soothing voice. Entice her to come to you."

"How do I entice her? I don't have treats."

"With your voice. Make her feel comfortable."

To my surprise, Noah does it. He gets down on the floor and speaks to the dog in a slow, soothing tone that could very well put me to sleep if I'm not careful. "Peanut," he croons gently. "Come here, Peanut."

She yaps again.

"Keep going," I whisper, not wanting to ruin the moment.

Noah sets the phone down on the floor, giving me a solid view of his ceiling. "Come here, Peanut. That's a good girl. Yes, come here. Do you miss your momma? It's okay."

I stop swinging, my feet going still while I listen to Noah soothe the dog into silence.

"That's a good girl," he says.

"You've done it?" I ask quietly.

Noah picks up the phone and carries both me and the dog back to the living room. "She's not biting."

"She's not barking anymore either."

Noah smiles down at the dog, then moves the camera so I can see her too. Her fluffy little body is shaking, but maybe that will stop once she realizes Noah's safe.

Because he *is*. His abs have nothing on this sweet, soothing side. It makes me want to contract an awful cold and let him be sweet to me like Joe Fox is to Kathleen Kelly in *You've Got Mail*.

"Thanks for the advice," he says, nestling down on the sofa and continuously petting the back of Peanut's head.

"You would have gotten there eventually on your own."

He looks down at the dog with skepticism. "I don't know about that."

"Bree is coming back, right?"

"Yeah." He looks at the phone, pulling his attention from the dog. "You thought she was *gone* gone?"

"Just checking. She's kind of our leading lady and the photoshoot is only a few days away."

"She'll be there. They just went to dinner. If I know my

sister, she's already booked the spa for the next two days to prepare."

I scoff, and the dog barks.

"Shhh, Peanut. It's okay, Peanut."

"I better go."

Noah looks up again. "See you tomorrow."

"Good night, Pennybags." I grin, not giving him a chance to argue the name before hanging up. I don't expect him to know that one. I only found it with the help of Google.

Millburn Pennybags, the name of the Monopoly man.

Dropping my phone on my stomach, I lay back in the hammock and swing it gently with my foot. I need to prep the rooms for Noah's cast and crew. He's booked the whole house for two nights, and I haven't really told Otto why yet. He knows I'm working for Noah, just not how many hours or why I took the job.

The door swings open and Otto sticks his head out. "Whatcha doing out here, Cattywampus?"

"Trying not to fall asleep."

"That's dangerous."

I pull myself up and walk toward the door.

His concern mirrors Holland's from earlier. "Are you working too hard? Maybe you should stop one of your jobs. The new one seems to be asking a lot from you."

"It's not too much," I tell him, passing through the door he's holding for me. "We're slow now anyway, and Noah won't need me after July, remember? It's short term."

"I still feel weird about you working for him."

Since when did he feel weird about it? He never said as much to me.

"That family needs a reality check. A TV show? Seriously? No one cares about their lives that much."

"Well, enough people do, or they wouldn't have been able to

carry five seasons. Six, if you count the spin-off his sisters are doing now."

Otto makes a scoffing sound and shuts the door behind me.

"Noah Belacourt isn't a bad guy, you know," I say carefully.

"He's got a decent head on his shoulders if he thought hiring you was a good idea. I have to give him credit for that."

I stand at the base of the stairs, feeling like there's something he wants to say. My mom hated rich people, and my dad was somewhat indifferent. But Otto and my mom agreed about this. They thought the wealth was wasted on people like the Belacourt family. "Are you okay?" I finally ask.

"I don't want anyone to take advantage of you, Kit Kat."

"Noah isn't perfect, but he's not like his parents." It was hard to imagine Mrs. Belacourt, with her five-inch stilettos and cold indifference, and see where Noah's warmth and consideration came from. Probably from a nanny. "I saw an opportunity, I took it, and it won't last forever. You don't need to worry."

He crosses the entryway and pulls me into his arms, the smell of saltwater and Irish Spring soap coming with him. "It's my job to worry. I'm the first to admit that kids aren't always like their parents. Just look at Grandma's house. *That's* what I grew up in."

I'd only been to my grandparents' house in Georgia a few times, but it was in a small, cramped suburban neighborhood with no character and zero land. Otto's free spirit grew up in that. It was a good example of the way a child could grow and be different from his family. I love him and his open mind, but I can understand his hesitance regarding the Belacourts. I want to give him peace. He clearly has enough other things on his plate.

I squeeze him once and pull away, starting upstairs. "Noah's a good guy," I reiterate. "It's just a job."

Otto grunts, heading for the kitchen. But I know his grunts. I can read them like a book, and I'm pretty sure I put his worries back to bed. Now I just hope Noah doesn't prove me wrong.

But I don't think he will.

CHAPTER 15

Noah

I'M NOT sure if Sunset Harbor is prepared for the chaos of a photoshoot on our beach. Scratch that—I'm not sure if my resort is prepared for it. The way we boated all the people and equipment in, the rest of the island can remain blissfully unaware of what we're doing here.

The resort patrons who are told the beach is closed today will be less pleased. Their vouchers for the spa or golf course or restaurant will ease that pain, I'm sure.

People are tracking footprints all over the sand, setting up two of the shoots while our hair and makeup artist, Melanie, has commandeered one of the beachfront villas for the models. She's in there now, directing their hair, makeup, and wardrobes. Bree is still in the house with her personal glam team, and her dog is right here on the beach with me, following my feet so closely I'm afraid I'll step on her. There have been two close calls already.

Mateo approaches with an iPad and a grim expression.

I know something always will go wrong—law of nature or whatever—but today it seems like one thing after another. Three of the models contracted food poisoning sometime in the night —including the redhead with freckles—so we're short a few people. The outfit we planned for Bree is missing, so she had to find something else to wear. Then the skies were ultra cloudy this morning, which can be great for lighting I guess, but not great for the sunny vibes we're trying for.

Thankfully the sky has cleared up. Mateo's brow is still stormy.

"What is it now?" I ask.

"The castle. The schedule's kind of tight. When is Cat arriving?"

"Any second now." I scan the beach but don't see her. I take another step toward the surf to look around the group gathered there, and Peanut jumps in front of me. I almost trip over her, so I lean down and scoop her up, letting her little shaky body rest against my chest.

"It's a dog," Mateo says.

"My sister's dog. She's nervous." She trembles in my arms, so I hold her tighter and run my fingers behind her ears. I figured out the other night that this move calms her pretty quickly.

"Right." Mateo looks at us another second too long before returning his attention to his iPad. "They're almost finished with the volleyball net. Christine is happy with the lighting, so we'll start over there once the models are ready. Oh, speak of the devil—Cat!" Mateo raises an arm to get her attention.

I follow the motion and have to catch my breath. She's coming down the stairs, and I work to keep my jaw from dropping to the sand. She's in white high-waisted shorts and a plain yellow tee that's tied at the waist. So simple, yet so cute. Her blonde hair is waved, blowing away from her face, and a red scarf is rolled up and tied around her head like a headband. It looks like the sodden thing she pulled out of the ocean the day I saw her a few weeks ago, and I have the weird desire to run my fingers through her hair.

"We need that castle now," Mateo mutters, even though she's too far away to hear.

"I'll tell her," I say, starting toward the stairs. "You can do something else."

Mateo stands there watching me. I can feel the heat of his stare on my back, but I don't even care if I just gave away my hand. Nothing matters to me right now as much as seeing Cat.

I meet her at the foot of the stairs. She kicks off her Birkenstocks and loops them over her fingers. "Hey, Elon." She grins, showing me a set of straight teeth when her gaze drops to my arms, her eyes warming. "And hello to you, Peanut. Where's your mom?"

"In New York, I think."

"Not your mom, Musk. Hers."

"Nice nickname. But could you pick someone less... what's the word?"

"Rich?"

"Not the attribute I was thinking of." I pull a face and she laughs.

Cat steps closer, reaching to pet Peanut. "She has you wrapped around her little paw, doesn't she?"

"She might." I can't breathe. Cat is leaning forward, her shoes dangling from one hand while she runs her fingers through Peanut's thick, fluffy fur. Her hot pink nails stand out against the dog's sandy color.

Cat leans down to look into Peanut's little face. "You have the sweetest uncle, Peanut."

The scent of her shampoo rises to meet me, and I inhale quietly.

She looks up, squinting against the sunlight, and her face is way too close to mine. I need some space so I can breathe again before I get too drunk on her and say something I'll regret later.

"You ready to make a sandcastle?" I ask.

"Yes. Where do you want me?"

In my arms.

It's a really good thing those words don't actually leave my mouth. I clear my throat and start toward the water. "Over here. We have all the equipment ready."

"Equipment?" she repeats, following me toward the water. There are a handful of beach chairs and an umbrella set up beside a bucket and shovel, with a few other beach toys.

"I thought you'd need a little help with the turrets."

"True," she concedes, surveying the bucket and tools. "These are great."

"Do you have much sandcastle experience?"

"Not recently, but it shouldn't be too hard."

Cat tosses her shoes to the side and checks out the tide before selecting the place for the castle, then gets to work. I set Peanut on a blue and white striped beach chair in the shade of an umbrella and kneel to help.

Cat sits back on her heels. "What are you doing?"

"Helping."

"Don't you have more important things to do?"

I glance over the beach. "Not really. Mateo is handling the coordinating. Christine is the visionary behind everything. Melanie is getting the models ready. Gina is up at the house with Bree."

She observes me, her blonde eyebrows pulling together. "And Alonzo?"

"Probably with Bree."

"Then why do you have their dog?"

"She followed me down the steps this morning." I scoop sand into the bucket and pack it down. "I think she may have imprinted on me or something."

"That's really sweet." Cat leans forward, smoothing out the sand that will be our castle base.

I flip the bucket and release a flawless tower.

We're getting another tower finished when the sound of a shutter clicks rapidly behind me. Cat glances up, then her gaze shoots to me. "What are they doing?"

Christine walks toward us, taking pictures. She gestures for Alex, the guy who's manning the video camera on a motion steadying device, to follow her. "Ignore us and just keep doing what you're doing."

"This is a prop," Cat says. "We aren't the models."

"I'm just using you for lighting." Christine talks while looking into her camera, adjusting things as she goes. "I want to test a few things before they get down here and we roll for real."

I look at Cat, who is a little unnerved. "You okay?"

"Yeah. We need to make a walkway between these towers."

"You are detail-oriented, aren't you?" I ask, unable to keep from smiling down at her. She's taking this sandcastle very seriously for something we intend to destroy during the shoot.

"That's what makes me such a great assistant." She grins at me and the sun sparkles on her, shining off her eyes. She looks down at the sand and starts forming the walkway.

Clicks go off around us, but we ignore Christine and her cameraman.

Cat shifts around the castle until she's kneeling directly beside me so she can better reach her walkway. I could move, but I don't. Her shoulder presses into mine and she leans forward, forming a little mound on top of one of the towers. Pinching the sand, she forms a little creature.

"What is it?" I ask.

"I'm offended you can't tell immediately."

"Peanut?"

"Bingo."

"Lucky guess. That thing looks nothing like a dog."

Cat scoffs, leaning away and laughing. "Don't worry about sparing my feelings."

"I'm not." She playfully swats my arm. I reach for her hand and take it before it can make contact. "Careful there, or you'll ruin the castle too early."

"Fair point, Lex."

I sit back and appraise her, still holding her hand. She hasn't tried to reclaim it yet, so I don't bother releasing it. Her small hand fits so perfectly within mine, it's kind of jarring. "Why villains, Cat? What is with the rich villains?"

She looks up, her eyes sparkling. "Um, because you're a villain. Obviously."

"Oh, right, I forgot about my master plan to take over the world. Hang tight while I check in with Pinky and the Brain."

"Who?"

"It's an old show—you know what? Never mind."

My feet are starting to fall asleep from sitting in this position too long, so I let go of her hand and move to stand. There's noise coming from the wooden staircase, and I see the group of models making their way down, Bree just behind them with Alonzo and Gina.

"Hey," Cat says, getting up beside me and putting her hand on my forearm. I'm not expecting it, so it stuns me into silence. "I didn't mean to offend you."

"You didn't."

"I'll quit with the villains. Though in my defense, Musk and Trump and Bezos... yeah, okay, I get it." Her nose scrunches adorably and her fingers squeeze into my skin.

I have the impulse to run a finger down her brow to smooth the wrinkles. I reach for her, taking the pad of my thumb along her forehead like the baboon in *The Lion King*. Except this does wonders and her skin instantly goes back to normal. "I'm not really offended, you know."

"That's good."

"I just don't relish the comparisons."

Her eyes are glued to mine. "I'll come up with better ones."

"Tony Stark works."

That makes her smile. "Oh yeah?"

"Or Steve Rogers."

"He's not rich."

"Bruce Wayne."

"I'm sensing a theme, here."

"Clark Kent."

Cat lets out a laugh, her fingers squeezing my arm. "Fine. I get it."

"Or, you know, Noah also works."

"Everyone to the sand pit!" Mateo calls through a megaphone. "I need players on the volleyball court, spectators on the sidelines."

People start moving toward the net. Cat drops my hand and takes a step back.

We turn to find Christine and Alex right behind us, still filming. "Perfect," Christine says.

Cat looks suspicious.

I feel that way too. "I thought that was just for lighting."

"It was cute, Noah. I think you'll like it." Christine lifts her hand in a placating manner. "We don't have to use it, but you might want to. If you're going to bring your girlfriend, you might as well get some mileage out of it."

Cat is quick to speak. "Oh, I'm not—"

"She's not—"

Cat shakes her head. *"We're* not—"

There's a beat of silence while Mateo's voice carries from the other side of the beach, calling out directions.

Christine narrows her almond-shaped eyes at us, tucking straight black hair behind her ear. "Okay. I misread the situation, but the footage is still great." She turns for the volleyball court and Alex falls in behind her.

I pick up Peanut from her little perch on the chair, afraid she'll panic if I leave her behind. "If they really wanted a good shot, I could have taken my shirt off. Done a few push-ups."

She gawks. "You're that into yourself, Belacourt?"

"No." I can't contain my grin. "I figured you are, since you like to watch me in the mornings."

I start toward the group, holding the small dog.

Cat hurries to catch up. "I don't *watch* you. I pay attention so I know when to make your smoothie. Distinct difference."

"Whatever you want to call it." I flash her a grin, noting the way her cheeks blush a furious pink.

Bree is in position on the volleyball court when we reach them, and the guy we've chosen to play her love interest is on the opposite side. She's wearing a pink swim top and shorts, her feet bare, her long dark hair in a beachy wave. She runs toward us and nuzzles her face close to Peanut without quite touching the dog.

"There's my baby. Alonzo panicked when he couldn't find her this morning."

"She followed me down here," I tell her. "I should have let you know."

"Don't stress. Just don't plan on stealing my dog." Bree looks beside me. "Oh, Cat. Hi, again. I *love* your scarf."

Cat's fingers trail the tail of the scarf that's hanging over her shoulder. "Thanks. It was my mom's."

I look at her quickly, but she averts her gaze.

Bree probably doesn't know that Cat lost her parents. I want to ask her more about the scarf—was that the one she went into the ocean to save?—but now isn't the time.

"Places!" Christine calls. She holds the camera up and takes a few shots of Bree's lover boy before adjusting something on her camera. Bree skips back into place and catches a volleyball someone tosses to her, then serves it over the net.

Christine takes a few more shots before lowering the camera and frowning at the group gathered along the sidelines. "Where are the blondes?"

"Blondes?" Mateo asks, hurrying to her side. "We had two and a redhead, but they all got food poisoning."

"There's no variety," Christine says, looking at the depleted group of models, thanks to whatever they ate for dinner last night. We've brought in various women of color, but I see what she's saying—they're all brunettes. Every single one of them. She glances up, right at me, before her gaze slides to Cat.

I know what she's thinking. I also don't know if Cat will understand that it's within her power to turn Christine down. There have been a handful of times that she's come to the house to assist me or gotten on the phone in the evenings—like FaceTiming during my barking dilemma the other night—that made me wonder if she was acting out of kindness or only doing it because I pay her and she thinks she has to.

"We need someone to offset Bree so she stands out on camera. Otherwise, she won't catch the viewers' eyes straight away."

Cat is listening, but I don't think she's caught on yet. Besides, by Christine's logic, Cat should be the one starring in these ads. As the only blonde, she'll stand out in every scene.

"What do you say, Cat? Do you mind jumping in?"

Her head whips toward Christine. "Me? I'm not dressed for it."

"You blend in perfectly. Even the thing in your hair"—Christine does a twirl with her finger toward Cat's head—"is the right color. It matches the color scheme."

Cat developed the color scheme, so whether it was just a product of being colors she likes or the fact that this palette has been in her head, she really did dress for the cameras today. Unintentionally, obviously.

"I'm not trained."

"You were a natural when I was testing earlier. Why don't we give it a shot, then go from there?" She looks at me. "What do you think, Noah?"

"If Cat would like to do it, I think it's a great idea." I try to hold her blue eyes. "If you'd *like* to," I reiterate.

She looks flustered, glancing from the makeshift volleyball court to me. Does she need permission to back out? I want to tell her she doesn't need to do it, but before I can open my mouth, she's nodding.

"Okay, I'll do it." She looks at Christine. "Tell me what to do."

CHAPTER 16

Cat

THE VOLLEYBALL SCENE wasn't terrible. It's something I know well, and we basically just had to play a low-key game of two on two with a lot of smiling and laughing while they filmed and took pictures. But now we've moved on to the picnic scene, and I've suddenly forgotten how to have a picnic with friends. Maybe because these models are gorgeous and my face feels under-dressed in comparison. Or maybe my body is too awkward for relaxed fake picnicking.

Either way, I'm blowing it, and Noah is watching the whole thing unfold from behind the camera with that adorable fluffy dog in his arms. Alonzo is here now, but Noah is still holding the dog. It's by choice, and it's one of the cutest things I've ever seen.

I still can't get the sound of him soothing her through Face-Time out of my head. It was a side of Noah I'd never seen, and I really liked it.

Most of what I've seen of Noah this summer have been sides I hadn't seen before. The teasing. The attention to people's needs. Has he always been so thoughtful and I never noticed because I was too busy being bullied by his sister and hating his family? Or is this a more recent development?

Bree reaches across the sand and squeezes my knee. She flashes me a smile while we wait for makeup to finish touching up some of the girls' faces. This Florida heat is *melting* us. "You're doing great."

"You're being nice," I counter, my back sticky and my shoes totally gone. "This is so not natural for me."

Bree shrugs one shoulder. She's still in a swim top and shorts, her long dark hair perfectly waved. She's a mermaid wearing her legs, a natural at all of this. "You're fooling everyone, then."

Alonzo walks toward us on the phone, his eyebrows raised high, his eyes wide. "Yes, if you'll just hold a moment," he says, then pulls the phone away and hits a button, probably to mute it. He gives Bree a meaningful look. "Do you have a second to take this?"

She goes still. "Is it..."

"Yes," Alonzo says, unable to dampen his smile.

Bree is on her feet and rushing toward him immediately. She takes a deep breath before accepting the phone and starting toward the other side of the beach, away from the noise and waves and people. "This is Bree Belacourt," she says.

The makeup girl reaches me, and I stand so she can do her job. She adds mascara because I probably didn't have on nearly enough, then fixes up my lips. They still look natural though, thankfully. At least in my phone camera.

Noah walks toward me when the makeup girl moves on. "How's it going over here?"

"I forgot how to eat sandwiches, I guess."

"You don't have to actually eat anything, you know." He glances sidelong at the food. "It's probably heavy on the sand right now anyway."

Oh, good point. "It's just so awkward. All of it. I'm not a natural at this whole modeling thing. I just keep thinking about where my hands are and what my face is doing. They'll probably need to edit me out when we're all wrapped."

Noah chuckles, shaking his head, then leans down to let the

dog onto the sand. She walks away for a bit and then back, where she sits right on top of one of his feet.

"Needy little thing," I say.

Noah looks at me from under his lashes. "I don't mind it. She's grown on me."

Are we talking about the dog or me?

There's a shout from the other side of the beach. Bree stomps toward the stairs, her face streaming with tears.

Alonzo rushes behind her. "Don't leave, Bree. We have to finish the shoot!"

"I... *can't!*" she wails, running for the stairs. Her face is red and splotchy, her tears so heavy it's a wonder she can see anything at all.

Noah curses under his breath, then takes off after his sister. Peanut gives a yelp when she realizes she's being abandoned, so I lean down and pick her up, but I'm not the one she wants. I watch Bree tear up the stairs toward the resort and—probably—their family home, Alonzo a few steps behind her, Noah at the bottom.

Gina—short dark hair and a pencil skirt, even out here—is following Noah, but the rest of the group appears too stunned to move.

Peanut barks, her yelp sad and high-pitched right in my ear. "You want your mom?" I say quietly, watching Bree disappear in a fit of tears.

I reluctantly follow.

THERE IS nothing anyone can do to convince Bree to return to the beach. She has received bad news, apparently, and she's devastated. Alonzo took the dog from me when I reached the Belacourt house, but he returned to Bree's room to comfort her.

Noah, Gina, and Mateo are now standing on the back porch,

talking with Christine and Alex and going over something on one of their computers. They have to reevaluate the whole thing because Bree is in no condition to be the face of their app launch campaign. Either way, she's straight up refusing to leave her room.

Maybe it's salvageable. Maybe they can still use the scenes they've already shot and piece them together in a shorter commercial than the original concept. The stills will be usable for ads, for sure, so not *all* is lost, I hope.

Bree's wails travel downstairs from her bedroom. I simultaneously feel bad for her and annoyed that she's put her brother in this situation. What happened to *the show must go on*? Yeah, she's gotten bad news, but is it really so awful she can't put on a smile and film just *two* scenes to finish the campaign?

There's that Belacourt entitlement I loathe.

I pull a LaCroix from the fridge and pop it open, taking a long pull. The sparkling cold water is refreshing. The back door slides open and Noah steps inside, closing it behind himself. He's looking at me warily like I'm Peanut on the day they met, approaching like he's afraid I'm going to snap at his hand.

"What's the problem?" I ask, setting the can on the counter.

"Aside from Bree suddenly being indisposed?"

I shake my head. "I know you don't want to be heartless, but sheesh. You can't pull out the contract and remind her what this campaign means and how much work it took to get ready?" I have an appreciation for that part after helping him for more than a week with preparations. That's not counting all the work they did before I arrived in Noah's life.

"We have no contract," he says. "She was just helping out, so we can't really do anything about that."

"You should have written up a contract."

"I will next time." He shoots me a smile. His face is relaxed, his brown eyes affectionate when they lay on me. I can't help but feel the tenderness there, like I really am Peanut and he's won my affection with his kindness.

Also, I'm fairly certain he has no intention of forcing his sister to sign a contract next time. Even if he had, he probably wouldn't force her into working while she's such a wreck.

It's just too much to hold his gaze. I look away and see that everyone on the back porch is watching us. They're waiting for something. Gina's arms are crossed over her chest and she's looking at me like I stole her lunch from the breakroom fridge and left just the carrots.

"Why is everyone staring?" I ask.

Noah doesn't look behind him. He knows what I mean, which sends trepidation through me.

"Tell me what they want, please."

"You." He speaks gently, but the word is full and rich, moving over my skin with a volley of shivers. I have to remind myself that *Noah* doesn't want me. That group on the deck does. "They want you to take over, Cat. There's a lot of good shots from volleyball and the picnic scene and... and us building the castle together."

"You're trying to sell *romance*, though, and I've just been the giggly girl on the side."

He pauses. "Alex showed us the shots he captured while we built the castle. It actually works for the narrative."

"It works."

"With the right music, yeah."

His words sink in, past the shallow barrier and into the deep. He means it works with *us*. We are the romantic couple in this scheme. "What about the guy who played the love interest alongside Bree?"

"He'll become one of the group."

Because Noah will take his place. His brown eyes cut through me, his concern palpable. He's worried about me. I'm still trying to wrap my mind around how it will work. "You aren't even in the volleyball scene," I say. "Or the picnic."

"They can cut me in." He clears his throat and looks away. "They have a few shots of me during those scenes. I'm not in the action, but they have me on camera watching... and smiling... anyway, it works."

It's like they planned this.

"Did Bree really get a call, or is this all just an elaborate hoax?"

Noah laughs, the sound coming from his belly, which answers that question. "You think I'm that manipulative?"

"No, I don't."

"There are easier ways of kissing you, Cat."

My stomach drops clear to my toes.

The kiss in the surf. It was *my* idea.

"You don't have to agree to this," he says. "There are other options. We still have everyone booked for another day of shooting. We're only asking because it's the easiest way to salvage the footage we already have."

And time, and money. We're losing daylight and still have two scenes to shoot and no leading lady. I want to say no. It's not my thing, and I don't feel like I'm good at it. But the way Noah is looking at me now makes that impossible. He's hopeful, and it does something weird to my stomach. I don't think I could refuse him anything, which feels reckless and dangerous and exciting.

Besides, his sister just bailed on him, and after watching all the hard work he's put into this campaign, I can't be the reason it doesn't get wrapped up now. I want to help him. He deserves to have someone put him first.

"Okay."

"Okay?" he repeats back to me, clearly surprised.

I nod, warming up to the idea. "Yeah, I'll do it. But you owe me."

"You'll be paid, obviously."

This suddenly feels icky. "That's not what I mean, Pennybags. You already pay me well enough. Now you'll owe me a *favor*. Totally different."

His smile is gentle. It feels just for me. Intimate, even.

"Do you have a swimsuit under that?" he asks. His gaze stays on my face.

"No. Why?"

"Because you'll need it for the final scene. We have extras in wardrobe."

"Okay."

He turns around and gives a nod to the group waiting outside, and they visibly relax. Even Gina looks relieved, which is saying a lot, because so far she has seemed like she's made of stone—impenetrable, blank expressions, the whole thing.

Bree's wails continue to trail down to us from upstairs, so I head toward the door. "I guess we better get moving."

It takes about twenty minutes to find a swimsuit that fits well and matches the rest of the group, though they let me keep my own shorts on. I guess the narrative is that now I've taken my shirt off and I had this swim top on the whole time, which makes sense for what they want us filming later.

I can't think about that. I let them mess with my hair and brush something powdery over my nose and direct me back to the beach.

There's a team building a big bonfire on one end of the beach while another sets up lighting near the surf.

Christine and Alex have explained the situation to the other models. They're being positioned near the bonfire while the sun begins its descent. It's still pretty high in the sky, making me think we have time.

"We have about an hour of good lighting left, so we need to move quickly," Christine is saying while Alex moves a few people over, getting them drinks. A sound guy sets up music so the people dancing can move to the same beat. I probably look as lost as I feel right now.

Gina sits back in a chair a good distance away, watching the whole thing, but Mateo approaches. "You know the concept, Cat. Hot guy you've met on Scoutr, date's going well, your friends like him. You like him. There are possibilities." He looks me in the eye to drive home his point. "You know the drill better than most of these people."

"Right." He's right. I helped develop it. I know it well.

"Just pretend Noah is some hot guy you met on Scoutr, and things are going well," he repeats.

"Just pretend." I look across at Noah, where Melanie is messing with his hair. Unnecessarily, I might add. It looked good already.

"Let's roll," Christine calls, holding her camera up.

"Flirt," Mateo says. "Give him *the eyes*."

I want to yell at him to shut it because he's getting in my head, but then I look across the newly blazing fire where Noah is watching me, and my skin prickles at the attention. *Flirty eyes, Cat. Just flirty eyes.*

I have to kiss him tonight. My lips on his lips. When's the last time I kissed someone? Last year? I need a breath mint or a time machine so I can brush my teeth. I've never been so happy I chose to skip the garlic hummus at lunch.

My body moves toward the group against my better judgment, since it's late June in Florida and too hot for a fire. Noah is like a shirtless beacon, standing out amongst the guys. He's watching me, giving me the eyes Mateo recommended and laughing with the guy next to him like they're old friends.

"You *like* this guy, Cat," someone calls to me.

Right. Flirt. On camera. For the purpose of a national ad campaign.

Get out of your head, Cat.

I breathe out, then I search for Noah's attention again. He's starting to look worried, which is the last thing we need. If we don't get this shot correctly, they'll make us redo it until we do. I'm hopeful we won't have to use tomorrow's shooting day now that we're almost finished. If we can get everything wrapped tonight, we can be done.

With that in mind, I send Noah a smile. His dark brown eyes track my movements, and I sink into his attention. I move around the fire while he steps away from the guy he was talking to until we meet in the middle. We don't have to talk—the ad will have voiceover and music. I just need to act.

"Hug her," someone calls, probably Mateo.

Noah doesn't hesitate. His arms reach for me while I tenderly step into them. My hand flattens against his abs, which are warm and ridged beneath my fingers. His fingers press gently against my spine until I'm pulled close to his side, and all I can smell is that black and white cologne ad mixed with salty air and thick warmth and comfort.

I'm *enjoying* this, which is terrifying.

But, right now, I get to pretend it's okay.

Right now, at least, this guy is all mine. I'm not in danger of losing my home and livelihood or standing way too close to the ocean. I'm just a girl on a beach who is into a guy who is also into her. Noah's smiling down at me like I hold the moon. His smile is burning and focused and warm.

This acting thing might not be so bad after all.

I tilt my head back to look into his eyes, letting a smile fall over my lips, and lean into him. His mouth is so close, his expression roasting me like a bird on a spit. All I have to do is reach up a little, tilt my head a bit, and we'd be—

"That's a wrap!" Christine calls, grinning. "You two are perfect."

My body freezes. Holy crap. I almost kissed him. Almost for real kissed him while I was so wrapped up in the scene.

"We should have gone with them from the beginning," Alex says, looking into the screen on his camera.

"Yeah, it's hard to argue with real chemistry."

I laugh a little too loudly, pushing against Noah's chest. "Chemistry. They're so funny."

He catches my hand, yanking me back. "I don't know what's funny about it."

Woah. Okay. That felt real. Did he miss the memo about wrapping the scene? Maybe he's trying that method acting thing—living the role even off-camera. The way he's smoldering down at me has my skin feeling hot and sticky.

"Let's move to the water," Christine calls. "We only need Cat and Noah for this part. Thanks everyone. Hang out in case we need to grab another scene. I think Noah plans to have dinner ready?"

"Yeah," he says, clearing his throat. "We have food coming to the house, and your rooms are all booked for tonight, so feel free to stick around."

We start toward the ocean. Waves crash and roll, drawing away and leaving flawless sand behind. My steps slow the nearer we get to the ocean. I don't like being this close to the water. It makes me uncomfortable. Logically, I understand I'm safe, but my chest still feels tight and my breathing speeds up anyway.

My parents drowned in unforgiving water. My mom, taken by a rip current, and my dad, who jumped in to save her unsuccessfully.

I haven't swum in the ocean since.

Well, except when I saved Mom's scarf, but I'm still convinced something else possessed my body that day.

"Ready?" Christine calls, directing one of the lighting guys to move with the big circular reflector thing.

I watch Noah's back move as he walks ahead of me, the muscles shifting with each step. His feet hit the shallow waves first, and my heart speeds up.

I can do this. I'm not going to be dragged out to sea if I stand in a foot of water. It doesn't even have to be a whole foot deep. We just need the waves to crash on our feet.

Noah turns and sees my hesitation. His dark brows pull together, and he looks from me to the water. "Hey," he calls, his attention shifting to Christine. "What about a shot of us walking on the beach first? Like we're leaving the bonfire."

"I like that." She glances back to the fire. "Let's get everyone back there. They can be partying in the distance, maybe a little out of focus."

Mateo turns back for the group to give them directions. Noah steps right up to me, takes my hand, and looks into my eyes. "We don't have to do anything you're uncomfortable with."

"I can do this," I whisper, but it's pitiful. I don't sound strong or resolved.

His fingers slide between mine, taking my hand. He's tall and broad and his voice is nothing but business. He's the owner of this company. This entire operation is under his command. The king of Scoutr. When he talks to me, I think I can believe him. "I stand by what I said."

Something about his confidence and assurance makes me feel like I can do anything.

CHAPTER 17

Noah

IT'S clear from her hesitation that Cat doesn't want to be in the water right now. She avoids the shoreline—she's already made that clear to me. And we do have everyone booked for another day of filming tomorrow. We can start over. Bring in a new couple. Film again.

It's not the end of the world.

Cat's hand tightens around mine. She draws in a breath like she's preparing for battle, then lets it out slowly. "Okay, I'm good. We can do this."

"Do you promise to say something the moment you're uncomfortable?" I press. I spent a lifetime doing things to keep others happy, and it culminated in a mental breakdown. I won't force that on anyone else if I can help it.

"I promise."

I give her hand a squeeze and wait for Christine's direction. It looks like everyone is back at the bonfire and the music is going again, because people are laughing and dancing and swigging drinks just like before.

"Okay, let's roll," Christine says. "Walk south, take slow steps. Then, Noah, take her hand."

Cat pulls her hand from mine, and we turn the other direction. I grip her shoulders and scoot her over so I'm standing on the inside, closer to the ocean.

Cat looks up at me with surprise and appreciation, her blue eyes glowing.

It almost makes me lose my footing. "Ready?"

"Sure am," she says.

We start walking on the beach away from the bonfire, the waves crashing farther down and running over our toes. I reach closer and hook my pinky around hers, tugging slightly. Cat looks up at me, smiling. After a few steps, I maneuver my hand around hers so I have the whole thing in my grasp. I pull her closer to my side while we walk.

"Running out of beach," Alex says.

"Go deeper for the kiss. I want your ankles covered," Christine says.

Deeper.

"You okay?" I whisper.

"I already promised," she reminds me.

Right. Because Cat isn't breakable. She's tough, strong, independent—all the things I've long admired about her. If she says she can do it, I trust she's telling me the truth.

We walk inward until there is a solid eight inches of water. It's refreshing. I've been heating up since Cat started touching me, so it's a welcome reprieve. "This doesn't have to be weird."

"It's not weird, Hot Guy from Scoutr. Thanks for swiping right."

I can't help but chuckle. She's playing a role, that is abundantly clear. I'm just going to enjoy this. My fifteen seconds with Catalina Keene.

I graze her jaw with my fingers, brushing her hair over her shoulder and exposing her neck. She looks up into my eyes. I want to capture her in my gaze and keep her there forever. Having Cat's full attention is wild and heady. I don't think about the cameras or the models at the bonfire or the way the sun is dropping lower in the sky and turning the clouds pink and orange.

I just think about my fingers on the space between her shoulder and her neck and the way her collarbone dips right there.

Cat's hands slide up my chest. She's not speaking anymore and neither am I, like we have an unspoken agreement to get lost in the moment and not think about all the people watching us.

I *don't* think about it. I only have her in my head, and there's no room for anything else.

She grips the back of my neck and pulls me down toward her until my lips land on hers and they press together softly. It's a sweet kiss, testing the boundaries. Pushing and pulling and moving gently. I try to appear calm, but my body is going wild. It's not enough. I want more of her.

So does she. Her hand slides into my hair, pulling me closer, while my arms go around her back. She tilts her head, deepening the kiss while waves crash at our feet. I flush hot from her touch, meeting the cold sea in a tornado of sensation.

A hurricane of heat and fireworks and desire blow through me with torrential force. I can't get enough of this feeling. Cat is filling my head and my heart. I've spent my life buttoned up and watching my every move, careful of how I look, act, talk, behave —on constant watch to control the way others perceive me. With her, I don't feel like I have to remain so vigilant. I can skip my ab workout. I can eat an extra cheeseburger. I can tell a stupid punny joke. I can be *me*.

My hands slide down her back, pulling her against me while she tilts my head the other direction. I'm Play-Doh and she's molding me into exactly what she wants. I could do this all day.

There's the faint sound of someone calling to us, but I ignore it. My brain space is taken up with the taste of Cat and the feel of her skin beneath my fingers.

She breaks the kiss, lowering a few inches until it's clear that she'd been on her tiptoes.

"Lean against him," Alex calls, his direction sending faint bitterness into the moment. "Yes, just like that."

Cat's head rests against my chest, and her hand splays over my heart, where I'm sure she can feel it trying to break free of its cage. I tighten my hold, resting my chin on the top of her head. This isn't for the cameras though. I just want to hold her.

But I'm also her boss. And I'm paying her *a lot* of money.

Despite how much I crave to make this moment last, as soon as they call scene, I lower my arms and step back. I try to catch her gaze, to see if I can read the same fire in her eyes I feel in my chest, the smoldering remnants of our collision. But she's avoiding my face.

That's not a good sign.

"That was perfect," Christine says, looking at the screen on her camera. "I think you'll be really pleased, Noah."

I force a smile and watch Cat retreat out of the water, wondering if that kiss was the best thing that's ever happened to me or the biggest mistake.

THE RESORT'S kitchen had a heads up for tonight's crew dinner, so the food is waiting for us when we finish gathering our things on the beach and trek up the stairs to my house. Bree isn't crying so loudly anymore, which is good. She doesn't need these random models spreading the news that she's had a mental breakdown—or whatever that was. When I followed her up to the house earlier, she wouldn't let anyone into her room except Alonzo. All he'd said was that she had bad news.

My guess is that the producers in Nashville chose to go another direction. I hope it's not more drama with her Manhattan friends or a guy she hasn't told me about. Career rejections are painful, but there will be other opportunities.

Cat stands at the kitchen island, pulling foil off trays and arranging tongs and serving spoons in the dishes while Mateo sets up the plates and silverware. The models and crew start filling plates and carrying them outside to the large table on the deck. Gina steps out of the office in the back room and heads my way. When did she leave the photoshoot and come up here? I haven't even noticed her. She's been quieter than normal.

"Do you have a minute?" she asks.

"Of course."

I follow her around the corner into what was once my dad's office, but now is just a desk and a bunch of shelves filled with generic books. My parents moved to New York City full time about five years ago and this house—what was once our family home—became a summer vacation place they visit every so often.

Gina perches on the edge of the desk, her arms crossed over her chest. "How are you, Noah?" She tilts her head to the side, her eyes laced with concern.

"I'm good." My shirt is back on, which is a good thing, or I'd feel too vulnerable for this conversation. I slide my hands into my pockets. "Being out here has been good."

"That's such a relief. As much as I don't mind taking on extra responsibility around the office, I'll be glad to have you back full time."

"Me too. Maybe we can get Dr. Stein to sign me off sooner—"

"I don't think the board will go for that." She cringes. "They were dead set on two months."

"If Dr. Stein agrees, why would they argue?"

Gina looks away in thought. "It's possible. You wouldn't want to rush their decision and have it turn out poorly, though. It just seems like a big risk to me." She focuses on me, tilting her head, her short bob swinging with the motion. "You seem better, but not... not entirely yourself still. Am I misreading the situation?"

Better, yeah. Still an anxious mess? Depends on the day. I suck in a breath and let it out slowly. "You're not wrong."

"Maybe it's better to give it more time so you don't return prematurely and burn out again. But you know yourself best, Noah. I'll support whatever you want to do."

She's right. If I rush the board, they might think I haven't given it enough time. It hasn't even been one full month since the incident, and they originally prescribed two. I should at least wait until the time is halfway over. I have weekly Zoom meetings with Dr. Stein, so I can check in with her in a few days and see what she thinks. I haven't had any huge anxiety attacks since coming to Sunset Harbor, so I think things are moving in the right direction.

Cat's laugh floats from the kitchen, joyous and bright. It's no wonder I feel lighter when I'm constantly surrounded by sunshine.

Gina straightens. "I'm going to take off, since we don't need to be here tomorrow anymore."

"I'll have someone drive you." Who can man the speedboat? Mateo, maybe?

"The ferry is fine with me."

"Have Mateo take you to the ferry, at least. It'll only take a minute."

She nods, then approaches and squeezes my arm. "It's good to see you looking so well, Noah."

I smile at her, and she walks away to find Mateo. After Gina leaves, I pull out my phone and see a string of texts, one from my sister and the rest from her assistant. I open the thread and scan them. Shoot.

BREE

I'm so sorry, Noah. Don't hate me.

ALONZO

> The producer called her. She's crushed. They decided to go a different direction and Bree is convinced she's ruined her one shot here.

So, I was correct. It doesn't make me feel any better, though.

ALONZO

> Between you and me, it's not great. But there will be other producers.

> I think we're going to leave. Bree wants to be alone and the house will be pretty full tonight.

> Scratch that. We can't get the plane until Tuesday. Don't let anyone come upstairs tonight. I'll keep her company. She really is a mess.

I text him back.

NOAH

> You guys need dinner? I can bring it up.

ALONZO

> We're good. I got food earlier, and Bree won't eat.

NOAH

> Can I help her at all?

ALONZO

> Be here for her. I didn't hear the whole conversation, but I think the producer was pretty brutal. She keeps talking about auto-tune, so I think they must have told her she can't sing.

He can't be right about that. If there's one thing Bree can do, it's sing. I don't think I'm biased either. She has a pure tone. I would've thought they'd recognize the Billie Eilish vibes and pick her up straight away. Something's not right here.

> **NOAH**
> Let me know what I can do for her.

> **ALONZO**
> Will do.

I release a long sigh, letting my head drop back.

"Oh, sorry. I'll come back—" Cat is turning out the door.

I stand up so fast my vision sparkles on the edges. "Wait, Cat."

She turns back, grimacing. "I didn't mean to interrupt."

"You aren't. Gina left."

"I was just going to ask if you want me to make you a plate."

She's so thoughtful, standing in the doorway, one shoulder up while she grips her elbow and waits. She's back in the yellow tee, tied at the waist, and her cheeks and nose are rosy like she got a little sunkissed. She said something about dinner, but I can't help thinking about the waves crashing on our feet, my heart thudding like a drumbeat, her lips devouring mine.

"Pennybags?"

And there it is, crashing away like the fantasy it was. I clear my throat and hope it clears my head. "I'll be out in a second."

She hesitates in the doorway, then looks around. "Do you use this office?"

"No."

"I didn't think so."

"Why?"

"Because the most I ever have to do in here is dust the books."

Right. Because she cleans up after us. "It was my dad's, but he took everything important out when they made Manhattan their regular residence."

"Are you planning to move in?" She still hovers by the door, peering at me like she can see the turmoil dancing over my skin.

I shake my head. "This will probably forever be a vacation

house. I have a condo on the mainland, close to work. That's where I usually am."

She runs her fingers along the edge of the bookcase. "Except for this summer."

"Yeah. Because..." My body goes numb. She can't know I got put on a time out from work. Nothing would make me less attractive than being related to a toddler, with the emotional capacity to match. "I just want to be out here this summer."

Cat steps into the room and crosses her arms. "You know your dimple pops when you're lying? It must be something you're doing with your jaw."

"I don't have a dimple."

"It's small, but it is there, my friend."

My friend. That's new. "How do you know I'm lying? Maybe the dimple pops because I'm happy to see you."

"Nah, it's definitely a lie detector. You don't have to tell me the truth, but you should know I can see right through you."

It's a really good thing that's not true, or she'd know how often I think about her.

I take a few steps toward where she's leaning against the door jamb. "Did you eat?"

"Not yet. I wanted to make sure everyone had what they needed first."

Including me. "You should get a plate before it gets cold."

"I will. You coming?"

"Yeah."

She stands there, looking at me. Hesitating. "Are you okay?"

Is that why she won't leave? She's worried about me? At least I don't have to worry about things being uncomfortable between us after the kiss. She's eliminated that fear entirely. "I'm fine. It's Bree. She's just... I don't know how to help her."

Cat glances up. "Is she still here?"

"Yeah."

"Take her some food?"

"She's not hungry."

"Has she faced a similar situation before? What did your mom do to comfort her when you were younger?"

My mom. That's a good thought. I try to think back to what she would do. "Bree faced rejection tonight. When that happened to my sisters in high school—boyfriends breaking up with them or when Olive didn't make the dance team—my mom would put on a movie and pop some popcorn. The girls would veg out and watch movies all night."

"Any specific movie?"

"*The Notebook* was a favorite."

She sighs. "You can never go wrong with Ryan Gosling."

"Hey," I say through a grin.

She matches my smile. "You're hot too, Pennybags, but I stand by it."

"Fair enough." I hold her gaze for a moment. "Thanks for the idea. Thanks for everything you've done today."

"It was nothing. Come eat before it gets cold." She turns, hurrying from the room before I can say anything else. I'm glad she doesn't seem uncomfortable because of the kiss. I felt sparks and the magic there, but as long as she's my employee and I'm paying her a ridiculously high salary, I can't do anything about how I feel, anyway.

So I swallow down my feelings and head to the theater room. It's time to hunt for *The Notebook*.

CHAPTER 18

Cat

THE RUG I ordered for Noah's room is long and heavy. I just finished cleaning the house and the rug was delivered early this morning, sitting in the entryway and taunting me. I hoped Alonzo would be around to help me carry it upstairs, but he and Bree had taken off to the beach this morning with Peanut and they haven't been back since.

It's been three days since the photoshoot. Bree is still withdrawn. She didn't even greet me this morning, just walked past me in the kitchen like a depressed zombie. Alonzo followed her, looking concerned. Something's definitely going on there. It makes me feel bad for thinking she should have just bucked up and finished shooting the ads. Whatever happened, it has messed with her mental health.

Kind of like how kissing Noah has messed with mine.

Okay, let's go back to the moment in the surf with the water rushing our feet and my hands all lost in his hair and the way he was gently holding me and letting me move his head whichever way I wanted. I've never felt so much like molten lava in my life. Kissing him was a heady, full-body experience.

I can't let it get to me. He's Noah Belacourt, billionaire extraordinaire with his pick of women, not someone who lives full time on the island. Besides, he's my boss.

It meant nothing. It was just a kiss. It didn't *feel* that way, but

I know those to be the facts, and if I repeat them enough, eventually I'll start to believe them. Besides, I just need to get the man out of my head. He's not *real*. He's from a different world. I just work for him, and that whole kissing situation was part of the job.

The way he'd looked at me when I'd found him in the office that night, concerned and stressed, made it clear he was trying to find a way to let me down easy, that the kiss hadn't been anything special. If it had been, that conversation would have gone differently.

I've done what any self-respecting person would do in my shoes. I've been avoiding him.

But I still need to do my job, which means moving this heavy rug up the stairs and setting it up in his room, preferably before he gets home from kayaking with Tristan.

Getting a good grip on the plastic-wrapped rug, I heave, pulling it toward the stairs. How does it weigh more than Otto's Volkswagen Beetle? With enough pulling, pushing, and leaning, I maneuver the rug all the way to the bottom of the stairs. The house is ultra air-conditioned, but sweat still beads along my hairline and down my spine.

Who needs a gym when you have an extra large rug? It takes much longer than I'm willing to admit to get the thing up the stairs, then I crawl along the floor, pushing it toward Noah's room like a kid playing with a train.

I'm sweaty and exhausted, but it feels good to sit in the middle of Noah's floor and unwrap the beastly thing. I wrestle the plastic off and toss it into the hallway, then unroll the rug. It's thick and soft and luxurious. Once I get it positioned on the floor, I lay down on it, just to catch my breath. It feels like laying on plush silk—if that's a thing—so I starfish out, running my hands along the smooth fibers. After cleaning the entire house and lugging this up the stairs, I'm beat. I close my eyes for just a moment and feel my body melt into the rug.

Noah

CAT IS SLEEPING on my floor, and it's the cutest thing I've seen all week. Even cuter than the animals I saw this morning in the wildlife refuge while I was kayaking with my buddy, Tristan. And we saw *otters*.

I lean against the doorway, arms crossed over my chest, and debate how to handle this. Cat's face is so relaxed. I don't want to disturb her. She works so hard, which is clear from the way she never stops moving. She's constantly running my errands or taking my calls in between her other jobs—cleaning other houses or rooms in her B&B or grocery shopping for Otto. She must be so tired.

I can't wake her up. Not when she clearly needs sleep. But I'm wet and salty from taking a swim after kayaking, so I need to change.

Cat starts to stir, solving my dilemma for me—but then she settles in again.

Great.

I move around her to get a fresh set of clothes from the dresser. I'll take them downstairs to change.

When I finish pulling shorts from my drawer as quietly as possible, Cat sits bolt upright.

"Oh my gosh. How long was I out?"

"I'm not sure." I keep digging around for a shirt to give her a second to wake up. "I just got back."

She groans, rubbing her face. "Sorry. Your rug is just *so* soft. I couldn't help myself."

The rug? I glance down and notice it. My attention had been elsewhere before. It's a solid blue rug, thick and heavy from the look of it. Hold up. She carried this thing upstairs on her own?

She couldn't have. It takes up almost the entire room. "How did you get it up here?"

"A little muscle." She crinkles her nose. "And a lot of determination."

No wonder she's exhausted. I'm impressed by her tenacity. "It looks good. You chose a nice one."

"Yeah, I did." She runs her hand along the long fibers. "You don't even need a bed anymore. This thing will put you right out."

I chuckle, pulling everything I need from the dresser and stacking the pile neatly on top of it. "Good to know. I'll have to test it out later."

"Come on in, the water's nice." She smiles up at me sleepily, then seems to think better of it and scrambles to her feet. "I mean, alone, obviously. I wasn't inviting you to do anything other than lie on your new rug. Or sit on it. You don't have to lie on anything."

Wow, she rambles when she's nervous. Have I ever seen Cat nervous before? I don't think so. Even at the shoot she wasn't nervous, just unsure.

"You know what? I'm gonna go." She starts for the door.

"Cat?"

"Yeah?" She spins around so fast she loses her balance and almost goes down.

I reach for her arm to steady her. It would only take a quick tug to pull her into my arms, so I drop her arm immediately and take a healthy step back.

"This might be presumptuous of me, but I was starting to consider you a friend," I say.

Her face softens.

So I push on. "But it has felt a little tense the last few days. I don't want everything that happened at the photoshoot to ruin that for us."

"Oh, gosh, you don't have to worry. I'm not going to be

weird about it, I promise." She looks down at the rug, her bare toes skimming over it. "It was just a kiss, Belacourt. We're still friends."

Just a kiss. That's not true for me. It feels a little like an arrow to the heart to hear her say it.

"Actually, speaking of kissing, you know what?" Cat says with more enthusiasm. "You should go out with my friend, Jane. You know Jane Hayes right? She works for the mayor now, and she's gorgeous and single. She's super fun." Cat gets into the idea the more she talks about it. "You guys might totally hit it off."

If she's trying to send the message that she's not interested, I'm reading it loud and clear. It hurts. "I'm not really in the market for a girlfriend."

"You don't have to marry her," Cat says. She's looking so earnest; I don't have the heart to refuse her anything. "I just thought it might be worth trying out. You know, to see if there's a connection."

"Like chemistry?" I ask, using the word they used a few days ago at the photoshoot to describe me and Cat. "Speaking of chemistry, I got the first looks for some of our ads. Nothing is finished yet. They're just preliminary concepts if you want to see them."

"I really do," she breathes.

"Okay." I pass her and lean over my desk chair to open my laptop.

"I can wait until you change," Cat says, eyeing my swim shorts.

I glance over my shoulder and catch her eye. "That would be great. I'll just be a minute. Feel free to take a seat." I grab the stack of clothes I'd pulled out earlier and let myself into my bathroom, shutting the door behind me. I start the shower because I was just in the ocean and want to rinse, but I'm in and out pretty fast. A stopwatch could probably clock me in under five minutes from the moment I step into the bathroom until the moment I come out.

Yet *still*, when I enter my room towel drying my hair, I find Cat laying on my bed, totally asleep. I toss the towel into my laundry basket in the closet and ease the door closed again, then sit on the desk chair to pull up the ads. I have to focus on something else, because if I look at Cat asleep, my brain goes rampant with the memory of her in my arms.

Not that looking at pictures of us kissing helps at all. Christine is a mastermind. She's so good at what she does. The videos are still being edited—as are most of the photos—but the ads Christine sent over for general direction are fantastic. Me and Cat at the bonfire, shoulder-to-shoulder building a sandcastle, walking in the surf, kissing with the waves at our ankles. They're magical and hazy and romantic. They make me want to go on a date, so I think the ads are working.

"Oh my gosh!" Cat sits up fast, her hands pressing into her cheeks. "Why didn't you wake me up? How long have I been out?"

"About an hour."

"Seriously?"

I chuckle. "No. Probably like ten minutes."

Cat yawns, then crawls to the edge of the bed and sits there cross-legged, looking at the computer screen over my shoulder. "That looks good."

I haven't turned back to face the screen yet, though. I'm gauging the tired lines on her face. "I think I'm working you too hard."

"You aren't. I'm just not sleeping well."

I swivel on the chair to fully face her. "Anything I can help with?"

She gives me a lazy smile. "You want to come read me bedtime stories, Belacourt?"

"If it would help."

"Someday when you're my assistant, we'll work it into the contract." Her gaze falls on the computer and her eyes brighten. She stands up and comes closer until she's leaning over my shoulder, looking at the images Christine sent over. "Wow, these look legit."

"Like real ads." I scroll through the few photos we have so she can see them all.

"Seriously," she says quietly. "We look good."

I turn to look at her, and her face is right there. She's so close I could lean forward and kiss her. I want to. I've already had a taste, and I know how electric it would be.

Cat turns her smile on me and freezes. Her blue eyes lock on mine. The feeling of her in my arms is so fresh. The buzzing energy between us crackles and sparks, but I need to throw a bucket of water over myself before I do something stupid. Acting on this feeling would be insanely inappropriate. I'm her boss. She deserves better than to be taken advantage of while she works for me. Especially when I know how tired she is.

I'm not even sure she would welcome it, anyway. Despite our chemistry, Cat hasn't done much to indicate she would be interested in me romantically.

Like now, when she takes a solid step back to put more space between us. She looks down at my lips for a beat, then clears her throat. "What do you think about that date with Jane? It's a great idea, right?"

Wait. She looked at my lips first. She *must* be interested, right? She was thinking of our kiss too and her cheeks are rosy. Does that mean this whole date with Jane is a test? Or maybe she's fighting her feelings, like I am, and this is a way to push me away. I really hope that's the right answer.

Well, fine. If she wants me to date her friend, I'll date her friend. I know Jane from school, but I haven't really talked to her in years. She's nice, pretty, and if nothing else, it'll be good to catch up. It'll prove to Cat that I'm not trying to date her while I'm her employer, at least. If she gets jealous... no, I won't go there. Because why would she?

"Okay."

"Okay?" Cat repeats, blonde eyebrows arching. "Like, yes?"

"Sure. I'll go out with Jane."

She stares at me for a second, just long enough to make me second-guess myself.

"Great," she says. "That's great. I'll just—"

The door slams downstairs, followed by the clicking of stilettos on the tiled entryway.

"Bree's back," I say. It's been a tough few days of emotions and romcoms and a lot of popcorn, among every other takeout option the island offers—and some they don't. Thank heavens for Mateo and the speedboat.

"Is she doing any better?" Cat asks.

"Not really."

"I better get out of your hair then."

I don't want her to leave. "You don't have to go. If Bree's still in a mood, we'll just be watching more romcoms and eating our weight in popcorn this evening. You're welcome to join us."

"Has it been helping?"

"I don't know about helping, but it isn't making things worse. I still can't get her to open up about whatever they said to her on that phone call, but it's clear she's feeling pretty rejected."

"Poor Bree." Cat starts toward the door and I move to follow her. "As fun as romcoms and popcorn sound, I better go. I need to pick up another Sunny Palmer book before the bookstore closes."

"Need to?"

Cat gathers up a wad of plastic covering I'm assuming was on the rug, then starts down the stairs. "Yeah, it's a need. If you ever read one of her stories, you'll know why. I was kind of avoiding romances for a while, but she sucked me right back in."

"Noah?" a woman calls from the entryway.

It's not Bree. My sisters have very distinct voices, and I can easily tell them apart.

Cat freezes halfway down the stairs, her eyes locked on the entryway and whoever just arrived.

I hurry past her to find Olive there, looking at her phone, her bleach-blonde hair falling over her face. She pushes her sunglasses up on her head. "Noah?" she calls again, her attention still on her phone. "You home?"

"Yeah."

She looks up and a grimace spreads over her face. "Hey. I heard about Bree. I'm here to help." Olive looks past me to where Cat is frozen, midway up the stairs. "Catalina Keene?"

Cat's a statue, clutching the plastic like a life preserver and staring at Olive. She doesn't respond. She doesn't move. She definitely doesn't look happy.

Concern leaks into my chest. "Cat?"

That breaks her from her spell. She visibly shakes her head and adopts a bland expression, crushing the plastic to her chest, but her face is still chalky and pale. "I'll see you later, Belacourt."

Cat doesn't say anything to Olive. She just slips her feet into the sandals waiting by the door, tosses her belt bag over her shoulder, and walks out, carrying the plastic with her.

Olive stares at the closed door, then faces me. "You and *Cat Keene*?"

Her shock isn't about the right thing. She's not even surprised Cat ignored her. This isn't promising. I knew their friendship had disintegrated in middle school, but I didn't realize they disliked each other so strongly. "What was that about?"

Olive's lips press into a firm line. "You don't want to know," she says quietly.

"On the contrary. I *very much* want to know." I have a

sneaking suspicion that whatever Olive doesn't want to tell me might have to do with why Cat couldn't stand me just a few weeks ago.

I'm just barely getting her to consider herself my friend *now*. If Olive sets us back to square one, she'll have to answer for it.

Olive brushes past me and lets herself into the kitchen. She opens the fridge and pulls out a Limoncello LaCroix—which I only stock because I noticed Cat drinking them—and pops it open. "Let's talk about Bree. I want to know everything."

"I'd rather hear an explanation about—"

"I *can't* right now, Noah." She speaks so fiercely it stuns me. Olive closes her eyes and grips the edge of the counter. She meets my eyes again, pleading. "Later, please. Can we talk about Bree now? Is she home?"

Silence sits between us. I won't push her, but there is definitely something she's not telling me. "No. She went to the beach with Alonzo. I don't know when to expect them back, but we've been spending our evenings in the theater room with takeout and romcoms the last few days."

"Takeout and romcoms." She smiles. "Feels like high school again."

"You're welcome to join us."

"Whatever I can do to help Bree." She sighs. "I brought Celine. I hope that's okay. She's on the phone outside with work."

"Sure." At this point, what's another awkward, uncomfortable situation? This is part of the reason I always stay in my suite at the Belacourt Resort next door. You never know when your sister is going to show up at the house with an ex-girlfriend. I'd be packing my bags to head over there now if Presley James wasn't using the suite to hide out. She's my friend, and she needed help, so I helped. Now I'm only slightly regretting it.

No, that's not true. Even if I knew lending Presley my suite would lead to me staying in the same house as Celine, I still would have done it.

But I don't have to be around Celine either.

I turn back toward my room. "You can be on Bree duty tonight, then."

Olive doesn't argue as I make my way toward my lair and the games on my computer waiting for me. It's time to check out from reality.

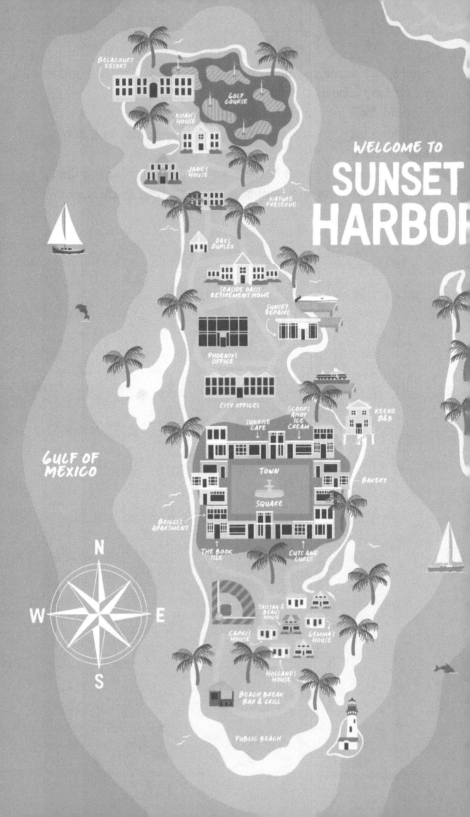

CHAPTER 19

Cat

THE SHORT DRIVE back home to the B&B is a blur. The streets are full of a montage in my head—Olive at thirteen mocking my hair, Olive and her friends at school turning their backs on me and not talking to me, Olive in the Belacourt house now, looking like Barbie and saying my name like it's an accusation. Back and forth, my brain jumps around in an unpleasant cycle between the past and now. It's been more than ten years, but I see her *once* and I'm back in that uncomfortable, gawky age before braces, when Olive made me feel low and poor and inconsequential.

I thought it was in my past. It *was* in my past. I have a solid support system in Otto and excellent friends: Ivy, Holland, Jane. There are people in my life who love and appreciate me for me and always have. Olive doesn't deserve the brainspace she steals, and she doesn't deserve to send me into a panic merely by existing in the same room.

That doesn't stop my brain from doing its thing, hyper focusing on her and how I feel around her.

I slide the golf cart right into place between Otto's cart and our house, then grip the steering wheel with both hands and lean forward until my head is resting on my fists.

Distraction. That's what I need right now. I sit up and toss my belt bag over my shoulder. I'm going straight to the bookstore to load up on delicious Sunny Palmer romances and forget myself in them tonight. Maybe they're not realistic, but I need a little less real life right now and a little more fantasy.

I can't stop thinking about kissing Noah, which makes me walk even faster. I thought there was a connection when we kissed, which is just ridiculous. How could I honestly fool myself into feeling anything for a Belacourt? Self-preservation alone dictates I'm better off considering Noah off-limits. I only set him up with Jane to force a barrier between us, and I'm feeling better about that decision now. I can't fall for a guy who's dating my friend.

I'm halfway to the bookstore, but I pull my phone out and find Jane's contact while I walk.

She picks up after one ring. "Hey, Cat."

"You need to go out with Noah Belacourt."

"Come again?"

"For your dating thing. You're still doing it, right? Trying to date the entire island."

Jane laughs. "It's not really like that."

"I know. You have a whole system for testing romance tropes." When Jane first told me her plan a few weeks ago, I thought her idea was a guaranteed way to get her heart broken. But maybe she's onto something. She's more likely to find Mr. Right by dating consistently than I am by burying my head in work. "Have you found *the one* yet?"

She hesitates. "Not yet."

"Okay. Perfect. Want to try the billionaire trope? Noah fits the bill. Or you can go with my favorite plot device: only one bed."

I shut my eyes. Why did I suggest *that* of all things?

"I've already done that one. Not so successfully." Jane sounds distracted. "What happened? Is the personal assistant thing not working out?"

"He's a great boss. He's really kind, actually. I think you'd get along and, if nothing else, he would be a considerate date. He won't talk about himself all night or make you pay for him because he pretends to leave his wallet at home or smell like over-fermented cheese. Also, he said he'd be interested in going out with you. Sooooo..."

"Done and done. Send me his number?"

"I'll text it to you. How's the Fourth of July bash coming along?"

"It's coming. You'll be there right?"

"Of course. Otto's been talking about the breakfast all week. I think it's the one day every year someone else makes breakfast for him."

"He'll have to load up on the pancakes. There will be plenty."

"Don't tell him that or he'll bring Ziplocs to take home extras."

"Okay, noted. Listen, I've got to run. Thanks for the Noah tip."

"Let me know how it goes!" I say, because I'm a glutton for punishment. Now that this is proceeding, I need every single detail I can get. I hang up the phone when I reach The Book Isle. It's one of my favorite places on the island since it's stuffed with books in an inviting way. It's full of cozy nooks and reading crannies, comfortable chairs and places to curl up and read. It's no big store just wanting your money, though I'm sure they *do* want my money.

The bell chimes above my head when I step inside and go straight for the romance section. Sometimes I really can't put up with the whole genre in general. My realism steps in and makes me want to throw the book when the guy is being more amazing than men *really* are, but on days like today, I just want to feel some dang butterflies, okay? Sue me.

"Hey, Briggs," I call, rounding the bookshelf out of sight and scanning the spines lined up on the shelf.

I hear him lower his cup to the counter. "How's it going?"

"Oh, you know, just need a little escapism tonight."

"In the romance section?" I can hear the smile in his voice. I've known him too long not to hear it.

I pop my head back around the bookshelf until I can see him—sandy brown hair, glasses, T-shirt draping nicely over his chest—and point right at his face. "You don't get to judge me, Briggs Dalton. I remember when you tried to kiss Britney Keegan at the homecoming dance."

His laugh rings through the empty bookstore. "I'd never been rejected so publicly. Bring it up again and I'll tell Noah Belacourt you used to have a crush on him. How's that job working out for you?"

Island gossip is its own living, breathing, active little thing.

"A crush on Noah? Oh my gosh, never," I call, locating Sunny's books and pulling out the two I don't own. I make my way toward the checkout counter, wrinkling my nose. "You're mixing me up with half the cheer squad."

"Right. Of course. You dated Jake Humphries." He takes the books and starts to ring me up. "How is he? I haven't heard from him in years."

"Jake turned out to be a tool." Luckily, his parents sold the family mansion and moved to Connecticut a few years ago, so I don't ever have to see him again. After he chose sorority girls over honesty and fidelity, I cut him off and never looked back.

Maybe sometimes I glance back a smidge, like small peeks, just to remind myself why it's a bad idea to mess around with rich, entitled men.

"Good riddance?" Briggs asks.

"Yeah, good riddance." I pay for the books and take the bag from him. "It's good to see you, as always."

"Same, Cat."

I walk into the warm, humid air and swing my bag on my

arm. A text came in while I was talking to Briggs, but I hadn't noticed it.

HOLLAND
I haven't seen you in days. Are you still alive?

CAT
No.

HOLLAND
Cause of death? You're being overworked? Not enough Holland time? Lack of information about the craziness that is my situation with Phoenix?

CAT
All of the above. I need a debrief. Has the wedding happened? Fake wedding? Is it a real wedding when it's a fake marriage?

HOLLAND
Not for a few more days, but yes, it's a real wedding even though it's a fake marriage. It's a lot. I'll call you later.

How are things with Noah?

I stop walking and look down at my phone. Should I tell her the truth? We kissed and I saw stars—in a good way—but he stepped back so fast when it was over that I'm pretty sure he doesn't see me that way. Then, to solidify my point, I suggested he go on a date with Jane to put some space between us, and *he agreed*. If that doesn't say "I'm just not that into you," nothing else will. I need to be wise and read the signs and back off.

Besides, he's a Belacourt.

Let's focus on that side of things.

CAT
Olive is back. I saw her today.

My phone immediately starts to ring. I answer it and continue walking home.

"My gosh, Cat. Why didn't you *lead* with that?" Holland says.

"Because I want to put it from my mind."

"Hold on to it for a second longer so you can give me all the details, then put it away. Did she see you too?"

"Briefly."

"Did she immediately apologize for being your middle school bully and ruining your life?"

"My life isn't ruined."

"It felt that way in seventh grade though, right? Eighth grade? Whenever that was."

"Eighth. It's in the past, Holls. It's not still affecting me." Or was it? I straight up froze on that staircase when she walked into the house. Seeing Olive sent a flash of anxiety and fear through me. Which is weird, since anxiety isn't something I face on a regular basis.

"Have you quit your job? How long is she here for?"

"I don't know. I kind of ran away before I could get any useful information out of her or Noah. But I'm not working for Olive, so I'm not quitting. I need this money too much, anyway."

"Cat, my client's here," Holland says, her voice dropping to a whisper. She must be at the salon. "I have to run."

"Okay. I'll talk to you later."

I hang up the phone and slide it into my pocket, then stand in front of my happy yellow house. Otto and my dad bought the house together fresh out of high school, using an inheritance from their grandmother. It was the perfect partnership, because my dad was the responsible one who crunched numbers and ran the business, and Otto was the free spirit who made guests feel like family. Dad went off to California on vacation, met and fell in love with my mom, and brought her back to Sunset Harbor. She was pretty much the female version of Otto, so they became best friends straight away. The three of them managed the B&B and turned it into a successful, viable business that had been running strong for a decade before I ever entered the picture.

I can't help but look at the B&B and see the love.

My parents are in the bones of this house. They're in the yellow paint and white shutters and azaleas that bloom bright pink in the spring. They're in the hammock out front—the best place to read at the end of winter—and in the view from the back window looking out to the ocean. It was open *all the time* when my mom was alive so she could smell the beach. They're so ingrained in every inch of this property that the idea of losing this house gives me a stomachache.

Which is why we won't.

I walk up the porch stairs and push the door open. The house is quiet. Our next guests don't arrive until tomorrow, then we'll have a full house until the week after the Fourth. Otto's probably around here somewhere, and after the mental jungle gym I went through today, I'm kind of craving the reassurance he so openly gives me.

Water is running in the kitchen, so I head that way until my feet come to an abrupt halt in the doorway. Otto is by the sink filling up his reusable water bottle. That's not the strange thing. He's also wearing all black. And *shoes*. Actual shoes that fully cover his feet.

I didn't know he even *owned* full on tie-the-laces shoes. Even when he skates, he's either in flip flops or Vans slip-ons.

Who is this funeral director and what did he do with—wait. There was one time Otto dressed up like this. One time. We have a picture together in front of two caskets, and he's wearing these exact shoes.

"Otto?" My voice is little more than a whisper.

He turns to face me so fast, water flies from his bottle and douses the counter. "Cat."

I want to ask him who died, but my tongue stopped working.

I'm staring open-mouthed. His black button-down has long sleeves that are rolled up the forearms, and those are unmistakably slacks.

His wide eyes are pinned to me. "This isn't what it looks like."

"Then what is it?"

"I just... I, uh..."

"Otto, you look like you're about to attend a funeral."

His shoulders visibly relax. "No, it's nothing like that. Well, maybe a funeral for my pride." He quirks a smile. "I thought it was time I started acting like an adult."

Okay. That's weird. "You've been an adult my entire life."

"Well, now I need to act like one. I had a meeting today." He's looking around the room, searching for a way out of this conversation while I stand in the doorway and stare.

I'm so uncomfortable. This is not us. This is not the basis of our relationship. Otto built a strong foundation of trust with me from the beginning, making it clear I can go to him for anything, that I can bring him my questions, and he'll answer them implicitly. The day I asked if he filled my Easter basket or if the Easter bunny did, he looked me in the eye and replied, "Do you really want me to answer that?" and I knew I didn't. Because Otto would never lie to me.

Until now, I guess? Or do lies of omission not count to him? Why isn't he telling me the truth? That hurts more than whatever secret he's trying to keep firmly wrapped up and close to his chest.

The pain in his face is vivid, mottling his cheeks and shifting his eyes all over the place. I want to let him free of this situation as much as I want to run and bury my head under my pillow and cry.

"I thought we had a banker at our kitchen sink. You should probably warn a girl before you dress like you have a desk job."

A smile falls over his tanned, wrinkled face. "You wouldn't believe how uncomfortable this is. My feet need to breathe."

"Can they breathe elsewhere?" I try to joke, to lighten the heaviness on my shoulders. "We don't all want to deal with the ramifications of those being cooped up in shoes all day."

"You got it, Cattywampus."

Okay, we're back. But there's a chink in my comfort I don't want to think about. A chip in the perfect façade that was once our relationship.

Otto brushes past me to head upstairs.

"Hey," I say, because I can't help just digging the teeniest bit. "I saw a letter from Killigan Hammer the other day. Everything okay?"

His face is blank. "Of course."

"The cancer isn't back?"

His head tilts to the side, his eyes softening. "I'm free and clear, Kit Kat."

"It looked official. We don't have any bills or anything? I should look at the budget if we do, and arrange—"

"No bills. Sheesh, Cat. You're starting to sound like your dad." His eye has a bit of a twinkle—I love hearing when I remind him of either of my parents—and he keeps trudging up the stairs. "We paid them off over a year ago. We're good." His voice disappears with him.

It's bittersweet, though. Now I know, without a shade of doubt, that my uncle is lying to me.

But why?

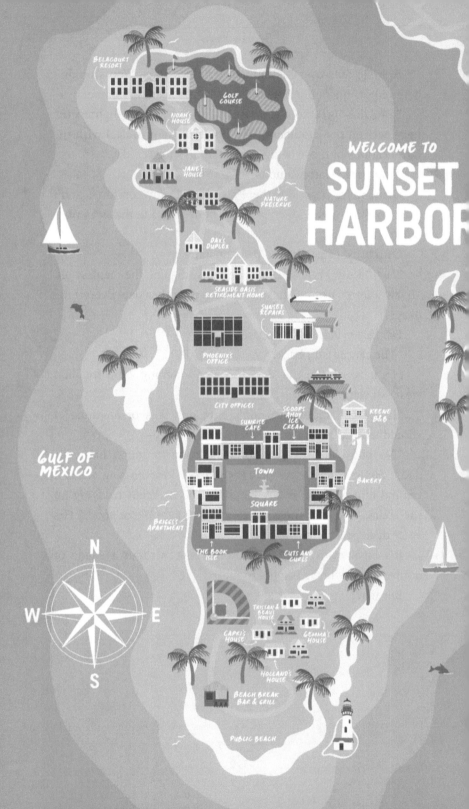

CHAPTER 20

Noah

TRISTAN PALMER and I have been friends our whole lives. It made things a little awkward when my sister crushed on him in high school and he had a girlfriend, but we never let anything get in the way of our friendship. He's a good kayak buddy and a better listener, which I didn't realize I needed until I'm kayaking alone and anxious, since Tristan had to work and couldn't make it out with me today. I need to call him once I'm back on shore.

I row toward the beach, irritated by my steady anxiety as it flows but doesn't ebb. It's annoying that it's still plaguing me after an hour out on the ocean, when kayaking is one of the things I do to take a break from the anxiety and soothe my fears. I love being in nature and letting go. I read an article once about how experiencing awe is good for the soul, how awe can be found anywhere outside. It's a mix of reminding myself that I'm such a small part of this big world and also experiencing the beauty and grandeur of Mother Nature.

Today, awe isn't doing much for me. My heart hammers when I pull my kayak onto the sand and drag it to the resort's locker tucked against the side of the hill. I punch in the numbers to lock it away and pull out my phone. I'm not going to swim today. My heart won't calm down as it is.

I don't want to go up to the house, either, when I know Cat

won't be there and two of my sisters will—with an ex-girlfriend in tow.

This is why you don't date your sister's friends.

It's been four days since Olive showed up in Sunset Harbor with Celine, and Cat has been weird ever since. She still comes to the house every day and completes the lists I provide each evening, but she's like an ultra polite ghost—moving around silently and disappearing the moment she's through with her tasks. It's a stark difference from the way she'd been hanging out with me more and more in the last few weeks. I miss her.

Not even beta testing the new open world game we've been developing is helping. I don't like feeling like I'm somehow, even inadvertently, causing Cat discomfort.

That must be why my anxiety is skimming at a steady low burn. My heart is beating like an idling Jeep, humming with more power than normal. It isn't going into overdrive or anything, so there's probably nothing to worry about.

But still. I start walking down the beach and dial Tristan's number.

He picks up, much to my relief. "Hey, man."

"How's work? You missed a calm day on the ocean."

Tristan groans. "Don't rub it in. Are you at the reserve?"

"No, just the resort's beach." I rub a hand over my face and close my eyes.

"What's wrong?" Tristan asks.

How can he tell? Did I sigh without meaning to? I haven't really talked to him about the anxiety, or getting kicked out of the office until I get a handle on my mental health, but it's not really the sort of thing I want to discuss over the phone. "Just trying to juggle a lot of things at once, I guess."

"Any balls you can drop for a while?"

Are there? I've handed the work ball over to Gina almost fully, but the sisters and Cat...? There's not much I can do about that until Olive leaves. I don't know what happened between them, but something obviously did.

"I don't think so. I want my sisters to go back to New York, but I can't kick them out. This house is just as much theirs as it is mine."

If only they would stop talking about our parents' arguments and the family chat I've silenced—but that won't happen.

"You can stay with me," he offers.

I smile, glancing up at the resort my family owns. He's a good friend for offering. "Thanks. I might just move into the pool house."

"Right. The pool house. Because you have multiple houses on your own property." Tristan laughs. "Just leave Sunset Harbor for a while, man. What's keeping you here? The ocean? They have ocean in Costa Rica, too."

Running off to another gorgeous island sounds more than incredible right now. I doubt Scout's board of directors would even consider it a red flag for me to up and leave, because they commanded me to take time off. What's more calming than a trip to the Caribbean? When I picture myself checking into the Belacourt Resort in Costa Rica, however, I don't picture myself alone.

"Cat," I tell him. She's the person keeping me here. There's no way I'd leave her halfway through the summer. She's probably not anywhere close to hitting the number she needs to pay off Otto's medical bills. Money aside, I don't want to be away from her. I've enjoyed spending time with her so much I'm pretty sure her distance is part of the reason I've been so off-centered the last few days. "I promised to hire her until the end of July. I can't just leave now."

"You could give her jobs from a distance."

"She's a personal assistant, man."

"Take her with you, then."

"Yeah, if only," I mutter. "Things have been going great until Olive showed up. I don't know why—"

"Seriously?"

My heart thuds. The Jeep is revving now. "What?"

"Olive's here? She's one of the sisters staying at your house?"

"She got here a few days ago."

He gives a humorless laugh. "No wonder Cat is being weird, then. Didn't Olive bully her? That has to be awkward."

I stop in the middle of the beach, heedless of anyone who might be lying in the cabanas or walking through the sand. "What?"

"Remember? It's been a while, so it's hazy, but I thought Olive bullied Cat pretty badly in middle school."

"They were friends."

"For a little while, yeah, but things went south."

"How far south?"

Tristan sounds like he's sucking the air through his teeth. "Man, it was a long time ago. I can't remember the details."

I do, though. I remember Olive being Cat's friend for a while. I remember being with Olive at Sunrise Cafe when we ran into Cat and having milkshakes together. I remember saying Cat was cute—I'd lowkey been crushing on her for a while and just wanted to feel out my sister to see if Cat had said anything about me. The next thing I knew, they weren't friends anymore. Olive hated it when I liked her friends. She's possessive. But *bullying*? He had to be thinking of someone else.

Except it made sense. When Cat had seen Olive for the first time, she froze like a deer in headlights then walked out of the house. Olive avoids the topic whenever I bring it up, and they tiptoe around each other like there's actual dislike there. Or shame. Whatever a decade-old feud brings up in mature adults.

I must have gone too deep into my head because Tristan's calling my name.

"Noah? You there?"

"Yeah. Sorry. I had no idea, but it explains a lot." I rub a hand through my hair and start to pace again.

"Maybe give Cat a few days off?" he suggests.

"Good idea."

"Sorry, man. I figured you knew. It wasn't really a secret."

How did I not know? Was I so in my head back then I didn't notice, or did Olive keep it from me? She is cunning and intelligent and possessive. Not a great combo for a thirteen-year-old, I guess. Though it makes her a killer businesswoman now.

"Thanks for telling me. I better go." So I can call Cat or Olive or just vomit. I'm not sure yet which direction my body is going to let me go here.

"Okay." Tristan sounds worried. "Call me if you need anything."

"For sure." I hang up and run a hand through my hair. My heartrate isn't slowing down, and the kayak didn't help at all. I pull up my email and send a message to Dr. Stein, telling her about my physical symptoms. She's mentioned medication a few times, but I've been wary of trying them. Maybe it's time to test something out. My mind is racing, my breathing is irregular, and I just want to claw out of my body.

I put my phone away so I don't watch my inbox for a response. I can't tell if the pulsing in my ears is my own heartbeat or the waves crashing behind me.

I think I need to go for a run.

SOMEHOW, I end up in the middle of Sunset Harbor's town square. I'm a block from Cat's house, and my feet carry me her direction before I consciously decide I want to go there. It's pretty stupid, actually. I'm into this girl, right? So I'm going to show up at her house at the end of June after a run when it's hot and humid and I'm sweating profusely?

Not a great look, Noah.

I press forward anyway. The sun beats down on me with suffocating heat. It feels good to push myself. I like that I can't tell anymore if my crazy pulse is from anxiety or exercise. At least for a little while, I get a break.

I walk when I hit Cat's street because I need a minute to decide what to say. I *still* haven't figured it out when I round the corner and find Otto outside, waxing his surfboard in the open unattached garage. He looks up, and his face tightens when he notices me.

I lift my hand in an awkward greeting.

He waves me over. "Cat's in the middle of a jam session right now."

Did I hear that correctly? I wait for him to continue, but he doesn't. He just smooths the wax over the board.

"A jam session?" I ask, hoping he'll clarify.

"Blackberry, I think. I'm not sure if she has enough. She was fretting."

"Oh." She's making jam. That makes sense. "How are you, Otto?"

He nods slowly. "I'm well enough." He stops waxing the board and shoots me side-eye. "I worry about my little girl, but as far as she reports, things have been going well while she's working for you."

"She's been an enormous help."

"I know."

It feels like that awkward moment before a school dance, hanging out with a girl's dad while I wait for her to come down the stairs. What does he want me to say? What is it he's holding back from saying to me? I clear my throat and speak the truth. "Cat is an extraordinary person and a hard worker. You've done a great job raising her."

Otto peers at me like a seer. Is he a witch? A warlock? I must have spent too long in my game the last few days, because I'm seeing magic where there isn't any.

"That girl raised *me*," Otto says quietly. "She has my whole heart. Don't break hers, Belacourt."

My throat is dry. This *is* the Dad Talk, and I'm totally not expecting it. Why would he say anything like that to me unless he thought I was dating Cat? It doesn't add up.

His skin is tan and wrinkled, his shirt open and flapping in the warm breeze. I can't imagine how terrified Cat was to lose him to cancer. Now he's healthy, strong, and wary. "Kitchen door's at the back of the house. She won't want to step away from the stove right now."

He's giving me permission to go see her. It's symbolic, I think, since I don't really *need* his permission, but I'm grateful for it. Somehow that makes it mean more. I nod my thanks and leave, following the shaded path between the unattached garage and the house, tall bald cypress trees lining the way.

Cat is humming along to the radio. She's blurry through the screen door, standing at the stove, stirring something in a large pot. When I walk up the steps, I can feel my body coming down from its run. My heart rate is slowing, because even just being this close to her is calming. Cat *is* a trip to Costa Rica. She's the break from working full time. She is our small island at sunset on my family's cove. She's wholesome and good.

My feelings for her run deeper than a crush. They're real. It hits me with force while I stand on her back porch, listening to her hum along to Post Malone and stir at the stove. I want her in my life. I want *this* image in my life forever.

Just maybe without the screen door between us.

She looks up as if she can sense me watching her, then squints. "What are you doing here?"

I cross the deck and pull the door open, stepping into the

kitchen. It's small, so I'm closer to Cat than I realized when the screen door slams shut behind me. "Just out for a run."

"I can see that." She gives me a once-over, but I still look at her face. Her arm doesn't quit stirring the whole time.

"More jam?"

"Blackberry this time." She checks her timer, then looks back at me. "I wanted to make a crumble too, but I ran out of berries."

"Who knew you were such a homemaker?"

Her face freezes in a weird smile. "Not yet. Homemaker implies I have a family, right?"

She wants that? "I don't know the definition. I guess, to me, it just means someone who makes a house a home. It looks like you've done that here for you and Otto."

"My mom did it first." She pulls out a huge metal bowl and sieve insert, then picks up two hot pads to grip the sides of the pot. Water is heating in a charcoal-colored speckled pot on the back burner while Cat lifts the jam and pours it slowly through the sieve and into the bowl. "She made this place a home. Otto and I just kept it up."

"Did she teach you how to make jam?"

Cat glances at me before focusing on her jam again. "Yeah. I helped her a lot in the kitchen. They're her recipes I'm following."

"She sounds lovely."

"She was," Cat says simply. When she puts down the empty pot, we both stare at the sieve, watching the jam drip slowly while it catches most of the seeds.

"Listen, Cat. I feel like things have been off the last few days. I just wanted to apologize for any uncomfortab—"

"It's fine," she says brightly, pushing past me to pick up the empty jars. "Don't worry about it."

"I have been worrying about it, actually." Over-worrying. Since Tristan's revelation, my brain has been going haywire. "I don't want to be the reason you're uncomfortable. If my sister is causing you any awkwardness, we can work around her."

"Like, you'll tell me when she isn't home so it's safe to come by?"

I shrug. "Yeah. Or I won't give you any jobs at the house. You don't have to clean while she's there or drop things off. I'm always happy to meet you elsewhere. Besides, we both have to head out of town tomorrow anyway. I doubt she'll return after that."

Cat nods slowly, her eyes searching mine.

"For what it's worth," I say, my voice dropping, "I didn't know about your history until today."

Cat straightens. "What?"

"I didn't know. I knew you guys stopped being friends—"

She scoffs. "It was a little more volatile than that."

My throat is dry. My hands are shaking. I hate that *my sister* did this to her, and I had no idea. "How bad was it?"

Cat removes the sieve and sets it in the sink, then starts funneling jam into a jar. "Pretty bad."

I feel responsible. If I hadn't had a crush on Cat, would she and Olive still be friends?

"Were my parents notified? Did you take measures with the school?"

"Otto got involved and had to meet with your parents and the vice principal. It was messy, but Olive let it go after that."

"Cat—"

"I really don't want to talk about this anymore." She fills another jar, then turns to me, her ladle hovering above the bowl like she's not quite ready to let go. "You *really* didn't know? Olive didn't come home from school every day and tell you some new humiliating story about me?"

"Not about you."

"Hmm." She keeps peering at me. "I figured she bragged about her conquests."

Conquests? That word choice is so specific and gross. I want to be a kid again so I can pull thirteen-year-old Cat into my arms and comfort her. Or pull adult Cat into my arms now and do something more.

I shake away the thought, but another one comes quick on its heels. "Are you busy?"

She looks at her jam with her eyebrows up.

"No, I mean after this." I gesture to the whole jam explosion in the kitchen. "I should go home and shower anyway."

"I just need to seal these jars and clean up." She hesitates. "Then I'm free."

"Perfect. Meet at my house—no, we can do the entrance to the resort—when you're done here. Wear clothes you don't mind getting dirty."

She looks intrigued. "Why? What are we doing?"

"You'll see." I start to back out of the kitchen, taking a mental heart picture of the way Cat is looking at me now. "Come hungry."

She gives me a half smile. "I always do."

CHAPTER 21

Cat

NOAH TEXTS me right before I leave to tell me it's safe to meet him at his house. I'm relieved he's figured out I don't want anything to do with Olive. She must have left for a while.

Or for good? *Please* let her leave Sunset Harbor for good.

I'm still trying to wrap my head around the fact that Noah had no idea his sister was a monster. Shouldn't it have been obvious when she was born with horns?

After getting to know him this summer, I can believe his ignorance. If he'd known back when the bullying was happening, he probably would have tried to put an end to it. He is nothing if not courteous, so it all tracks. For as long as I've held animosity toward this family, it's weird that I didn't even question Noah's revelation. If anything, it calmed me, which makes me feel like I can trust him to tell me the truth. It resonated, which is refreshing.

He's refreshing. Is that annoying? Probably. I shouldn't think about him like that because it's dangerous. But Noah can be a friend, even if kissing him sends me into a lightheaded mindspin. That's normal when a guy knows how to kiss, right? Well, Noah knows how to kiss.

I let myself into the house and come to an abrupt stop when I find Bree standing in the entryway, frowning, her dog in her arms.

"Hey," I say, closing the door behind me. If she's here, is Olive nearby? Maybe they came back because Olive forgot her broom and cauldron.

Bree can pretty much read my frantic searching because she says, "Olive's not here. She went to the beach a while ago with Celine."

I notice the designer luggage piled against the wall. "Are you leaving?"

"I'm going home." She strokes Peanut between the ears, and the dog nuzzles into the touch. "Hey, listen, Cat. I'm sorry about bailing during the photoshoot. Alonzo told me they asked you to step in."

"It all worked out."

She gives me a sad smile, brushing her dark hair over her shoulder. "It did for the ad campaign, at least. I'm grateful you stepped in and saved it. I wasn't thinking straight."

"Noah said you got some disappointing news."

She scoffs. "That's putting it lightly. My dreams were crushed."

I can tell. She still carries an aura of sadness, which makes me want to hug her. We aren't really at that level, so I hang back. I'm surprised at myself for wanting to hug a Belacourt who isn't Noah.

"I don't know the situation," I say, "but it sounds like a job thing and not a relationship rejection. Is there no other way to accomplish your dream? When Taylor Swift couldn't get her own masters, she produced them again herself, right? Made it work despite a rejection." What goes without saying is that Taylor had the connections and finances to make that work. But Bree isn't lacking in either regard.

Bree narrows her eyes slightly. "Noah didn't tell you what I was trying to do?"

"No." I mean, I was the one who sent her flowers in Nashville, and now she's suspicious after my Taylor Swift example. I'm starting to think it might have something to do with the music industry, but I'm not going to say as much.

She sighs. "It's not the kind of thing where I can just put out a Bree's Version and stick it to the man. I need *the man* for this."

Taylor has a song for that, too.

"Do you, though?" I ask. "I guess I figured there's always a way to accomplish your dreams when you have enough motivation."

Bree looks down at her dog, her dark eyebrows pulling together. Her long hair is flawlessly curled and cascading over her shoulders. She looks like she's dressed for lunch in Manhattan with her ribbed high-neck tank and designer jeans, which is maybe where she's headed now.

"I hope you find a way," I tell her as footsteps tap down the staircase.

Alonzo and Noah appear with more bags and pass us to take them outside. I feel Noah's arm brush mine as he passes. My eyes linger on his retreating back, watching the muscles shift beneath his T-shirt as he effortlessly carries a bulky suitcase in each hand.

"Thanks, Cat." Bree slides her sunglasses on. "Try not to break my brother's heart, okay? He seems tough on the outside, but he's a softie."

That comes out of left field. Does she know her brother? He doesn't seem tough on the outside. He's kind to the bones—it shows in his smile and the way he listens to people. Yes, he's a bigwig businessman billionaire, but he's not scary.

I totally misjudged him. He's not really a buttmunch at all. Maybe his new nickname will be Bleeding Heart Belacourt.

Brawny Belacourt

Broad-shouldered Babe Belacourt.

Makes Me Want to Brush My Lips All Over His Belacourt.

I'm getting away from myself. Otto has ruined me for normal names. This is entirely his fault.

Also, *me* break *Noah's* heart? Is she for real?

I look through the open door where Noah is walking away, but he doesn't look like he heard her. "We aren't dating," I say quietly.

"I know." She doesn't say anything else, just gives me a little smile and goes out to the golf cart where Alonzo is loading up all the bags. It takes a few more trips to empty the foyer. By the time they drive away, I've made my way into the kitchen and gotten a LaCroix from the fridge. I pop it open and let the bubbly water run down my throat. I need to cool off. Get myself under control. Why would Bree warn me like that unless she noticed the way I looked at Noah when he came downstairs?

He comes back inside after seeing his sister off and shuts the door. "You ready to go?"

I glance down at the old Pink Floyd tee and cut-off shorts I'm wearing. "I better look this terrible for good reason, Belacourt."

"You look perfect." He passes me to pick up a few empty gallon ice cream buckets and leads the way to the back door. When he reaches it, he turns to look at me, his brown eyes deep. Their focused attention makes me breathless. "You coming?"

You look perfect.

I take another drink and put the can on the counter. "Coming."

NOAH LEADS me down the coastal path past his house, heading away from the resort. He's swinging the empty buckets in his hand. I have to slide on my sunglasses because the early afternoon sun is glaring down at us.

"Are we about to enter your secret lair, Lex?"

"No, that's back at my apartment." He glances at me. "You really don't know where we're going? Jake never brought you here?"

"I try not to think about him. But no, he never brought me here."

"Bad breakup?"

"He cheated." I tilt my head side to side. "If you can call it that. He ghosted me, so we never actually had a breakup. Technically we could still be together."

Noah stops walking. "Seriously?"

"He quit talking to me after he left for Yale. Stopped answering the phone or texting me back. When I started seeing pictures of him with other girls, I realized what had happened."

"Brutal. It's definitely cheating."

"It felt that way at the time."

"I know how it feels to be cheated on, but I haven't been ghosted. There must be a lot of unresolved feelings there."

The warm breeze runs through my hair while waves crash down on the shore below our path. Clear water spreads out below, the waves small and harmless from up here, the light blue water a perfect foil for the lush greenery. "Not anymore. I decided to resolve them myself a few years ago so it wouldn't hang over me forever. I don't like the guy, but I'm over it." Otto was dying, so other things mattered a lot less at the time.

"And if you ever see Jake again?"

"I don't know. I'll probably have to force myself not to punch him in the throat, but mostly just so I don't hurt my hand."

"I'll punch him for you," he mutters.

I laugh, but when I catch his steely gaze, it looks like he isn't joking. A wave of chills rushes down my arms.

"Okay," he says, pulling his gaze away from me. He stops at a break in the shrubs, where the dirt path shifts down toward the ocean. "We're here."

I look from the path to Noah, then my eyes snag on the tall

brambles lining the walkway and curving down the side of the hill. *Blackberries.* A whole entire cache of plump, juicy blackberries. Enough for another vat of jam and a couple of crumbles, at least.

"How did I not know this existed?" I ask, very much in awe.

"It's not accessible unless you live in one of these houses or stay at the resort."

Okay, now it makes sense. I dated Jake back in high school for nearly a year, but we never came down this way. If we went to the beach, it was one of the public ones.

Noah holds out an empty ice cream bucket to me that looks at least a decade old.

I take it, feeling like I'm seven again. "My mom and I would use these to gather blackberries, too."

He sends me a half-smile before reaching high and plucking a berry. He pops it in his mouth and closes his eyes. "There it is."

"What?"

His smile twinkles in the sunlight. "The taste of summer."

I can't take this anymore. He's so sweet. I want to jump the guy and kiss him senseless. So I do the smart thing and walk down a bit to start picking blackberries, leaving a healthy distance between us. Enough space that I can't lose my resolve and maul him.

For the next thirty minutes, every time Noah finishes his section and takes a step closer to me, I take another step further away. His focus is on the high berries and mine is on the low ones. It's like a snail-paced game of cat and mouse, only I want him to catch up to me as much as I know it would be a bad idea.

"How are things going with Otto?" he asks. "Have you made enough to help out with his bills?"

I let out a slow breath and pluck another berry, dropping it in my bucket. "Not enough, but I'm almost halfway. I can't wait to approach him with this huge sum of money and wipe away all his stress."

"He doesn't know you're doing it?"

"No. He still won't tell me about the debt."

Noah turns to face me. "Have you considered that he might have already taken care of it?"

"Yeah, but he mentioned selling his VW Bug, which was a dead giveaway. I straight up asked him if we had any bills from the cancer institute, and he told me they were taken care of a year ago. The bills I found spanned the last six months, at least. He's trying to hide it."

"Poor Otto." Noah resumes picking.

"Poor me. Otto's never lied to me before. It kind of rocked me."

"He must feel like he has a good reason."

"I'm sure he does, but it's not good enough." I reach for a berry and prick my finger on a thorn, hissing through my teeth while I pull my hand away.

"You okay?"

"Yeah. It's nothing. Hazard of the task." I shake my hand out. "I talked to Bree for a minute. She seems pretty sad."

"She got her hopes up. I wish I could tell you more, but she asked me not to tell anyone."

"Don't worry about it. I don't want to pry." Though, in all honesty, I was hoping he'd divulge a little more. A girl can't help but be curious. "I'm guessing your family is careful about the things they share with people, anyway."

"Generally speaking, yeah. I don't worry with you."

My stomach hums with butterflies.

"It's just not my secret to share," he says.

"Understandable."

I turn to ask if his bucket is nearly full like mine is, and he's standing right next to me. How'd he close the gap so seamlessly? I reach for a berry from his basket and chew on it, letting the sweet tartness burst in my mouth.

I'm nodding like this was the confirmation I expected. "Okay, these are going to make the best crumble."

"Do I get to make it with you?"

"Absolutely."

I reach for another berry, but he grabs my wrist lightly, his teeth gleaming down at me. "Eat your own hard-earned berries, Cat."

"Fine." I reach up and pop the berry in his mouth. He grows still. My finger brushes his lip, immediately throwing me back to the ad shoot and how velvety and pliable his lips are when they're crushing mine. "There you go." My voice is scratchy, my mouth dry.

I don't want anything in the world right now as much as I want to kiss him.

But he is my boss, and not interested, and Olive's brother, and disgustingly rich, and so so so hot.

I lean closer, picking another berry from his bucket. My self-control is a thing of the past. The sea air and berry sweetness and earthy brambles are going to my head. I hover with this berry for a minute. He opens his mouth for it, but I pop it into mine, chewing around my smile.

Noah puts his basket on the ground, then takes my full basket and sets it next to his. He grips the hem of my T-shirt and pulls me closer until my chest presses against his, his eyes on mine the entire time. "You're trouble."

I should be stopping this, but I want it. "Only if you want to save any berries for crumble."

"Like I said, trouble." He slides a hand to the back of my neck, making my skin prickle.

"What do you have going on tonight?" I ask. Energy buzzes between us. I want to touch him, but I'm afraid of being zapped. "Dessert first? We can make the crumble right now."

Noah freezes before his mouth gets any closer. He closes his eyes and lets out a breath. "A date with Jane."

Seriously? I can't even be mad because I set them up... and for good reason, right? At the time I had reasons. Now I can't remember what they were.

Noah steps back, putting distance between us. "I better get going."

"Yeah, of course. Jane." I pick up the bucket of berries and fall into step beside Noah, feeling like I walked out of the house without my keys. I'm missing something.

Some*one*. Noah. I let that sink in. When I'd suggested the date with Jane, I was trying to protect myself by erecting a barrier between us. I've never been so annoyed with my past self and her sense of self-preservation. Barriers are stupid.

We make it back to his house after an uncomfortable walk along the sea path, and the whole time I'm cursing myself for setting Noah up with Jane in the first place. The girl is hot. I love her to death. She's funny, smart, gets stuff done. She's threat level one, and I just set up a date between her and the guy I'm falling for.

Noah gives me the second bucket when we reach the house. "Sorry I can't be your sous chef. I'll help you eat the crumble, though, if you want."

"Sure."

Olive is leaning against a stool at the kitchen counter beside another girl. They both look up when we walk in. "Hey, Noah. Want to go grab dinner..."

She trails off when she notices me behind her brother.

"I have plans," Noah says.

"See you," I say to Noah, walking past Olive without a word.

She stands up. "Hey, Cat."

My heart is hammering. It's an entire construction site in my chest, and it's wicked uncomfortable.

"Cat?" she calls again.

I ignore her, because I'm not in a place where I can face this right now.

"Wow," the other girl says. "She's kinda rude."

My blood simmers when I reach the door. I don't even bother turning back to address how insanely imbalanced her perception is. I just let myself out and slam the door behind me.

CHAPTER 22

Noah

JANE HAYES IS BEAUTIFUL. She's smart and kind and a little goofy, but in a good way. If my brain wasn't completely occupied by Cat Keene, maybe I'd consider going out with her for real. But our date is—while not unpleasant—just fine. The entire time I'm thinking about blackberries and Cat's seed-studded teeth after she ate too many and grinned, squinting into the sunlight. I'm thinking about leaning toward her when we finished picking berries and how she let me. I'm thinking about her finger brushing my lip when she fed me a berry and it kills me. I'm dead. I just want Cat.

So badly, in fact, that even though I spent the whole drive home after the date with Jane telling myself to be chill, I'm sitting in my golf cart in front of my house and texting Cat.

Is it too late in the evening? Yes.

Do I care? No.

NOAH

> How'd that crumble work out?

Someone slides into the seat next to me and a smile spreads over my face, until I glance over and see that it's Celine.

Eww.

"Did you and Olive have fun at dinner?" I ask, willing my

phone to buzz with an incoming message. A call. Anything to get me out of this conversation with my ex.

It's completely still.

"We stayed in," she says, pressing her shoulder into mine. "Why have you been avoiding me?"

Um, let's see. Because of the awkward break up, or the fact that she cheated on me with some photographer, or the fact that every time I see her she talks about how much she misses the trips we'd go on or my apartment in the Upper West Side and not *me*. I don't say any of that because Celine isn't stupid. She messed up, she knows it, and she wants the perks of being my girlfriend again.

To be clear, I'm under no illusion that she actually wants to be my girlfriend. She just wants the perks.

I know this, because the first time she reached out to me after we broke up was just after *Forbes* did a feature announcing me as a billionaire.

She's the definition of a gold digger.

I didn't know that little tidbit in the beginning, when she was sweet and laughed at all my jokes and fit in so well with my family.

I know it now.

I've also figured out that women who fit in well with my family are the type of women I need to be wary of.

"Don't do this, Celine," I say, trying to gently turn her down.

"What?" she asks innocently. It sends a pang through my chest that I have to actively ignore.

"We aren't getting back together. You're wasting your time."

She straightens. "You're with that girl, aren't you? The one who works for you?"

"Cat and I are friends."

"If you stopped paying her, would she still be your friend?"

Celine is trying to dig at me, but it won't work. The truth is that I don't know the answer to her question. If I had never offered Cat a job, maybe we wouldn't have developed this friendship. But we have, so I don't have to think about that. Besides, that's not really the point Celine is trying to make. "She's not after my money."

"How do you know?"

"Because I know her."

Celine stands up and rolls her eyes. "It sounds like you're avoiding the question, which makes me believe you think she wouldn't be around if she wasn't getting a salary."

Her words send a pang through my stomach. "She's not greedy, Celine."

"Everyone's greedy."

"Cat isn't. She's facing a huge medical bill, and I'm just trying to help her out."

Celine's eyes flash. "So, like I said, she's after your money."

My gut ties itself into knots, tangling worse the longer this conversation goes. "I convinced her to take the job, not the other way around."

Skepticism moves across her face. Her straight nose wrinkles while she looks sidelong at me. "I'm sure she made it feel that way."

What?

Celine walks away, leaving me in my dark driveway with questions and doubts. No, that isn't fair. She's projecting herself onto Cat and they couldn't be more different.

I still feel unsettled.

My phone buzzes, indicating that a text came in two minutes ago.

CAT

About to pull it out of the oven, so I don't know yet

NOAH

I'll help you taste test

CAT

> Come over

She doesn't have to tell me twice. I back out of the driveway and go straight to Cat's house, immediately sloughing the discomfort Celine planted in me. I'm there in minutes.

When I arrive, knocking before letting myself into the house, she's not alone. Otto and his golf cart are gone, but there's another family at the table—two teenage boys and their parents—eating crumble with vanilla ice cream and groaning in pleasure.

Cat must not have heard me come in, because she's leaning against the wall in the dining room, grinning at her guests. She's wearing a pink checkered apron, her blonde hair up in a messy bun on her head. "Good, then?"

"I'll take seconds," the younger teen says around a full mouth.

"Manners," his mom scolds. "This is plenty, Miss Keene. Thanks for sharing with us."

"I don't mind at all." She catches my eye across the room and her smile grows. "Hey."

Just wants me for my money *indeed*. This girl doesn't have a single gold-digging bone in her body.

"Hey." I sling my hands in my pockets to keep from reaching out for her while she crosses the room.

"Come on, let's get you a plate."

I follow her into the kitchen. She dishes up two plates of blackberry crumble, topping them with a scoop of vanilla ice cream. It smells like warm, tart, sugary, berry heaven in here, and my mouth is ready for a bite when she hands me the plate.

The crumble tastes as good as it smells. I lean against the counter, digging in. "This is heaven."

Her smile is so wide, you'd think I told her she was the most beautiful woman I know or something. She is, but I didn't say it. "It's my mom's recipe. She was such a good baker."

"You could sell this at the farmer's market, Cat. Seriously, it's good."

She leans against the counter, dragging her fork through the crumble and spearing a berry. "I don't need to sell it. I'd rather share it instead."

"Just like your jam. Do you often distribute it to old women?"

"Usually," she says around a bite. "My book club likes jam. I take jars to Mrs. Finnigan and Mrs. Rojas when I clean their houses, too. But I also give it to young people. Everyone likes jam," she adds defensively.

My plate is empty way too fast. Cat reaches for it, but I bump her out of the way with my hip and rinse my dishes before putting them in the dishwasher. "That exceeded all my expectations." As did seeing her with her guests, wearing her cute apron with the white frills, her hair up off her face and her cheeks bright from the praise and probably the heat of the oven.

I can't look away from her. "I'll pay you for a jar."

She rolls her eyes. "You pay me enough. Take as much as you want."

That eats at me. The transactional component of our working relationship grates. I want her to treat me like anything but a boss. There's no way I'm taking her jam as though it's included in our assistant deal. "This isn't part of your PA responsibilities, Cat. I'd love a jar, but only if I can pay for it like a customer."

"No one else does."

She has me there. "But you give it to them freely. I'm *asking* for some. It's different."

Cat crosses the room where the jars of deep purple jam are sitting in rows on a dishtowel. She plucks one from the front and brings it to me. "As my friend, I'm giving you a jar for free, just like I do with all my other friends." She uncurls my fingers, then pushes the warm jar into my palm. "Happy birthday."

"My birthday isn't until September."

"Happy *early* birthday, then." Her hand is still on the back of mine, holding it in front of us. "How was the date?"

"Jane is great," I say, unable to tear my mind from her fingers pressing into my skin. "But she isn't you."

Cat's hands tighten. She's watching my face. I can see the turmoil jumping around in her head and the longer she doesn't speak, the more antsy I am to break the silence.

"How easy would it be for you to get away tomorrow?"

She drops my hand and steps back until she's leaning one hip against the counter and facing me. "I have to clean guest rooms, but I don't have anything else going on."

Is this asking too much? I don't know. But I want her with me tomorrow when I have to face my family. When was the last time I'd wanted anything so much?

"I have to attend a birthday party for my aunt on the mainland, and I was hoping you'd come. It's hard to face my family sometimes, but I think it would be easier with you there." I'm suddenly extremely self-conscious about presuming she's a good enough friend to come to a party like this with me. I fall back on our work-related relationship to smooth the weird, unlabeled emotions. We call that digging my own hole. Yes, I don't want her to see me as a boss, but maybe I don't know how to put myself out there without it. It's a crutch. "Christine said we can stop by and see all the finished ads while we're in the city, too. They have some printed, which is always the best medium to see them in."

"A family party? Like with your parents?"

I cringe. "They'll avoid each other, but they'll both be there." My breath already feels shallow at the thought of dealing with my parents in person. Okay. We're friends. She *just* said so herself. "It's selfish of me, but I was hoping you'd be there to make it better. If I have you, I have an excuse to not sit around with my mom all night and a reason to leave early."

She hikes up a blonde eyebrow. "I'm your scapegoat?"

"Only if you feel like you can sacrifice an entire day."

She looks at me, searching with her blue eyes. I can't tell if she's annoyed by my request or disturbed or confused or intrigued. She certainly doesn't look thrilled. Her face is stone. Granite. Carved from rock by a master of stoic, an impassive lack of feeling. "What time?"

My shoulders relax. She's willing. "We should head out by nine at the latest." I clear my throat. "It'll take about two and a half hours to get there."

She nods. "Okay, I can do that. I'll ask Otto to cover me if the Morgans aren't gone in time."

"We probably won't get home until really late. Like, early hours of the morning late."

Cat's eyes wrinkle suspiciously. "Okay. Will your *entire* family be there? All of your sisters?"

"Yeah. Actually… Olive will be traveling with us, so if you don't want to come…"

She hesitates before shaking her head. "It's fine."

"I'll tell her to give you space."

"Thanks." She picks up a spoon and digs a bite out of the pan. "Will your aunt be okay with me crashing the party?"

"I get to bring a plus one, so you aren't crashing."

She peers up at me. "A plus one? How fancy is this shindig?"

"The invitation mentioned cocktail attire. Do you have something to wear, or should we shop before—"

"I have something," she says, chuckling. "Even island girls go out sometimes. Occasionally. Okay, fine, very infrequently. But it happens."

"Probably more often than I do."

"Um, unlikely, Mr. Billionaire Hot Shot Ladies Man."

"That's a mouthful."

"It's also true. You can't hide from a giant *Forbes* spread."

A smile curves over my mouth. "I thought you got your info from *BuzzFeed*."

"They are equally reliable sources."

"Do either of them say how much of a nerd I am? Because I wasn't kidding about that secret lair, Cat."

She straightens, pushing away from the counter. "Say what? Where is it?"

"In my Manhattan apartment."

Her eyes go round. "You're serious right now. What's in it?"

"I want your respect too much to tell you that."

Her eyes gleam. "It has to do with whatever was on your computer monitors, doesn't it? Warlocks and Vikings and lots of code."

A scoff rips from my throat. Guess I didn't pull the plug fast enough. "You're unbelievable. How much did you see before I ripped out the power cord?"

"Just those things." Her smile twinkles with amusement. "It was enough to know that I have no idea what it was."

"Good."

"Come on," she says, stepping close and taking my arm in both of her hands. "Tell me what it is and I'll give you seconds."

My gaze drops to her lips before I realize that she means a second helping of dessert.

She notices.

"Maybe someday," I say, my voice hoarse, "after I've proven to you how cool I am first."

She gives my arm a pat and steps back. "You've already done that."

"We'll see after you meet my extended family," I mutter. "I'm really glad you're coming."

Cat looks at me warmly. "We'll have fun. I'll protect you from the aunts who want to squeeze your cheeks."

If only my aunts were so wholesome.

"My mom adores Celine, too. It'll be nice to have someone with me so she won't try to shove my ex in my face all night."

"You dated Celine?"

Have I not told her that? "For about six months, yeah. We broke up well over a year ago."

"She's friends with Olive?"

"It's how we met," I tell her. But she doesn't seem jealous. In fact, she doesn't even seem bothered. I'm glad she can sense—I hope—how Celine isn't a threat. How my gaze doesn't follow Celine around a room.

Cat smiles softly, nodding like she understands.

I imagine walking into the Apollo Lounge with her on my arm and being able to tell people she's with me. Can she tell I want this to be a real date? I don't say it outright, because I don't want to push her. When I hinted earlier that I'd rather have gone on a date with her instead of Jane, she didn't say anything.

Besides, I'm still her boss.

But there is that kiss, and that moment at the blackberry brambles, and I'm not ready to give up hope yet. I just need to wait out this job, and then I can ask her out for real.

Until then, I'm going to be the best platonic guy friend she's *ever* had.

CHAPTER 23

Noah

DR. STEIN HAS COME in clutch. She emailed me back sometime during my date with Jane to set up a telehealth appointment, but I didn't see it until I got home from Cat's house last night. She gave me a phone number to text her, so here I am at seven the next morning sitting at my desk and waiting to be let into the Zoom meeting.

For some reason, my stomach is queasy.

Anxiety really is the pits sometimes.

The screen comes to life and Dr. Stein shows up, sitting at a brown desk. Her black hair is extra curly and bunched behind her head in a claw clip. Shelves of knick-knacks and little stacks of books are artfully arranged behind her. In the center of the screen, just behind her head, is a large, soothing abstract painting of calm blue and cream and gray. I already feel more hopeful.

She's good at her job.

"Good morning, Noah. I'm sorry we couldn't meet yesterday. How are you today?"

"Better?" I say it like a question, then lean back in my chair and shake my head. "It comes and goes."

"Okay. Why don't you start at the beginning for me? I think when we ended last time, you were doing your best to support Bree during her difficult time."

I go back about a week, because that's the last time I filled her in, and tell her about Olive coming home to comfort Bree and how it's thrown Cat. I tell her about the family group chat that explodes every day, how I swipe into the message thread to get rid of the notifications and then back out again without reading anything. I tell her about my shortness of breath at the beach and how kayaking did nothing for me.

"Being in nature or going for runs has helped historically, correct?"

"Usually," I confirm. "I couldn't seem to bring my head back down to earth yesterday. My breathing was shallow, and that thing was happening where I could hear my heartbeat in my ears."

"You mentioned feeling better this morning. When did those symptoms lessen?"

"Yesterday afternoon. I went to see Cat and spent some time with her, and the symptoms weren't as bad then."

"But they didn't leave completely?"

"No. I still feel it all," I tell her, a little ashamed I can't get a handle on my emotions.

Dr. Stein looks down at her iPad, then raises her eyes to me. "Do you have an event coming up? A circumstance that might be triggering this extended anxiety attack? Or could it be the presence of your sisters in the house that is bringing up some discomfort in connection to your parents' divorce?"

Extended anxiety attack. That sounds like a barrel of fun. "I'm not sure. There's a party for my aunt tonight. Both of my parents will be there."

She smiles softly at me, full of kindness and understanding. I appreciate her patience while I gather my thoughts and continue.

"My sisters being home has been a lot, too. One of them has a difficult past with Cat, so there's been some discomfort this week. I didn't know—that is, no one ever told me my sister bullied Cat in middle school. It was years ago, but I can't seem to let go of the guilt associated with that."

"Cat is your personal assistant, correct?"

"Yes, but she's also my friend." Which is putting it lightly. She's so much more than that to me.

"Putting blame on yourself for actions out of your control will only increase your discomfort, and it isn't fair to you. While it's understandable that you want to protect your friend and be a support to her, you can also let go of responsibility for actions that another person made—even one so close as a family member."

That was far easier said than done.

"Right now, what I'd like to address are your immediate feelings. Have you considered the medication we've talked about?"

My stomach seizes again, sending a queasy feeling through my gut. I've seen the way my family has abused prescription medications and alcohol, and it's kept me from ever being interested in either of those things. I've opted for holistic remedies instead of the anti-anxiety medication Dr. Stein mentioned at our first meeting.

"You have expressed concerns in the past, so I want this conversation to be open and honest. There are medications you can take on an as-needed basis for panic attacks. They could help you in situations like this where you know a trigger is coming—a meeting, a family party, anything big. But I think you could benefit more from a consistent, small dose that would keep you regulated. You could feel less symptoms all the time, instead of trying to determine when you'll need it and when you won't. Your triggers appear consistent enough to make this a safe medical option."

I sit there silently, feeling the lightness in my limbs and the pulse in my ears and the uneasiness in my gut, and I want it to go away. I don't enjoy feeling this way, and though I know it's been part of my life for a long time, it has only gotten out of control in the last few years. I'm ready for it to be gone.

I'm ready to feel like me again.

"We would start with a very conservative dose, if this is what you choose to do, then go from there."

"Okay."

She waits a moment, giving me room to continue. When I don't, she starts to lay out instructions about lowering the dose and testing it out for two weeks before taking the full pills. I appreciate her cautious approach. With my weekly appointments this summer, she'll be checking in with me regularly too.

I can stop at any time. It feels important to remind myself of that.

"This won't take immediate effect, Noah," she reminds me. "You still need to utilize the coping mechanisms we've discussed when you attend the party with your family, or work meetings, or anything else where you start to feel the symptoms we've gone over."

I nod. There are a few things I can do—for instance, I can always walk out the door—but I'll have Cat with me, and she has been a steadying presence from our first day together this summer.

She *is* anti-anxiety medication.

I also know I need to figure myself out, and Dr. Stein is monitoring me closely enough that I feel safe giving this a chance.

"Can I start Monday?" I ask her. "I have to leave for the airport fairly soon."

"Of course." She smiles into the camera. "Don't hesitate to reach out when you need to, Noah. I'm glad you emailed me yesterday."

I am, too. It's so hard to reach out sometimes, to feel like what I'm going through is worth an appointment when I'm so used to putting on my big kid pants and dealing with the pain or the inconvenience. Now that I have reached out to her, I can already feel the weight lessening.

Not the stomachache, though. I have a feeling that will persist until the party tonight is behind me.

We sign off, and I check my email to see if there are any updates on the open world game or the dating app I need to address before taking off for the day. Now that the bugs are worked out and the ad campaign is complete, we're getting close to releasing the dating app that I'm hoping will reduce the amount of catfishers out there.

I've seen the ads Christine finished with our graphics team, and they're good. Like, really good. I'm hoping they'll entice other people too. I would buy anything that used Cat as a point woman on their ads.

I, very intentionally, do not open the game on my computer, even though I have an hour to spare, because I know how easily time passes when I get sucked into it. Mateo tells me they're still working out the kinks before the game can be brought before investors, but I've been playing it for two months now and it seems nearly perfect to me. They brought my vision to life.

I pick a suit for the party tonight because there's no way I'm letting my mom's stylist dress me again, then pack up everything I'll need and zip it into a travel garment bag.

Then I pull out my phone and text Cat.

NOAH
Don't forget your license

CAT
What about music? Do you have that covered? Two and a half hours is a long time to be stuck with your sister.

NOAH
Entertainment is covered.

She'll probably be glad to learn there are TVs on the plane. She can plug in to one of those and ignore Olive all she wants.

I head downstairs and hang my suit bag over the back of the sofa. Olive is sitting at the table with Celine and what looks like artfully arranged power bowls. The blueberries and sliced strawberries are fanned out with oats and seeds and some sort of honey or agave drizzled over the top.

"Where did you find those on the island?" I ask. They're easy to get your hands on in Manhattan—not so much in Sunset Harbor.

Olive leans to the side, taking a picture of her and Celine leaning together with their bowls. She reaches forward and pushes her bowl over an inch, then takes the picture again. "Perfect."

"Ollie?"

"Oh, I made them." She digs in, putting her phone down. "Dash's chef taught me a few good ones."

Dash: her boyfriend the movie star. He was a lot more down to earth than I'd expected when we met for the first time, despite things like having a private chef. We get along pretty well. Neither he nor I like being around my bickering parents, so we often escape on the occasions we're all together and find a game to play. He's a nerd too, so it doesn't take much to get us to search out a TV and a couple of controllers. "Will he be coming tonight?"

"He has a press thing downtown, but he's going to try to stop by."

I pull a banana from the fruit bowl and peel it, leaning against the counter. It's debatable whether addressing the bullying now is a good thing when we all still have to fly to the city together. At this point, I don't care if she knows that I know.

"Cat's coming," I say, taking a bite of the banana. "I would really appreciate it if you gave her space."

Olive's head whips my way. "She's coming to Tootsie's party?"

"Is she your date?" Celine asks, her mouth full of chia seeds and fruit. "Or is this part of her 'work' responsibilities?"

"She's just a friend." I spear Olive with a look. "Please give her space."

Her brown eyes lock on me. "She told you."

Olive's too intelligent not to note the difference in me between now and yesterday. Then I was ignorant and confused. Now I'm angry. "No. Someone else did."

She bristles defensively. "I tried to apologize. She just walked right out."

"Can you blame her?"

"It's been over ten years."

"Ollie. Can you blame her?" I repeat.

She is so stubborn. She got it from my dad and it's not her best trait. Her gaze drops to her bowl before lifting to me again. "Not really."

"Okay, then please give her space. You can't force her to accept your apology or want to be around you."

"I just hoped we'd all be adults about it now."

Implying that Cat is childishly holding on to the past? "No more digs, okay? I'm serious. Or you can find your own way there." I polish off the banana and toss the peel in the garbage.

She turns her glare onto her breakfast. "You know, I've moved on. It would be nice if she could too."

"That's her business, not ours."

Celine nods. "It's true, Oll. Forgive yourself. You can't force her to do it, but you can free yourself from the guilt."

And there it is, the faint shimmer of goodness in my gold-digging ex-girlfriend. There was a reason we dated for six whole months, thin as it was.

I'm guessing Olive filled Celine in on her past with Cat.

Olive takes a bite of her breakfast, ignoring both of us. If I can handle the rest of my family this seamlessly, maybe the rest of the day won't be as bad as I've feared.

Or maybe defending Cat just comes naturally to me.

"You know," Olive says, turning in her seat to face me. Her freshly highlighted hair falls over her shoulder. "I wasn't going to say anything, but you brought it up, so it's fair game now. You claim she doesn't want you for your money. But the first opportunity she gets, she's taking your private plane to Manhattan for an exclusive party." Her eyebrows hike up. "Sounds a little suspicious to me."

Celine drops her focus to her bowl, looking mighty hard at the blueberries there. Little snake.

Defenses die on my tongue. "My relationship with her isn't anyone else's business."

"Mom won't agree with that. The party is probably being covered tonight. You're not going to be able to avoid pictures."

"I'm not ashamed of her," I clarify. "We're just friends, so we don't have anything to worry about."

Olive rolls her eyes. "Sure."

"Ollie."

"What?" she snaps. "Celine said Cat needs money, and now she's hanging out here all the time—"

"It's called *working*."

"—and then she's leading in your ad campaign and coming to family parties—"

"Olive," I bark. "Honestly, stop. You don't know her and you don't know the situation."

Her eyes spit fire. "I don't want my brother to be taken advantage of. Or, worse, hurt because some girl wants revenge after what I put her through over ten years ago."

Ah. So she's being protective. Taking blame. It's oddly comforting to hear she has a reason for being so ridiculous, that it's not coming from sheer mean-girl-ness anymore. Maybe providing a little more information about the situation would give her enough cause to step back and quit worrying.

"Do you remember how her parents died and left her with her uncle?"

Olive nods, her face a mask of hesitation.

"His name is Otto. A few years ago, he got cancer. I don't know if you'd heard, but it was pretty bad. He went through a cancer treatment center right on the mainland for chemo and surgery. He's in remission now, but they were slapped with some pretty hefty medical bills."

Olive's shoulders deflate, the fight gone from them. "So Cat needs money to pay her uncle's medical bills or... what? They lose everything?"

"Yeah. The house her parents raised her in. Their B&B. Her home."

She's careful when she asks, "Have you considered the possibility that she manipulated you into helping her?"

"Honestly, no. She's not like that. It didn't even cross my mind." My gaze flicks to Celine and back to my sister. "I've had plenty of people take advantage of me, Ollie. I know the signs."

Celine glares.

But Olive understands. "I just don't want to see you hurt because of something I did when I was young and stupid."

"She holds that against *you*, not me."

Olive rolls her eyes. "Great."

"She's gone through a lot," I say. I can't imagine losing my parents, dealing with a bully, almost losing my uncle, then possibly my house. "Cut her some slack."

Celine makes an irritated scoff, but Olive ignores her. My sister nods, rising with her half-full bowl and carrying it past me to the sink. "I'm not evil, you know."

"I know." I pull her into a side hug. "You're only part evil."

Olive laughs, but the sound is strained.

"Or middle school you was, apparently," I mutter.

She rinses her dishes. "I really tried to apologize to her, but she wouldn't let me."

"That's her choice," I say softly. "Can we just make the best of today?"

"Yeah," Olive says. "Did you hear the latest? Mom *cut Dad out* of the family portrait that was hanging in their Manhattan place."

My stomach churns. "That was an oil painting."

"Yeah, and now it's a ruined canvas. She wants to do a photoshoot with just her and the kids to replace it." Olive rolls her eyes. "Probably better to humor her. They won't live together again, and she wants a family picture on the wall."

I have to get away from this conversation. "Be ready to leave in an hour?" I ask.

Olive nods.

"Be on your best behavior," I warn.

She scoffs. "I've grown up, Noah."

I look at her with reservations. I also never thought she'd be capable of bullying.

Prove it, sis.

CHAPTER 24

Cat

RIDING across the bay in the Belacourt speedboat and piling into Noah's SUV takes no time at all, thanks to the way people seem to move out of the way for him, literally and figuratively speaking. Our travel is so seamless, I almost wonder if he's got some sort of billionaire smile that gets people to move faster when he flashes it.

Is it the way he talks? Walks? The way he dresses? His Mercedes G-Wagon?

I slide into the front seat and settle in, popping open my sparkling water and taking a sip. I've got two cans of LaCroix for the drive and earbuds, just in case Noah's "entertainment" isn't enough to keep his sister out of my head.

I've tried to let the past go. I really have. To be honest, I kind of thought I already had. But when I see Olive, my whole body flushes hot and cold at the same time. It's probably a mix of residual shame, anger, and humiliation.

That doesn't make my feelings any less real. I don't know how to make them go away.

"So where is this place?" I ask while Noah pulls onto the road.

"The Apollo Lounge. Have you heard of it?"

"No."

"We were there a few months ago," Celine says from the

back seat, her voice suggestive. "They did a speakeasy night that kind of reminded me of that club we went to in London, Noah."

His cheeks are pink. I don't think I want to know what took place at that club or why Celine is bringing it up now.

"I guess I see the resemblance," he says, pulling onto the freeway and heading north. His attention turns back to me. "My dad knows the owner, so we have family parties there occasionally. It's a nice place. On the smaller side."

Noah's elbow sits on the arm rest, but his non-driving leg is going wild. It's bouncing around like it can accelerate us fully with Flintstone power. My instinct tells me to reach across the console and take his hand to calm his knee, but I curl my fingers around the seat instead. Celine and Olive are sitting right behind us. I don't need them getting a front row seat to me being rejected in case Noah takes my gesture the wrong way.

There's the possibility he'll read into me trying to calm him down and assume I'm making a move.

Blackberry bramble moments aside, this man is my boss.

Time for a subject change.

"Do you like road trips? Otto took me on a road trip to Georgia to visit my grandparents right after I graduated high school, and his car broke down on the way there *and* the way home." I patted the dashboard. "This baby seems unlikely to leave us stranded in the middle of hickville for two days."

Noah turns a weird expression on me. "Yeah, she's pretty reliable."

"You do know we aren't going on a road trip, right?" Celine asks.

Noah pulls off the freeway, his face whipping toward me. "You thought we were *driving?*"

"You didn't say otherwise." Panic starts at the base of my gut, swirling around as I look up and watch an airplane take off in the blue sky ahead of us, angled toward the clouds. Why are we at an airport?

"I'm so sorry." Noah sounds panicked. "I thought I mentioned that we're going to the city—Christine's office is there. It's just second nature for me, so—"

"Hold up." I twist my torso to better face Noah. "Where are we going?"

"The Apollo Lounge."

"Where is it, though, Belacourt?"

He swallows, looking like he just ran over a bunny. "Manhattan."

The world goes silent. "What?"

"We're flying."

"But... *what*?" I repeat, trying to wrap my head around this sudden change in expectations. "I brought LaCroix!"

"You can bring cans of liquid on this flight, Cat. You won't need to, though, because they have it on the plane." He pulls the car onto the side of the road and turns to face me, ignoring Celine laughing in the back seat. I don't know if Olive is laughing too because I'm actively ignoring her. "I'm so sorry I didn't make that clear. Obviously, you don't need to come if this is a dealbreaker. You can drop us off and drive back to the ferry."

He's giving me an out. I look into his dark brown eyes, two pools of rich chocolate that are ringed with concern. The signs for traveling like this were there—his reminder to bring my license, talking about Christine's office, how he has the entertainment covered.

I'd actually asked if he had the music sorted out. It's so cringey I wish the seat would swallow me whole.

Noah's stressing out. His knee is prepping for a rocket launch, and his eyes are boring into me like they can read my mind if they only stare hard enough. The man clearly hasn't been trying to trick me into getting on a plane. This is obviously not a big deal to him. But, I mean, flying somewhere to attend a party and then flying home on the same day? That's wild. Is this something people do?

I guess billionaires do.

Oh my gosh. Wait. I can bring the LaCroix on the flight? That must mean... "Do you have your own plane?"

He looks abashed and turns his focus on parking the SUV. His cheeks pink while his gaze flicks to me and away again. How can he be so humble and *so filthy rich*? At least his knee isn't bouncing so hard anymore.

"You do. It's your plane. That's why you know there's LaCroix on board."

"It'll be cold," he says weakly.

"You hate sparkling water," Olive says. "I was wondering why it's in your fridge."

"Cat likes it."

My whole body goes warm. How does he know this? Am I that obvious? I love the stuff, but I had no idea I was the reason he bought them for his fridge. It makes me feel fizzy. I'm warm and bubbly like a LaCroix left in the sun.

"We should get going." Noah says it like a question and waits for my answer, turning off the car.

Am I doing this? Am I letting Noah Belacourt whisk me away on a plane to attend a party just because he's worried about facing his family alone? I won't leave him stranded, that's for sure. He did say he'd get me home tonight.

Okay, there's also the tiny little detail titled *I Want to Go to a Party with Him*. I'd read that book, over and over again. Every moment from Noah inviting me when he was fresh off his date with Jane to now has been a dream. The guy went out with Jane freaking Hayes and missed *me*. What world is this?

One where he's my boss. I need to write it on my hand, because it's really easy to forget when I can see and feel and smell him.

No, I'm not a vampire. It doesn't matter how good he smells. I can resist.

He's still staring, waiting, so I clear my throat. "Let's go."

Celine lets out a disappointed sound. She really doesn't want me here.

Tough.

The girls start to get out of the back seat. Noah reaches for my hand, squeezing my fingers. "You really can take the car home. I can Uber back later tonight."

"I want to come with you." It's the truth, too. I don't mind this change of plans. Flying to New York City is a vast step up since I was prepared to sit in a car for two and a half hours with my middle school nemesis and Noah's ex-girlfriend. "You've improved the trip already."

"Okay. I don't know why it didn't occur to me to make sure you realized... anyway, I'm sorry."

I squeeze his fingers. "Come on, Pennybags. You worry too much."

He lets me pull my hand free and slip out of the car. I swear I hear him say, "You have no idea."

THE FLIGHT IS PASSING QUICKLY, which is all thanks to the fact that we have this plane entirely to ourselves and I don't have to quietly fight over armrests or wait until the flight attendants show up to get a cold LaCroix. The seats are plush, crafted from luxurious leather in a variety of configurations that mean I don't have to face Olive or Celine for the whole flight, instead sitting directly across from Noah. He's spent part of the time working on something for his app launch party while I read *Summer Fling*, since I've already finished this month's book club book.

After an hour, though, I'm done reading. I lower the book and watch Noah work. "I thought you were going to entertain me."

His eyes flick up. Somehow, just that look heats my blood. Okay, maybe it's better to read.

"What did you have in mind?" he asks.

So many things we cannot or should not do. Also, anything that keeps us on the opposite side of the plane from his sister would be good. "Anything."

"We can put on a movie. Play a game?"

"Do you have Battleship?"

"No, but I have checkers."

"Done."

He gets up to retrieve the game and returns with a travel-sized wooden board, the squares stained in contrasting shades. We each pull out a drawer on opposite sides of the little board and retrieve the pieces, then proceed to set up.

I arrange all my pieces on the dark squares. "When's the last time you saw your parents?"

"Over a month ago."

"And the rest of your family?"

"I saw Tootsie—it's her birthday party we're heading to—and my grandmother a few months back at a charity dinner in the city. It's been much longer for most everyone else." He sits back, waiting for me to perfectly center my pieces on each square. "My family is busy, but we make it a point to come together a few times a year to celebrate each other."

"Sounds like you're close." I can't remember the last time I saw my grandparents, aunts, uncles, and cousins at the same time. No, I can. It was the trip we took when I graduated high school. My grandparents send cards and call me on my birthday, but we don't see each other often.

Maybe if one of us had a private plane, that would be different.

"We're as close as we can be while we all travel frequently and don't live in the same place. I haven't called Manhattan my regular home in a while."

"But you like it there?"

"I love the city. Florida is home, but there's a lot of good food and culture and people in New York."

"Why didn't you open the Scout office there?"

"I did. That's where we started, but my heart is down in Florida. I spend a lot of time in Sunset Harbor throughout the year, so it made sense to keep both offices running. I don't love my apartment on the mainland as much as my Manhattan flat, but it was a quick buy, and I could change it if I wanted to."

"Bring in a decorator or buy a whole new place?"

"Depends on how long I want to stay there, I suppose." He gestures. "Ladies first."

"Black goes first," I counter, leaning back in my smooth leather seat and eyeing him. "I can't imagine not feeling settled. You bounce all over the place, so which one is *home*?"

He picks up his checker piece and taps it on the table, looking at me. "I haven't really settled, I guess. Manhattan is the place I've made my own, but..." He looks at his sister, then back to me. "Sunset Harbor has been feeling like home again lately. I always spend time there. My suite at the resort gets regular use, but this summer has been different. I can't explain why."

He finally moves his piece, so I slide one over too. "Maybe because you're at the house full time. You're not really bouncing anywhere."

"Could be." He moves another. "There are a lot of good childhood memories there."

"And not-so-good ones," Olive pipes in, clearly listening to our conversation.

Noah ignores her.

I move my piece. "If you're happy being a nomad, then you're happy being a nomad."

He doesn't say anything else. Maybe because his sister is listening, maybe because he doesn't owe me any explanation. I want to ask him what about his family makes him so anxious, because he's been bouncing his knee so hard I'm worried he'll hit the table between us and send our game flying. But I don't want to make things uncomfortable between him and his sister.

So I reach under the table and press the tips of my fingers to his knee. It immediately stills under my touch. His entire body seems to turn to granite. "What's going on?" I ask quietly, pressing with my fingers so he'll know what I'm referring to.

His leg immediately freezes. He's still for so long, his eyes running over my face. He wants to say something, I think. Or he's calculating the best way to say it.

"Contention is hard for me," he says quietly, slowly. "It's not something I do well with."

"I've seen you handle uncomfortable situations. You were so good with Bree when she bailed during the photoshoot."

"I'm uncomfortable when people argue. At work, I can defend my employees and manage disputes easily. But when people in my life aren't happy with each other, I get so uncomfortable in my own skin I just want to claw my way out."

"And your parents' divorce has been far from amicable." He must be automatically dialed up to high levels of discomfort anytime he's around them.

"That's putting it mildly."

My heart goes still. This means he's probably set to high when he's around Olive and *me*. The last thing I want to do is cause him this much distress, but I do it by being around him. And he still wanted me to come on this trip? Knowing my past with Olive and that we'd be forced to travel together?

His parents' contention must be extremely awful if he's willing to endure this plane ride in order to have me there.

I move my checker piece and smile up at him. "Just call me a shield, because that's what I'll be until we land in Florida again."

CHAPTER 25

Noah

CAT HAS BEEN a fantastic shield so far, and we haven't even been in the city for a full hour. We climbed into our car—I had Mateo order two so we could take one and Olive could go elsewhere with Celine—and started toward Manhattan. Cat's wide eyes absorb everything, gawking at the Brooklyn Bridge and craning her neck to see the skyline. It's been so distracting and adorable I'm not even stressed about seeing my parents tonight.

Well, I am when I think about it, but that isn't often.

My knee has stopped nervously bouncing altogether. When Cat touched it on the plane, it was like pressing a magic button. Something about the amount of control she seems to have over herself makes me feel like she has things well in hand, including me. She is strong and sturdy and an excellent friend to have as a support.

Also, I'm definitely falling for her.

"Okay, hot shot," she says, leaning away from her window while the driver takes us toward Christine's office building in the heart of Soho. "Time to come clean. Are the bagels here really the best?"

"You're telling me you've come to New York for the first time and the thing you're curious about is the bagels?"

"I mean, I wouldn't mind checking out Lady Liberty or

seeing the hotel from *Home Alone 2*, but yeah, I'm curious about the bagels too."

"They're good," I tell her, unable to dampen my smile.

The car comes to a stop. "We're here, boss," our driver says.

"Thanks, Paul. I'll text you when we're ready to leave."

He nods. I get out and move around to open Cat's door, but she's done it herself and is halfway out of the car. I'm not used to that. Most of the women in my life patiently wait for me to help them out. But Cat's not in five-inch heels, either. She's sporting her usual brown Birkenstocks and I kind of love that about her.

She's so comfortable in her own skin. There's no sense of her trying to change to fit in better. She's Cat. Take it or leave it.

I'd rather take it. Claim her. Like, *belong* to her. Not some weird ownership thing.

We take the elevator up to Christine's modern exposed-brick office. The receptionist tells us to head straight back. It's one big room, like an old warehouse that has been gutted and stripped and filled with glass, metal, and supple leather furniture. A pair of clear glass offices stand on one side, a conference table on the other, with groups of chairs and freestanding desks scattered about in half of the room. An empty corner is set up as a photography studio with light pouring in from the layers of windows set in each wall.

Christine eyes us from her office and puts a finger up, her phone pressed to her ear. She says something into it and hangs up before coming out to greet us.

"I can't wait to show you everything," she says, leaning in to kiss me and Cat each on the cheek. "Alex finished the videos yesterday."

I haven't seen those yet. "You have the posters, too?"

"In here." She leads us to her office and holds the door, then crosses to a table and rifles through a stack of printed posters before pulling out a few for us and flipping them over.

Cat sidles up right next to her and watches Christine flip through the photos she selected for the ads. Since it's for a dating app, the photos are mostly me and Cat in cozy positions or me watching her with adoration in my eyes.

I swallow. Can she see how authentic these pictures are? Because then I'm in trouble. I've been good at keeping a healthy distance between us lately. Or so I thought.

The entire time we're looking at the pictures, she doesn't give off nervous or awkward energy. "These are gorgeous, Christine."

"I'm glad you like them. You know, for an amateur, you did great."

Cat shakes her head. "Bree would have been better. I'm just relieved I didn't mess everything up."

"Real chemistry shines through the lens, Cat," Christine says, looking between us. "That's part of the reason these are so stunning. You can feel what Noah's thinking when he's looking at you. And that *kiss*? Magic." Her eyes flick to me. "Has Alex sent you the video?"

"He might have, but we were traveling." I'm glad she's changed the subject and that Cat is standing in front of me so I can't look into her eyes and find any discomfort there.

Christine circles her desk and drops into her seat, typing away. "I've got it. Hold on, I'll pull it up."

Cat shifts, looking through the stack of photos again. She stops on the one where she's in my arms just after we kissed, her head buried in my chest. Her eyes are closed, and she looks so blissfully content. My chin rests on her head, my eyes down, and a soft smile touches my lips, so faint it's more of an essence than a curve.

"It looks good," I say, my voice hoarse.

She drops the stack onto the table like it's made from hot coals. "Yeah."

"Okay, I have it." Christine shifts the monitor so we can both see it. We crowd around her desk and watch the video. It's more of the same from the photos, but the emotion is different. I can feel how much we want each other in those clips. It's really satisfying when we come together in the waves and finally kiss. And I mean *kiss*. Cat is all in. I'm all in. It doesn't look like we're doing it for the cameras but because we are feeling the moment.

The room just bumped up a few degrees.

I'm in shorts and a plain navy tee, but I still feel like I need to pull on my collar and fan myself.

"Wow," Cat says.

Christine watches us. "This will be all over social media in a few weeks. Right, Noah?"

"Yeah." I clear my throat. "My marketing team is planning to go hard with the sponsored ads on release day."

"I can't wait," Cat says quietly. She doesn't say anything else.

We chat for a few more minutes about the shoot before I realize Cat is clearly bothered by something. She's distant, not paying attention to the conversation. Was it the ads? Hit with the realization that her face will be plastered all over social media? Annoyed by the way I look at her in the photos?

I need to get her alone and make sure she's okay. "We'd better be on our way."

"I'll see you next month," Christine says.

"Did we have something else scheduled?" Mateo usually doesn't forget to tell me things, but I haven't seen anything on my calendar.

Her black eyebrows pull together. "That family shoot your mom booked."

Oh. So, that's happening then. "Without my dad, I'm guessing?"

Christine bites on her lip. "Sorry. I figured you were told."

I give her a bright smile. "I'm sure I have an email about it somewhere. I'll see you then."

Cat seems to snap out of her funk and pulls Christine in for a hug before we head out. We have a few hours left before we need to get ready for the party. We don't have time for a tour of the Statue of Liberty, but we can see Kevin McCallister's hotel. "Are you hungry?" I ask when we step into the elevator.

"Starving."

"Okay, let's go eat."

THE AWKWARDNESS HAS DIMINISHED SOMEWHAT with the help of pepperoni pizza and hot soft pretzels. I took one bite of pizza and threw my slice away, my queasy stomach rejecting it. The closer we get to the party, the sicker I feel, which is a red flag, but I'm trying to low-key monitor the situation. This is kind of like the day I freaked out at work. I felt it building until it reached a head, until I couldn't take being in that boardroom with the advertising team, who proceeded to watch me lose my mind.

Cat chews on her pretzel while we walk through Central Park, heading toward the corner near the hotel. The path is straight, lined with tall trees and literary statues the size of a truck. Warm air cocoons us, thick with moisture and heat. I'm glad I'll have time to go home and change before the party, because this walk is making my back sticky with sweat.

"I can't believe we're walking through the place where Kevin McAllister made friends with the bird lady."

If she loves that, the hotel we're heading to is going to blow her mind.

"What's your favorite Christmas movie?" she asks, then takes another bite.

We weave down the path toward the road, the tall, curvy elm trees providing shade and reprieve from the heat. "Maybe *Elf*? I love how wholesome it is. *How the Grinch Stole Christmas* is a classic, though. Is yours *Home Alone*?"

"Yeah."

"Which one?"

"One and two. I refuse to acknowledge the rest of them."

I chuckle.

"What kid doesn't love the idea of having to defend their home against a couple of bad guys? Plus, all the snow makes his house look so dreamy."

We reach the end of the path and turn on the sidewalk. The hotel is up on the corner across the street, but we can't quite see it from here.

"Maybe we should go over what you expect from me tonight," she says. "What is my job exactly?"

Hold up. Job? The word floats uncomfortably between us. Did she only agree to come because of her position as my personal assistant? My steps slow, the idea rocking me like a boat in hurricane season.

Cat turns around to face me, the warm breeze blowing a strand of blonde hair over her face. She drags it back behind her ear. "What's wrong?"

The way I see it, this can go one of two ways. I can pretend to sneeze and keep walking beside her like nothing happened, or I can shut down the expectation that I wanted her to come to Manhattan because she works for me.

There's nothing I can do about my feelings for her while I'm her boss, but I can kill the idea that she has to obey my every command.

It's also possible to show her that I don't have work-related feelings about her, even if I can't act on them. Besides, she's the one who launched us into friendship with her jam gift.

"Didn't we decide to be friends?" I ask.

She searches my face like I have an answer key written in the dimple she *claims* pops when I lie. No dimple now, huh?

I take a step closer. My body feels jittery, my stomach still sick from nerves regarding the party tonight, but I don't care about any of that when I'm next to her. "I didn't invite you because you work for me, Cat."

"Oh."

The hair comes loose from behind her ear, so I move to brush it back again, my fingers dragging over her skin. Our kiss is fresh, the video replaying in my head on repeat. It was electric, buzzing like the energy between us now.

Cat's head tips back while she looks into my eyes. "I didn't mean it like that."

"How did you mean it, then?" I'm leaning closer. Her lips are so pink and plump and kissable. Probably salty from her soft pretzel. She licks her lips like she can read my mind, and a wave of attraction falls through me.

Then something warm and gooey splats on my forearm.

Cat yelps, jumping back.

I glance down at the black and white muck slipping over my skin. Yes, ladies and gentlemen. That is bird poop.

When I look up, I don't see the offender, but there are plenty of pigeons hanging out on the nearby lamppost and waddling around the sidewalk like they don't give a crap what anyone thinks about them.

Or maybe they give them too freely. Looking at my arm now, I'd say that's more apt.

Thank you, rat-bird, for killing the moment.

Cat's grin widens. She pulls the napkin from her pretzel and hands it to me.

"Thanks," I mutter, using it to wipe the bird poop as well as I can. I've done a decent job and ball the napkin up, tossing it in the trash.

"I didn't mean that, by the way," Cat says, chewing another bite of the pretzel when we keep walking. "I meant, like, how can I help you be more comfortable around your family? Any ex-girlfriends I should help you avoid or situations where I should step in? Though, judging by the way you and Celine act around each other, ex-girlfriends don't seem like a problem."

"No, they're more of an irritation than a problem."

She nods, half of the pretzel hanging from her hand. I can't even look at it or I feel like I might vomit.

Which is weird because, up until now, being around Cat has only eased my anxious feelings. Today, it doesn't seem to matter what she says or does. My queasy stomach and thudding pulse keep increasing with each passing hour.

But in regard to her being here? Even if I'd known I'd be fighting an extended anxiety attack all day, I would want her by my side. "Just so long as you understand I don't want you treating this like a task. You're invited to attend the party, Cat. You aren't there as an employee."

Her head dips side to side. "Invited by you."

"As my plus one," I finish, holding her gaze as best as I can while walking down Fifth Avenue. "Because I want to spend time with you." The words are out there between us. There's no taking them back. Maybe it's my discomfort that makes me reckless.

We've reached the street corner, the hotel visible now, but Cat doesn't see it. She's grown still. She watches me, trying to read between the lines. Is she picking up on the kiss and the photoshoot and the way I was looking at her in those ads? Or the way I'd taken her to the blackberry brambles and pulled her close? Or the way I almost kissed her before the bird assaulted me just now? Or how seeing her is the best part of my day *every day*?

Clearly, I've bypassed subtle entirely and embraced sending clear messages. I'm falling for this girl hard. Part of me wants her to see the raw emotion on my face and read it for what it means.

The other part of me is terrified she'll run away if she does.

When the silence stretches beyond comfortable, I give up and gesture across the street. "The Plaza Hotel."

Cat whips around, gasping quietly. "Kevin's hotel?"

"The very one."

Her smile is so wide as she takes in the large stone building and its columns. Green copper lines the windows and ornate gold streetlamps light the doorways. It screams early American elegance. "Can we go inside?"

"We can try."

We cross the street and mount the red carpeted steps. There is a sign near the front door permitting only hotel guests past that point, but I'm hoping previous guests count, too. From one hotel owner to another, I understand wanting to protect the privacy and comfort of their guests, but I'm crossing my fingers they'll be okay with us looking around.

The doorman opens the door, then looks us over. "Can I help you?"

"Noah Belacourt," I say, cringing internally that I'm using my name to get around their rules. I'm also a lot less formidable in shorts and a T-shirt than I am in a suit. At least the bird poop is pretty much cleaned up. "It's been a few years since I stayed here, so we aren't current guests. My friend was hoping to get a look inside. I understand if that is against protocol."

The doorman's face clears. He works in the hospitality industry, so it's no surprise he immediately recognizes my name. "Of course, Mr. Belacourt. Right this way."

Cat shoves her arm behind her back, hiding the pretzel.

"I can take that for you, miss, if you're finished?" he asks.

"Oh, thank you," she says meekly, handing him the pretzel. "That's so nice of you."

He carries it away, pinched between two fingers.

Cat presses close to me, bringing a cloud of something faintly sweet. Her shampoo, maybe? "I wasn't finished," she hisses.

"Why did you give it to him?"

She looks up, her shoulder still pressing into my side. "Yeah, right. Like I'm going to walk around the freaking Plaza Hotel with a half-eaten soft pretzel."

That pulls a chuckle from me. "We'll get you another one." Or maybe we'll go for bagels instead. She mentioned wanting to try them, and the Upper West Side houses the best bagel shop in the city.

"You've stayed here before? Why would you do that when you have Belacourt Hotels in the city?"

"My sister and I did our own Christmas a few years ago." I shrug. "We kind of had a *Home Alone* theme."

"Bree?" she asks.

My stomach clenches. "Olive. I've always been closest to her."

Cat nods distractedly, then looks up and gasps, taking in the whole foyer and its tall, gilt-edged ceiling lined with glittering chandeliers. "This is amazing." Her gaze swings to me, eyes full and warm. "Thank you."

"Anytime," I whisper. I mean it one hundred percent.

CHAPTER 26

Cat

THE PLAZA TOUR was followed by a pit stop for a warm bagel smothered in chive and onion cream cheese—for me, since Noah still wasn't hungry—and yes, it lived up to the hype. I bought extra bagels to take to Otto.

By the time we reach Noah's apartment, we have about thirty minutes to get dressed before we need to leave for the party. I put on the blush pink midi dress I got for a wedding earlier in the summer. It runs high in the front, sweeping across my collarbones and dipping in a V in the back, but the best part is how it fans out when I spin. The curls I put in my hair this morning have fallen, but they're like gentle waves now, which is okay. I pin back one side and look at my face from every angle to make sure I'm satisfied. This is when I need Holland to work her magic and give me a great hairstyle in under three minutes, but she's a little far.

At least I had thought to toss mascara in my purse, because the New York heat melted my face off today, and I need a little pep.

Noah hasn't come out of his room yet, so I take a minute to examine his apartment. It looks like a man's home, for sure. The camel-colored leather sofas sit on a navy rug surrounded by dark wood floors and a charcoal-colored statement wall. The TV is enormous, of course, and everything looks specifically chosen to give the feeling of a comfortable, calm place to relax. All blue and brown and dark wood and bright light. The windows are open, proving that we are way too high in the air right now.

I cross the room to check out the bookcases flanking the TV when Noah steps from his bedroom. "You ready?" he asks.

I glance back and almost run straight into the wall. Um, hello *GQ*, have you met Noah? He's in blue trousers, brown shoes, and a crisp white shirt open at the collar—effortless and cool. Nothing about him looks casual, but at the same time, he's so relaxed I would imagine he's just heading out to dinner with a friend. A super expensive fancy dinner on the Upper East Side, but still just dinner.

"Am I overdressed?" I squeak.

"No." His eyes run over me, making my muscles clench. "You look perfect."

I lift a bare foot and wiggle my toes. "Perfect, huh? Now I know you would say that regardless of what I put on."

His smile looks... different. It's soft, like melty chocolate left in a sunny window. I'm trapped in it. My body screams to step forward, closer to him, but my head bleats a warning cry.

Don't even go there, Cat. The last time I dated a wealthy guy, he dropped me the moment I wasn't convenient anymore. That's all I was to Jake back in high school—his island girl. Someone he didn't need anymore once he reached Yale. I'm Noah's island PA, and I would consider myself Noah's island friend now, too, but I will *never* be his island girl. My heart deserves better than that.

A nomad with three homes (that I know of) and offices in two different states and no permanent house on the island—his family home doesn't count—isn't going to stick around for a relationship. He's not looking for that.

So I break the stare, despite how much I want to fall into it instead, and move toward the couch to slip on my heels and fasten the thin strap at my ankle. "I'm ready when you are."

THE APOLLO LOUNGE is the bougiest club I've ever seen. It's tucked beneath a fancy hotel, down a secret side entrance. The room is long and narrow with orange-toned dim lighting. The wood-paneled, barrel-vaulted ceiling is lined with chic Edison bulb fixtures. A long copper bar runs along one side of the room and a continuous leather bench dotted with velvet pillows lines the other. There are groups of square velvet benches and leather chairs. The place screams luxury and so do the people filling it. My blush pink dress and white heels suddenly feel too light and airy for this sultry bar. I should have worn black.

Which is only further proved when we move deeper inside. All I see are dark sheath dresses and chic skintight numbers that probably cost more than I make in a year. They all blend into the atmosphere; even Noah in his navy pants and crisp white shirt fit in seamlessly. I stand out like a fur coat on the beach. In July.

Noah is tense. He holds himself straight, like his abs are contracted, his movements stiff. I can't tell if it's the light or something else, but his mouth is tight, his skin kind of pale.

It's probably just the lighting.

"You okay?" I ask quietly.

His eyes scan the crowd. "Just looking for my parents and hoping they aren't near each other."

Right. Because he has difficulty with conflict. My clothing choices don't even matter anymore. All I want is to protect him.

"Cat," Bree says, approaching us with her eyes bright and round. "We need to talk."

"Um, hey sis." Noah blocks Bree from dragging me away. "You aren't taking her into a den of wolves without me."

Bree rolls her eyes. "Then follow us." She slides her arm around mine and pulls me toward a group of sofas that aren't occupied yet.

"Your family parties aren't small," I say. There are so many people here. Despite watching episodes of *The Belacourts*, I don't recognize most of them.

"Not usually," she agrees, plopping down on a sofa and bringing me with her. It's a deep russet velvet that is just as silky as it looks.

Noah sits on my other side, kitty corner to me. "What's wrong, Bree?"

"Nothing." She tucks her chin, looking at me. "I took your advice."

Oh, crap. What was my advice again? There was something about Taylor Swift and taking charge. Was that *really* only yesterday? It feels like a week ago. "I didn't even know the situation," I start.

"You said the right thing. I'm guessing Noah told you—"

"He didn't tell me anything."

Bree glances at her brother with suspicion.

"I didn't," he confirms.

She looks at me earnestly, then lowers her voice so she's not overheard. "I had an opportunity to be part of a country music duo, and they decided to go another direction. The manager called when we were at the beach to tell me, and he wasn't nice, to put it lightly. He said all these things about my voice that sent me into a spiral."

"How awful."

"Well, yes. Alonzo tried to convince me to try again. Said all these things about it only being one man's opinions. Anyway, rejection is hard."

"It is hard." I've had my fair share. From Olive when I was a young teen to being ghosted by Jake in college to various things since. It's never easy to be told that, essentially, you are not enough.

The truth is, all of those situations—Bree's included—have nothing to do with personal worth and everything to do with the other person. That can be hard to remember in the moment, though."

"*So* hard," she says, driving the point home. "Anyway, when we talked before I left Sunset Harbor, you said something that stuck with me and I haven't been able to stop thinking about it."

"It's been like a day," I say, laughing. Though I'll admit it feels much longer.

"I still haven't been able to stop thinking about it. I decided I don't need a manager. I have Alonzo, and he gives me great advice. I'm going to make an EP on my own and put it out myself. I don't need a middleman. I can afford to produce a professional track, so why should I allow anyone else to tell me if I'm good enough?"

I have no idea what an EP is, but I'm guessing it's some type of album. "That is really empowering, Bree."

She straightens, her smile bright. "Right? I *feel* so empowered."

"Do you have songs already?" I ask.

"Yeah. More than I need. Now I just have to narrow them down and find someone to produce them."

"And a marketing guy," Noah says, his business acumen kicking into high gear. "Might be worth using what connections you have to get into podcasts and radio shows? You'll have a lot of work to do to make up for not having a label, Bree."

"I know," she says. "I'm okay with that. I'm Swifting this."

There's a beat of silence before Noah says, "Like Taylor? She's not a verb."

Bree looks at me. "Yes, she definitely is."

"Noah," a woman says, her hands jangling with diamond tennis bracelets and golden bangles. She's wearing a charcoal-colored dress that shimmers in the light, and she doesn't have nearly enough wrinkles for what might be her age. It's hard to tell. "Introduce me to your friend, darling."

"Tootsie," he says warmly, rising to kiss her cheek. *The aunt.* "This is my friend, Cat."

I stand beside him. "Happy birthday," I tell her. "Thank you for letting me join."

"We're always eager to meet Noah's friends," she says, giving me a wide smile of perfect teeth. Her hair is so big I wonder if it got blown out in Texas. "Tell me about yourself."

"Oh, there's not much to tell." I give a little chuckle. "I've known the Belacourts for a long time."

"She grew up on the island with us."

Tootsie nods slowly, looking between us with a flicker of interest. She glances behind me and raises her hand. "Nancy, over here, darling."

Nancy Belacourt. Noah's mom. She steps around the crowd and comes to stand beside her sister, giving me a long, slow once over. She's wearing a violet sheath dress and extremely tall heels. Her makeup is flawless and her mouth flat. "Hello."

"Mom," Noah says, leaning forward to kiss her cheek. "You know Catalina Keene."

She doesn't show a flicker of recognition, despite the fact that I've been cleaning her house for a few years now.

"Her uncle is Otto Keene," he continues.

"Who runs the B&B," she says, connecting the dots. "In Florida."

Can she not say *Sunset Harbor* or *the island*? Florida sounds so distant with her edge of distaste. I paste on a smile. "Yes. Otto's been running the B&B for thirty years."

"Not alone though, I think." Nancy screws her eyebrows together. "There was another couple before. Died in a tragic accident."

"My parents." I try to sound nonchalant but fail. It comes out like a raisin in a bowl of chocolate chips. I'm supposed to be keeping things not stressful for Noah, though, so it's time to alter the course of the conversation. "This lounge is incredible."

"Thank you," Tootsie says. "I've always liked to pretend I'm sneaking down here for an illegal drink in the twenties."

"You should have said," Nancy says. "You know how much I love a good theme."

"And how much Tom hates them."

Nancy tips her glass against her mouth. "Well, that goes without saying."

"Speaking of Dad," Noah says, "is he here?"

Nancy throws back the rest of her drink and looks away, frowning.

"Not yet," Tootsie says. "Go on and get this girl a drink." She leans in and lowers her voice. "I'll take care of your mother."

She shoos us away, so Noah slides a hand behind my back, his fingers on my bare skin, and directs me to the bar.

He leans against the counter, waiting for a bartender, and I climb onto a stool. We're almost eye to eye now. I smile at him. "You're doing great so far. I'm starting to think you didn't need me at all."

"I need you." His gaze is hot on my face.

I look away.

"What are you drinking tonight?" he asks.

"Club soda with lime. It's my go-to. At least while the night is young. You?"

"Probably ginger ale."

"Hard drinker."

"Tonight I'm just trying not to puke," he mutters. "My stomach is in knots."

"Are you that nervous?" I reach for his arm, tugging until he steps a little closer. His face is still looking tight and pale, but again, I don't know if that's just the lighting. "What can I do?"

"You're doing it," he whispers.

"I'm literally just sitting here."

"You're *here*. You're with me." His eyes are so hard I can't look away. "Trust me. You're doing it."

"Okay." *I need you.*

The bartender approaches so Noah orders our drinks.

"Noah!" a guy calls, forcing him to turn around.

Noah lights up. "I didn't think you'd make it."

I get a good look at the guy and nearly fall off my stool. Here in the flesh is one of the biggest Hollywood stars in America. He's British, naturally, with a super smooth, deep accent and a million-dollar smile. Dash Malone. Olive's boyfriend.

Of course, Olive is standing right beside him.

All of a sudden, my club soda with lime is looking extra interesting.

"Cat," she says, coming right up to me. Is this a calculated play because she doesn't think I'll be rude and ignore her in front of her ultra famous boyfriend or the rest of Noah's family?

She's right, but that's not why I give her my full attention. I do that because of Noah and my strong desire not to heap more trouble on his plate. If he can't stand conflict, then I'll do my best to be as conflict-free as possible. Even if I have to fake it.

"Olive," I say, trying to give her a smile. I probably look like I'm chewing on metal.

She looks at me for a beat. "Can we talk?"

CHAPTER 27

Cat

GREAT. This whole Olive-begs-for-forgiveness thing is going to happen *now*? In a bunker that has been repurposed as a smooth twenties speakeasy-type club and full of her friends and family? That better be her objective, at least. I don't expect her to grovel, but a little begging wouldn't go awry. The air is thick with fresh lime and Chanel No. 5 as a group of older women press together on the sofa nearest us.

Olive watches me expectantly. I can see why her shows have so much drama. Choosing public parties to hash out issues must make for good television. She could have pulled me aside any time during the last week on the island, or even when we traveled to New York. But those options wouldn't be nearly as dramatic as doing it now when we're supposed to be celebrating her aunt.

Are there hidden cameras here? Or is Olive just pre-programmed for creating a scene?

I look at Noah, who's watching us nervously, then back at Olive. I won't let this become a scene, and I certainly won't be the reason Noah stresses *even* more. "Sure."

Olive almost sags in relief. She starts walking toward a shadowy, empty corner. I pick up my drink and follow her.

Once we're away from the men, I lower myself on the seat beside hers, clutching my glass like a lifeline.

Her dress is black, matte, and low cut. She embodies class, even with her platinum blonde hair that's obviously from a salon and fake eyelashes. "I'm not going to try and butter you up or anything like that, because I know how much you despise me. With good reason, I know." She takes a sip from her wine glass and shakes her hair from her face. "I don't have an excuse for my behavior toward you when we were kids. I'm sure you're looking for a reason, but I don't have one to give you. No one died in eighth grade or hurt me or treated me unfairly or anything like that." She gives a little shrug that is not nearly enough to feel any sort of catharsis here.

Something about her dismissing her behavior as unexplainable heats my blood. I'm the one who doesn't want a scene here, though, so I force my voice to remain steady. "You just woke up one day and decided it was nice and sunny and the weather was perfect for ruining someone's life?"

"No." She takes another drink, wrestling with herself. "I was jealous, okay?"

I scoff, grateful I didn't take a sip too, because it would have sprayed all over her.

"I was," she insists, putting her glass down on the low table in front of our sofa. "You had this perfect life, and I didn't. When I saw how my brother was into you, it scared me, okay? He was my closest friend and only ally in my house. Zoey was always doing her own thing and Bree was too young to get it. It was just me and Noah against the world."

As much as I don't want to understand, what she is describing sounds a lot like me and Otto.

"If he had started dating you, then I would have lost him," she says. "I needed to put a stop to it. I'm not saying it's right. It's just how I felt then."

"Back up." My brain couldn't wrap around her logic. "Noah liked me, and that's why you pushed me away? No—" I shook my head. "You thought my life was *perfect*?" Had Olive missed the memo about my parents dying a few years before all this went down? I'd been a mess, so depressed I was put on medication and treated like a glass doll. By eighth grade I was feeling normal again, but it was a heavy road to reach that point.

"Your uncle *adored* you, Cat. He treated you so well, and it made me so jealous. My parents pretty much ignored me all the time, and their fighting was out of control."

My heart pangs, thinking of middle school Noah in a storm of arguments. Is that where his discomfort with conflict comes from?

"They had always fought," she clarifies, "but it got pretty bad around then. I had to watch your uncle respect you and love you and want to be around you, which was hard. When Noah wanted you too, I just couldn't take it."

"You chose the wrong way to handle it."

"Yes. I did." She scoots a little closer like she's going to reach for me, then thinks better of it. "Which is why I'm sorry. I'm *so* sorry. I wish I could take it back. I wish I would have just told you how I felt and dealt with it. But I wasn't in therapy then. I didn't have examples of healthy conflict management in my life, and I didn't know what to do except lash out." She heaves a sigh. "You don't have to forgive me, but I want you to know how deeply I regret being that monster to you."

Great. There goes my heart, reaching out for her. In a way, it's kind of comforting to know I was right in one regard—that she'd acted out because she's entitled and selfish. It tracks with the way I've been imagining her all these years. But that feeling is gone as quickly as it arrives because she's right. Otto does adore and respect me. His attention became much more localized after my parents died, but he has been there for me, loving me like a dad since day one.

I'm sure her parents love her too, but her home life can't compare to mine. If I had grown up in a toxic environment, would I be the person I am now? Maybe she got the mansion and the huge resort and the private beach and her sweet sixteenth in Cabo with her friends, but I had Otto.

This isn't even a case of both of us finding the grass to be greener on the other side, because I never wanted her life. Some of her money, maybe, but never her life.

The most satisfying thing is Olive calling herself a monster. She *was* one. I don't really think she is anymore.

She's waiting, watching me for a reaction.

"I tried to forgive you a few years ago," I say, "but I think it was more like pushing it under the rug. My uncle got sick, and some of the things I was hanging onto from my past just stopped mattering to me at all, so I shoved them aside. You haven't been this looming, evil thing in my life. I feel like you should know that. I've never wanted to be around you, but your bullying didn't stop me from living."

She nods.

"But, all that said, I realized I never actually let it go when you showed up in Sunset Harbor and I had a physical reaction. I felt sick when I saw you, like I was thirteen again. Anyway, it proved I was still holding onto it. I guess it felt unresolved to me because I wanted justice for the way you acted."

"You want justice?" she asks, straightening. What is she expecting? Me to dump a bucket of pig's blood on her head? This isn't *Carrie*.

Hearing her accept the way she acted and apologize is enough for me. I don't expect us to ever be friends, but I also don't feel the weight of our past hovering anymore.

"I think we're good now. I guess I just wanted an apology."

"I tried—"

"Where it felt *real*. Authentic. This felt authentic, Olive."

"Okay."

I can tell she wants to say more, and I'm glad she doesn't. I stand up, taking a drink of my bubbly lime water. Now that the awkwardness is behind us, my whole body is humming with the vague realization that her brother was into me back in middle school. Like, *what?* He was a grade above us and so quiet then. I remember him hanging out with Olive and me once or twice, but he kept to himself mostly.

"Olive? When you said Noah was into me, what did you mean?"

She goes still, her fingers turning white against her wine glass. "He hasn't told you?"

"I don't know. What is there to tell me?"

Olive takes a long pull from her glass, then lowers it, shaking her head. "It's not coming from me, Cat. It has to come from him."

"If it's in the past, does it really matter?"

She lifts her eyebrows. "Our entire conversation has been about the past, hasn't it?"

"Touché."

"If you want to know more, just ask him," Olive says before heading back toward Dash and Noah and leaving me with questions.

The music has been turned up during the course of our conversation, but I didn't notice it until now, or how the crowd had multiplied. People are chatting, drinking, dancing. But there's a clear path to Noah, where he leans against the bar talking to Dash Malone. His eyes flick up, pinning me in place. He looks at me like I'm the most important person in this room.

It starts a warmth in my belly that fizzles and spreads, like my feelings for him have multiplied to fill the space left behind when I released my anger and hurt regarding Olive.

Maybe Noah isn't going to stick around, and I still refuse to be his island girl, keeping him occupied until he gets back to his mainland girl or his Manhattan girl. Except, we're in Manhattan now and he's only looking at me. Knowing Noah, that's not really how he would operate anyway.

Maybe, just this once, I can put aside my concerns about

longevity and just enjoy this night with him. Once we're back in Sunset Harbor, I'll protect myself again.

For now, I'll pretend I'm his.

Noah

IT IS SO hard to breathe in here. I feel like I'm going to vomit. Dash is talking to me about the latest update to *Warhammer 40k*, but I can't even focus on that. Olive has been talking to Cat, and I'm not over there protecting her.

Okay, it looks like the conversation is over. Olive is walking back over here. It didn't come to yelling or blows or anything. It looked impassioned for a hot second there, but now they both seem cool and collected. That's a good sign, right? Or will Cat rue the day she ever agreed to work for me and come on this trip and become part of my life?

Because she is part of my life now, and I'm not planning on letting her go.

Olive slides under Dash's arm, sipping her wine. He says something else to me, but there's ringing in my ears, and I can't really focus on anything except Cat, who is looking at me from across the room. Is she okay? Does she need space, or should I go to her?

Man, my head is throbbing. When did that happen?

"Noah?"

I glance back at Dash, who looks amused. "Yeah?"

"I asked if you made any progress on your game."

My game. The one I've been keeping from Cat so she doesn't see how ridiculous I am. I look back to find her coming our way. "Some, yeah. I'll send it to you."

He claps me on the back. "You're the best. I had some ideas—"

"Let's get together and talk it over once you've played. I think some of it will change after you see Jason's latest updates."

Dash goes still, looking confused. I don't know if I've ever cut him off before, but I need this conversation to die now. Cat is almost here.

"He gets a little high-strung at family parties," Olive says, trying to explain my rudeness.

Dash relaxes. "Don't we all?"

I imagine Cat doesn't. Her family probably eases her stress, not adds to it. That's how Otto is, certainly.

"Hey," Cat says, sidling up right beside me, holding her empty glass.

"Want another drink?"

She puts the glass on the counter and shakes her head. "I'm good."

I look between her and Olive, waiting to see what happens, for the awkward and thick discomfort to take over. For one of them to roll their eyes and walk away. I've been around for years and years of sister/girl drama so I know it couldn't have wrapped up so easily.

Cat can probably sense what I'm feeling. She slips her hand around my arm. "We're good now."

"You and Olive?" I say, because I need some confirmation here, and it's a little hard to believe.

She shrugs. "We talked it out."

I look at Olive, and she nods. "It's over."

It can't really be that easy, right? Not that this was easy. It was years in the making and a week of discomfort leading up to now.

Someone taps a mic. We all swing our attention to the lone man holding a microphone and grinning like someone handed him the keys to a new Lamborghini. He's in a suit with an open collar, his silver hair combed back at the sides—Dad.

"I just wanted to take a second to thank everyone for coming out to celebrate my beautiful sister-in-law, Tootsie."

Cheers and clapping fill the room. Dad's gleaming smile is wide. He puts an arm out and a lanky blonde steps under it, a woman who really can't be much older than Bree. Okay, now I really might vomit. She is for sure younger than me.

"Kara and I are glad to see so many friendly faces," he says, beaming down at the woman under his arm.

Kara must be the girlfriend and is very new here. She doesn't know these faces. Who is Dad trying to fool? Himself, probably.

He unhooks his arm from around her and raises his drink. "So drink up—the tab's on me tonight—and put your glasses in the air for Manhattan's most unforgettable woman, Tootsie!"

The cheers drown out Mom's angry footsteps as she crosses the room and yanks the microphone from Dad's hand. She steps away from him, her back to Kara entirely. A lock of brown hair loosens from her twist and falls forward. She brushes it aside smoothly. "As the host of this party, I would like to make it clear that—as was stated on the invitation—we already had an open bar. So heroic gestures to prove manliness are not necessary tonight." She gives a little laugh that matches the awkward chuckles around the room.

My pulse thrums faster. My stomach is nauseous. My head pounds.

"Hey," Cat says, her fingers gripping my side. "What's wrong?"

I shake my head. Sweat has broken out on my hairline, and my vision is swimming. My chest is tight. Can you have a heart attack from anxiety? Is that a thing, or just something they put in movies?

Mom is still talking into the mic. I've stopped listening, but judging by the awkward silence and the rising music, someone is trying to signal her to stop, which is never a good sign.

"Talk to me," Cat says, her attention solely on me. "Should we leave? Let's go."

I don't want to make a scene. Last time I walked out of the room when I felt like this, it ended with my board of directors saying I appeared mentally unstable and perhaps not fit to do my job. What will my family think if I run away now?

"Which means it's probably a great time to tell you all that we are giving ourselves a clean break," Mom continues, yelling into the mic to be heard over the music. "That's obvious with teenage Barbie on Tom's arm, I think, isn't it?" She cackles, and the music gets even louder.

"Is your mom drunk?" Cat asks.

I look at her—into her concerned blue eyes, her bent blonde eyebrows and pinched lips. "Probably," I say, searching the sea of blurry faces for a way out. It's becoming increasingly difficult to breathe.

"We're selling everything, so the house in Park City is up for grabs, Jimmy," Mom says, pointing to my dad's friend somewhere in the crowd. "Linda, I know you've always eyed our Sunset Harbor house. You want it? It's yours."

What? I look at Olive, who's gaping at Mom. Her gaze swings around the room, probably to Bree, then finds me again. Did anyone know about this? Has Mom told Zoey? I don't think my older sister has even arrived yet.

Oh, she's here. Zoey is making her way through the people, directly for Mom. Her dark hair is styled back, slicked away from her face and gathered behind her head in a curly explosion. She takes the mic. "No one is selling anything tonight. Grab an extra drink and enjoy the party, everyone. Happy birthday, Tootsie!"

The room is overdoing it with the applause, probably to drown out my mother's embarrassing monologue. Zoey ushers her to the bar—probably not the best idea. My older sister catches my eye, widening hers like she's trying to say *what the heck was that?*

But I can't respond. I can't bring myself to cross the ten barstools between us, either, because I think if I talk to my mom right now and have to hear her complaints about Dad's girlfriend, I'll lose it completely.

Noise pushes against me. My stomach rolls.

Oh, no.

I think—

Cat grabs my hand, yanking me through the crowd. She doesn't ask, she just pulls, and I let her. Someone says my name as we pass, but I keep my gaze on the back of Cat's head while she weaves through the people and breaks out to the other side. The door is just ahead. I can make it.

My stomach rolls again. I'm not gonna make it.

Cat's hand tightens, and she moves faster, getting me outside and away from the party. We push through the door and climb the steps up to the sidewalk, the streetlamps and taxis filling the street with light. Warm air hits me like a stuffy wall, and my stomach rolls again.

I pull my hand free, jog toward the edge of the building, and vomit.

So long, dignity.

CHAPTER 28

Cat

MATEO IS A SAINT. Three minutes after Noah threw up on the side of the building, he threw up again. His skin was clammy, his eyes glazed, his attention gone. I've never seen a face pale as quickly as Noah's did at the bar. I'm glad Mateo and I exchanged contacts weeks ago, because without him, I'd have to go back inside and beg one of the Belacourt babes to help me. He texts me Noah's address, the door code to get inside, and his favorite foods while he's sick. I'm not sure if this is anxiety or the flu, but there is definitely something wrong.

We make it back to his apartment when a text rolls into my phone. I push Noah into his bathroom. "Shower and get in bed."

"Okay," he says weakly.

I pull out my phone and go back to the living room.

MATEO
I assume you aren't flying home tonight. Should I reschedule the flight?

CAT
Probably a safe assumption

Noah had mentioned that this Manhattan apartment is the place that feels the most like home to him, so I'm guessing it's where he'd want to be sick if he had a choice.

MATEO
Let me know when you're ready to come home. I'll arrange everything.

CAT
Have I told you lately that I love you?

MATEO
I'm taken, but thanks

CAT

So, this hot and sour soup you mentioned?

MATEO
Any Chinese restaurant will do. He loves them all.

You probably have your hands full, so I can get some delivered.

I'll get an Instacart order in, too.

CAT
You order the soup, I'll take care of everything else

MATEO
You got it.

By the time I'm finished filling an Instacart with all the things on Mateo's list and a few on mine, Noah is out of the shower. I give him plenty of time before knocking on his door.

He's laying in bed in the dark. I carry in the largest bowl I could find in the kitchen and sit on the edge of his bed, the bowl in my lap. "How are you feeling?"

"Dead."

Certainly explains his pale skin earlier. "Is this body sickness or anxiety sickness?"

"Both, I think." His eyes open lazily and sweep over me, half-glazed.

I push the bowl toward him. "I brought this in case you can't make it to the toilet. You sleep. I'll be around if you need anything."

"Cat." He presses his fingers to my wrist. "You can still take the plane home. It can come back for me."

"I'm good, Belacourt. Don't worry about me. Just sleep."

He looks like he's about to argue, so I lean forward and tuck his blankets in, then brush his damp hair from his forehead.

"Cat." After a full day of anxiety, I'm guessing his body is shutting down.

"I'm here. Don't worry. Just go to sleep."

He listens, or he gives in. Either way, his breathing grows deep and even pretty quickly. I gently slip off his bed and sneak out of the room, closing the door behind me.

I cross to the window and look out over the layers and rows of buildings stacked up on each other, their windows lighting white and yellow against the dark sky. Otto needs a warning, and I have the sneaking suspicion he's not going to be happy, so I pull my phone out and call him. When he answers, there's noise behind him, like he's at a party or a restaurant or something.

"Otto? What are you up to?"

"Just, you know, stuff. What's up, Cat?"

That felt like avoidance. "You know that road trip I went on with Noah and his sister today? We ended up flying, so I'm in New York City right now."

He's quiet for a second. "For real?"

"Yeah, for real. But here's the deal: we left his aunt's birthday party early because Noah got sick. He's in bed now, and I think he might have the flu."

"And he's your ride home."

"Well, yes, but it's more than that. I can't abandon the guy."

"Cat," he says in a warning tone.

"What would you do differently?" I ask.

Otto's silent. He's moving, then a door shuts, leaving the noise behind him. "Nothing, I guess. You can't abandon him. I get that."

"I don't know when I'll be home to help at the B&B. We have the Morgans staying there now and another family is checking in Monday. Should I find someone—"

"I can cover for a few days, Kit Kat. Just do what you need to do, and we'll be here when you get home."

"You're going to turn over the rooms?"

"I've done it before," he says defensively. "You aren't the only person who can make a bed."

"I know. I just hate making you do that."

"You aren't." He sighs. "Has his sister been around?"

"Olive? Actually, we talked tonight. Put the past behind us."

He's quiet. I'm sure he's reliving the moment in the principal's office with Olive's parents and how little they did to stop their daughter from being a monster. "You okay?" he says softly.

My eyes are dry and my contacts need to be taken out, but I know that's not what he means. Good thing I put my backup glasses in my bag when I packed for the party. There's not enough clothing in there for a few days in NYC, so I might start to smell, but at least I'll be able to see.

The fact that I'm thinking about my dried-up contacts instead of the way Olive used to make me feel is proof that our conversation was good for me, even though I only agreed to it for Noah's benefit. "Yeah, I really am. It was good to make peace. Freeing."

"As long as she means it."

"She's grown up, Otto. I think she means it. Either way, I feel better, and that counts for something."

"It counts for everything." He gives a chuckle. "You know, if your boss is footing the bill for a trip to the city, you should take advantage of being there."

Your boss. He doesn't realize how much more Noah has grown to become for me. "I'm not going to use him."

"Not like that." He scoffs. "Geez, Cat. You know me. I just mean you should use the time to see a few things."

"Like hit up some cool hip clubs?"

He laughs. "No. Don't meet a guy there. Then he'll take you away from me."

"No one can do that."

"True. You'll never leave this island."

"You'd have to drag me away."

"Well, I won't be doing that." There's someone talking behind Otto, and he swears. "Got to go, Kit Kat. Love you, and I'll see you when I see you. Don't worry about us."

He hangs up before I can say anything back, like who is *us*? That's bizarre and suspicious. I pull up my Find My Friends app and check his location. Weird. It looks like he's at the Belacourt Resort, which means he must be golfing. After spending the last month with Noah and some time with Bree, my animosity toward their resort and their name in general has lessened significantly. I think Otto's has, too. But it's still weird to see him there after so many years of keeping his distance.

Why wouldn't he just tell me what he was doing? Unless he's trying to hide something... or someone?

The sound of retching comes from Noah's door. Okay, he's definitely sick. I put my phone away and head in to help him.

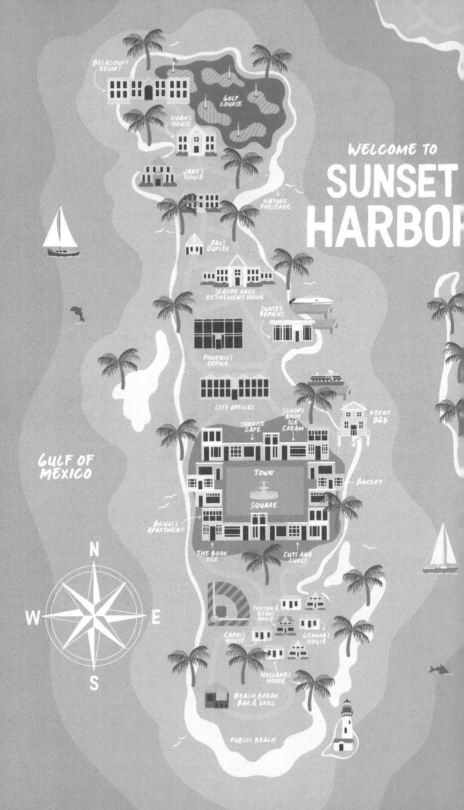

CHAPTER 29

Noah

I WAKE in the middle of the night. I know that because it's dark and silent—as quiet as it gets in the city, at least. I've lost count of how many times I've been sick, or how low I've felt every time Cat has come in to help me. She's washed my bowl and changed my sheets and now I can never face her again. I know it's been at least an entire night and a day and then a night again, because I've been hazily awake off and on.

There's also the snippets of memory floating around in my head. Moments when I think I told Cat that I love her and never want her to leave. I was sitting on the bathroom floor, my head over the toilet, and she was pressing her cool fingers to my forehead.

Hopefully that was a dream.

Now I'm ravenous and alert. I rub my eyes and sit up, growing completely still when I notice Cat in the chair in the corner of my room. She's curled up with a blanket, her feet on the ottoman and her head resting on the armrest. There is no way that's more comfortable than the couch. I need to fix this.

As I slowly sit up and wait for my head to stop spinning, I realize I'm in no shape to carry her anywhere. My hands are braced on the edge of the mattress, my head hanging down while I wait for my blood to even out.

"Noah?"

My body constricts. Has she said my name before now? It has a crazy effect on me, but I do my best not to react.

She rises, leaving the blanket and picking up black-rimmed glasses, sliding them on before coming to stand in front of me. She's in one of my T-shirts, so long on her it hits her mid-thigh, and I'm struggling to swallow. I've never been more attracted to anyone in my entire life.

"You okay?" she asks, her voice low from sleep.

I lift my head. "I'm actually hungry."

"That's a great sign," she says. "Does hot and sour soup sound good?"

I can only seem to gaze up at her like the angel that she is. I want to pull her close, so I grip the mattress harder. "How did you know?"

"Mateo."

"Of course."

She turns away. "I'll go heat it up."

I reach for her hand, tugging. I don't have much strength right now, so I know she's willing when she turns back to face me. "You should go to sleep," I say, admiring the glasses and her rumpled hair.

"I can heat some soup first."

"So can I. You've done enough."

"It's just soup."

"It's the middle of the night."

"It's like eleven."

"What?" I look at the clock, and indeed, it isn't even midnight yet.

"You slept for almost twenty-four hours. It makes sense you'd be hungry now."

I'm still holding her wrist, my fingers running along her velvety skin. I thought my pride wouldn't allow me to face her again, but it's surprisingly easy. She makes everything feel that way. "It's too much. Everything you've done is too much. I can't believe you stuck around."

She grows still. "I wouldn't abandon you."

"Clearly."

"Listen." She frees her hand to brace my shoulders, standing between my legs. The hem of her shirt—*my* shirt—brushes against my knees. "It's really not a big deal. I would stay up with anyone I care about."

She cares about me.

"As for all the other stuff—"

I groan.

"—I've seen so much worse. I'm a maid, remember? I don't get grossed out very easily."

"That's not as comforting as you think it is. I've had my eye on you for a long time, Cat Keene. Now that we're friends, this isn't really how I want you to see me."

"Tough. It's over now and, like I said, I'm not going anywhere."

"You mean I get to keep you?"

She laughs. "You don't really want that. You're still delirious."

"Maybe a little. But I know how I feel about you." I'm feeling reckless and heady and will probably regret this tomorrow. "If you feel even remotely the same way, I don't want to pretend anymore."

Her fingers dig into my shoulders. "Why were you pretending?"

"Because you work for me. I'm your boss. It's not appropriate to try and date you while I'm paying you so much."

She freezes. "What do you mean?"

"When you're finished earning the money you need for Otto, then I can ask you out."

"So it was just a charity thing," she says, and her voice has a weird quality.

"No."

"Why else would you say you can't date me while you're paying me *so much*?" She drops her hands and steps back. "Not just paying me, but *overpaying* me? Seriously, Belacourt?"

Not Noah. *Belacourt* again. It feels like a demotion. "Just let me write a check, Cat. Let me help you so you don't have to worry anymore."

She takes another step back.

I immediately regret the words. I'm not thinking straight.

"It's late," she says, "and you're hungry. I'm going to heat your soup." Her words are clipped, a message to quit talking while I'm ahead. I give her five minutes in the kitchen before I follow her in there and sit at the counter. She gives me a steaming bowl of hot and sour soup—my comfort food—and a glass of Gatorade.

"Just do what you can," she says.

I take one bite and my stomach doesn't want it, so I chase it with Gatorade and wait.

"Want toast?" she asks.

"I don't have bread."

"I ordered some." She moves into the kitchen and makes me toast.

The whole time I feel like we're hanging out in limbo, where she's upset but still feels like she has to care for me.

I don't like this, so I stand up and circle the island to reach her. "Cat." I take her face in my hands and wait until she looks at me. "I said something stupid, okay? Can we please forget it?"

"It's not what you said," she says weakly. "It's how you feel. You can't just wave your checkbook and erase my problems."

"Actually, I can. For this problem, at least. I haven't tried to, because I respect you too much and it's obviously not what you want. But I can."

She looks at me but says nothing.

"The only reason I haven't offered before is because I knew

you'd say no. I also figured it meant you wouldn't work for me anymore and, selfishly, I've really enjoyed having you around."

Cat steps out of reach and my hands fall to my sides. "Is this all just charity? You hired me to pay Otto's bill and create jobs to keep me busy? Did you ever even need an island PA?"

"You've earned that money, Cat. Don't diminish the work you've done. You were crucial to the success of the ad campaign. Without you, we wouldn't have gotten such incredible shots. But before that, even, you were imperative to the creative process."

"You were humoring me."

"You think that?" Now I'm annoyed. "I asked for all those opinions because I value your feedback. You're smart, you're our demographic, you're a consumer. The things you said were useful and relevant. You were immensely helpful."

She closes her eyes.

Time for all or nothing. "I have liked you for a long time, Cat."

"You mentioned that last night."

"Crap. That wasn't a dream?"

She gives me a soft smile, filling my chest with hope. "No. Apparently, you've been into me since middle school. Caused a lot of problems with that crush, Belacourt."

"I would have kept it to myself had I known."

"Even now?"

"No." I swallow, my throat going dry. "Now I want you to know I have a crush on you." I step forward, but my head is light.

Cat considers me for a beat. "Then show me your secret room."

"What?"

"The secret room. The Vikings you hid on your computer. Give me a reason to believe you can trust me. You didn't tell me

Bree's secret, which makes me think you're good at boundaries, but I also need to know you trust me."

My heart thuds. Cat stuck around even after I made a fool of myself at Tootsie's party with an anxiety attack and the flu. She has stuck around despite being angry that I want to pay away all her problems. If she hasn't left for those reasons, maybe this won't turn her away either.

At some point I have to take a leap of faith.

"Okay. Follow me." I lead her to the bookcase to the right of my TV and find the fake *The Lord of the Rings* book. "This is the key. It's a dead giveaway, since it's a trilogy and this isn't thick enough to hold all three books."

"Not a dead giveaway to all of us," she mutters.

I pull the book, which is really a lever, and the bookcase swings open. Inside, I slide up the dimmer until there's enough light to see into my little den.

"You're serious," she says, stepping inside. Her eyes run over the shelves of Funko Pops and LEGO creations of Hogwarts Castle and Rivendell. Her gaze moves to Aragorn's sword hanging above my computer, then the framed *The Lord of the Rings* movie posters and the enormous map of Middle Earth on one wall. The Death Star hangs from the ceiling, the Millenium Falcon a few feet away. There's a glass frame holding Viking arrowheads I bought in the UK a few years ago. It's a nerd's treasure trove.

I try to see it all through her eyes, and I'm guessing most of it doesn't make sense.

"Where's the Viking thing?" she asks.

I sigh, pulling out the desk chair and powering on the computer. It takes a minute to pull up the game, and I'm grateful to sit. When it comes on the screen, I swivel to face her. "A few guys at work are helping me create a game."

"Like Vikings meet wizards?"

"Kind of." I make my character walk through a tavern and

then through a village, showing her some of the graphics. "It's at the beginning stages. I'm hoping to build that department once the dating app is launched. Maybe open an office entirely for game development." I swivel in the chair to face her, nervous about what I'm going to find. Cat has always been cool. She's the kind of effortless who does what she wants and wears what she wants and always seems so comfortable in her own skin.

I couldn't be that person in a million years. I overthink everything. Stress is my longtime companion. It's a turn-off for a lot of women, but they put up with me for the other perks, like Celine can attest to. My name comes with money, spotlight, entrance into places otherwise closed to the public—like Kevin McCallister's hotel.

"This is really cool," she says, her eyes dancing around the room again, taking in the minor details—"speak friend and enter" painted in Elvish above the interior of the door or the glass-encased pipe Gandalf would have used in filming if his had broken. It might be a backup, but it's still the real deal.

And, no, I will not say how much I spent on it at auction.

Is Cat pulling my leg? I look up at her, and her eyes are jumping between my computer screens before slowly tracking each of the things in the small room.

When her gaze falls back on me, it's warm. "I love this."

"Do you know what any of it is?" I ask.

"No, but it's still cool." She crosses to the map of Middle Earth and peers closely.

"*The Lord of the Rings*," I tell her.

"You really like that one, don't you?"

"It's some of the best storytelling of all time."

"Hmm. You're saying it's better than *The Shop Around the Corner*? Or *You've Got Mail*?"

I stare at her.

"What? Those are romantic comedy at its finest," she says,

perching on the edge of my desk. "I tell you what. We watch your favorite movie—"

"Trilogy."

"—then we'll watch mine. After that, we can debate."

"It's apples to oranges."

"It's your favorites to mine."

She's not running away. I told her I like her, showed her who I really am, and she's *not running away*. "Should we start now?"

Cat gazes down into my eyes like she's reading my soul. "Yes."

It feels like she's agreeing to more than just a movie marathon. I'm waiting for the penny to drop, for Cat to laugh at my interests like my sisters do or some of my ex-girlfriends have. Celine doesn't even know this room exists, because we never reached the point where I could bare my soul to her. I'm waiting for Cat to tell me it's a cute pastime but bores her. I'm waiting for things to go wrong.

But they don't.

We leave the secret room and go to the kitchen to retrieve my cold toast. "I like the glasses," I tell her.

"I know."

My face cringes. "You mean I already said something earlier?"

"I believe your exact words were something about a sexy librarian."

I shove the toast in my mouth so I don't have to come up with a reply. I'm starting to worry about what other things I revealed while in the throes of delirium, but at this point, there's nothing I wouldn't want Cat to know about me. Apparently, I've confessed my love for her and her sexy glasses, showed her I'm a professional nerd, and she's still here.

"Olive mentioned your parents have fought for a long time," she says, leaning her hip against the kitchen counter.

"Most of our lives."

"But they waited so long to divorce."

"I'm guessing they considered their relationship as more of a partnership than a marriage. When the partnership outlived its usefulness, they dissolved the company."

"The company being their marriage?"

I shrug, taking another bite of toast and waiting to see how it feels on my raw, empty stomach.

"Was she serious about selling the Sunset Harbor house?" Cat won't look me in the eye.

The toast hovers just before my mouth. I'd forgotten about that. I put it down on the plate. "I don't know."

"So you don't know if you'll have a home on the island anymore?"

This hurts her. I can see that right away, but what I don't understand is *why*. "I think it will hurt my sisters more than me. When I'm around, I usually stay at the resort anyway."

"Right. When you're around."

"What's wrong, Cat?"

She looks ready to say something, but then looks away and smiles. "Should we start the first movie? I'm wide awake now."

"There's a projector in my room if you don't mind lounging on my bed. I promise I'll stay on my side."

"That sounds amazing," she says, heading for my room.

I think I just won the lottery.

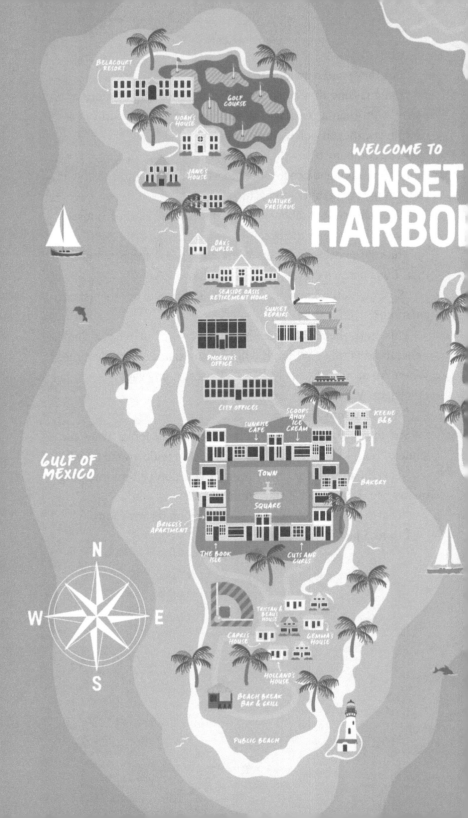

CHAPTER 30

Cat

PRETENDING I'm Noah's only lasted a few hours, then it became too painful to bear. Just when I had entered the bargaining phase, convincing myself that maybe we could make it work despite his off-island home and constant work and travel, he drops the bombshell reminder that he *doesn't* live on the island. He doesn't even care that his family house is being sold.

It felt like a personal affront. I tried to shove that thought away while we watched his favorite movies in his massive bed. The state-of-the-art projector made it feel like a movie theater. Noah's room is much more comfortable though, which is why I'm totally okay watching *The Lord of the Rings* like this.

Or at least the first one. I fell asleep. On his bed. Beside him. Unintentionally.

It was like two in the morning though, so can you blame me?

When we woke up the next morning, Noah was still in his I-can't-leave-the-house-in-case-I-need-a-bathroom phase of the flu. We hunkered down and spent the entire day watching the rest of the trilogy after I called Mrs. Finnigan to reschedule her cleaning. We didn't have time to fit in my romcoms before we had to leave for the airport, but I'm okay with that.

His movies were not at all what I was expecting. There were a lot of times he had to pause the movie and explain relationships or what was going on. Honestly, between you and me, I was here for it.

When Sam and Frodo finally made it to Mordor, I was *invested*. It wasn't just a bunch of elves and dwarfs dancing around, fighting each other. The themes were deep and meaningful and rewarding.

But things between me and Noah? They've felt easy and effortless and it took all I had not to climb into his arms to show him how I feel. I've exercised restraint while we watched movies and drove to the airport and during the entire flight home.

I deserve a medal.

We landed back in Florida and took his speedboat to the dock outside his resort.

It's warm and balmy as Noah steers us into place at the dock. The island looms in the darkness, and I feel peace as we come to a stop in front of it. We're home.

"Are you okay being on a boat like this?" he asks.

"I can do boats; I just struggle with swimming. I guess I feel protected in a boat. Who knows why my psyche can handle one and not the other."

"Probably has something to do with your parents not being in a boat when it happened, right?"

"Probably." I take my glasses off and clean the water from each lens with my shirt.

"Have you ever tried to overcome your fear?" he asks, getting up to tie us to the dock.

"A few times." We're stopped now, our boat rocking gently with the waves. "Otto was bent on fixing the issue when I was like fifteen. He wanted me to be his surfing buddy. I agreed to try, but I had a full-on panic attack when we got out in the water, so he stopped pushing it."

"Do you wish you'd kept pursuing it?" he asks, wrapping the rope around the cleat.

"Sometimes, when it's really hot, I just want to jump in the ocean. But honestly? It's not a make it or break it thing in my life. I know my limits. I'm not holding on to residual trauma with my parents' deaths. I'm just afraid of the ocean's whims and fancies, and that doesn't make me less of a person. I've made my peace with not being perfect, I guess." I spread my arms out. "This is who I am. Take it or leave it."

He stares at me in awe and fascination. "I wish I could be more like you."

My arms drop. "How? Accepting your shortcomings?"

"No. Not looking at them like they're shortcomings."

He's right. That's how I shifted my thinking, and it's never bothered me since. I stand up, moving toward the center of the boat so I can hand him the bags. "Then change the way you look at yourself, Belacourt. You realize a lot of people struggle with anxiety, right? It's not some weird taboo thing."

"In my family, it is."

I laugh, the sound wrenching from my gut with force. "Have you met your family? They might not talk openly about it, but they all have their issues. *Everyone* does because none of us are perfect. Look at Bree's reaction to her bad news while we shot the campaign. Someone with their life together would have been able to table the pain for later and finish working. I haven't even met Zoey, but judging from your reality show, she's a perfectionist. Olive needs constant outside reinforcement, and we won't even get into your parents. None of them are perfect. There's no way they expect that from you too."

Noah's expression is a blank mask while he absorbs what I'm telling him.

"Having anxiety only ruins your life when you let it," I say. "You aren't less of a person, or less of a man, or less of a boss for it."

"Tell that to my board of directors," he mutters.

"Why?" I pass him a bag and he puts it on the dock.

He takes a deep breath like he's gearing himself up for something. "It's why I'm on the island, Cat. I had an anxiety attack, kind of like the thing you witnessed at Tootsie's party, except we were meeting with investors. I ran from the room and we lost the account because they thought I was unhinged. My board told me to take two months off to get a grip, which is why Gina has stepped in and helped me run things."

"And why you don't go into the office much."

"Right. I'm on a time out."

The boat rocks, so I grip the back of a seat, letting his words sink in. If I thought we wouldn't work out before, we definitely won't now. There's no way he'll be able to make time for me when he's no longer forced to be on the island. Something about that—the fact that he had to be removed from work in order to be here so much—kills me. It's my home, my happy place, the best little piece of paradise in the world.

If we can't see eye to eye on that, we're doomed from the start.

So why bother trying? I don't want to set and bump the volleyball of our relationship if it's just going to spike out of bounds no matter what.

This wakeup call is good, because I was starting to melt toward him again. I can't let myself listen to feelings that have no legs to stand on. It'll just end in heartache later.

I pick up another bag and hand it to him.

He takes it from me. "What did I say wrong?"

"Nothing." I hand him the last bag, then climb out, ignoring his offered hand.

"I can tell you're unhappy."

"It's fine." I lean down to pick up my things.

"Cat."

I stop, closing my eyes, and drop my bag on the dock. "Can we not do this? Someone forced me to learn what Orcs are yesterday, and now I have to go scrub my brain."

"I didn't realize you hated the movies."

"I loved them." I meet his eyes so he'll read my sincerity. "Seriously. Didn't expect to, if I'm being honest, but now I'm thinking I'll be Sam for Halloween this year."

"Not Arwen?"

"She's pretty, but Sam is the real MVP."

He smiles at me like I said the right thing. "Cat—"

"I really can't do this right now," I say, almost pleading. "It'll be too hard. Can't we just be friends for the rest of the summer while you're here, then go our separate ways and not have to deal with heartache on top of saying goodbye?"

He's frozen, his face carved from granite. His chest isn't even moving, so I'm wondering if he's holding his breath.

"Please?" I ask. I don't add that I've lost enough in my life, that I'm unprepared to love and lose him, too.

"Okay."

"Friends?" I ask, to make sure he heard me.

Noah nods. "Friends."

As we pick up our bags and climb the stairs toward the resort, I can tell that things are already different between us.

I'm racking my brain for something to say that will pop us out of this funk when we pass the restaurant at the resort, and I stop dead in my tracks. It's dark outside, but the windows glow from the candlelight and the dim bulbs above the bar, perfectly highlighting my uncle inside.

Otto is here. He's dressed in all black and smiling at someone sitting at the bar. Because he's *behind* the bar shaking a martini mixer. The world starts to tilt, this vision not lining up with what I know to be true. Why is he acting like he's working here? He cannot... Can he actually be a Belacourt bartender?

"What's wrong?" Noah follows my gaze until he notices Otto. "Oh."

"Did you know about this?"

"No."

I search his face and see truth. When I look back at Otto,

he's staring at me, his wide eyes proving he's not happy to be discovered.

I start for the door when Noah takes my hand. "Come the back way. It's better."

He leads me around the side toward the kitchen entrance. The door swings open and Otto is there, hands up in surrender. "It's not what it looks like."

"Is this why you've been sneaking away and wearing black dress shirts and not telling me where you are? I thought you had a *girlfriend*, Otto!"

He looks abashed. "It's not a big deal."

Not a big deal that he was sneaking around and lying to me? I take in his combed hair. "Do you even *golf*?" I burst.

Otto cringes.

"Why didn't you tell me?"

"I didn't want you to panic."

I grow still. Is he finally ready to let me in on his secrets? "About what?"

Otto closes his eyes and runs a hand over his face. "I need the money, Cat."

I wait. The silence sits around us. Noah steps back, giving us space.

"Some bills showed up a few years ago—"

"A few *years*? Seriously?" I didn't realize they were so old.

"Cat. Listen. They're from Killigan Hammer, and they're big. I didn't want to worry you, so I've been chipping away at them. But then we had a few slow months, and I couldn't make the payments, so I've been trying to even things out by working here."

"I know."

He looks up at me. "What?"

"I found the bills. I already know. I've been saving too. It's why Noah hired me this summer, to help out."

Otto frowns, looking over my shoulder to where I'm guessing Noah is standing.

"I have almost enough to cover half of the bill, Otto. By the end of July, I'll have enough to pay the whole thing."

He looks between us, his scowl growing, then shakes his head slowly, his eyes not leaving mine. "No."

"No, what?"

"No, you aren't paying my bill. It has nothing to do with you."

"Um, yes, it does. If you're getting a final notice on it, then that means our house is in danger, which has everything to do with me."

"Not when the house isn't in my name."

The world rocks around me. I couldn't have heard him correctly. "What are you talking about?"

"When you signed all those documents to take over the B&B while I was dealing with chemo, you got ownership of the house. It's all yours, Cat, entirely in your name. If the bank comes for me, the house would still be yours."

"I don't understand."

"I did it to protect you. I had no idea what the treatments were going to cost us or if I would even be around to pay them, and I didn't want you saddled with a huge debt, especially if I'd died." He shrugs. "You already owned your dad's half of the house, so I just signed my half over instead of waiting until I was dead."

"But it's *your* house. Your money. You aren't dead yet—you have a lot of life to live."

Otto just shakes his head. "You are my life, Cat." The soft way he says it has me melting into a puddle.

I cross the rest of the deck to fall into his arms and let him squeeze his love into me. "It's me and you against the world, Otto. I don't care who owns the house. I'm helping you pay off this stupid bill and then we can talk about the future."

"Good," he says, kissing the top of my head. "I've been thinking about joining Phil and Hank on an extended surf trip once Phil's hip heals."

"You should do it. The guests can suffer from my cooking."

He laughs. "You're a better cook than me and we both know it." He clears his throat. "We'll talk about the bills later, but you aren't paying them. I won't accept your money."

We'll see about that. Otto gave up his life to raise me. I can pay one bill.

He looks over his shoulder. "I need to get back."

"I'll see you at home."

Otto heads inside, and when I turn around to find Noah, he's gone.

The gate at the end of the path swings open softly. No, not gone. The tense feeling in my chest eases.

He's waiting for me.

CHAPTER 31

Cat

WE'VE BEEN HOME from New York for two days and things are already strained, which means I've thrown myself into my favorite pastime: scrubbing. Mrs. Finnigan's house has never sparkled so brightly. My back aches and my little baby triceps are sore, but this is what I do when I need to feel in control. It could be so much worse, like an addiction to cocaine or painkillers or—*yuck*—running. At least this coping mechanism leaves me with a clean house.

I'm itching to have a go at the guest bathroom grout once our guests vacate. Those clean white lines and shiny tiles. To feel my fingers turn to raisins and have the room smell like bleach while the sea breeze laps at me from the open window. It's a drug.

And a distraction. Noah is trying not to press me, I think, because his list of tasks each evening are not even lists. It's been one bullet point each day: see if Mateo needs help with the app launch party.

Guess what? Both days, Mateo told me he has everything well in hand.

The evening before the third day, when Noah texts me that exact same thing, I'm a bit fed up. I sit cross-legged on the chair at our dining table and chew the last bite of the panini I made for dinner.

> **CAT**
> You're telling me to do that so Mateo can tell me he doesn't need me, right? I'm not charging you for these days because I'm not actually doing any work.

> **NOAH**
> You're on call. You get paid

> **CAT**
> Don't be ridiculous

> **NOAH**
> I'm doing what any employer would do

> **CAT**
> Fine, then I guess you're not my employer anymore

> **NOAH**
> Don't do anything rash, Cat.

> **CAT**
> Rash? I'm saving my relationship with my uncle. He's not happy about our arrangement. He's looked it up. Even the wealthiest men don't pay their assistants this much

It's been a sticking point for Otto. He wants me to quit and still refuses to accept my help with his bills. He won't accept the argument that I'm paying him back for the years he raised me and all the stress and money that went into that.

I take my plate to the sink and start pulling out ingredients for berry overnight oats for tomorrow's breakfast. Otto walks into the kitchen when I'm pouring oats into the mixture.

"You quit that job yet?" he asks.

"Did you quit yours?"

Otto makes a gruff snort.

"What if we make a deal?" I offer, stirring the oats. "We'll go fifty-fifty on the bill."

He grunts.

"*Otto.*"

"What?"

"You can't give me a house and then not accept *any* help."

"Half of a house. Your dad left you the first half."

I roll my eyes.

He bends down to tie his shoes. Now that I know about the bartending job, he hasn't bothered to hide his uniform from me. Seeing him in trousers and button-down shirts makes me think of my parents' funeral every single time. I hate it.

Otto lets out a sigh, getting to his feet, and lumbers over to kiss the top of my head. "See you later, Cattywampus."

"Have a good night."

I watch him leave and finish assembling the oats before pouring them into a glass container and putting them in the fridge. Once the house is quiet—the guests are all out—I slump in a kitchen chair and sigh. My phone has gone off a few times, but I don't have the energy to argue with Noah about money right now. Not when I'd rather be hanging out, watching his intense movies and letting him explain how Orcs are made.

Yeah, it's gross. I know. I think I'm smitten.

I sneak a look at my phone.

NOAH

I'm tempted to deposit money into your account

CAT

That's an invasion of trust and privacy

NOAH

I thought it was called a grand gesture

He has me there. Can we pretend none of this is happening and curl up in his movie room with Jimmy Stewart and *The Shop*

Around the Corner? No, because we need to understand each other first. He needs to understand me.

> **CAT**
> I value you and your friendship, Noah. This isn't a pride thing. It's mine and Otto's issue. We have to work it out on our own.

> **NOAH**
> I just want to help

If we were married, yeah, maybe I'd hand over Otto's account information and let him have at it. A lifelong commitment to have and to hold would be sufficient for me to feel comfortable accepting his help to erase a debt of this magnitude. The whole what's-yours-is-mine jazz is about more than shared accounts—it is a byproduct of the ultimate commitment and pledging entirely to one another.

But *now*? Fresh on the heels of admitting we have feelings for each other? It's a relationship death sentence. Besides, I value *him*, not his bank account.

> **CAT**
> If you paid it, I would feel like I owe you. I don't want a relationship built on a foundation of favors.

> **NOAH**
> You want a relationship?
> I see your point now. I really do

Do I want a relationship? Probably shouldn't have phrased it like that right after telling him we should only be friends. The correct answer is *yes, of course,* but the smart answer is *no*.

Be smart, Cat. Save yourself future heartache.

Noah's golden heart is in a good place though. I get it. If I had ninety-two thousand dollars sitting around, I would have already paid it off.

I straighten in my seat. I don't have the full amount, but I have some of it. Noah gives me checks every other Friday like a normal job, so the money from our first month is sitting in my bank now.

If I pay Otto's bill—or at least what I have so far—he can't argue with me about it anymore. He won't accept the help otherwise. This isn't the same situation as Noah wanting to pay it off for two reasons. First, I'm Otto's closest living relative. Second, despite his insisting he was happy to sacrifice to raise me, he *did* sacrifice and he did raise me. He gave up the opportunity to leave the island whenever he wanted for sick waves with his buddies because he had a nine-year-old at home. He did that for me. Because I love him so much, I want to do this for him.

I don't have the full amount right now, but I can pay half of it and get the "final notice" taken off the envelope.

Otto hasn't moved the medical bills, so I find them quickly and call the automated number, glancing at the clock. Just in time. They close in ten minutes.

The computer-generated system gives me the runaround, but I finally get a human on the line.

"How can I help you?" she asks.

"I want to make a payment on a bill."

"Can I have your name and the account number, please?"

"I already gave it to the computer system. Do you need it again?"

"To confirm your identity, I need your name and the account number again."

I rattle off the information.

"You have a zero balance on that account, ma'am."

She must be confused. I double check the last bill that's sitting in my hand. "I'm showing a balance of $92,410.06."

The woman hums. "That is the amount for the most recent

payment, but you are now showing a zero balance. Is there anything else I can help you with today?"

"Wait, hold on. You mean someone paid it?"

"Yes, ma'am."

"Who?"

"I don't have that information, ma'am."

"When was it paid?"

"Just a moment." She keeps humming while she's looking at the information. "It appears it was paid on July 2nd."

Yesterday. Noah. It had to be.

"Is there anything else I can help you with today, ma'am?"

"No, thank you." My hands shake as I hang up the phone. Did we not just go over this? Why did he *let me* say all those things? I push my phone into my pocket and get directly into my —no, Noah's—golf cart, and head straight for his house. My blood is boiling, overheated from Noah's audacity. I can't believe he went over my head and took care of the bill, knowing I didn't want him to. When I reach the house, I ring the bell three times too many.

It swings open to reveal Noah in shorts with no shirt. The porch light is working against me, sending golden light over the ridges on his abdominal muscles while his face holds cautious excitement, like he wants to take me in his arms but he's waiting for permission.

The universe hates me.

I swallow my flaring attraction, shoveling it under the welcome mat. I'm here for a reason. "Asking to take care of Otto's bills is one thing, but going over my head and doing it? That's crossing a line."

"What are you talking about?" Bless his heart, he looks confused.

"The medical bill. It's gone. Someone paid it."

It only takes a second for him to connect all the dots, and his eyebrows shoot up. "It wasn't me."

I guffaw in a really unattractive way.

"It wasn't me, Cat. Someone else must have done it."

"Who else has that kind of money? I don't. Otto certainly doesn't. No one else who's aware of our situation can afford to do that." I'm fighting tears. I just want to crawl into his arms and let him hold me, but instead I'm feeling small and lied to. "What else am I supposed to think?"

He takes a step forward, the muscle working on his jaw. "Definitely. It makes sense to jump to this conclusion. But, Cat, I mean it. I did not pay the bill. I wanted to, but I didn't do it."

"Would Mateo have done it on your behalf?"

"No."

I feel so defeated. It's such a small thing, but my pride is really caught up in it. Now that I'm here looking at him, his brown eyes soft and brow bent in concern, I know he's telling me the truth. Why would he have asked permission to pay it an hour ago if he'd already done it? He's not manipulative.

Noah steps forward, cupping my cheeks to raise my face. He brushes his thumbs over my scowling forehead, and I can feel the tension ease slightly. "I can help you get to the bottom of this if you need to know."

I nod, his hands moving with my head. He seems to sense how much I crave comfort and pulls me close, wrapping his arms around me. His chest is warm and hard beneath my cheek. I should be elated the bill is gone, but it just feels icky on a different level, like someone has crossed a boundary into my personal space without permission. Walked into my room and tried on my clothes. Stepped into my bathroom and cleaned the toilet. Used my *shower scrubber* on their own back.

You just need to ask before you do these things.

Noah's voice is a low purr as he continues. "Or you could choose to be grateful for the gift, and—"

I step back, missing his comfort immediately. "That's a lot of money, Belacourt. I'm not just going to move on with my life like it didn't happen."

"The person might wish to remain anonymous."

"Because the person is you?" I ask, heart in my throat.

"No, it's not me. But I might have an idea—"

"Who?"

He hesitates, rubbing a hand over his chin. "I don't know for sure. I shouldn't give you a name unless I'm certain."

I shake my head and take another step back. "It doesn't add up."

"Cat—"

"No, this is... I don't know, but something doesn't add up."

He looks ready to argue, hurt flashing in his brown eyes.

"I believe you didn't do this, but I need some time to figure it out." I can't shake the weird feeling buzzing in my arms and stomach. I want to step out of my skin and into a more comfortable set. I need to get away. It's too hard being here with him when he's *not* holding me. "Honestly, maybe it's a good time to break this off. We don't need the money anymore, which is the real reason you hired me in the first place."

"Cat, don't do this," he says, his voice low. "Of course I need you."

I cringe because he sounds hurt. He doesn't need me in a professional capacity, not when he has Mateo. We both know this. "It's not *you*. I don't like how I feel right now. We should dissolve our professional relationship so I can focus on my other jobs again." I turn to leave, halting at the golf cart. It's his. I toss the key on the seat and start walking down the driveway, crying in earnest now.

"Just take it, Cat," he says. "I'll get it back later."

"It's okay." My voice is high. I try to sound normal, but the tears are obvious in my tone.

He lets me walk away, probably in a chivalrous move to give

me the space I asked for. But every step feels like it's chipping away at an open sore and tearing me in two.

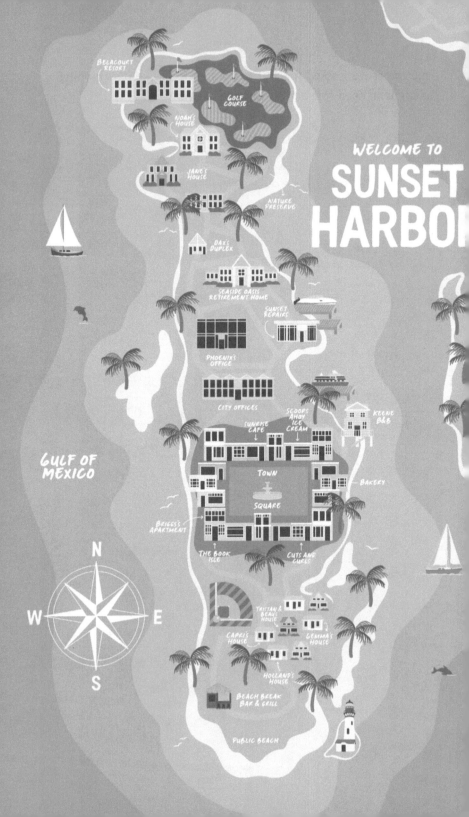

CHAPTER 32

Noah

SUNSET HARBOR MAKES A PRETTY big deal out of the Fourth of July. They do a pancake breakfast, parade, dance, fireworks—the whole shebang. I was hoping Cat would want to go to the festivities with me, but since our working relationship ended, I didn't ask her. Sometimes a little breathing space goes a long way. I didn't want to rush her into any decisions, even if keeping my distance has felt like taking a cheese grater to my emotions.

I've seen Cat off and on all day at the various festivities. She's been polite, but there's been a solid wall of ice layering our brief conversations. I'm assuming for self-preservation. It's taken everything in me to respect her boundaries and refrain from taking a blowtorch to her frozen castle.

I also found out who paid Otto's bill, but I don't know how to tell her.

With my app launch coming up, I tried to fall back into work and let it consume me, but it wasn't the distraction I hoped for. Mateo picked up the medication Dr. Stein prescribed, so I started that a few days ago. It's too early to tell if it's going to help, but I'm hopeful.

Now the fireworks are over. I'm sitting on the dark beach while a bonfire blazes in front of me, feeling for the first time like I have control of my life and also like I'm missing the one thing I want most.

Tristan is here with the girl he's been dating, Capri—well, hoping to date. From the look of it, things are going well in that department. Watching them together makes my stomach clench. I want that to be me and Cat, too. Not just friends. I don't want to be *friends* with her, and it was a stupid thing to agree to in the first place. Why would I let her put me into the friendzone when I know we could be so much more?

Now we're worse than that. I wouldn't call us enemies, but Cat might. Judging by the way she looked at me today though, I have a feeling she's more hurt than mad.

Tristan is chatting with someone else now, but his fingers are playing with the ends of Capri's long, dark hair.

I want that to be me and Cat. To fall headfirst into the stage of the relationship where you just can't keep your hands off each other. I yearn for it so badly I think I might vomit.

Maybe I should just come clean. I could tell Cat the truth, beg for her forgiveness, and explain my plan.

If she forgives me and things keep going well for Tristan, we could double. Take the yacht out. Start building our couples' relationships on the island.

Okay, one thing at a time.

I stand up.

Cat left like twenty minutes ago, so she can't be far now.

Let's be real. Nowhere on this stretch of land is very far.

"You leaving?" Tristan asks. His arm is around Capri, and she gazes up at him with a tender smile. Yeah, there's no way they're staying single for much longer.

"Yeah. I'd better run."

"See you around, man."

Hopefully sooner rather than later, when we're on that double date. Cat is in my future. I can taste it. I can almost taste *her*.

I wave at the few people I was chatting with closer to the fire and take off. Cat was polite all day. The lack of vitriol must be a good sign. Maybe she's hurting as much as I am with the distance between us.

Distance with Cat is not what I want for my life. I want *her*. If I don't lay it all out there now, I'll miss my shot.

I pull out my phone while I'm walking away from the beach and call her.

"Hello?" she asks, a little breathless.

I'm just glad she answered. "Are you busy?"

"Um... not really."

"Can you meet me at my house? I know you don't... that things are different, but I'd really like a chance to talk. To explain."

There's silence.

I stop walking, my voice dropping. "Please."

"Okay." There's a beat of time before she says, "I'll be there in ten."

It takes too long to locate my golf cart. The moment I find it, I race home, toward her.

Cat is sitting at my kitchen island when I get home. I'm glad she felt comfortable enough to let herself in, at least. I lower myself on the barstool beside her.

"Will you let me explain everything before you get angry?" I ask.

"Yes." Her hair is still half-up, like it was all day, the red scarf that led us to our watery collision last month tied around it. Her skin has a glow from the sun, but her eyes are wary, the blue dimmed. "Who was it?"

I take a beat. "Olive."

Cat's jaw clenches. "You told her about my situation?"

"No. Well, yes, but not how you think. She was worried I was facing a gold digger—"

Cat's frown deepens.

"I explained it was a short-term job we mutually benefited from—which is the truth, like it or not. I needed help around the island so Mateo wasn't spread too thin, and you needed help to pay off Otto's bill. I realize I shouldn't have told her, but I thought I was absolving you with the information."

"Go on," she says tightly.

"Olive was grateful you forgave her at Tootsie's party. It was a huge weight off her shoulders. I didn't know she'd been holding on to the guilt for so long—I mean, I didn't know about any of it. Clearly it was a burden you relieved for her. She wanted to do something nice for you."

"To pay me back?"

"No, that's not how she said it. She doesn't want you to know it was her. She just wanted to be a good Samaritan and bless your life, since she knows she really screwed up all those years ago."

"She's atoning," she says flatly.

"I don't know, Cat. I know my sister, though, and she wasn't trying to ruffle feathers. She was hoping the hospital would let you know a foundation had come through and cleared some debts, that yours was one of them. I guess you called in before the hospital could reach out to you."

Cat closes her eyes and leans forward on her bent arms.

I'm tempted to rub her back, but I'm not sure she wants me touching her now. "It's the truth, Cat. My sister's boyfriend has a foundation that does this—pays off hospital debts for uninsured people all over the country. He partners with different hospitals to offer debt forgiveness, too, even for those with insurance when the bills are outrageous or the insurance refuses to help. It's not like Olive went in and just wrote a check. She utilized Dash's foundation, made a donation—larger than the sum of your bills—and submitted Otto's situation. It could have happened to you even if Olive didn't know." I smile with faint self-deprecation. "The whole thing was approved and expedited because she's dating Dash, but Olive went through the proper channels."

Cat glances up. "Dash Malone does this?"

"Yeah. He even goes into some of the hospitals dressed up as Superman occasionally. He has a big heart."

Her clear blue eyes peer at me. "So Olive paid it through the foundation," she repeats, as if saying the words will allow them to sink in.

"The money was Olive's, but the foundation did the legwork. She wanted it to be anonymous." I clear my throat. "Does Otto know?"

"I haven't said anything to him. I wanted more information first."

"So… are you going to let the hospital make the phone call? They'll tell him about the foundation and how his debt is cleared. He can quit working at the Belacourt and go back to surfing all day."

She sits up, looking at me. "Keeping Olive out of it."

"She wants to stay out of it. I know you want to tell him, but she really wanted this to remain anonymous. Do you think you can forget you know, for her sake?"

Cat's nodding, looking in the distance. A little furrow pops between her brows, so I reach forward and smooth it out. She turns to look at me.

"Maybe we can be friends again," I ask, my heart in my throat.

"I'm not working for you. I'm not letting you pay me." But she doesn't say no.

There's a week worth of work she hasn't been paid for yet, but that's a debate for another day. "We can discuss a fair wage, but you need to be paid for the work you did."

She doesn't argue. We can figure that out later. Right now, I need to tell her how I feel. I can sense her softening toward me, and I can't hold my feelings in anymore.

But I don't want to do it here. This house has more negative associations for me than positive ones, and if my parents are selling it, I don't want it to be the place where I confess my feelings to her. No, that'll be my favorite place on the island.

"Will you come with me?" I ask, holding my breath. "I want to show you something."

Cat only nods.

I lead her outside and down the path away from the resort. I put in the code and unlatch the gate just behind my parents' house, the one that takes us directly to the cove. Other families use it sometimes. My dad gave the code to a few other locals years ago, but right now it's blessedly empty.

The staircase leads to a sharp, steep decline onto the beach. It's dark, so I pull out my phone's flashlight and we descend in silence. Once our feet hit the sand, I reach for Cat's hand to help her over the rocks at the base of the stairs.

"What is this place?" Her voice is normal now, the animosity and hurt gone. It gives me so much hope.

"I've always called it Pirate's Cove, because that was its purpose for a lot of my young life, but I think my dad named it Belacourt Cove at some point."

Nothing can rival Tom Belacourt's love for his own name.

"Is it private?"

"Yeah. It's where I have the few good memories from my childhood, before my parents started fighting so much. We used to bring picnics down here in the summer and play in the water until our shoulders were red and our fingers were raisins."

It's a small cove, not much more than a little beach and a lot of waves at this point in the evening. In the daytime, there's much more sand.

"Will we be stuck down here if the tide comes in?" she asks.

"The tide is in as far as it usually goes in July, but as long as we can get to the stairs, we'll be fine." I turn off my flashlight, letting the stars shine over us. We're cloaked in darkness, but the full moon glows on the stretch of white sand, making it possible to see each other.

"This could be super creepy with the wrong person," she mutters.

"Or romantic with the right one?"

Her eyes cut to me. "I don't think you're supposed to be romantic with your friends."

At least we've made it back to the friendzone. We're heading in the right direction. "You can if you're trying to get that friend to date you."

"Okay, let's dial it back," she says, a little worried. "I thought we decided—"

"Not we. *You* decided. I realized I don't have to sit back and let you slip away. Not without fighting for you."

She's silent, her round blue eyes locked on my face.

"I've liked you for a long time, Cat. You're smart and funny and beautiful and you are unapologetically you. I've been envious of that and admired it. It's one of the things I really appreciate about you."

"I'm not sure this is a good idea," she whispers.

I press on. "When I came to live full time on the island this summer, I was feeling lost and alone, struggling to get a handle on my emotions and my purpose. You popped in, the same as before, but so much more too. You brought the sun to me, Cat. No, you *are* the sun. You brighten my world. You don't make me feel any less for having trouble with anxiety or my imperfections. You're just you, and you let me be me. I sought perfection for so long, I didn't see what I really needed until you showed me."

I slide my hand down her arm until I find her fingers, interlacing them. "I don't feel broken when I'm with you. I don't feel like I need to be fixed."

"Oh, Noah," she says. "You're not broken."

I suck in a breath, dropping my voice. She called me by my name. Not Bruce. Not Belacourt. Not Moneybags or whatever that one was. "Say it again."

"You aren't broken?"

I shake my head.

"Noah," she whispers.

Two steps is all it takes to close the distance between us. My hands are lost in her hair and around her waist, pulling her close to me. I pause just before reaching her lips, my heart hammering, breathing rapid. I'm waiting for her to tell me it's okay, that she wants this—but I don't have to wait. Her breath is hot on my mouth as she crushes her lips to mine.

Not for the cameras. For me. This kiss is entirely us, and my body is exploding just like it did the last time. A flurry of fireworks makes my nerves dance while her lips tangle with mine. I break away, my breathing ragged. I've cracked my heart and opened it to her entirely.

"I love you, Cat."

CHAPTER 33

Cat

NOAH *LOVES* ME? My chest fills with heat and I jump, wrapping my legs around his waist while he holds me up. I frame his face in my hands, kissing him with all the restrained emotion I'd been keeping at bay. It's like I've been filling a power bank since that moment we shared in the surf and now it's time to expend all the energy in one kiss.

The uncertainty surrounding Otto's bill and who paid it has made me feel icky and unfinished. Even through that, I trusted him when he said he didn't do it, which I was right to do. I can appreciate Noah's healthy respect for boundaries, and it certainly explains why he needed to confirm with Olive before sharing his suspicions with me. While I don't love what Olive did, I can understand it and I can accept it. She wants to make her peace, just like I did.

She did Otto a solid, so I can return the favor and keep her secret. It was a good Samaritan move. No one needs to know who the Samaritan was.

Noah squeezes me closer, angling his head to kiss me deeper. He is so strong and good, his heart clear and wholesome and full of me, apparently. It's too much to believe—too good to be true.

Or maybe I'm one of the lucky ones, and I get to be wholly and truly loved by a good man. Kissing Noah again is everything

I've been dreaming about since that kiss during the photoshoot weeks ago. It's everything I've been dying for each time I've seen him since. His lips are soft and pliable, giving and honest and true.

And the way he makes me *feel*? I'm alive.

Our kiss slows, the feverish pace falling to a crawl. "You're a good man, Noah."

"I didn't scare you away?" he says between kisses.

"You can't. I realized I loved you in New York. I was just too scared to say anything."

He breaks away, looking at me. "That's why you didn't abandon me while I had the flu?"

"I couldn't abandon you."

"I figured that out. You stayed. It was when I realized how special you are."

"That's when you realized it?"

"Nah, that would be more like ninth grade." He grins. "You keep surprising me, Cat. Every time I think you can't possibly do anything to surprise me again, you do. I'm impressed with the way you forgave Olive, and the way you cared for me, and how hard you're working to help your uncle."

I close the distance, kissing him again, holding his face close to mine and exploring his lips entirely. I want this moment to last forever, to kiss him until the sun rises, then again until it sets. But we are two different people with different paths. Are we driving into a storm here? Enjoying the moment but destined for pain ahead? I lean back, then unlock my ankles and let him lower me back to the ground. "You're still leaving, aren't you?"

He's breathing heavier. "What do you mean?"

"You're going to let your parents sell this house. You'll live on the mainland or in Manhattan, and you'll work a lot, and it won't be the same."

He's surprised or confused, his brow bunched together. "That was your problem? That I don't live here?"

"My life is here, Noah. It will be such a challenge to leave." I swallow, my chest pounding with the truth that while my life is here, *Noah* is my home. As hard as it will be, I can sacrifice if it means we could be together. He's worth it.

"I know that."

"I don't want to," I say quietly. "I'm happy in my little B&B with my uncle and my friends around me and the beach everywhere I turn."

He listens to me, letting me feel what I need to. Allowing us to marinate in the moment, to determine our true feelings.

"But... For you... I can find a way to make it work." The words are out, and I don't feel the impending doom I expected. Sadness, but not doom. "The way I feel about you is more important than where I live."

"Cat," he says, almost like a plea, "I don't care where I live. I don't want to be anywhere that you aren't."

I'm shaking my head. "That's not fair, either. If I force you to stay here, someday you'll grow to resent me for it."

"Not if it's my choice." He pulls me close.

"That's my point, Noah. It's not your choice. I'd be making the choice for you."

"You aren't." He looks earnestly at me. "I told Mateo to get my mainland apartment ready to put on the market days ago. I made an offer on a house down the street."

I'm speechless.

When did he have time for this? I guess when personal assistants help run your life, you can find the time. "Your parents' house?" I ask.

"No. I wanted to start fresh. Let my sisters buy that one. Or they can sell it to a family who might actually use it. I want my own place, where we can make our own memories."

"You'll be giving up Pirate Cove."

"Technically, it belongs to the resort. Dad just never gave them access."

"So you're moving to Sunset Harbor?"

"I am. On my own, even though you weren't really talking to me. Is that enough to make sure you don't worry about me resenting you?"

"It's enough."

"Maybe, when the sale goes through, you can help me decorate? I'm hopeless."

"Only if you pay me. I don't come cheap, either." I squeal when his arm comes under my legs and he sweeps me off the ground. I'm laughing while Noah carries me farther away from the surf, then sets me down on the powdery sand. He joins me, and I wonder if he had the same idea I did, because he starts kissing me, and it doesn't seem like he's going to stop until the sun comes up.

CHAPTER 34

Noah

IT'S BEEN two weeks since Cat agreed to be my girlfriend in the middle of our make out session on the beach, and I'm legitimately the luckiest man in all of Florida. I have the girl, Dr. Stein signed off on me returning to work two whole weeks early, and my open world computer game is coming along so nicely, Jason—the lead developer—thinks we'll be ready to approach investors by September.

There was an anxiety attack nestled in the middle of all that when my parents led a Zoom meeting with me and my sisters to discuss who wants which property. It was nice of them to give us first dibs before putting everything on the market, but it's *never* fun being with them together. I got through it, and I'm still here. Still fine. Still growing and learning and adapting.

Everything is set for the launch party for our new Scoutr app. It hit phones early this morning and already has enough downloads to give my team a reason to let out a long, relieved sigh. When we first developed the software to fact-check information on the internet, it was heavy on my mind that utilizing it with a dating app was imperative. There are too many people lying on the internet, and both men and women deserve a little extra faith in knowing exactly who they're meeting up with after they match with someone online.

I'm just hopeful it works past the beta testing stage, but so far, so good. Because profiles get a gold rim around their profile picture with a little star after Scout has done its job and their info checks out, we made the whole launch party themed gold.

Mateo has outdone himself. The Belacourt Resort's dining room has been transformed, the tables and chairs pushed into different arrangements from the norm to promote mingling. Deep black tablecloths cover everything, making the candles flicker brightly, with gold table runners, plates, and some sort of golden fabric hanging from all the walls.

It feels like we're standing inside a jewelry display case—black velvet, bright gold jewelry, and stunning diamonds.

People mill about, but I can't keep my gaze from the door, watching for Cat. We'll have less traffic tonight than normal because the island is still recovering from a tropical storm we got a few days ago, but I've never minded an intimate party. Most of the people who matter already live on the island, and the rest made it across the bay safely. I nod to Tristan, standing on the other side of the room with his arm around Capri. He smiles before being pulled back into conversation with Holland and the guy who came with her. My gaze jumps to the door again, but Cat still isn't here.

I lift a wave to Otto behind the bar as he mixes a drink for Gina, and he nods back. He's working through the end of the summer because he likes the tips, but I wonder if there's another reason—I saw him flirting with Chef Gotier in the kitchen last week. She's a little brash, but if anyone could mellow her out, it would be Otto. Those Keenes are like happy little sunshine pills.

"You know," I say, coming to sit on a stool beside Gina. "I wondered if we'd make it to this day."

Gina takes the drink from Otto, and he moves on to the next person. She sips from the martini glass, raising her eyes to me. "I knew we'd make it. You have the Midas touch, Noah. Everything you touch turns to gold." She puts out an arm, indicating the decorations she had a hand in choosing.

"Nicely done."

"I'm serious. What are we doing next? A line of natural baby diapers? Producing music? Filming a pilot for the CW? Whatever you have up your sleeve, I am here for it."

I chuckle. She's being ridiculous, but the music producing idea isn't too bad. "Video games."

She waves it off. "I meant *after* that."

"Probably more games, if I'm being honest. I'm hopeful here, Gina. We can build that department."

"Might as well make it its own company, then."

She might be onto something. "Table the idea, but I want to circle back to it after the launch."

"You got it." Gina takes another sip of her drink.

I have her full attention, but I don't know how to vocalize how grateful I am for her. She kept the office together while I was trying to figure out myself. She stopped me from making foolish decisions, and she's level-headed. She could easily replace me as CEO while I take a less hands-on approach for Scout and Scoutr, giving me more time for Cat and the video game department. "Listen, I was wondering if we could meet sometime this week. I have a proposition for you."

She shakes out her short, blunt bob. "If it's more responsibility at the company, you know my answer already."

I bite back a smile. My instincts, as always, were right with Gina. "Does Tuesday work?"

She smiles. "Tuesday is fine."

"Enjoy tonight," I tell her. "You've earned it."

I meander closer to the door, watching for Cat and sipping my drink. Appetizers circulate on trays held by waiters in all black, but I stop by the table holding cocktail glasses of shrimp and plates of crab-stuffed mushrooms.

"Hey," Dash says, coming to my side and pulling a shrimp

from a cocktail glass on the table. "You never sent me that updated game."

New York feels like months ago, it's hard to believe it was only a few weeks.

"I forgot." My cringe shifts to a smile. "You guys sticking around tonight? I have it ready to go on my computer at home."

"Olive wants a few days at the spa, so she booked one of those beachfront villas." His grin spreads. "You busy tomorrow?"

"Not anymore." I clink my glass to his and take a sip, my eyes on the door.

Perfect timing. Cat steps in, wearing a pale blue dress that brings out the color of her eyes. Her hair is arranged behind her head in a gentle chignon, and she's in the same shoes she wore in Manhattan. I put my glass down and cross to her, ignoring Dash's chuckle. I'm certain I hear him say "smitten" but I don't care because he's right.

And I don't have to try and hide it anymore.

Cat

THE RESORT'S dining room looks completely transformed, but none of the gold or candlelight or famous party guests snag my attention. It is wholly on the man coming my way. He's in a black suit that is cut so fine and perfectly fitted, I can practically see the outline of his abs through the jacket.

Okay, not really. But I can picture those babies perfectly no matter what he wears. Tonight, he's sleek and suave and I'm sure—yep, there it is. A whiff of cologne. The man still smells like a dream.

A daydream, since this is real life and he's really pulling me in for a quick kiss.

Too quick, to be honest. His lips are warm on mine, molten and sensual, then they're gone again and his smile is beaming down at me.

"Good evening, Mr. Pennybags."

"Mister?" he says, eyes twinkling in amusement. "I've been upgraded."

"He's always been a mister. I was just more informal before now."

"You're going to tell me who he is, right?"

"Who, Millburn?" I stare at him, having trouble focusing while his fingertips graze my arm, never stopping in one place, sending shivers all over. "You haven't Googled it yet?"

His fingers grow still. "I didn't think of it."

A laugh escapes my gut, louder than ladylike, but Noah doesn't seem bothered by it. "Millburn Pennybags is the Monopoly man."

He blinks at me. "How did you know that?"

"I googled rich men and he popped up."

It's Noah's turn to laugh. "You mean you went out of your way to find names to tease me with?"

"It was fun." My grin spreads now. "You're easy to tease. My favorites were the ones that got a reaction though, so that's what I was looking for."

He leans forward and kisses me again. "It worked."

I glance around the room until my gaze rests behind the bar. "I should go say hi to Otto."

"Okay. I'll mingle for a bit."

Noah squeezes my hand as I walk away from him and approach the bar. Otto is mixing a drink for someone else but lifts his eyebrow to me. "Club soda with lime?" he asks.

"I'm that predictable?"

"Yes."

"Make it an Old Fashioned. No rocks."

Otto lifts both eyebrows. "Since when did you start drinking bourbon?"

"Never. I want my limey water, and I don't want to be judged for it."

He chuckles, shaking his head. After serving another couple down the bar, he brings me my drink.

I smile at him. "I heard you still haven't put in your two weeks' notice. Aren't you and Hank meeting up with Phil soon for that fishing trip? Or surfing trip? What did y'all settle on, anyway?"

"Both. That's what time off is for."

"You like working here."

He doesn't answer, just smiles at me.

I nod, accepting this new fact about him. "Okay. That's cool."

"We can talk about this at home," he says, "but I've been thinking about other ways we can improve things at the B&B."

Otto's been thinking of improvements. This ought to be interesting. "Like what?"

He leans forward, his hands bracing the counter. "Hiring high school kids. That's how you got your start, Kit Kat. We could bring in a few kids to manage the turnovers, handle the gardening. It's called outsourcing."

"What would *we* do, then?"

Otto stares at me for a few beats. "I just wondered if we should be thinking ahead. Ways to keep the B&B running even if we aren't both there."

There's a niggling of something weird down in my stomach telling me change is on the horizon. Otto has talked for years about taking off with his buddies, following the waves and the fishing. I don't think he'd leave forever, especially if he's having fun bartending here—and let's be honest, he'd miss me too much—but it won't be just me and Otto against the world anymore.

It'll be me and Otto and Noah and our whole network of friends and family, which is good too, in a different way.

"We both know how long you've been dying to start a family," he says softly. "The B&B can stay alive without you in the building, you know."

"Otto," I hiss, turning to make sure Noah isn't listening. "We've only been dating for like two weeks."

His smile is warm, his eyes crinkling. "I'm just thinking of the future. If you train the maids now while you're living at home, it'll make things easier for you someday when you move out."

A little premature? Maybe. Then I catch Noah's gaze across the room and my stomach squirms with the need to be over there and in his arms, and I think, *or maybe not.*

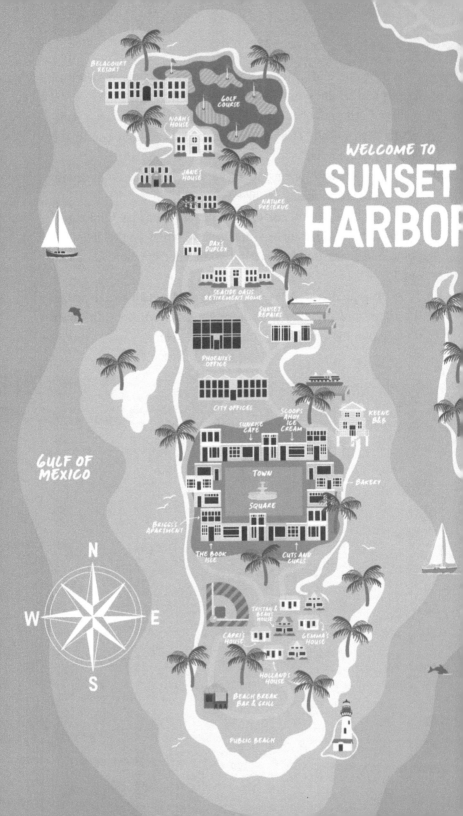

EPILOGUE

Cat

EIGHT MONTHS LATER

THIS IS IT. This is the day I completely change who I am at my core. It is a beautiful, sunny April day in Sunset Harbor. The sun is out and warm for the first time in what has felt like months. My skin soaks in the rays and I drop sunglasses over my eyes, taking in the resort's private beach in all its sun-drenched glory.

I can see why people wake up early for this. It's beautiful, it's rich, it makes me feel alive. Noah has been running on the beach for years, and he is constantly talking about the awe found in nature.

Now, he's finally convinced me to give it a try with him. He believes I'll love it if I only try.

I want to believe he's right.

Want to.

"You ready?" he asks, leaning over to make sure his shoes are tied.

"No."

Noah chuckles, pulling me in for a morning kiss. I cup his face and hold him so he can't leave, kissing him long and slow.

When he finally breaks away, I sigh. "Can't we just do that all morning?"

"Cat."

"*Fine.*"

Noah takes off down the beach, and I follow him. His pace is ridiculously slow. I know it's with me in mind, and I'm grateful for that.

The next thirty minutes are absolute agony. I'm huffing, my lungs are screaming, and my legs are sore. "Are we almost done yet?"

"Cat," he says, not even a hitch in his breath. He checks his watch. "We've only been running for four minutes."

"Four?!" I stop, resting my hands on my thighs and struggling to breathe.

Noah circles back, jogging in place, before coming to a total stop. "You aren't going to finish this run, are you?"

"I *did* finish the run. Right here." I look up. "I love you, man. I tried. I really did."

Noah laughs deep from his belly. "Okay, babe. Let's do something else. Want to kayak?"

I glance at the sparkling water just behind him, the way the cerulean waves are crashing on the white sand. "It *sounds* fun."

"You'd be sitting in a boat," he says, like that will help. Maybe it would. I've never actually tried it.

"I don't know if I can."

"It's up to you." He puts his arms out. "We can walk, kayak, go back up to the house and make pancakes. Your choice."

The sun soaks into my skin, and I know I'm not ready to go inside. I want to be out here more, longer, with him. "I kind of want to try it, but I'm nervous."

"What if you situate yourself in the kayak on the sand, and I'll push you into the water? Then you don't have to walk through the waves."

We'd been working on it the last few months, me being comfortable walking through the waves. Noah is always right beside me, gripping my hand tightly, and some days are better than others. With a life vest and a boat, I wonder if kayaking is something I could handle.

I heave out a breath. "Sounds doable. What if we get out there and a manatee knocks us over?"

He smiles. "Then I'll put you back in the kayak. But you know that's unlikely."

"Not impossible," I mutter.

He stops me with a gentle hand on my waist. "This is your call, Cat. Entirely your call."

My body leans into his touch. I feel the safety there, the knowledge that he's a strong man and a solid swimmer and he's already saved me from the ocean once—even though I didn't need saving. He has done it. If we get the kayaks far enough out, there won't be any rip currents to pull me away.

I give him a nod and he presses a tender kiss to my temple.

We return to the resort's beach and pull a two-person kayak out of the locker before carrying it close to the water. Noah sets it down and helps me get into it. My knees are bent, my feet pressing into the footrests, both of the double-sided oars in my hands. I squeeze my eyes closed and take a deep breath while Noah pushes us into the water.

I've always had a fear of being like my parents—the ocean pulling me out to sea and pressing me under the water until I couldn't escape. Sitting on top of the water, safe from rip currents, feels different.

The life vest helps, too.

Noah pushes us out through the clear turquoise water until he's knee deep, then climbs in behind me. The kayak rocks, making my heart thud with the motion.

"Cat, will you hand me the oar?"

I give it to him wordlessly without turning around.

"You okay?"

I nod.

"Catalina."

"Yes," I say weakly. "It's scary."

"We can stop right here."

Deep breath. "I want to do this."

He waits a moment longer before saying, "Okay. Let's head toward the cove. It'll be a short ride."

"Sounds good."

Noah teaches me the best way to hold the oars and how to paddle in rhythm with him so we conserve our energy. We head out on the water, and I can feel my anxious energy sloughing away the further we get from shore. Yes, some of my fears are illogical. Isn't that the point of anxiety? It doesn't always bend to logic.

When we fully leave the resort's beach and curve around the edge of the small cove, Noah comes to a stop. I do too, my arms burning from the exercise. It burns in a good way, though, and I'm starting to see the appeal to this whole kayaking thing. Water glitters around us, lapping gently around the boat while the sun beats overhead.

"This is beautiful."

"Isn't it wonderful? I love being out here. It helps me feel so human and small. I appreciate the world a little better."

I turn just enough to see him. "You're such a romantic. Look at you gushing."

His grin is wide. I can't see his eyes beneath his sunglasses, but I know they're on me. "Wait until I take you to the nature reserve."

"I've been there loads of times."

"Not with a kayak."

That's true. I sigh, leaning back and breathing in the salty air.

"Hey, Cat?"

I try to turn in my seat again until I can see him and nearly drop my oar.

Noah has a black box open with a brilliant ring in the

middle, somehow outshining the sunlight gleaming down on the ocean around us. "I love you, Cat. I want to spend my life with you, and I want you there cooking breakfast or still asleep when I get home from runs. I want to take you to Paris and raise children with you here on the island. I want our lives to be entwined. I want you forever."

"Noah," I say, my breath just a wisp, caught by the breeze and carried away.

"Will you be my wife?"

"You planned this for the middle of a *run*?"

"I planned this for the cove, but it's so peaceful out here, I didn't think anything could top this."

"What if you drop it?!"

"I won't." He's so confident, I believe him. Still, a little crazy.

"I can't kiss you out here, Noah."

"I think we can manage. What do you say?"

"Yes!" I scream. "Of course I'll marry you. I already have most of the wedding planned anyway."

"Poor Mateo."

"He supports most of my ideas."

Noah laughs, reaching for my hand. I hold it out so he can slide the ring on—a huge sapphire on a gentle band. I love it so much.

I twist in my seat as much as I can and Noah leans forward, bringing my face flush against his, kissing me with sweet tenderness.

"Thank you," I say against his lips.

"Come on." He leans back. "Let's go. Otto wants to see you right away."

"He can wait a while." I grip my oar again and grin so wide my cheeks hurt. "I have some plans involving you and the beach at the cove."

"Next stop: three kids."

"Six," I counter.

Noah's chuckle wraps around me like a warm embrace. "We can debate that later. Let's just start with one."

"How about we do this wedding first?" I say.

"As long as it's sometime this year."

I lean back, basking in the sun and glorious happiness. "You read my mind."

If you aren't quite ready to leave Cat and Noah, sign up for my newsletter to get a *bonus* epilogue set another four years in the future! https://BookHip.com/WVPQBZP

Read the next book in the Falling for Summer series all about Noah's friend Tristan and another island local, Capri!

The book is always better than the movie. But occasionally, life is better than the book.

Ten years ago I made a mortifying, life-altering mistake. Now, this once seemingly insignificant choice is threatening to wreck my entire existence. And possibly throw Tristan Palmer—my next-door-neighbor and the guy I've had a secret crush on for the entirety of my life—into the fray unaware.

The mistake?

I am Sunny Palmer. As in the anonymous, best-selling author of over a dozen beloved romances and renowned thief of Tristan's last name. Okay, not renowned yet, thank the high heavens! But that news will spread like wildfire if people discover that this introverted book nerd is the woman behind the pen name. And the fact that my first book, *Secret Crush*, is Tristan's and my fictionalized love story leaves zero room for calling it anything but what it is—a travesty of greatest proportions.

That's why NO ONE can know! *Ever!*

So it's wretched luck that when I finally visit Sunset Harbor, the small-town island where I grew up, I run into the still heart-stopping, book-boyfriend-worthy man himself. And shockingly, Tristan seems intent on reminding me what the island has to offer. Because that's what *friends* do.

Logic demands I resist his charm and guard my secret at all costs, which is why it's vastly unfortunate that Tristan Palmer was and always will be ... my greatest weakness.

FALLING FOR SUMMER

Summer Ever After by Kortney Keisel
Jane + Walker

Beachy Keen by Kasey Stockton
Cat + Noah

Plotting Summer by Jess Heileman
Capri + Tristan

Summer Tease by Martha Keyes
Gemma + Beau

Beauty and the Beach by Gracie Ruth Mitchell
Holland + Phoenix

One Happy Summer by Becky Monson
Presley + Briggs

Rebel Summer by Cindy Steel
Ivy + Dax

ACKNOWLEDGMENTS

You want to know what's just as fun as this series? The authors who wrote it with me. I have had such a blast working with these ladies to develop Sunset Harbor and all its intricacies. I don't think it would be easy to write such an involved series with just anyone, but these ladies made the process smooth, seamless, and respectful. I'm so glad to have found them all! Thanks for being so wonderful Kortney, Jess, Martha, Gracie Ruth, Becky, and Cindy.

Thank you to my beta readers: Brooke Losee, Nancy Madsen, Emily Flynn, Maren Sommer, Rebekah Isert, Rachel John, Katie Rowles, Martha Keyes, Brooke Hampton, Jamie Morris, and Kerry Perry. Thank you Jacque Stevens for your edit and ideas. Thank you Karie Crawford for your editing and polish. Your notes are the best, in all the ways. I'll check in to ellipses anonymous soon…maybe after the next book…

Thank you to all the ARC readers, bookstagrammers, and readers who leave reviews, post about the book, or tell your friends to pick it up. Special thanks to the Summer Cheerleaders. You ladies have been so fun to work with!

Thanks to Melody Jeffries for the cover. You killed it on this entire series—they are so perfect.

Final (and most important) thanks goes to my bestie, Jon. My hilarious kids. My dog who always seems to know when I need a little love. My house is so full of love and I'm grateful for everyone in it—chief of all, my Heavenly Father.

ABOUT THE AUTHOR

Kasey Stockton is a staunch lover of all things romantic. She doesn't discriminate between genres and enjoys a wide variety of happily ever afters. She publishes both contemporary and historical novels, and all of her titles fall under clean romance. She loves reading, chocolate, and period dramas, but nothing tops her very own prince charming, their three children, and their sweet goldendoodle.

Made in United States
Troutdale, OR
07/10/2025